GW00503021

In The Eye Of The Storm

Every Storm Starts with Rain

Cleo Crombie

DEDICATION

This book is dedicated to my mum for always believing in me. For my husband Ibrahim for supporting my dream. To my little sisters Rhianne and Shanice for inspiring me. To my dad, Aunty Angela, and Grandma for always encouraging me, and to my Granddads who aren't here to see me shine. Also, special thanks to my mum and Rhianne for being my unpaid editors, and to Bia W. Andrade for designing my front cover.

LOE LIVE FOREVER. FOREVER LIVE LOE

IN THE EYE OF THE STORM

1

HOME COMING
ISLINGTON 2056

My stomach churned anxiously so I could not help but be sceptical about the whole situation. I had this funny feeling inside me. Like tiny little spiders were spinning a web around the inside of my stomach to trap the wild fluttering butterflies. Something didn't feel right, but then again *nothing felt right anymore.*

I sighed loudly and accidentally caught my mother's eye, so I lowered my gaze to the dining room table. She had set it annoyingly meticulously with her precious bone china dishes, and sterling silver cutlery placed upon dainty little place mats. The crystal flutes stood almost majestically on a finely woven crochet table cloth, a family heirloom that was trimmed with 14 carat gold thread.

My tummy rumbled again, *painfully*. But this time I was sure it demanded the food going cold in front of me. The kids were eating some glowing solar sweets that lay loose around the large cake in the middle of the table. I grabbed a berry bomb and I rolled the tangy cherry flavoured orb around the inside of my mouth until it exploded into a sour fizzy sherbet. It wasn't enough, after the day I'd had only hot food could rid me of the aggressive thumping between my eyes and the tight knots of nauseous air invading my stomach. Irritated, I yawned as I looked up at the Union Jack clock above the dining room table. It was already nine thirty, but I had barely been home for an hour. The Diminishing Rights Bureau was flooded with soldiers before I'd even arrived that morning. I *had* expected their arrival of course, but I didn't expect the sheer number that came to us for assistance or the line that spanned out of our office, outside of our building and trailed halfway down the street. They weren't rejoicing or celebrating considering the fact that they had finally returned safely to their *homeland* after years of guerrilla warfare in the desolated waste lands of World War 3. After all they were home now, back into the welcoming bosom of the motherland, the country that they *most likely* had been born in. Back to the kingdom that had nurtured them, raised them, loved them, and moulded them into the men that they now were. They had fought, they had killed and they had suffered in the name of King George VII of Great Britain. But upon their valiant return they found that the land they once loved no longer belonged to them. It was now a place where their families may no longer live and where their homes may no longer exist. A strange but surreally familiar place and if they ended up sitting in front of my desk at the Diminishing Rights Bureau, they no longer held any economical social status whatsoever. My family and I had found out about the soldiers return early last night when an emergency transmission interrupted the semi-final of *'Who wants to marry an English heir.'* The VTV screen suddenly went black and the three-dimensional holograms flickered in front of us until they disappeared moments later. After a long beeping sound, a familiar voice boomed through the electro-transmitter.

'This is an important announcement... I repeat this is an important announcement... Viewing... will continue in due course.' Another long beep followed drowning out every other noise in the room and immediately drawing everyone's attention to the British Fundamentalist Party logo hovering in front of the screen.

'The day we have all been waiting for has finally arrived,' the news reader announced as his face flickered into focus on the virtual television screen.

'World War 3 has come to an infinite end and our brave British soldiers have safely returned home.' The VTV buzzed and flickered for a moment.

'I can now officially say with the upmost certainty that they are *all* back on *our* beloved British *soil.*' The news reader smiled making his eyebrows twitch as a flush of rosacea clouded his cheeks.

'I am overjoyed and honoured to be able to state that every *unforgotten* soldier should soon be in the arms of their loved ones.'

I remember the correspondent's cheesy grin as his face started to flicker again when it began to disappear. The portly news reader winked at his audience. 'In the words of our prime minister every great British soldier has come home a hero and will be awarded the prestigious medal of honour for their services to Great Britain and his Majesty King George VII.'

I rolled my eyes and sighed loudly. *I had heard that one before,* we all had but still *I* was the only one in the room that didn't seem to be elated by the news.

I stared blankly as the VTV switched to sponsored adverts like it always did before normal programming resumed after an emergency broadcast. I didn't believe the announcement and I wasn't going to pretend to be happy about it, not for my mother's sake or anyone else's. Maybe it was my job that made me so sceptical or it could just be down to the fact that the BFP can only be described as a bunch of lying, fascistic, corrupted MPs, or in my own word's greedy chauvinistic bastards. There had already been two *'end of war homecoming announcements'* earlier this year, not to mention one the year before. Each time my mother had gotten just as excited, and every single time her precious son never returned home. On every joyous *homecoming* occasion the government had only bought back a small largely *Caucasian* fraction of their troops, and continued the World War in the wastelands without further explanation.

'Mummmy... Can we eat now?' My little sister Déjà whined from further along the table.

'Déjà...' my mother said coldly. 'Why would

4

you even ask me that? You *know* we're waiting for your brother.

'I'm sure we could leave him a plate.' Maxwell, my mother's partner of fifteen years quipped as he skimmed the rim of his champagne flute with the tip of his finger making it sing. My mother firmly ignored him and besides the low hum of the VTV, an awkward silence had settled around the table. After a few minutes of quiet my grandfather suddenly kissed his teeth and abruptly rose to a stand. He picked up the long carving fork and forcefully stuck it into the chicken with the gusto of a healthy young man; he then quickly began slicing the bird gracefully with the carving knife in his other hand.

'Daddy, what the hell do you think you're doing?'

'Chuh!' my grandfather said as he looked up. 'What it look like Marcia?' My granddad said stopping his artistic carving mid slice. 'You blind? cyan yuh see we hungry?'

'Daddy, put the knife down!'

'Hush up nuh Marcia,' my grandfather said dismissively as he continued to slice the cold meat.

'Stop cutting!' My mother said coldly as she smoothed the table cloth around her plate with her long fingernails.

'So, wham, you want mi die of starvation?' my granddad hissed as he continued to cut the bird into sections.

'I, want *you* to wait for your grandson!' My mother screamed, abruptly standing to her feet.

'Now put the knife down!'

'Relax yourself nuh!' My grandfather said sternly as he stopped cutting the chicken into sections and began to make a start on the lamb. 'Mi soon done.' My mother suddenly lunged across the dining table towards him.

'NO!' My mother screeched making everyone jump at the shrillness of her voice. 'Don't you dare touch that bloody lamb!' She hissed, carelessly snatching the large knife from my granddad, and pointing it at him.

'Do you have any idea how much blue quid that cost me? Two bloody weeks' worth!' She shouted as she pointed the large knife at the roasted leg of lamb before haphazardly dropping it in the gravy boat. 'I got the lamb especially for Ryan! It's his favourite.'

'Lahd Jesus gimme strength!' My grandmother exclaimed making my mother turn towards her.

'We're not waiting on Jesus' mummy so there's no point calling his name.' My mother ranted with wide crazy looking eyes. 'Were waiting on Ryan, my first-born child, your grandson mummy, remember him?' She spat after taking another gulp of red wine straight from the bottle.

Everyone sat silently staring up at my mother, her drunken rants were nothing unusual or out of the here ordinary.

'Marcia, listen here!' My granddad shouted while waving the carving fork around with a stiff aggressiveness. 'You *will* show *mi* and yuh mudda sum damn respect you understand!'

'Respect Daddy... You want to talk to me about

respect?' my mother scoffed. 'You have no idea what it's like to lose a child at war!' She shouted pointing a finger in my granddads face. 'To not know if he'll ever come home!'

'Marcia, calm down nuh!' My grandmother said fretfully.

'No, I won't flipping calm down Mum!' She said wiping her snotty nose with the back of her hand. 'I'm talking about my son, my only son!' My mother spat as she began to sob. 'Nobody knows how I feel... Nobody understands what it's like to always be waiting to hear something... anything!' I got up and tried to put my hand on her shoulder.

'It's alright mum,' I said attempting to comfort her and control the situation.

'No, it's not alright Raine! Nobody understands what I'm going through!' she sniffled shaking me off, and like after every empty homecoming announcement I could sense another one of my mother's major episodes coming on.

'Don't you care about your brother?' She said suddenly looking up at me. 'Don't any of you care that he's coming home today?' She asked looking around the table. 'After four long years of dodging radiation bombs, GMA's, bullets and God knows what the fuck else, and *you* his family can't even wait till he gets home before you stuff your bloody faces?' my mother took a slow deep breath and a large sip of her red wine, this time from her glass. She was shaking a little as she wiped a tear away from her cheek and slowly sat back down in her seat. My mother had retreated into herself and her slender fingers began to methodically trace the white table cloth around her plate.

Once again, a silence settled around us like a thick layer of dust in a long-forgotten room. The only sound to be heard was the low muffled sniffling from my mother's lowered head and the low music from a show on the VTV.

'Mummy… Daddy…' My mother finally said after several minutes of awkward nothingness. She raised her head showing us how her puffy bloodshot eyes were. 'I'm sorry, it's just I need his homecoming to be perfect you know?' Her voice was broken and hoarse. 'How do you think Ryan will feel when he sees we couldn't even wait for him to come before we started eating?'

'He will know we were hungry.' My Uncle Kenny said slowly. It was a dry joke but it cracked the stiff tension in the room and made everybody chuckle. Everyone that is, except my mother who gave him a look that could kill.

'Marcia de children them hungry let we eat nuh,' my grandma said sensitively as she put her hands over her eldest daughter's fidgeting fingers. 'Ryan will understand and whatever time him come will be special because he will be home.' My mother wasn't even listening, she was staring at the army green cake that read 'Welcome home Ryan' sitting in the middle of the table.

'The adults can wait a little while longer, can't we?' my Aunt Pamela said encouragingly, trying to appease my mother.

'I bloody can't!' My Uncle Kenny said kissing

his teeth, making my grandmother glare at him from across the table. My Grandfather commanded the VTV to turn onto BBC to watch the 10 o'clock news. He had to turn up the volume to hear over the escalating clink and clanging of the fine silver cutlery now being used.

'Good evening and welcome to the BBC 10 o'clock news.'

'They should be here by now,' I mumbled to myself as I looked back at the clock above the dining room table. It was now, way past curfew and I was getting more agitated by the minute. I looked towards the VTV as my little cousin and two younger sisters ran past me racing to use the double microwave. Generic footage of families being reunited for the first time in years repeatedly flooded the screen, and after a few minutes of watching happy ending sob stories I glanced up at the clock again. I noticed that my mother's eyes keep rolling in my direction, and I caught her glare.

'Why do you keep looking at the time?' She asked me coldly, 'have you heard from your father?'

'Huh?' I said confused making my mother huff loudly, as if I was trying to irritate her on purpose. 'I hadn't heard from my father since he arrived at the military base that morning, and I knew he should've called me hours ago to let me know whether he had found Ryan or not, like he usually did. *What was taking so long?*

'See there, you just did it again.'

'What?' I shrugged innocently which made my mother mutter something under her breath and cut her eye at me.

'Your clock watching!'

'Ohhh that… Sorry its nothing,' I said breaking my eyes away from her intense stare and looking back towards the VTV.

I was worried, and desperately trying not to show it.

'Do *not* lie to me Raine,' my mother said narrowing her eyes at me. I rubbed my thumping forehead, and sucked air in through my teeth. I knew exactly where this conversation was going.

'Raine, Leoni, Montrose, don't you dare kiss your teeth after me!' My mother hissed as she continued to stare at me, her eyes burning holes into my face until I couldn't take it anymore.

'What Mum!' I shouted making everybody look up from their food.

'What the hell do you want from me?' she narrowed her eyes even smaller until they looked like little black jewels behind her slit eyelids.

'You have that twinny feeling, don't you?' I shook my head and sighed to myself.

'No,' I lied as I tried to distract myself by dishing out a plate of food before I lost my appetite. I shovelled rice, potatoes, chicken, and lamb onto my plate and as I looked up my mother was still looking at me.

'Raine, baby,' she said too smoothly for my liking. 'You can tell me the truth I won't ask any more questions; I just have to know. You do have that funny feeling, don't you?'

You're already asking questions, I wanted to say, but I groaned loudly and leaned back in my chair instead.

'No mum I don't *that* funny feeling!' I snapped after a few seconds of wide-eyed staring.

'You're lying Raine,' she said coldly. The soft expression was gone and the narrow-eyed stare was back. 'Don't play the fool with me I can tell when you're lying. I *know* you feel something, what is it? Just tell me?' My mother looked more desperately manic with every loaded question. 'Is it that Ryan isn't coming home? Is he close? Has he contacted you? Is he hurt? Is he...' My mother's voice trailed off as more tight knots began to form in my gurgling stomach. I held my breath for a few seconds until the hot rush of nausea passed. I knew why she was asking. Every time we were told Ryan would come home; I just knew that he wouldn't come. My mother was right; I did have a feeling but this time it was different and I didn't know why, or how to explain it. I picked at the lamb on my plate as wind curdled in my stomach. 'Well?' My mother asked eagerly as she watched me chewing my mouthful of food until I swallowed. I looked up at my mother blankly; I mean what did she want me to say? *I don't think Ryan's coming home mum? He was exiled in the depths of the forgotten wastelands or worse still Ryan's dead and he communicates with me from beyond the grave? I wasn't psychic I didn't know what these bloody feelings meant.* When Ryan and I were little, we used to be able to tell when one of us was hurt or in trouble, the usual *twin* thing you hear stories about, and my mother never entertained or encouraged it up until recently. Nowadays she clung to these occasional supernatural feelings as if they were the indefinite future. When

Ryan was first sent to war I had horrible nightmares, like I was at war with him. They felt so real it was like I was actually there. I could smell the death and decomposition from rotting corpses, decapitated bodies and soldiers running and diving in front of me shooting guns. I could hear the deafening sound of air raids and land mines going off close by. Buildings fell around me and I could hear the wild howls of dogs in the distance. They, the dogs were always chasing me and my only inclination was to find Ryan. But would I die and wake up before I could get to him, every single time. The dreams used to really freak me out but at least I knew we were still connected, that is until they stopped abruptly. Ryan had been away at war for almost a year at that point, and I suddenly didn't know whether he was dead or alive. But after every government homecoming announcement I just knew that he wasn't coming home. At first my mother thought I was just being negative. It wasn't until the 5th announcement three years later that she started to pay attention. I hadn't felt anything remotely *supernatural* since the nightmares, that is until today. Something was different.

'Raine?' My mother snapped pulling me out of my thoughts. The look of apprehension on her face told me she had obviously been waiting for an answer.

'Yes Mum…' I said as calmly as I could. 'What the hell do you want me to say? After all the years of us arguing and all the drama it caused, I stopped telling you the truth because you didn't want to know! And now I'm just supposed to tell you? I…'

Ding Dong. the sound of the doorbell made everyone around the table jump.

'He's here!' My mother screamed excitedly jumping out of her seat. 'Quick!' She said frantically lighting the candles on the big round cake. 'Everybody stop eating, and… and look surprised,' she paused to swig the last of the red wine draining the bottle. 'Oh, and fix the food on your plates so it looks like you haven't started eating yet. Kenny! Get ready to open the champagne.' She tried to fix up the chicken by pushing the stuffing back up into the bird and placing the loose skin back into place over the decapitated breast meat, she turned the leg of lamb over in its dish and then interfered with the surrounding vegetables.

'I guess I'll get the door, shall I?' I said standing up, as everybody else was too busy looking at my mother who was too occupied with the dinner table's presentation to answer it. I rolled my eyes as I quickly left everyone in the stifling dining room, and walked down the long dark corridor into the still coolness of the front of the house. I walked slowly as my heart beat grew more erratic with every step. I was feeling nervous, and as I approached the front-door I could see a few distorted silhouettes behind the frosted glass window. I paused for a moment to think. I was about to see my twin brother for the first time in four years and I had absolutely no idea what to expect… or what to say to him. What if he was different somehow? Disfigured, dangerously temperamental or even shell shocked. I took a deep breath as I lifted my arms and shakily began to undo the lock.

2

RECONCILIATION

'Open up! We have a warrant to liquidize your occupancy!' I jumped back from the front door startled.

'WHAT?' I called confused.

'Open up and stand clear for the reclamation of your property!' The voice was ruff and serious. I peered through the thin panel of transparent glass next to the door. I gasped and held my hands over my mouth. RECON'S! Where the hell was Ryan and my dad? Instead, big black figures dotted the front garden holding huge laser guns.

'Erm... I think there's been some sort of mistake.' I called from where I thought was a safe enough distance away from the door.

'No mistake. Now open up!'

'Why! What do you want?' I asked trying to buy time to think.

'Your blue papers have expired, and we have a

red order to liquidize your occupancy!'

'What? That can't be… blue papers don't expire!'

'Open this door, now!'

'But… we haven't even been served with an amber order!' I said panicking, 'plus this is a legal region and you're in an established gated commune! You're in breach of section 21 of the Historic Citizenship Rights Act! This is against the law.'

'We are the law!'

I jumped back a little further as a dark figure bellowed through the door. 'Recon enforcement is entitled to raid every region and you are now in direct violation of the Reconstitution and Reconciliation Act of 2031!' My knowledge of the law didn't seem to be doing me any favours.

'But I don't understand why you're here…'

'You have three seconds to open this door!'

'But… you… you, you can't do this to us!' I stuttered.

'ONE…'

'Please wait I…'

'TWO.'

'We can talk about this… we've… we've got blue quid… loads of it!'

'THREE.' A huge bang penetrated the front door blowing it clean off its hinges. I was thrown backwards and I landed hard and heavy sliding on the varnished wooden floor. Before I could move a flood of bodies rushed towards me and I was pulled upright and pinned against the passage wall.

'Don't move!' I couldn't move anyway. I felt dazed but I could still feel a large hand pressing down on the back of my head and another one holding my hands and arms together above it. A foot kicked my legs wide open and I was pulled off the wall as another heavy pair of hands patted down the ins and outs of my body lingering on my breasts, my arse and inner thighs. My mind was still trying to clear the fog and the high-pitched noise in my ears, but I was suddenly aware of the screaming, shouting and shots coming from the back of the house. I tried to struggle out of the large Recon's grip but he shoved a spasm stick into my back and threatened to use it. Tears flooded my face as more large boots thudded past me and thundered down the hallway and up the stairs. My head was throbbing and salty tears invaded my mouth as the house suddenly fell eerily quiet. After a few long minutes I was forced down the hallway towards the back of the house. I was shoved into the dining room where my family were sat on the floor faces pointing downwards and backs against the wall. A Recon Enforcement Officer in the centre of the room motioned towards my family with his gun. I took a few slow foot steps towards them and as I did so I could feel the crystal glass and bone china braking into even smaller fragmented pieces underneath my feet. Silver cutlery lay discarded everywhere as did the dining chairs. Ryan's homecoming dinner, and my mother's family pictures and possessions lay strewn amongst the debris. The table was on its side so I had to walk around it, I stepped over the joint of lamb which still looked succulent even as it lay upturned on the floor. I walked around the legs of the table and shrieked when I saw Maxwell lying face down on the floor in a growing pool of blood. My little sisters and cousin were crying, and my Aunty was trying to quieten them in the corner. I stepped around Maxwell trying not to look at his dead body and squeezed in between my two little sisters. They were both crying silently as their dad lay in front of us like a piece of unprepared meat. I put my hand out towards my mother but she didn't take it, instead she just looked at me coldly.

'You knew this was going to happen.' She whispered callously before she looked back towards Maxwell's lifeless body as more Recons suddenly thundered into the room. One of the new Recons who was short and stocky bent over Maxwell and checked for a pulse. He sighed loudly.

'Bloody hell Charlie what the heck have you done now?' Charlie's round face went as red as a tomato.

'It wasn't my fault Rich... I mean the bloke... It was him!' All the Recons looked from the tubby finger pointing towards Maxwell's motionless body and then back to Charlie's red bloated face. 'He was absolutely everywhere he was, ask Gaz he was here!'

'Don't flipping look at me mate.' A voice retorted from the other side of the room. I couldn't see this Recon as he was out of my line of sight.

'But seriously Rich, he was all over the ruddy place,' Charlie continued, 'and when I say all over the place, I mean bleeding everywhere. Jumping all over the blooming gaff he was! Like… Like a bloody crazy gorilla or something, puffing up his chest and giving it all that!' Charlie turned his right palm into the shape of a mouth and made it chatter rapidly. His stubby fingers hit his thumb which was acting as the lower jaw. 'Scared for my life I was… so I had no choice but to put him down.' He said putting his hands onto his chest before throwing them up in the air. 'And I hold my hands up mate, but trust me… it was complete and utter self-defence, I seriously thought he was going to kill me.'

'You're lying!' Déjà screamed.

'Shut your dirty little mouth!' Rich roared pointing the gun at Deja's face. I immediately reacted by putting my arms up in front of my little sisters. Skye, who was the youngest, buried her face into the crook of my arm as she cried quietly.

'You!' Rich spat as he shone the laser of his gun over my face. 'Keep her under control or I will.' Rich moved the gun away from us as he turned back to Charlie.

'Now where was I?' Rich said scratching his head.

'Errm…. My case of self-defence Rich,' Charlie said nervously.

'It was a rhetorical question you fat bastard, anybody would think you of all people could do this job without killing someone every flipping five minutes!'

'Blimey Rich, I'm sorry… I just… panicked.'

'Ooh, you just panicked.' Rich mocked in a high-pitched voice.

'Well in future, if you just panic, and you feel like you need to defend yourself, you paralyze him with your Mortis rod Charlie, or try shocking him with your spasm stick. You can even knock him about a bit if you like, but for Pete's sake don't bleeding kill 'em!' Rich said condescendingly, and even though he wasn't even half the size of Charlie he stared him down until Charlie practically shrunk into the wall behind him. 'Krew's going to have you for this one... You know that don't ya?' Charlie looked down at the floor without offering a reply. 'You really fumbled this one Charlie! You know the damn rules, no fatalities before testing the bloody cargo!' Charlie's big burly frame shrank smaller still as he stared down at the floor. 'I mean sometimes I actually have to excuse myself for thinking that you're slightly retarded.' Rich said casually still standing over Maxwell's lifeless body. 'We may still be able to test his DNA, buts he's almost useless to us now.'

Check his DNA for what? I thought as I watched him studying Maxwell's body beneath his feet. Then Rich suddenly groaned loudly. 'Bloody Nora!' Rich said as studied the device in his hand, you've seriously cocked up now you know that? Your utter stupidity has affected the stats of this month's quota.

'I'm sorry Rich... I don't know it just kind of happened, you know?'

'No, I don't bleeding know Charlie!' Rich snapped as he looked at the two other Recons in the room. 'It just happened he says, well the loss is coming out of your cut!' The Recons chuckled and something sparkled which caught my eye. Turning my head slightly to the left I could see a gold tooth, and that the Recon it belonged to was black.

'You're taking all the heat for this one, cause bugger me if I'm filling out anymore flipping paper work to cover your bloody mistakes! Not with the audit and inspection coming up...' I looked up at Rich then, right into his ugly heavyset face. *Is that all we were to them, paperwork, and numbers?*

'Come on Rich, we don't even have to mark this one down on the books... like the one last week.'

'Don't be stupid you fat tub of lard, you heard the bloody brief in the van, this one had to be kosher!'

'But Rich...' Charlie's last protest fell on deaf ears. Rich had caught me looking at him before I could quickly turn away.

'What the flip are you looking at ay?' I didn't answer him and I kept my eyes on the floor.

'Oi... sweetheart,' he said waving his fingers at me. 'Have a look lads, she's gone all shy on me.' They all chuckled as I heard the bone china crunch underneath Rich's feet as he walked across the room. 'Didn't I just ask you a question?' He said as he stood over me. I kept my face down as my heart beat began to accelerate but still, I didn't look up. He knelt in front of me and grabbed my jaw hard in between his thumb and fore finger, pulling my face up to meet his. His breath smelt of second-hand smoke and cheap alcohol. 'Now, I'll ask you again luv, and you will answer me this bloody time.' I stared into his watery blue eyes and said nothing as he bought his face closer to mine. 'What the hell were you looking at?' Still, I said nothing and he suddenly took a long sniff with his nose pressed hard against my cheek. 'What, see something you like did ya?' Rich whispered into my ear as bought his face closer still. I looked away from him and I caught eyes with my Uncle Kenny and my grandfather who were sat in the corner to my left. Rich suddenly pushed his sweaty forehead hard against mine. 'Look at me when I'm talking to you,' he hissed grabbing my hair. He dragged me up to a stand and thrust me into the middle of the room. He grabbed my neck and suddenly stuck his mortis rod into my side rendering me helpless as a cold paralyzing sensation shot through me. I grunted loudly. 'She's a pretty one isn't she lads?' Rich took his finger and started to trace the outside of my body. 'I hope you're taking notes Charlie' he said smiling. 'This is how you control a bitch,' he hissed before slowly licking my right cheek.

'Enough! I demand to know who is in charge of this... this farce!' My grandfather announced using a radiator to rise unsteadily to his feet. I could see my grandmother out of the corner of my eye pulling at his arm as she tried to shush him.

'Alright, calm down gramps,' A tall ginger recon, skinniest of the lot stepped in front of my granddad spreading his arms as if he was waiting to catch him.

'Move from in front ah mi! This country was built on the backs of my fore farda's, and I will not sit here and let you disrespect my family!' Most of the officers laughed at that, except the big black Recon with the gold tooth.

'Listen here bwoi!' My granddad said wagging a bony finger in the skinny ginger Recon's flushed face. 'I have been in dis country since 1986, and I am a naturalised British citizen, so I demand–'

'Who you calling boy, ay?' The skinny Recon said aggressively.

'Daddy just sit down please.'

'Yea come on Daddy don't be stupid, Mummy needs you.' My Uncle Kenny and Aunt Pamela protested. I couldn't see much; Rich had my head pointed towards the ceiling with the mortis rod still poking into my back. The floors above were quiet now. There were no more thuds from toppling furniture or thundering steps from upstairs. I had no idea what they had done to my great grandmother who was bedridden in her room on the first floor.

'Look gramps, I'm giving you one last chance to sit down and shut the hell up!'

'Listen here, you likkle bwoi, I will not sit down you hear mi! Mi no my damn rights and you cyan come inna my yard and just… Just kill up people soh!' My grandfather said pointing at Maxwell's lifeless body. 'It's not right, unno treat we worse than horse shit, tarass!' The ginger Recon grabbed my granddad's arm and tried to pull him but he resisted, grabbing onto the radiator. 'This whole country went to de dawgs a long time ago! But dis… dis ah de last rahtid straw!' My granddad hissed struggling, his patois becoming thicker with every animated sentence.

'Who the hell are you calling a bloody dog?' The

Recon demanded aggressively grabbing my grandfather's other arm, and yanking him away from the wall.

'Let mi go bwoi! Yuh dutty crawny John Crow!'

'Talk the king's bloody English you senile old twat...' The Recon said shaking my grandfather violently. 'Do I look like I understand your bloody nig nog lingo–' the Recon tried to stop himself as his words trailed off, but it was a little too late, he'd already said it.

'Leave it out Gaz!' The big black Recon said sternly.

'What do you mean leave it Goldie?' Gaz griped, 'I'm a Level 5 Recon Enforcement Officer and that black monk... I mean old bastard needs to know his bloody place.' He continued to protest, though his voice was much more submissive than it had been a few seconds earlier.

'He's an old man, you bloody tosspot, now I said leave it before you get on my fucking nerves!'

'Listen to Goldie.' Rich said impatiently, 'I've got enough on my plate without having to deal with him breaking your ugly mug tonight.' Gaz huffed loudly, glancing down at my grandfather who was still held firmly in his grip. 'Put him down, Krew will be here any minute, and we still got a lot more runs to do tonight.

'Who the hell is dis Krew, is he de one in charge here!' My grandfather interjected loudly interrupting Rich. 'You deaf crawny bwoi? Him seh unhand mi!' Gaz released my Granddad's frail body with one hand and grabbed his spasm stick with the other.

'You cheeky old cun...'

'I am Mr Krew... the one in charge here...' A tall pale man said smoothly, as he suddenly floated into the middle of the chaotic upheaval. His deep assertive voice filled the room, and Gaz pushed my granddad onto the wall, putting away his spasm stick as he shrank back into his idle position against the wall. I craned my neck to see the stranger as the grip around my throat was loosened, and Rich nodded for me to return to my place in between my sisters. This man definitely wasn't a Recon officer, and instead of a uniform he wore a suit. One of the Recons quickly retrieved an upturned chair and the suited man brushed the seat with a gloved hand and sat. He then looked at my grandfather who stood small and inferior amongst the large intruders.

'Mr....?'

Rich instinctively leaned forward.

'It's Alexander, Mr. Krew sir.' He answered quietly.

'Ah yes, Mr. Alexander.' Mr. Krew smiled showing an immaculate set off shiny white teeth. 'I'd be grateful if you'd oblige me and please take a seat.' My Granddad was breathing heavily, still gripping onto the radiator.

'Not before I know what is going on.' Mr. Krew interlocked his fingers and placed them on his crossed knee.

'Please be patient Mr. Alexander, and all will be explained. I am now going to read you your rights so I would really appreciate it you took your place.'

'You,' Gaz said suddenly pointing his gun at my mum, 'help him.' My mum didn't move and my Aunt Pamela tried to get up in her place. 'Not you, I said her!' Gaz snapped pointing the gun in my aunt's face. A loud cough from Rich made Gaz look up as if out of a trance. He looked around before lowering his gun.

'In future, keep that animal locked up in its cage if he cannot behave himself out on a raid.' Mr. Krew said glancing at the corpse in the middle of the room.

'Aye, aye sir,' Rich replied saluting him. 'Gaz put a flipping lid on it will ya!' Rich hissed nodding his head towards the dead body in the middle of the room which Krew had yet to mention. 'In fact, get on your plug and call clean up.'

'What?' Gaz protested as he backed away and allowed my Aunt Pamela to help my Granddad lower himself onto the floor. 'But Charlie was the one who…'

'I don't care!' Rich said marching towards him. 'Just do it!' Gaz pulled a face and skulked out of the room.

'Sorry Mr. Krew sir, he just gets a bit too excited you know.' Rich chuckled uncomfortably under Krew's stare. Krew rolled his eyes as he looked down at his hand where a telekom, a tiny computer small enough to fit in the palm of your hand, sat positioned on a strap wrapped around his wrist. The device worked through thought recognition brainwaves and could only be encrypted to its owner. The wearer connected to their telekom through an earpiece called a plug, which worked in conjunction with the mainframe or independently. With this expensive device you could do almost anything... Krew plugged himself in and his eyes shimmered as he took a deep breath.

'Scroll 58,' Krew said as he held out his hand, and luminous words began to drift up and out of his palm like the holograms you see on the VTV. Krew cleared his throat then began to read. 'Under the Recovery, Reconstitution and Reconciliation Act of 2031 and the Preservation of Sovereignty and Anti-deprivation Act of 2032, passed lawfully and democratically by the Conformed British Fundamentalist Party. You, the Alexander family will be immediately sent to a secure facility to be tested, processed, and deported to the most direct place of ethnicity. These actions are deemed necessary by all members of parliament in the continuing struggle for economic cohesion, international sovereignty, and supreme entitlement. You do have the right to reclaim all household assets, goods, and the contents of your bank accounts once all debts due to the government are repaid in full including any interest owed.' Krew cleared his throat. 'And last, but by no means least, you the Alexander family still retain the right to remain silent as anything you do or do not say may be used against you in an ethnic cleansing immigration court of law.'

3

SOUTH OF THE RIVER

'Right, everybody up!' I was awoken by the light of a torch burning through my eyelids. The same Recons from the house were inside the van shaking each member of my family from an involuntary sleep.

'Wake up!'

'Huh?' I said confused before being violently shaken.

'Up now!' Gaz growled into my face before moving onto my mother who was propped against the inside of the van beside me. Goldie was trying to help my Aunty Pam and little cousin down the van steps. She avoided his hand leaning on the van door to step down; she then lifted Rico out of the van herself.

'Err... Rich...'

'What!' Rich shouted from outside of the van.

'Erm... This one's not waking up.'

'Gordon flaming Bennett! What the blooming

heck do you mean one of em's not waking up?' Rich exclaimed as he appeared in the doorway smoking a cigarette.

'Who is it?'

'Oh, shite on a stick… its Gramps,' Gaz said as soon as Charlie moved his bulky frame. He moved onto my grandmother and shook her repeatedly but she wasn't waking up either.

'It must have been the gas.' Charlie said as he stood upright and removed his hat to scratch his head. 'Too much for his heart I suppose.'

'Are you taking the piss Charlie, that gas is more harmless than one of your farts.' Rich shouted tossing his half-smoked cigarette and stepping into the van. I could do nothing but sit there and stare, my mother did the same and due to the situation, we went unnoticed in a shadowed corner of the van. My Uncle Kenny was helping my woozy little sisters out of the back and I saw the alarm on his face.

'Oh, bloody Nora!' Rich groaned as he took a proper look. He jumped back out of the van and spat a ball of phlegm into the distance before walking around the vehicle. I could hear his heavy footsteps trudging on the muddy ground as he walked around to the other side of the van. He stopped for a few seconds before walking back.

'What idiot left the gas dial on high?' He barked as he suddenly reappeared in the van's doorway and stood next to Goldie. There was silence as Gaz and Charlie looked at each other from opposite sides of the vehicle. 'Well! Who's flipping turn was it?'

'It's been on high since last night!' Charlie protested. 'You know… From that high security classified
transfer.'

'What exactly is your point, you fat prick?' Rich
said angrily peering into the van. 'Because unless I'm
mistaken the dial is supposed to be reset for every single job!'

'Why are you just asking us?' Gaz whined
loudly, 'Goldie was on this job too.'

'Because unlike you two Gaz, Goldie is *not* a
walking bell end!' Rich said lighting another cigarette.
'So, you tell me then,' He hissed after taking a pull,
'who left the flipping gas dial on comatose huh? Another hour or so and they all would've been dead.'

'I dunno do I?' Gaz snapped back.'

'Well, we don't make commission if they're
dead Gaz, so the rest better wake up.' Rich spat spraying saliva into the air.

'They will,' Gaz mumbled.

'And what about that one' Rich said nodding
his head towards my grandmother.

'She'll be fine' Gaz muttered bending down,
again trying to wake her.

'She better be!' Rich grunted taking another
long drag on his cigarette and looking in my direction.

'That's two losses tonight and neither one is
coming out of my cheque.'

'But I had nothing to do with this one Rich!'
Charlie piped up making Rich jump into the van and
push his lit cigarette into his bulbous face.

'There have been two bloody deaths tonight,

that's 7 this month alone Charlie… And your only job is to retrieve and transport cargo alive.' He spat grabbing Charlie's face hard between his thumb and forefingers.

'Gerald?' My grandmother suddenly moaned finally coming round. She grabbed my grandfather's hand and called his name again as Rich let go of Charlie's cheeks and shone his torch into her face.

'I told you she'd be alright,' Gaz said smiling at Rich.

'Well get a bloody move on then.' He said as he exhaled smoke and stepped out of the van.

'Gerald, wake up nuh man!' she cried stroking his face. 'Come now open your eyes,' she said as she kissed his cheek and let her head fall into his chest. I wiped the tears from my eyes as my attention was diverted to the ruckus outside. I could see my uncle trying to push past Rich and Goldie to get back into the van. Gaz stood in front of him blocking further entry. Rich hit my Uncle Kenny with his spasm stick and he immediately collapsed. It was as if he couldn't hold his own weight and he hit the ground with a hard thud groaning loudly. I could no longer see him but I could hear him as he began writhing around in the mud. I wiped the falling tears away from my cheek as I looked around. I felt completely numb. This was all wrong, it just couldn't be real, and I was sure I would wake up from this nightmare any moment now. I closed my eyes for a second and pinched myself. Unfortunately, I felt my long fingernails dig into my skin and before I could try again Gaz dragged me up to a stand.

'Come on, hurry up!' He barked as he forced me out of my daydream. Gaz was pissed, I could tell by the way he grabbed my arm and threw me out of the van. My mother was thrown out after me. My grandmother who refused to leave my grandfather's body was hoisted out of the van by Charlie as she cried and pounded him heavily on the back. We were lined up into single file and forced to leave Uncle Kenny shivering on the ground as the side effects of the spasm stick slowly subsided. Rain began to fall as we were led towards a huge dark bricked building with hundreds of windows and a sign that read Hermitage Hill Detention Centre on the front. All the windows were barred and as we approached, I could see thousands of hands reaching through the gaps as if they were trying to catch the falling rain. Flood lights suddenly lit up the courtyard and I turned around just in time to see the big metal entrance gates were being drawn shut. It was the only opening I could see in the tall metal fence that surrounded the building. The fence was crowned with spirals of electro-magnetic barbed wire that made me jump as they suddenly sparked in the rain. I shivered and wrapped my arms around myself finally accepting the fact that I wasn't going to wake up. I knew of this place… *Well,* I had heard stories. Many of my clients back at the bureau had either died, escaped, or been directly deported from Hermitage Hill. Most of the people that went in *apparently* never came out. I gulped at the thought as we neared the main building. We walked in silence listening to the squelch of our feet in the thick mud, we hadn't even been allowed to put on

31

shoes or coats to protect us from the wintery elements. The courtyard was now littered with other Recon officers also arriving in black raider vans full of captives. Looking back, I could no longer tell which one held my granddad or see what had happened to Uncle Kenny.

'Look where you're bloody going, you clumsy mare!' Gaz barked as I stumbled up the concrete steps. Still, I managed to get one last glance outside as I whispered one last goodbye to my granddad before the set of heavy doors slammed in my face.

The building was dark but warm inside and we were immediately led through a long narrow corridor and into a large rectangular room. We all kept inline and apart from our footsteps we were silent, not even the kids made a sound.

A lady in a grey uniform was sat behind a desk in the middle of the floor. She was leaning back on her chair obviously preoccupied because she didn't look up until she was addressed.

'Alright Sandy,' Rich said tipping his berry hat.

'Boys,' she replied as she looked up and smiled. 'It's a bit early for the first drop, isn't it?'

'Don't flipping ask!' Rich said grimacing.

'Must have been a *special* if Krew attended...' Sandy commented and Rich rolled his eyes.

'That was the last bloody thing we needed!' Gaz hissed from across the room. 'Now can you hurry this up Sandy? I wanna get back out there, and make up me lost commission!'

'Okay... then,' she chuckled shaking her head as she finished doing something on the screen in front of her.

'How many to handover?' Charlie did a quick count, a chubby finger pointing at each of us in turn.

'Two adolescent females, three adult females, one male minor and one OAP.'

'A bit light for you lot,' Sandy said raising an eyebrow.

'Well, erm–'

'Oh, just leave it out will ya.' Gaz whined from his stance against the wall behind us, cutting Charlie off before he had a chance to explain. He suddenly jumped aside as the door next to him unexpectedly buzzed open, and Uncle Kenny was pushed into the room. Goldie was following closely behind as he stumbled and landed on the floor in front of us.

'Make that eight... plus the adult male.' Charlie said nodding his head towards Uncle Kenny who groaned loudly as my Aunty Pamela helped him up to his feet. The woman, or *Sandy* as she was referred to walked around the desk and up and down our line until she stopped in front of me. She stared into my eyes for a moment before tapping something on the screen of the strange contraption in her hand. After a few seconds of fiddling with it she held out her palm and I looked from her hand back to her face confused.

'Palm,' she said impatiently, and I held my hand out as instructed. She placed the contraption over my palm and a red laser danced along its lines and tickled my fingers. She then used the contraption to scan my right eye. I blinked under the green light and Sandy lowered the device and looked at the screen. 'Turn.'

She said blankly, I didn't understand so I just stared idiotically as I turned over my outstretched hand. 'Around.' She said flippantly. I sighed as I complied, and she pulled my plaited hair up and scanned the base of my neck.

'Mummy... what's... what's going on?' I heard Rico whimper from further down the line.'

'Keep him quiet.' A Recon ordered as my Aunt Pam tried to settle him.

'Raine Montrose,' Sandy said drawing my attention back to her as she read off the contraption in the palm of her hand. 'You can proceed... Please go through the red door,' she said pointing towards the opposite side of the room.' I took a deep breath. There was a large red door in the middle of the wall and a larger blue door next to it.

'What about my family?' I muttered nervously looking back at them.

'Don't worry you'll see them soon,' Sandy said smiling deviously. I looked back at them again frozen to the spot. She was obviously lying and didn't want to leave them. I embraced my sisters Déjà and Skye who stood next to me, and tried to reach for my grandmother's hand.

'Come on move it!' Gaz said shoving me hard on the back of my head with his gun. I stumbled forward, and then step by step I walked across the floor with Gaz's gun still poking me in the back. I turned around trying to catch my mother's eye but Gaz shoved me in the back of my head again. I could hear Rico crying as I reached the wall at the end of the room and the large red metal door opened upwards in front of me. I didn't move until Gaz pushed me inside and I spun around just in time to see him blow a kiss before the metal door quickly plunged down.

'Mum!' I screamed throwing myself at the door and banging on it with my fists. 'Deja, Skye!' I started to panic and I fell to my knees trying to catch my breath. Suddenly I felt like the room was moving and a green light began to glow illuminating me in the darkness. Standing up again I realised I was in some sort of elevator. I closed my eyes as greens laser beams appeared and began to dance over my body. A thousand tiny pins and needles ran through me making me squirm as the lift continued its descent. The lift jerked suddenly as two long vertical panels extended out of walls either side of me and stretched the entire length of my body. Four metal robotic arms swiftly clamped two metal cuffs around my arms and legs so I couldn't move. I gasped under the heat on my skin as one of the robotic arms swooped around me cutting away my clothes with a laser beam. I suddenly felt the heat of the laser on my head and I gasped helplessly as I watched the strands of my hair float down before my eyes, like tiny fluttering feathers. I screamed and tried to move my head but it was no use and all I could do was bear witness to the falling strands as they settled lifelessly on the ground. The lift suddenly came to an abrupt halt and the robotic arms retracted into the long panels before they disappeared into the grooves of the walls. I could move again but the sudden weight of the cuffs clamped down on my wrists and ankles. I rubbed the areas of skins where my new metal constraints had already started to bruise. Suddenly a large projection of a man appeared in the black space above me lighting up the room.

'Greetings, and welcome to Hermitage Hill secure facility.' I could see the man's face and I instantly recognised him as Mr. Krew. 'We are an independently run government initiative whose primary goal is to create economic cohesion and international sovereignty. *You* are here because in one way or another you pose a threat to our ongoing mission, and may need to be weeded out of our progressive society.' The projection flickered slightly. 'It *is your duty* to cooperate with us in any way we see fit whilst under His Majesty's pleasure... And if you're lucky you will be deemed useful in our ongoing fight against international terrorism. In return for your service, you *will* be treated in a perfectly humane fashion.' Krew smiled as the projection flickered and disappeared plunging me back into total darkness as I wiped a solo tear from my eye.

'**Proceed!**' I jumped at the sound of the voice from overhead as another set of metal doors slid open behind me. I instinctively covered my nakedness. 'Proceed,' the distorted voice repeated, louder, deeper, more urgent. I turned around and investigated the dark opening. I could feel a faint breeze and I shuddered as I had the intrusive feeling that I was being watched. Hesitantly I looked out into the dimly lit tunnel ahead as overhead lights flickered on. I could just about make out another door at the other end of the tunnel. 'Proceed!' The voice boomed again, even louder and more agitated. It sent shivers through my spine and I took a deep gulp of air before I finally stepped forward.

4

AMAZING GRACE

I woke suddenly alert and I immediately sat up-right on the cold hard ground. A cold draft nipped at my body and I curled my limbs in closer to protect myself from the breeze. I was still naked and I couldn't remember what had happened after entering the dark tunnel. I grabbed at the white cloth that was laid beside me. It opened into a long cotton dress and I quickly pulled it over my head. It took a minute for my eyes to adjust to the darkness and when I looked around properly, it was obvious that I was in some sort of cell; I could see moonlight creeping in through a high barred window on the wall opposite me. There was an old-fashioned dirty porcelain toilet in a corner and above the broken sink sat a dusty mirror which through all the dirt and grime still managed to reflect some light. I stood upright inspecting my surround-ings. Even though half of it was covered in darkness I quickly realised that the cell didn't have a door. I ran to the nearest wall and traced my hands over it feeling for any grooves. After a minute of pointless searching, I pounded the wall with my fist and dropped to my knees. Feeling defeated I held my head in despair and was reminded of the fact that I was now bald. I raised my forearm to wipe away my tears and I accidentally scratched my face with the metal cuff around my wrist. I wanted to scream but I had no energy left, my body feeling like it had been beaten. I licked my cracked lips and my throat was so dry that I walked across the cell and turned the taps above the sink. They made a loud regurgitating sound but nothing came out. I side glanced the toilet, and I tiptoed and put my hands up through bars of the window in attempt to catch the light droplets of the falling rain. After a few minutes of licking rain water of my hands I walked back over to what I could only assume was my bed. I lay down on my side facing the wall, repelled by the odour that wafted up from the lumpy mattress be-neath me. There was no pillow to fluff so I tried to create a heap in the mattress by making a curve and forcing the head of it up against the wall, shivering I grabbed the blanket beside the mattress to cover my-self with. The blanket was itchy but surprisingly warm but I couldn't rest, unnerved by the murmuring, moans and distant screams floating through the walls. I tried to recall how I'd gotten inside the cell. Lost in my thoughts I turned away from the wall to look out of the barred window. The starry sky was clear now and the full moon had adorned the middle of the cell with light. I felt like I was getting too warm under the blanket and the warmer I got the more my skin started to itch. I ran my hands over my body and came across huge clusters of welts and hives. The relief from rubbing them wasn't enough and the sensation I got from itching them was addictive. My skin was suddenly on fire and I kept accidentally scratching myself with the cuffs while I tried to attack the inflamed rough patches with my finger nails.

'Don't scratch it, that'll only make it worse.' That's when I saw her. Had she been there all this time just watching me from the shadows? She must have been. The only thing giving her hiding place away was her short scruffy mop of blonde hair shimmering in the moonlight. She was sitting on a mattress in a shadowed corner on the opposite side of the cell and slowly, she brought her face further into the light. For a second, we just stared at each other, she had a pretty face from what I could see with big owl-like eyes.

'I'm Grace,' the girl said finally. I didn't take the opportunity to introduce myself feeling slightly violated that she had been watching me for God knows how long. 'I didn't want to say anything earlier... You kind of looked like you were going through something.' I rolled my eyes and there was a moment of awkward silence.

'So... What's your name?' She asked, trying to break the ice.

'Raine,' I said after a few seconds. I figured it would be better to indulge in conversation rather than lie alone in the dark.

'Stop scratching.' My new cellmate said interrupting my thoughts. 'Not unless you want scars.'

'What's wrong with me?' I asked desperately trying my best to ignore the urge to itch. Grace paused. 'It's just a side effect… from one of their tests ok… Look just try not to itch.'

'What test?' I asked fidgeting and Grace paused again as if she was trying to choose her words carefully. 'To see how long whatever, they dose you with wears off.' She said as if it was obvious.

'Why?' I asked bemused.

'I don't bloody know!' Grace snapped as she receded back into the shadows. 'Only God knows what they're testing us for…' She said quietly from her side of the cell. 'What I do know is… They haven't even started on you yet.' *Bitch…* I thought as I turned to the wall and resorted to scratching myself softly through my cotton dress. I felt like she knew more than she was saying, but I let it go and my mind quickly wondered onto my family. I hoped that they were all ok but it was doubtful, and I was dismayed by the fact that they were probably in one of these horrible cells. The same cells with the barred windows I had seen when we had first walked up to the building only hours before.

'What're you in for anyway?' Grace asked from behind me after a few minutes of silence.

'Being black,' I said scornfully without turning around, and I heard her snort through the darkness.

'What are you really in for?' She asked mischievously.

'What's that supposed to mean?' I snapped flippantly turning over to face her.

'Well, you don't end up in Hermitage Hill just for being black, they could've sent you anywhere for that.'

'What exactly are you trying to say?' Grace laughed cynically like she knew something I didn't know.

'What the hell is so funny?' I hissed in annoyance; her cryptic shit was really starting to get on my nerves.

'Wake up will you!' Grace said as she stopped chuckling. 'Look around! This isn't any ordinary detention centre... There's another reason you're here... and it hasn't got anything to do with race or status.' I kissed my teeth loudly sucking in cold air.

'What reason is that then?' I snapped as I sat up and crossed my arms.

'Well, I don't know do I?' Grace said innocently, making me feel certain she knew more than she was telling me. 'You're the one who just got here so... You tell me.' I paused for a moment... Maybe there was another reason why my family was taken. But what could it be? I pondered as Grace emerged from the shadows again, her large owl-like eyes just watching me. *Unless she was crazy*, I thought staring back at her. It's not like I hadn't heard of Hermitage Hill, I'd been working for the Diminishing Rights Bureau for three and a half years. Hermitage Hill was where the special security documents came from, all the high-profile cases that were forwarded to the Bureau's citizen legal advice department. They contained classified papers that were way above my pay grade.

'Shit!' I said to myself under my breath, how could I have been so damn stupid! I had no idea why my family had been targeted but my instincts told me that Grace was right! My family were legal last week and now we were in one of the most notorious detention centres in the whole of the United Kingdom. But why though? I took a few deep breaths trying not to let my mind run away from me. I squeezed the bridge of my nose in frustration and when I opened my eyes, I noticed that Grace was still watching me. The thin beams of moonlight streaming in had shifted towards my side of the cell but I could still feel her piercing stare.

'Why are you here?' I asked trying to divert the attention away from myself.

'Me?' she asked surprised as if she didn't expect me to ask her.

'Well, I'm a nobody... Just a Ghost... And Ghosts have no legitimate ties to this country so...' She trailed off and I squinted at her through the darkness.

'Didn't you just say that ending up in Hermitage Hill had nothing to do with race or status?'

'Well... that always plays a part I mean they are of course... the primary factors.'

I rolled my eyes; she was playing games with me and I was in no mood to entertain her. But I needed to know what she knew if I had any chance of finding my family and getting out of here, if that was even possible.

'Well, what did you do to end up in here then?'
I asked more specifically since she was trying to avoid
answering the question.

'I'm Afghani,' she finally said. 'Well, my mother was anyway…' She paused as she slowly leaned forward. 'When World War 3 erupted in the Middle East
anybody living in the UK with ethnic ties to any part
of that region was immediately seen as a threat to national security.' She paused again as she came even further into the light finally revealing the whole of her
face. 'Not to mention the fact was my birth was illegal… To cut a long story short,' she said sighing, 'after
the coalition, and the Liberation Riots my mother's yellow papers were revoked and she was red listed… My
father was English, and from what I was told he
wouldn't abandon my mother… So, they were both
taken in the middle the night.' Grace looked up as she
spoke, and I listened quietly nodding my head sympathetically just like I had been trained to do at work
when listening to similar stories of injustice and broken
lives. 'The Recons came for us when I was just two
years old.' She said holding up the two fingered piece
sign. 'But… Luckily for me I'd been hidden away with
my dad's parents in their countryside cottage a fortnight before.'
I was starting to feel sorry for her, realising how easy
my life had been 'I ran back to London when I was 14.'
She said before she went quiet.

'How did you end up *in here* though?' I pressed,
noting that she hadn't explained that part. She silently
looked out of the cell window at the full moon in the

clear midnight blue sky and I did the same. It had stopped raining now and there were a few minutes of silence before either of us spoke again.

'Get some sleep,' she said abruptly. 'We have to get up soon.' She quickly turned away disappearing beneath a blanket of shadow. I lay on my back and breathed slowly, watching my breath turn into steam as it escaped my mouth and curdled with the cold air. Unfortunately for me as soon as I lay down and was suddenly re-aware of how much my skin was irritating me.

'Come on, you might as well tell me?' I said restlessly as I sat up again, unwilling to accept a whitewashed little backstory. I knew there must be more to it, and I wasn't going to give up until I got an answer. 'Well?' I said again, 'I've got all night!'
Grace groaned loudly and didn't say anything for at least ten seconds. 'I joined the League of Equality when I was 16.'

'The League of Equality?' I repeated quietly. 'As in the LOE Society?' I said much louder than necessary. 'So, *You*, were a Loelife?' I asked in shock and curiously but she didn't answer me. 'Aren't they like, some vigilante terrorists?' I said lightly scratching a cluster of welts on my chest.

'The LOE fights for freedom and liberation!' Grace snapped suddenly reappearing into the light where I could see her.

'The League of Insanity more like.' I retorted sarcastically, remembering some of the stories I had heard on the news.

'Well, those so-called terrorists saved my life…
I would be dead if it weren't for the LOE!' Grace announced as she suddenly stood up on her mattress.
'What the hell have you done to fight the oppression of
the BFP?' She barked viciously. 'Or were you just content with living out your meaningless little existence as
long as the outside world didn't directly affect you?' I
didn't know how to answer that question so I just
stared back at her blankly. 'Look at you…you're nothing but a mindless drone… I can see that and I don't
even know you,' she spat as she pointed at me. 'You
believe whatever you're told to believe, like everything
you see and hear on the news. Happy to live out your
little irrelevant mediocre life because you thought you
were doing your little bit for society.' She attempted to
imitate my voice as she used both her hands to create
inverted commas. 'I've been in here nearly two years
now and I've seen girls like you before… The only way
you're getting out of here is on a plane straight out of
the UK or in a cheap wooden box,' she ranted nastily
as I sat there in silence. Tears stung at my heavy eyelids
as I thought about what she was saying to me.

'You don't know me! You think I don't know
what's going on?' I retorted angrily as I wiped my tears
away. 'I worked for the DRB office for years and I did
everything I could to help those people. I… I even vol-
unteered at the weekend's doing charity work at my
local millennial hospice.' Grace groaned loudly interrupting my train of thought.

'Oh, boo hoo hoo poor little black girl helping
all those people out of their unfortunate situations.

Open your eyes! The Diminishing Rights Bureau is a government funded organization is it not? Whatever role you played in their twisted society was pointless. You were nothing but a drone... just an irrelevant pawn on a chessboard!' I opened my mouth to say something but I couldn't speak, how could I defend my life when she had ripped it to shreds in less than 2 minutes? 'But... you're one of us now...' Grace said sinisterly, 'so you can't just sit and watch from the fenced off comfort of your cushy little life anymore.' I didn't respond and Grace continued to watch me during the few seconds of silence that followed. 'You need to realise that were in a civil bloody war!' Grace suddenly exclaimed as she threw her arms up into the air and began to spin in the beams of the moonlight in the middle of cell. 'You're in bloody Hermitage Hill for flip's sake!' She stopped spinning and dizzily stumbled closer, staring at me with big wild eyes as a million specks of dust floated around her unkept mane in the beams of moonlight. 'You're relevant now,' she said repeatedly making me wonder if she was just weird or legitimately crazy. 'But the question is what will you do with your relevance now?' She asked dramatically as she backed away from me step by step and got back into her bed. She lay down without saying another word and I sat alone in the darkness thinking. Was she right? Had I been living my life on the fence, blinded by corrupted headlines and false propaganda? I lay down and sighed loudly, finally relenting, and admitting what I already knew. I was assisting people with red papers, day in day and out to senselessly reapply for conditional yellow and orange work papers that I knew they would never receive. Helping single parent families who had loved ones lost at war apply for war widow support grants that I knew would never be approved. Countless faces ran through my mind when I tried to imagine their inevitable fates. The DRB turned away 95% of the people that applied for their help last year just because they did not fall within a certain criterion.

I sighed to myself looking up at the dirty ceiling above me. *Grace is right my job was pointless,* I thought as I turned onto my side and a single tear slid down my cheek, in fact my whole life seemed pointless. Now... more than ever.

***

I stirred abruptly from a troubled sleep and my eyes shot open as I reawakened back into my grim reality. A loud buzzing sound made me jump up in bed as my eyes adjusted to the light streaming in through the cell window. I covered my brow with the palm of my hand as I realised that Grace was standing in the middle of the cell.

'What are you doing?' I asked croakily, my mouth was so dry I could hardly speak.

'Just get up will you! I tried to wake you, but I thought you were dead...' She said casually as I groaned loudly and wriggled my frostbitten toes.

'Why?' I said rolling my eyes, not ready to get out of bed and face whatever was in store for me.

'Buzzer means up, and you better move before

it goes off again, I'm not getting punished just because the new girl doesn't know the rules!' She said as she bent down and practically dragged me out of bed to an abrupt stand on the cold stone floor next to her. A loud deep vibration suddenly shook the cell walls, and I almost jumped out of my skin as I clutched Grace by an arm.

'What the hell is going on?' I shouted as the buzzer abruptly stopped, leaving my shrill voice to disturb the sudden silence.

'Just shut up and let go of me!' Grace hissed shaking me off dismissively, as the wall in front of us slowly began to disappear, exposing a large void of space in front of us. My eyes widened and I could just about make out the large square landing lined with other cells all the way around it. An enormous surge of light suddenly shone down from above and I felt a rush of fresh air. I could now see the figures of other prisoners standing as we were in their cells bolt upright, heads straight with their arms by their sides. I could also see into the darkness below and I realised we must have been at least five storeys high. The buzzer sounded again and I followed Grace as she slowly walked out of our cell and onto the landing. Looking up I could see that some sort of skylight had been opened and soon a long line of women crowded the wide square landing in single file. The buzzer sounded again and step by step the queue began to move. We exited the landing and we were met by a male guard who led us through a long dark corridor that had no access to natural sunlight. As we walked, I noticed that the corridor was descending downwards and I could see a bright light spilling in through an open doorway ahead. We were led into a large white square room with huge round windows perched way too high up on the walls for anyone to reach. The room was enormous with countless rows of tables and benches on either side. Men were filing into the hall from two doors on the other side of the room as we were lined up against the tables. A guard instructed us to sit and we sat down in front of empty plastic bowls and cups already filled with what looked like water. As soon as the women were seated a queue of men filled the empty tables on the other side of the room. When everyone was in their place four more doors opened in the centre of each wall. These doors were much wider and accommodated the rows of squeaking trolleys that were now being pushed through them by other inmates. The servers slowly walked up and down the aisles pushing trolleys of what looked like vats of steaming gruel. A young girl with a blank expression on her freckled face pushed her trolley slowly around our table. Her wild curly hair covered the top of her eyes making her look incredibly forlorn and she ladled the concoction into each bowl with utter hopelessness. I looked around the room and noticed several dozen other prisoners with shaved heads like me and I searched as far as I could see for any signs of my family. I twisted in my seat craning my neck until I noticed one of the guards watching me from his post against the far wall. I quickly turned looking down at my empty bowl before glancing around my table. The girl opposite me poked at the gruel in her bowl lifting the skin off the top with her spoon and smelling it before letting it drop back down. The woman next to her waited till it was cold and she traced a grid with her spoon and sliced the now solid mass into chunks. The vat of gruel was getting closer to me as the teenage girl pushed it around to my side of the table. Nobody spoke so I guessed you weren't allowed too, and most of the other prisoners were eating silently without complaint. I was next and I watched the gruel slide off the ladle and plop into my bowl. My stomach rumbled loudly, the strange substance was lukewarm and I reluctantly began to eat. It didn't taste too bad; it was flavourless but at least it was food. I was starving and the last time I had eaten was lunch at work the day before. I didn't even get to take a mouthful of Ryan's homecoming dinner. I used my spoon to skim around my bowl several times as the buzzer sounded loudly to inform us that breakfast had come to an end.

5

WADING IN THE WATER

After that abysmal Breakfast we were taken to a huge room sectioned off into large tiled cubicles. We were then separated into groups of eight and herded into the showers. The cubicles were lit by a huge barred skylight in the ceiling and the sun shone through the bars exposing the brown stained tiles and the mossy green mould growing in the corners. Male guards stood watch from an aisle that ran through the centre of the room. The guard watching my group kicked a large tray full of blue soap, salt toothpaste and small disposable tooth brushes into the centre of the cubicle.

'Quick,' Grace whispered as the other women rushed towards the tray. 'People like to take extra.' She said as she lunged into the swarm of women. The tray on the floor was sliding beneath their feet as wrestling hands pulled it from all directions. Grace grabbed a bar of soap on a rope, a tooth brush and successfully grappled for a small tube of salt toothpaste. I did the same quickly grabbing the last tiny bar of soap and a tube of paste before a short stout woman could get to it. She cut her eye at me before returning to her space empty handed. I cut my eye back as I didn't even get a tooth brush. The Guard then instructed us to find a shower-head and face the floor. We silently obeyed and a loud rumbling sound shook the walls as ice cold water gushed out from the showerheads above us. I was immediately drenched; the water was so cold that I had to force myself not to screech and jump out. The light cotton dress I was wearing disintegrated into wet mush and washed away within seconds. I cowered beneath the showerhead and covered my naked skin as the streaming water slowly began to warm up. I began to rub the blue soap along my skin as I blankly stared at the drains in the centre of the tiled floor regurgitating dirty brown water and clumps of hair. As I rubbed the soap along my chest, I suddenly realised that the clusters of hives on my skin had gone. I searched my lower back but felt nothing, whatever they had infected me with had thankfully worn off. I looked around the cubicle as I continued to lather my skin. All the other women were washing except a woman at the front of the cubicle in the walled corner a few feet from the guard. She wasn't moving at all, she was just standing there, head bowed beneath the rushing water. The guards were distracted by conversation and I stepped forward discreetly trying to get a better look.

'Mum?' I called through the splatter of gushing

water as the guard's cackle echoed throughout the room.

'Raine what the hell are you doing!' Grace hissed from beside me.

'I think I can see my mum,' I told her quietly. 'I don't think she can hear me.'

'Well, you can't talk to her here!' She whispered shaking her head. 'Wait for recreation.'
But I couldn't wait.

'I just need to know if it's her,' I said as I quickly washed the blue suds off my skin. I stared at the woman for a long moment peering through the steam. I was sure it was my mother; she had the right complexion and the right frame and build plus her head was shaved meaning she hadn't been at the facility for long. I took a few deep breaths and when the guard wasn't looking, I dashed to the opposite corner of the cubicle to the horror of the other women. I had to stand right in the corner against the mouldy wall to stay hidden, because the guard was standing by the cubicle entrance on the other side of the wall. 'Mum?' I called again but she didn't answer me, 'Marcia!' I hissed her name attempting to get her attention but she didn't even flinch. Her face looked slightly distorted under the sheet of water so I leaned forward and pulled her body towards mine. SHIT! I whispered as she looked back at me with blank grey eyes. It wasn't her. I released the strange woman and she sunk back into the streaming water. I leaned back into the mossy corner as my heart sank down into the pit of my stomach. My mind suddenly drifted to the rest of my family and I thought about where they were at that very moment. I shook off my anxiety realizing I still had the obstacle of getting back to my position without being seen. The guards were out of my line of sight so I knew I just had to make a run for it and hope their banter kept them occupied. I counted to five and leaned forward but hesitated when I caught Grace shaking her head out of the corner of my eye. I kept my eye on her and as soon as she nodded, I ran across the cubicle trying not too splash too much across the wet floor. I slipped and hit the floor hard sliding back into my position on my arse. My feet hit the tiled wall and I struggled to quickly stand up.

'You're crazy!' Grace said as soon as I got to my feet.

'I made it didn't I?' I sighed under the safety of my showerhead.

'Oi...You?' My heart stopped and I froze under the lukewarm water as if I hadn't heard the guard who was now staring at me from the entrance of the cubicle.

'Raine this isn't a flipping game.' Grace hissed as I looked around. 'This isn't your privileged little life; you can't just do what you want!' The other women were silently staring at me, including the one I had mistaken for my mother. I lowered my head as I heard heavy footsteps stamping across the floor towards me and within seconds, I could feel a presence overshadowing my back.

'What the hell were you doing out of line?' He shouted into my face making me shudder beneath the shower head.

'Sorry sir... she's erm new, she don't know no better.' Grace spoke up, trying to defend me. He silently looked over my shoulder, and then slapped her with the back of his hand.

'Who asked you?' he spat viciously. Then without warning he grabbed my head and slammed my body into the mouldy tiles. 'No interaction in the showers!' He shouted as he dragged me back over to my showerhead. 'Do you understand?' I could feel him pressing his body against me, and see the other guards watching from the entrance of the cubicle. He suddenly held my head up to face the shower until I spluttered and coughed up water. My head ached and I felt dizzy.

'Come on Peirce, I think she gets it...' I heard another guard call from the doorway of the cubicle.

'Don't come on Peirce me!' He said pulling me forward out of the water by my neck. 'I'll say when she bloody well gets it!' He barked as he turned and slapped me on the arse before he finally walked away. I glanced at Grace and she shook her head and looked away from me. Glimpsing around the cubicle I saw that all the other women were still staring at me with a look of shock and disgust on their faces. I tried to put my face back underneath the water to wash away my tears but it was immediately shut off. Without the steam from the running water, we were swiftly exposed to the chilly morning air. I covered myself as best I could but most of the others didn't seem too bothered about being naked or cold.

Suddenly, I could hear the screeching wheels of a cart

being pushed along the central aisle of the room. It took a little while to get to our cubicle as we were in the furthest partition and I shivered until it came to a halt in front of the doorway. We were told to line up in the centre of the showers and we queued obediently as the drains bubbled and gurgled beneath our feet. The girls in front filed out of the showers one by one dipping their hands into the cart and retrieving a towel.

'Not you,' the guard in charge of my group said pulling me out of line as we filed into the central aisle. He snatched my towel away and forced me back into the cubicle. My heart began to race as everyone else left the showers. Grace paused for a moment looking back at me just before she left eyeshot. I heard the last footsteps leave the room and I was left alone for a moment as the guard followed them out. He returned before I even had a chance to think and he gave me an evil stare as he walked towards the cart and grabbed a towel. I watched him closely as he slowly approached me holding out the raggedy piece of material. I hesitated but he gestured for me to take it so I reached out cautiously trying not to expose my naked body. As soon as my hand was within reach, he snatched the towel away and laughed to himself. 'I think you need a lesson in how things run around here.' He chuckled looking me up and down. 'Put your hands by your sides,' he said smiling mischievously. I stubbornly refused and kept one arm over my breasts and the other over my crotch. 'I said… Put your hands by your sides!' The evil little guard repeated raising his voice. I glanced up at him and flinched as he slapped me hard across the face. My left cheek tingled from the sharp sting as I watched him drop the towel into the stagnant water that had collected around the drains. He picked it up and rung it into a long tight spiral. My heart was pounding but still I defiantly covered myself as he viciously hit my bare legs with the wrung towel laughing as I jumped away. He immediately hit me again, across my belly this time and I sucked air through my teeth to keep myself from making a sound. 'If you do not do as you're told I will enjoy making you scream.' He said callously as he wrung the wet towel and hit me again. I jumped back but still resisted so he grabbed me by my throat and choked me until I began to desperately pull at his arms. I couldn't breathe and I hysterically kicked him in the groin to make him loosen his grip. He let me go unfazed, the metal cuffs around my ankles preventing me from hitting him as hard as I would have liked. He watched me silently as I wiped the water from my eyes and caught my breath. 'Well, you're a feisty one, aren't you?' he said as if he was in awe of me. I flinched at his cold touch as he reached forward to grab my breasts. He pushed a cold clammy hand in between my legs and I clamped them shut as he forced his fingers into the crevice of my thighs. 'Be a good girl,' he whispered as he touched himself through his trousers with his other hand. 'And I won't hurt you too much,' he said just before he pushed me back against the tiled wall of the showers. I wanted to scream as he prised my legs open and forced his tongue into my mouth. I bit down hard and he slapped me again catching the side of my face with the back of his hand. 'I was going to be nice…' He whispered into my ear as he forced his fingers inside of me. I squealed in anguish and he sighed into my ear sadistically as I struggled to keep my legs closed. I held my breath as I suddenly heard footsteps approaching. Peirce abruptly let me go and stepped back leaving me to cower in a corner of the showers as another guard entered the cubicle.

'What the hell do you think you're doing Peirce?' He said glancing from Peirce to me as I lowered my head.

'Teaching that little bitch, a lesson,' he hissed gesturing towards me as I stood against the wall facing the floor.

'That's way out of your jurisdiction.' The other guard said assertively making me look up.

'Look she was out of line and she needs to be taught a lesson… you know what these Black bitches are like.'

'Watch it Peirce!' The other guard snapped as he glanced over at me. I looked away but not before noticing his uniform differed from the other guards, I had seen this morning.

'Come on mate you know what I mean, it's not like your fully one of em are ya?' Peirce said chuckling nervously as he turned around and smiled at me making my stomach turn.

'No, I don't know what you mean.' The other guard said coldly, 'could you enlighten me on the lesson you intended to teach this rebellious *black* bitch?'

'Forget it… It was nothing…' He said looking back at me again as if for reassurance.

'No Pierce please... I insist.' The guard said with a hint of passive aggression in his voice. There was a moment of silence, and I marvelled at this miraculous turn of events as Pierce anxiously ran his hands through his greasy blonde hair.

'Come on Jones...' Peirce said rubbing his hands together. 'I'm just having a bit of fun... you know?' He said jovially and even though his back was towards me, I could hear the smirk in his voice. 'All the guys do it...'

'Look Pierce,' Jones said stepping forward. I noticed that he wore a dark blue uniform with a visor whereas Peirce wore a lighter blue uniform with a baseball cap. 'You're new here so let me give you a little advice... Just keep your head down and do as you're told. You're already on thin ice so I suggest you leave her alone and piss off.'

'But I don't understand what the bloody problem is.' Peirce hissed walking towards Jones until they stood directly opposite each other in the middle of the cubicle. 'Unless... you just want her all to yourself?' he said agitatedly.

'Look you might get away with this on Jaime's watch but it's not happening on mine.' Jones said loudly making his voice echo throughout the huge shower room. There was silence for a long moment as the two men sized each other up.

'You can't tell me what to do,' Pierce said defiantly sloshing back over to me. I lowered my head wishing I could just disappear, holding my breath as he got closer.

'Leave her alone Peirce,' Jones hissed as his face twisted into an angry snarl. 'I won't tell you again!'

'I've heard all about you Jones,' Peirce said stopping in his tracks just a few feet in front of me. 'Now I don't know who the hell you think you are,' he said as he spun around. 'But you need to look the other way or one word to my father-in-law, and I'll have you–'

'You'll have me what?' Jones shouted as he marched across the cubicle towards us. 'When I'm on watch I run this wing you understand?' He barked into Peirce's face. 'Or do I have to remind you that you were demoted by that very same father-in-law, and that's the reason you're here instead of in that nice corner office on D wing hmm?'

Pierce growled loudly making me jump. He was staring right at me and it took him a few seconds to turn and walk away.

'This isn't over Jones.' He spat trudging passed him and out of the cubicle.

'Yeah yeah, alright Peirce just don't let me catch you on shower duty on my watch ever again!' Jones called after him as he marched out of the showers. I listened to the sound of Pierce's boots until they faded away very aware of the remaining guard's eyes watching me from beneath his visor. I looked at the floor and he cleared his throat as he began to walk closer, within seconds he was in front of me and I kept my eyes on his shiny black boots.

'There's no need to be scared,' he said as he slowly held his hand out to give me a towel. I stretched an arm away from my bare breasts and grabbed it. I turned away from him and quickly wrapped the towel around myself.

'Thanks,' I said quietly while still staring at the ground.

'You're welcome,' he said as he lifted my face to inspect the bruise Peirce had given me across my cheek, and the bump on my head. I flinched but didn't fight the gesture, and he gently cupped my chin in one of his large hands. I averted my gaze as he tilted my face upwards to meet his.

'Raine… Raine Montrose?' I was so shocked by the sound of my name that I thought I was hearing things. 'I knew it was you!' Still, I didn't look up. 'Raine… it's me.' He said as my eyes darted around in shock. I finally looked up at him meeting his gaze as he pulled off his visor.

'Sebastian?' I mouthed quietly not quite believing my eyes. 'Oh, my days Sebastian!' I screamed jumping into his arms. I hadn't recognised him with a full beard and I squeezed him tightly as it brushed the side of my face. Sebastian suddenly looked away embarrassed and glancing down I realised my towel had fallen onto the wet ground. I jumped down to retrieve it but Sebastian snatched it away, and went to get me another one.

'Don't want you catching nothing.' He said breaking the awkward silence as he threw the dry towel around my shivering body.

'How did you end up in here?' He asked me as I tucked the worn fabric over my breasts. Seeing Sebastian's familiar face had taken me to a happier place for a few precious seconds, but now back in reality, I stared blankly into his questioning eyes before responding.

'What am I doing here?' I retorted venomously as I averted my gaze. 'What the hell are you doing here?' I asked accusingly as my eyes bored into his. 'My whole family was grabbed during a raid but what bloody excuse could you have for working here!' I said heatedly as he rubbed his face with his hands.

'So much has happened since I last saw you...' Sebastian answered quietly.

'You don't fuckin say!' I hissed angrily searching his hazel eyes for an answer, 'What could have possibly happened to make you work for *them*!' I cried loudly.

'We... I didn't have a choice...' He said sighing hopelessly as he looked away from me.

'We? Wait hold on a minute,' I said my mind working like a clock as we stared at each other in silence. 'If you're here then... Where the hell is my brother?' The look on Sebastian's face made my stomach sink like a stone.

'Sebastian, where is he?' I demanded.

'I don't know.' Sebastian sighed loudly as he shook his head.

'Don't lie to me.' I spat agitatedly.

'Raine, you have to be quiet! this isn't the time or place...'

'Fuck that, Sebastian! You and Ryan signed up together, now tell me what the hell happened to him!' I screamed angrily and he hastily covered my mouth as my shrill voice echoed around the showers.

'Raine, keep your damn voice down!' He said coldly as he looked over his back towards the entrance of the cubicle. I nodded sheepishly, remembering where I was as my eyes welled up with tears. He gave me a few seconds to calm down before he removed his hand from my mouth.

'They took my family.' He said after a long gaze down at the ground. 'I had to take this job in exchange for their release…'

'Oh…' I said quietly as my eyes searched his face suspiciously. Was he telling me the truth? Could I trust him? Was he still the little boy I grew up with? My brother's best friend and my first secret crush.

'So… when did you get back from the waste-lands?' I asked and Sebastian paused for a few seconds.

'It's been almost 3 years now,' he said finally.

'Well, if you've been here for that long then… then what about Ryan?' I asked desperately as I grabbed his jaw and looked up into his face.

'I don't know… all I know is that he… he just wouldn't comply… he resisted, and we got separate-ed… I got sent back, and I just assumed that they sent him… to *the beyond*.'

'What the hell is the bloody beyond!' I de-manded, as Sebastian sighed, and then paused for a moment that seemed like an age.

'*Beyond* the front line…' I swallowed a large lump in my throat as I let go of Sebastian's chin. He gave me a sympathetic look and put a hand on my shoulder. I shook him off and turned away as I tried to come to terms with what he had just told me. He gave me a moment to myself, before he stepped back into my line of sight. 'Raine, you know I would tell you if I knew exactly what happened to Ryan for certain.' Sebastian said quietly, and my eyes lingered on his profile as I shivered from the cold chill in the air. I took in how much he had changed since I had last seen him. He was still tall of course with a hue the colour of smooth molten caramel. He was much stockier than I remember, with a full beard covering the lower half of his face, and a strange tattoo around his left eye. I wasn't sure if he was telling me the whole truth, and I didn't know if I would call his choice of submission totally pathetic. Or Ryan's choice to resist completely heroic. Because at the end of the day, Sebastian might have sold out to the government, but at least he was here... Alive. And he was the only one that could help me now...

'Sebastian,' I said watching him closely. 'I need to get myself and my family out of here.' He stayed silent but maintained eye contact. 'I need your help.' I pleaded desperately. Sebastian sighed as he looked up at the ceiling for a long time.

'Look Raine,' he said after looking at me for a long moment, 'I can get you out if we go now... You'll have a half day's head start. But I mean like, right now!'

'What?' I said conflicted by his bittersweet reply. 'You expect me to just leave my family behind?' I asked as he looked away from me. 'Why can't you help them too!' I pleaded frantically.

'Raine, I don't even know where your family is…. I would have to find them and that takes time.' He looked deep into my eyes. This is a risk I'm taking because… it's you. Do you understand that if I get caught, they'll execute me and my entire family?' I bit my bottom lip anxiously and nodded slowly. 'What I'm about to do for you I've never done for anyone, and with the influx of arrivals, we have a rare opportunity-ty… so if you want it you, have to take it now. Do you understand' What was I supposed to do? I couldn't just leave my family behind. My heart began to beat wildly as we stood silently staring at each other. His eyes left mine for a second, and after they darted around the room for a moment, I took a deep breath and slowly stepped towards him until our bodies were touching. There must be a way to get them out, I had heard of escapes, whole families even… I couldn't leave them! Tip toeing, I reached up to kiss him and he reciprocated the gesture by bending down slightly. His lips felt soft to the touch and when I closed my eyes, I seemed to forget my surroundings for a blissful moment. He didn't stop me so I lifted my arms up around his neck and allowed the towel around me to fall onto the wet ground. I then pressed my naked body against his uniform and within seconds I could feel him getting hard against my thigh. I took his arms by the wrists and lifted his hands to my breasts.

'Can you help them now?' I said looking up at him doe eyed and shivering under his cold touch. He suddenly snatched his wrists out of my grip and abruptly pushed me away.

'What the hell do you take me for?' His said turning his back on me, as he walked over to the trolley and retrieved yet another towel.

'What's wrong?' I asked feeling humiliated.
'Don't you want to?' I said thinking back to when he had taken my virginity at a house party on the last day of school. Our little romance ended almost immediately, especially after Ryan had caught us sneaking around a few weeks later...

'Of course, I want too...' Sebastian said taking a deep breath. 'Ever since we...' He trailed off. 'Just not like this! I don't want you to think that you have to do that for me to help the rest of your family... They're like my family too... I would help them if I could!' I kissed him again before he could stop me and he rolled his eyes and smiled down at me.

'It's just going to take some time to find them... But you're here right now, and this wing is not a good place to be.' He said as he held onto my shoulders and squeezed reassuringly.

'Why have they bought me here?' I asked hopelessly looking down at my feet.

'It could be one of a few reasons ... but, the less you know the safer you'll be.' Sebastian said still gazing down at me. 'You're going to have to trust me ok,' he said lifting my chin. 'Now tell me who's missing?' I listed all my family members and their current descriptions while Sebastian recorded my voice on his telekom.

'What now?' I asked as he tucked the device back into his pocket.

'We move.' Sebastian said looking down at me.

'Oh, you meant right right now?' I quizzed as my eyes widened, 'In the middle of the damn morning?'

'Yes! It's recreation time now and all the prisoners are out in the yard for exercise, they'll be all over the place for the next few hours. So, we must move now while we have the opportunity. Let's just hope you don't get called in for testing. If we wait until night-fall I won't be able to get you out of your cell.' I nodded remembering that the cells had no doors.

'What about Peirce?' I asked anxiously, 'He saw us together.'

'Don't worry about him, I know how to handle his sort.' He answered reassuringly.

'Your skin must be still raw over your tracker.' Sebastian commented as he touched the back of my head and felt around my hairline.

'Ouch!' I said batting his hand away as he touched the soft spot at the base of my neck.

'Sorry,' he said stepping back.

'When you arrived, they would've put a sensor chip into your neck.' I shrugged not able to remember most of my first few hours at the facility. 'The sensor chip's alarm sequence is activated when you stray more than a hundred yards away from the prisons secured perimeter. If you are not found on or around the premises it will activate the red alert and you will be tracked down. I took a deep breath as I tried to take it all in. 'You may feel a numbing or ringing sensation in your head.' Sebastian continued without taking a

68

breath. 'It will incapacitate you if the Recons sensors get within range. The closer they get the more the ringing will hurt, but I will plant a nasty little bug in the system to give you a good head start. They won't know you're gone until evening, but if you hear even a faint ringing in your ears you run even faster you hear me.'

'What if I don't get far enough? Can't you just take it out now?' I asked panic stricken.

'No there's no time, I don't have the tools so you'll bleed, and scream. But I can block the signal for a few hours, and they won't notice that your gone until they gather up the other prisoners for dinner and lock down. That should give you enough of a head start, so you won't get immobilized before you get to safety.' He said as he abruptly marched away from me. I nodded tentatively as I hurriedly followed him out of the cubicle, and over to another trolley which stood haphazardly in the middle of the aisle in between the cordoned off showers. 'But you need to get the tracker chip removed as soon as possible.' He said as he retrieved a pair of hard soled material shoes, a dirty beige bandana and a cotton jump suit and passed them to me.

'How?' I asked as he turned around politely while I dressed. He seemed to ignore me while mumbling to himself and fiddling with something in his hand.

'Head up, feet wide and hands out.' He instructed turning around to face me as soon as I was fully clothed. I obeyed him and kept my arms out in the air until they began to hurt. I looked at him as he swore to himself and strange beeps and buzzing came from the small device in his hand. The same device the woman called Sandy scanned me with when I had first arrived. The metal cuffs around my arms and legs suddenly began to rattle before they split open and flew in opposite directions hitting the outside tiles of the cubicles on either side of us. I sighed and rubbed the sites of sore skin they had left behind.

'Right let's move,' Sebastian announced as soon as he had retrieved the broken cuffs and dropped them in the shower's gurgling central drain. I quickly followed him towards the door. 'Stay close,' he said quietly as he looked down at his device then in both directions before stepping out into the hall.

'What if someone sees us?' I whispered cautiously before tentatively stepping out behind him.

'This is my watch,' Sebastian said quietly.

'I'm the wing Supervisor, so, I'm in charge for now… This little device will help me find a safe quiet route.'

'What about the AI, the cameras are watching us?'

'Don't worry about it.' He replied tapping the device again. I know a guy in the algo-systems department.' He said winking to reassure me. 'Just keep your head down and follow me closely, ok?' I nodded as a painful pang in my chest reminded me of my family.

'How are you going to find my Fam–?' I asked solemnly, thinking out loud.

'Never mind that now!' Sebastian interrupted tersely, looking down at his security device.

'How long will it take to free them?' I asked again after a few minutes as I tried to keep up with his long strides. He turned a corner and quickly strode down a long corridor with a metal security door at the end before he replied.

'I'm not sure... escapes usually take up to a year to plan... and they're not always successful.'

'A year!' I blurted loudly stopping dead in my tracks. 'To plan! I can't leave them here for that long! What if they all get deported, or worse?' I hissed hysterically as Sebastian walked back to me. He gave me a very stern look as he pulled me along by my arm.

'Raine, Hermitage Hill has 22 huge wings and I've got to search all of them... plus, we need the right opportunity or distraction.' He said relenting, instinctively knowing that I probably wouldn't shut up. 'I've still got to cover up your disappearance... *the rest of the guys are gonna be livid...*' He trailed off and I looked down at the ground.

'Look Sebastian,' I said pulling my arm out of his grasp. I know you're taking a huge risk for me... But I can't just leave my family in here forever.'

'Raine, listen to me,' Sebastian said as we came to another high security barrier. 'What good can you do for them in here huh? Give it a few days and you'll be drugged up to the bloody eyeballs... Trust me, we won't get another chance like this!'

'Drugged?' I said anxiously looking up at him.

'Nothing, forget I said it... I'm just getting you out of here today!' I saw his Adam apple leap in his throat as he used his handheld device to unlock the security door. We carried on in silence and soon Sebastian had led me to an unlit basement underneath an abandoned wing in a very old part of the prison. We stood still for a moment as Sebastian put away his device and pulled out his telekom. He held his hand out in front of us and the dark space retreated under a projected blue light as he cast some sort of image or hologram into the air. Whatever he was viewing was encrypted so all I could see was small random explosions of illuminous binary code.

'Sebastian, how are you even gonna get away with all this?' I asked quietly from beside him.

'It's safer if you don't know the details... but let's just say there's a few of us who are fighting the system from within, and this is just our little way of resisting.'

'Oh, I see.' I said, deciding that Sebastian's choice to submit to the system wasn't so pathetic after all.

'Try not to worry about your family,' he sighed finally looking up. 'I promise I'll find them and do all I can to keep them safe.' I forced a smile, and followed him as he quickly moved through the dim until he came to an abrupt stop. A stench suddenly invaded my nostrils and I realised we were standing at the top of a stairwell as Sebastian shone a light into the darkness. He suddenly grabbed my hand, and we descended into the dark spiral passage. I watched the light from his hand bounce off the mossy green walls as I lost all notion of how deep underground we were going. We continued marching downwards and soon we landed with a splash on wet even ground. I covered my nose and mouth from the rancid odour that seemed to seep from the walls as Sebastian silently studied his encrypted hologram. After a few seconds he marched ahead without warning and I hurried after him making sure to leap over the large puddles and piles of debris. My skin had started to itch and I felt jittery as I felt the drip drop of dirty water from the broken pipes that ran along the ceiling overhead. I was walking so closely behind Sebastian that I kept stepping on his feet. I held onto his shirt as I gazed into the open cells as far into darkness as the light from his plug would allow. I quickly glanced up as a pack of nestling rats darted under the exposure of artificial light glowing around us.

'What is this place?' I shrieked as I stepped on what I assumed was a dead rodent.

'You don't want to know.' Sebastian said calmly as we continued to quickly move through the underground maze. We carried on in silence and after a few more minutes of twists and turns Sebastian suddenly stopped in front of me. He then gently removed my grip from around his back and turned around to face me. Looking past him, I realised that we had come to a dead end.

'I can't go with you any further.' He said slowly.

'What? Sebastian… You can't leave me here.' I said looking around horrified.

'Raine, I have to get back, I need to plant the virus into the security system before you get shocked at the perimeter. *Plus, I need to tell the guys what I've done.'*

He looked away from me. 'Besides, I better show my face in the yard before anyone notices…' I quickly buried my head into his chest as my eyes welled up with tears. He let me stay there for a long moment before he gently pulled my head away from his uniform and wiped my tears on his sleeve. 'You're strong Raine… You've always been strong. Braver than me and Ryan anyway,' he said chuckling. 'You'll be fine I know you'll make it… You have too.' I nodded meekly as he walked over to the wall opposite us and began moving the large pile of stacked crates and metal sheets that lay against it. He put a ball of light in suspension mode, and it hovered nearby giving Sebastian just enough light to study the wall. He suddenly wedged open a large vent releasing a gush of sludgy fluid that seeped onto the floor. I stepped back as the puddle splashed my feet and I couldn't help but notice how the algae covered wall made the mossy grate practically undetectable to the unknowing eye. *How did he know that was there?* I thought as Sebastian beckoned me over. In a daze I slowly stepped forward as a faint gust of air caressed my face. 'All you have to do is keep crawling and never turn left.' He said as I gazed into the dark hole. 'The seventh turn on the right will take you up to the street above.' My eyes caught his stare and I tried to stop myself from crying again but it was too late. I couldn't hold back the shuddering sobs suddenly escaping my body.

'I can't do this by myself!' I said peering into the dark vent then back at Sebastian. 'And I can't leave them here!' I cried as I wiped the free flow of tears out of my eyes.

'You have to!' Sebastian said grabbing me by the arms and shaking me. 'Now... Do you remember what I just told you?' I closed my eyes and slowly nodded as I tried to stem the last of my falling tears. 'Good,' he said as he wiped my face with his other sleeve. Sebastian gave me a few moments to gather my thoughts before leading me closer towards the open vent. 'When you get out you run, you hear me.' He said taking off his visor and fastening it on my head. After he had adjusted it to my size he fiddled with the peak and a handy little light clicked on. 'You will need to find the LOE Society... They're the only ones that'll remove your tracking sensor. 'The LOE Society,' I said sniffling... 'The society of Loelifes?'

'Yes Raine...The nearest safe house is Brixton Tube Station, so you need to head north.' I tried to protest but Sebastian put a finger up to my lips. 'You will be safe there, trust me.' He sighed as he leaned forward and kissed me on the forehead. 'Besides, where else are you going to go? no one will touch you or offer you any help.' I sighed knowing Sebastian was right. I bit my lip as I was reminded of Grace. Here I was getting the chance to escape and I was attempting to negotiate to find the best hideout. Maybe she was right about me.

'When you come up to street level find Brixton Hill,' Sebastian continued. 'You'll be close so find that and it will lead you to Brixton Station.' Sebastian pointed to the ball of suspended light and the illuminated orb changed into a 3D map. He pointed out what street the tunnel would take me to and how far away I would be from Brixton Hill and Brixton Tube Station.

'Sebastian, how do you know all this?' I asked not able to concentrate on what he was saying. It was as if my brain had chosen this precise moment to catch up with the trauma, I had experienced over the last 24 hours. Sebastian didn't answer me, and we stared at each other under the blue light of the holographic map as I tried to gather my thoughts.

'Remember seventh turn on the right…' He said finally as he suddenly hugged me. He broke the embrace after a few seconds and helped me climb into the vent. It was cold and wet, and I flinched as I saw something scurry away from the light of the torch on my visor as I looked up ahead. I took a deep breath.

'Sebastian… I know I've asked for the world already, but can I ask for one more thing?' I requested as I turned back before he closed the grate. He nodded and leant his head into the vent to give me his full attention. 'My friend… Well, my cellmate Grace… I know I haven't known her for long, I just met her, but she helped me in the showers so if you could help her too…' I let my voice trail off. I had asked for so much already and I didn't expect anything more, but something told me that I had to throw Grace a lifeline if I could. Sebastian shook his head and smiled. 'Typical Raine always trying to rescue everybody… I'll see what I can do.' He said as he stood upright slowly closing the large grate behind me. He bent down and looked through the bars, but they were covered in so much moss and algae that I could barely make out most of his face.

'Thank you… For everything,' I said through the grate.

'You're welcome.' Sebastian said after a few seconds. 'Just take care of yourself.' He pleaded staring at me with unblinking eyes and I slowly nodded as a single tear slid down my cheek.

'Raine, you need to go now.' Sebastian urged quietly after a few more seconds and I turned around to glance into the tunnel ahead. I took a deep breath trying to ignore what was crawling through my fingers in the shallow murky water beneath me. I took a deep breath and without looking back I began to crawl. I stopped after a few metres as I heard Sebastian replacing the metal sheets and wood over the entrance to the vent behind me. When he had finished, I listened to his splashing footsteps as he began to walk away leaving me alone in the dark. I shuddered as the feeling of complete loneliness overcame me and I didn't move again until I could no longer hear the echo of his footsteps fading off into the distance.

6

IN PLAIN SIGHT

*T*ake heed this is an urgent announcement. There is a prisoner on the loose; I repeat there is a prisoner on the loose. The prisoner is a black female of illegal status. Do not engage, I repeat do not engage! The prisoner is a crazed escapee from Hermitage Hill and she is armed and highly dangerous. An earlier curfew is being enforced on the South side of the river with immediate effect. Anyone found on the streets after 6pm will be arrested. Anyone found consorting with the prisoner will be detained. Please note the Department of Recovery, Reconstitution and Reconciliation does not rule out the use of excessive force, those who are found harbouring prisoners will take full responsibility for themselves and their actions. This announcement was brought to you by Reconco the National Department of Recovery, Reconstitution and Reconciliation. Keeping you safe from international terrorism every single day.*

My stomach churned with hunger and I covered my

ears as the feedback from the megaphone speaker followed the announcement. I was exhausted so I dared not move from my hiding place until I had caught my breath. I sighed to myself as the sound of feedback from the megaphones posted on every corner continued to ring through the air. I smelled like crap after crawling through that disgusting drain and into the ancient sewers of old London. I was terrified by the harrowing sounds that drifted towards me through the tunnels and it hadn't taken me long to work out that it was leeches sticking to me as I crawled through the contaminated slush. It was time to move, I had only been out a few hours, but I had been running for what seemed like forever. It was early evening and I was getting desperate. The streetlights flickered unreliably against the already aubergine purple sky as I watched people rush to get off the streets. I tried my best to stay out of sight considering the state I was in; my white cotton jumpsuit was stained a shitty shade of brown and I stank to high heaven, but I was forced to run frantically down the abandoned streets. I didn't know what else to do but I knew I had to keep moving. I must have taken a wrong turn somewhere because I was completely lost. I ran down an empty road and quickly turned another corner but after just a few minutes of exposure I could hear the faint sound of sirens and barking in the distance. I panicked and thought about disappearing down another manhole, but I couldn't bear the notion of finding the source of the harrowing sounds I had heard earlier. Something told me I must be close but if I didn't find Brixton Tube Station very soon, I knew the Recons would get within range and would relentlessly track me down. I ran across a road and into a small park to hide but I knew I had to keep moving. I could see the lights of the Recon's vehicles shining into the bushes from the near distance. I stayed close to the metal fencing and soon I could see the small dancing beams of light from the Recons uniforms as they entered the park behind me. The chilling bark of the modified dogs made me shiver and I picked up the pace darting through clusters of trees and running straight into an open clearing. I stopped for a second looking around for a moment. I peered into the darkness and after squinting for a few seconds I saw a gate on the opposite side of the grass. I took off again bolting across the greenery and out into the road of a large intersection. I paused to think but a loud ringing suddenly invaded my ears as a dull pain pulsed from the base of my neck and down my spine. The tracker chip had been activated and it took all my strength to force myself to breakout into a run. I glanced back and saw the Recons had on gliding boots and they quickly skated down the road towards me. I could hear the patter of dog paws gaining on me and I ducked into a large church yard and kept running. I leapt over grave after grave trying to find another exit. The painful ringing was getting stronger, but I forced my body to keep moving. The bitter wind whipped at my face causing tears to stream down my cheeks as I sprinted towards a tall gate at the end of a walled garden. I approached the gate at such speed that I couldn't help myself from crashing into it. I stepped back and rattled the bars anguished to see that it wouldn't open.

'Arrrh!' I cried grabbing the locked padlock frantically. The sound of barking close by made me jump and I whipped around to see two hybrids rapidly approaching. Much more monstrous than normal dogs, they were genetically modified to be faster and deadlier and they were closing in on me as they leapt over gravestones and into the small garden. My stomach lurched as I watched them run around opposite sides of a water fountain in the middle of the green to get me. I had no escape and without thinking I let go of the padlock and leapt up onto the gate. The top of it was laced with jagged metal and barbed wire but I had no time to carefully work my way over it. I wedged my foot into the square handle and launched myself over the gate one leg after the other. I jumped down smarting my feet on the pavement as the hybrid dogs ran headfirst into the thick black iron bars behind me. They shook it violently banging their bulky bodies against it as they tried to squeeze their large heads through the bars and bite into the metal. The ringing in my head returned with fierceness and the searing pain shot down my spine as I caught site of the Recons gliding into the garden. The dogs ran back and began trying to jump over the gate as I forced myself to keep going. I jogged back to the junction. I had to stop to catch my breath and I doubled over exhausted. I put my hands on my knees and I noticed the large gash on my right forearm and that it was leaving a trail of blood behind me. I cursed silently as I looked around and noticed people watching me from their windows. I ignored them as I turned 360 degrees and high up on a building on the opposite side of the junction, I finally found what I was looking for. It was a sign that read Brixton Hill. I had finally found it and I let out a short-lived sigh of relief as I heard paws beating the ground again. The Recons were already out of the graveyard and back on my trail. I frantically sprinted across the junction and straight down Brixton Hill. I began to panic as I noticed that there was a blackout up ahead, but I knew it was too late to change course and I continued to make my way towards it. I ran straight into the darkness and my eyes were immediately drawn to the only source of light. I saw what looked like a scrap yard a little further down the road. A tall beacon of light flashed above the abandoned vehicles reflecting off the broken metal and glass. The sound of barking was getting closer and I carried on running towards it aware that the Recons could catch up to me any second now. There was no fence around the scrap yard, so nothing prevented me from running into the depths of the discarded vans and cars just as the Recon's lights penetrated the darkness of the blacked-out section of the street. I crouched by a pile of tires heaving and panting heavily, desperately trying to get fresh air into my lungs. *They're going to catch me!* I thought as I frantically looked around considering my next move. I could now see the beacon of light sat high on a pole on top of a building. I ran deeper into the scrap yard and made my way towards it. I diverted around a double decker bus but found myself blocked in by more vehicles. Cars and vans were piled on top of each other like some sort of barricade that prevented me from going any further. I ran back around the bus to find another way through and I froze when I saw the light of the Recons in the scrap yard. I heard the thud of heavy paws clambering over vehicles and panicking I tried to prise the bus doors open with my fingers, but they wouldn't budge. I fell onto the ground in pain as the ringing in my ears sent shockwaves down my spine. I forced my body to move as I tried to scramble underneath the bus in front of me. I crawled forward with all my strength but just as I was halfway underneath, I felt a hot searing pain in one of my legs. There was nothing to hold onto and I screamed in agony as I was dragged along the gravel and pulled from underneath the bus. My fingernails scraping through the dirt as I screamed. I was being dragged along the ground like a rag doll and I could see the other dog rapidly approaching from another angle. I covered my face and closed my eyes braced for impact, ready for death by genetically modified dog. But then the dogs suddenly yelped, the one coming towards me retreated, and the one attached to my leg released its lock jaw and clambered away. The ringing in my ears began to fade and the shockwaves pulsing down my spine abruptly subsided. My eyes fluttered as smoky fumes encircled me and crept into my nostrils. I covered my mouth to cough as I cautiously looked around. There was billowing smoke everywhere and I could hear shouting as I struggled to sit up. I groaned as I tried to move my injured leg and I leant against the bus heaving from the shooting pain.

My eyes were burning, and I began to feel dizzy, I was barely able to move my own body when somebody grabbed me a few moments later. I tried to open my eyes properly, but they were so heavy, and the toxic fumes were choking me.

'I've got a stray!' The figure shouted as I felt him kneel beside me and inspect my leg. The pain was excruciating but I couldn't even react to his touch. 'She's been bitten!' I heard him shout again as he covered my face with something, hoisted me up and carefully slumped me over a large shoulder. I still couldn't open my eyes, but the corners of my mouth curled into a slight smile as I let myself drift off into an uncontrollable sleep... I had made it.

***

I let my body drift in and out of sleep for a while, I don't know how long for, but I was comfortable. I was in that safe warm place, right in the moment just before you first open your eyes in the morning after a good night's sleep. I could hear my mum's footsteps coming towards my room and I opened my eyes before she had the chance to scream my name. *Where the hell was I?* I thought as my eyeballs adjusted to the light and darted around the large space in front of me. I shifted my head from left to right to see that there were several beds around me. I immediately noticed the drip hanging from my arm and the lack of windows in the large oval chamber. I rubbed my head confused, my mind was groggy, and I had to concentrate for a second as I rose up onto my elbows. I gasped from the sudden pain in my leg as the events of the night before hit me like a brick to the head. Groaning, I shifted myself backwards to lean back against the bed frame and only then did I notice the man standing at the foot of my bed.

'How are you feeling?' The man enquired as he stepped closer towards me. I didn't respond for a moment distracted by his robotic voice and the peculiar mask that covered his face.

'Where am I...'

'You're safe.' He replied, his pliable mask moving in unison with the muscles in his face.

'How long have I been asleep?' I asked groaning loudly.

'Over 48 hours.' The man said as he calmly approached the chair next to my bed. He paused standing beside it confidently, his stance making him seem at least seven feet tall.

'I slept for two whole days?' I asked wincing as I raised a hand to my head and felt the deep cut on my forearm.

'What is this place?' I asked again as I broke eye contact. I was being hypnotized by the flashes of green shimmering on the surface of his mask.

'You're in Brixton Tube Station, LOE Society territory and a safehouse for ghosts and runaways like yourself. But I gathered you knew that already.' *I left them behind! They'll never forgive me!* I thought as my stomach turned and a knot of guilt tightened inside me. I was safe but what about my family, they were still in that horrible place.

I noticed the man was still examining me and I swallowed hard under his intense stare. 'I suppose I should thank you...' I said quickly as I watched him suddenly open the curtain on a rail all the way around my bed. He then paused before he abruptly sat down in the chair beside me.

'Who are you?' He asked suddenly and I paused struggling to collect my thoughts.

'I... erm?' I muttered nervously as he continued to stare. 'Er, my... My name is Raine.' There was a long pause as he squinted at me, and I gulped as he silently glared right into my eyes.

'Phoenix.' the man said slowly as he nodded and tapped his fingers together. 'How long were you kept at Hermitage Hill... And more interestingly how did you get out?'

'How did you know I came from Hermitage Hill?' I asked anxiously, my heart beginning to race. Phoenix placed Sebastian's branded visor in my lap and opened his other hand to reveal a tiny fibrous metal square. I felt the nape of my neck realising that he held my implanted tracker chip. He dropped it on top of the hat as I lightly traced the sore patch where I found a small line of stitches.

'How did you escape alone though? That's my question. Tell me who helped you?'

'No one...' I said quickly peaking at him from out of the corner of my eye. 'I... I just saw a chance and I took it.' I looked down at the visor as my chest grew tight.'

86

'What... all by yourself?' Phoenix asked sarcastically, and I nodded in response keeping my eyes on Sebastian's visor. 'How long were you in there for?'

'Three years.' I blagged as I pressed the tracker chip between my thumb and forefinger to inspect it.

'You're lying...' He said blankly as he continued to watch me through his creepy mask. I dropped the chip and looked up at him innocently. 'Why are you lying to me Raine? I just need you to tell me how you got out and who you got out with....' Phoenix pressed calmly. I didn't know what to do, should I give up Sebastien's name? We never discussed it. My mind raced and I started to panic as eyes began to well with tears. Try as I might I couldn't hold them back.

'Tell me how you did it!' He demanded slowly.

'Or what? You're going to torture me?' I cried holding my face as my eyes filled with tears. Phoenix chuckled and I looked up at him through the waterfall of tears that were cascading down my cheeks.

'Don't believe everything you see on VTV.' He said sighing. 'Afterall there's more than one way to skin a cat.' He winked as I wiped my face with the back of my hands and watched him through glassy eyes. He leaned forward and I flinched as he retrieved the tracker chip and visor. 'I'm not going to hurt you,' he said as I continued to sniffle. 'Is it the mask?' he asked pointing at it. 'Is it freaking you out?' He chuckled as he pulled it halfway up his face. 'Look... Raine, you don't have to tell me anything right now.' He said as he rubbed his facial hair. 'But you will have to tell me...'

'I left them behind!' I sobbed, unable to hold it in any longer.

'Left who?' He asked curiously leaning forward. I heaved as I wiped my nose with the back of my hand, and in between sobs I relayed my story. I told about my family, the Recons, Grace, and Sebastien. When I was done, I sighed loudly and leaned back on the bed in relief.

'Hmm,' he said leaning into his seat. I glanced down at my twiddling thumbs, ready for judgement but instead of frowning, he curled his full lips into a handsome smile. 'Sounds like you were really brave.' He paused, his deep brown eyes squinting as he studied me closely. 'Many people wouldn't have made it all the way here.' He pulled the mask's peculiar material back down over his face as he glanced over at the masked man standing in the corner. It was the first time I had noticed him, and I assumed that he must have been a reader, analysing me for any signs of deceit as Phoenix questioned me. His hooded mask was very plain in comparison to the intricate one Phoenix wore, and he gave a slight nod before Pheonix turned back to me. 'You're not exactly what I expected from the first runaway to get out of that place in over 2 years. He smiled again exposing his straight white teeth as he stood up.

'I'm no one.' I muttered as I thought about the family. 'I was just in the right place at the right time.' I mumbled as I closed my eyes for a moment to stop the returning tears. I let a few seconds go by but when I opened them, Phoenix was still staring down at me sympathetically. I sighed forlornly under his intense gaze.

'Theres no such thing as coincidences.' He said broodingly before leaving me to listen to his heavy footsteps as he walked away.

***

It took me a month to recover from the infected dog bite on my leg, and as soon as I was released from the infirmary, I was escorted to a halfway house on the north side of Brixton station. After a whole month of being underground, I was allowed to go back up to street level, albeit briefly, and I took in the fresh air and the night time sky before being led back down again. The station was dark and dimly lit so I stayed close to the Inferior Loelife leading the way.

We passed various people going about their business and it didn't take long to get to our destination. I was led into a large open area with dilapidated shops surrounding the perimeter, and an ocean of tents that stretched almost to its entirety. I was on my own from here, directed through the mass of shelters towards the other side. I could see the Halfway sign flashing in the distance as I carefully waded through the narrow aisles in between the cordoned compounds until I reached the other side. I came to a large shop front covered in grime and graffiti with a flashing holographic sign above it. The glass windows were so filthy I could barely see inside. I looked around as I slowly stepped towards the entrance forcing the doors to automatically slide open. My eyes scanned the expansive space before I stepped inside. It was the pungent smell of body odour that hit me first, followed by the oval shelters that lined the room. It took me a moment to realise that they were rows of bed pods positioned in parallel lines on opposite sides of the room with an aisle running down the middle. I had heard rumours at work of how the Loelifes lived in strange subterranean eggs but I had never seen these apparent 'dome home' in the flesh before. I gawped as they glowed in various shades of colour in the total darkness. The room looked like a lair full of eggs laid by some sort of gigantic prehistoric monster. These domes were the only sources of light except for an illuminated hologram that read reception with an arrow floating in the mid-air, pointing to the far side of the room. It was late and eerily quiet as I made my way towards the girl staring at me from behind a desk under the reception sign. It had taken me a moment to notice her in the dim, but she was there alright, right in the corner beside the grimy glass window. I squinted at her before moving and she quickly looked away as I began limping towards her. She threw a suspended ball of light into the air as I approached, gazing up at me as if I had interrupted her.

'Write your name.' The girl said indifferently as pointed to a clipboard and pen in front of me.

'Ok.' I said narrowing my eyes at her, as she looked me up and down. She looked young, I'd bet no more than 16, and I wondered how she ended up at Brixton Station working for the LOE. I watched her type something down on an old computer keyboard and then waited for it to print out a small piece of paper. It had been a while since I had seen one of those, at the DMB we had virtual laptops hooked up to a system mainframe. After a moment the computer regurgitated a small scroll and she then passed me the small note.

'What's this?' I asked looking down at the digits on the small piece of yellow paper.

'Dome 45 is yours. That's the code to sync your plug to the pod.' She said as she pointed her hand towards the back of the shop without looking away from the computer screen. 'I don't have a plug,' I said looking down at her. I'd never had one, they were way too expensive and out of reach for ordinary citizens like myself.

'You'll get one,' she replied without looking up, 'when you've been assigned work.'

'Work?' I said as I fingered the little piece paper and stood watching her for a moment, but she didn't attempt to explain instead dismissing me with a wave of her hand. I sighed and hobbled back towards the main doors, running my hand along the graffitied glass for support. I then began to walk down the aisle in the middle of the shop floor. I was quickly surrounded by rows of dome homes, egg shaped pods that encased your bed and your entire life if you lived in an LOE run underground station. The numbers on the front of the domes illuminated as I walked by in the dark, and that told that dome 45 was further along the aisle and in the even darker part of the never-ending room. When I finally reached number 45, I held the small piece of paper under the light and punched the code into the key pad. The dome hissed as its rounded lid eased itself open and it lit up inside. I sighed as I took my shoes off and placed them in a draw underneath the door before getting into the bed fully clothed. I reached over and pulled the domed lid over my head until it clicked shut. The dome's lights slowly dimmed around me as I lay there on my back and tried to fall asleep. *What was I supposed to do now?* Was the only thought that ran through my head the entire night. My mind went around and around in circles trying to find a logical answer to a very relevant question. Before I knew it, it was already early morning and I could hear the room stirring to life as people began to move around and chatter as they left their domes. I watched the translucent shadows walking pass my pod as I pondered on my next move. Phoenix had made weekly visits while I was in the infirmary. I guessed the reader had confirmed I was telling the truth so he probably assumed that he could trust me. I wasn't sure if I could trust him, I was just hoping he would help me rescue my family. During his visits he continually plied me for information but I hadn't been at Hermitage Hill long enough to give him any valuable information. On his final visit he asked to scan my memories but I wasn't ready for such a personal intrusion. Nobody had been inside my mind before, I had never even used a plug, So I just wasn't ready for that. He was surprisingly gracious but then that was the last I saw of him, and as soon as I was well enough an Inferior Loelife turned up and cryptically escorted me to The Halfway. I wondered if the only reason I was even given a dome was because Pheonix believed I held more valid sub-conscious information.

Bang, bang, bang! I sat up as someone pounded loudly on the lid of my dome. I quickly blinked away my tears telling myself to get a grip as the knock came again.

'What?' I called as I lay back down and pulled the musty sheet over the upper half of my body.

'Induction in two minutes.' The voice said and I groaned loudly as I heard the footsteps walking away.

***

'Rent is due every Friday, unless you sign up to join the LOE Society and become a Minion.' The girl from the night before said five minutes later as she escorted the new additions to The Halfway around the dingy kitchen, toilet and washing facilities.

'What does becoming a Minion involve?' I asked unenthusiastically from the middle of the group.

'Cleaning, post, and basic guard duty.' The girl replied flatly without turning around. 'Of course, there are other ways of earning a living in the station, but… bear in mind that The Halfway reserves the right to evict any tenant that actively refuses to join the LOE Society.' *What does that even men?* I thought. 'That means even though every Ghost and runaway is given sanctuary in the station, we can't all be afforded the same privileges.' She said smiling at me as if she had read my mind. She sauntered into the grimy common room next and we circled around her. 'Now it's time to make your decision... to be or not to be a Minion and join up to the L.O.E.' She impatiently watched us inspect our greyish surroundings as we pondered on her question.

'But what if you don't want to join the LOE Society?' I asked boldly, 'do you lose your dome?' She narrowed her eyes at me as if I had said a dirty word, and then looked around at the large group standing in the middle of the room staring back at her.

'Like I said, there are other ways you can live her... and there is a trial period where you can make your decision. But the Halfway is for LOE members only. So, in the long run your welcomed to become a resident of the Pavilion.' The rest of the group mumbled amongst themselves.

'What's the Pavilion?' I asked, speaking up again.

'What you waded through to get to the Halfway.' She said curtly as she spun on her heels to look at me directly, making me wonder if I was annoying her.

'Oh,' I mumbled to thinking about the mystery inhabitants of the assembly of tents outside of the halfway house.

'Listen, joining the LOE is a good deal!' She said as enthusiastically. The dome homes at the Halfway give you a little slice of your own world for next to nothing... All you need to do is pledge yourself to the LOE.' She smiled mischievously as I exchanged glances with a few of the other outsiders. There was a long pause as we all looked at each other and she cleared her throat loudly, breaking silence. 'Anyway, my name is Toni and that was the full tour. SOOO, if you want to sign up to The LOE *now*, follow me. If not, rent is due this time next week, no exceptions, *and* your countdown starts now. In 29 days, you will have to make your decision!' She turned to walk away, and I watched as three quarters of the group followed her. I took a deep breath and hesitated before trudging behind them. Toni quickly led us up to the front desk to sign our lives away. But standing in the dwindling queue, I changed my mind. I needed to clear my head and think about it, so I made a quickly returned to my dome to get some rest, after all I hadn't slept. But unsurprisingly sleep seemed futile, my mind was turning too quickly to relax, and after an hour or so of trying to force myself into slumber, I decided to go for a walk around the station. I left my dome deciding to street level to get some *real* fresh air. But my empty stomach led me towards the kitchen at the back of the halfway house, even though I had no food to my name. The room was deserted, and I pounced on a half-eaten sandwich that was left discarded on the kitchen table. I began to devour it feverishly without even looking inside. It was slightly stale but I hadn't eaten since I left the infirmary so it would do.

'I was eating that!' I stop chewing mid swallow and almost choked on the food, too ashamed to turn around. 'Syke!' The voice said loudly before a stifled chuckle. I rolled my eyes and slowly turned around.

'I know you…' Toni said hauntingly, and I relaxed as I saw her standing on the other side of the kitchen, poking her head through the common room door. I continued chewing, although hiding the sandwich behind my back and dropping back down onto the plate out of embarrassment.

'Of course, you know me,' I said casually. 'You saw me come in last night and I was just on your stu–, your tour.' I turned to walk away but she ran past me and into the hall.

'I mean, I've heard about you…'

'Oh yeah?' I said eying her.

'Yep!' She said smiling as if it was an achievement. 'You're the girl that Phoenix's is renting the dome for…' Toni said as she blocked my path and sated me with a chocolate bar. I grabbed it and tore it open with my teeth. 'Or should I say getting the rent fee waved for,' She whispered behind her hand as if it was a big secret. *Maybe it was.*

'Excuse me?' I said wit my mouth full, 'what do you mean?' 'You're the girl that escaped from Hermitage Hill all alone, aren't you?' The first person to make it to Brixton Tube Station alive in like, over 5 years…' She ranted as she widened her eyes and gazed into mine, clearly exaggerating.

'Where did you hear that?' I asked glancing away from her intense stare as I gobbled down the rest of the chocolate bar.

'Well… you're practically famous now, so everyone knows about you Raine!' *She didn't seem this impressed last night!*

'Ok slow down, what was that you said about my rent?' I asked, but she just stared back at me with a curious expression on her face. She was pretty, with skin as smooth and dark as molasses.

'Are you and Phoenix doing a *ting* or what?' She asked ignoring my question. I kissed my teeth loudly and limped around her to walk away.

'Ok sorry, none of my business... wait don't go...' She said suddenly. 'I heard Phoenix talking to my dad about you this morning...' *Phoenix came to the Halfway for me?*

'What did you hear?' I asked curiously as I stopped and spun around on my good leg.

'Just that he'll cover the cost of your dome for 30 days... and that we should give you credit to buy food... so you won't have to rush into a work assignment, or pilfer stale half-eaten sandwiches out of the kitchen.' She made a face.

'Why 30 days?' I asked ignoring her last comment.

'Argh, weren't you listening on the tour?' She said rolling her eyes. '30 days is your grace period innit. That's how long you have, to join the LOE Society voluntarily...'

'Oh yeah of course,' I said nodding. I scrunched up the chocolate wrapper and pushed it into my pocket as I began to limp away.'

'If you come to the front desk, I'll give you your cred and show you to the market.'

'Thanks, but you don't have too...' I said smiling at her.

Toni shrugged as she broke eye contact.

'It's cool,' she replied smiling back. 'I've done my rounds for now so there's nothing for me to do around here anyway.' There was silence for a few short seconds.

'You still don't know who Phoenix is do you?' Toni asked with a half-cocked smile sliding across her face.

'Yeah, course,' I said acting casual, 'I know he's a high ranking Loelife... if that's what you mean.'
Toni laughed out loud and she shook her head.

'He's not just any high ranking Loelife,' she exclaimed with vim in her voice. 'He's like, *the* Loelife, especially south of the river.'
I thought about this carefully. If Phoenix was indeed as important as Toni said he was, then he could definitely help me get to my family. I had already planned on asking him but he never came back to see me in the infirmary.
'You have to tell me how you escaped from Hermitage Hill!' Toni squealed cutting right through my train of thought as we reached the reception.

'Alright.' I smiled as she practically bounced down in the aisle beside me. 'But first you need to tell me absolutely everything you know about Phoenix.'

***

I found out that Phoenix was in fact the Superior Loelife in charge of Brixton Underground Station. He had joined the LOE Society ten years ago at the age of

19 and had been fighting for The LOE ever since. He had worked his way up from Inferior to Superior faster than any other Loelife on record. Toni on the other hand was born into the LOE, it was in her blood. Her father, a longstanding Loelife ran the half-way house and it was where she had grown up. Her mother had abandoned her at birth and all Toni had ever wanted to do was become a Loelife, and supposedly make some sort of significant difference to the world.

My outlook on life was a little different, and it took me the whole month to sign up to The LOE waiting list and become a Minion. I did so almost voluntarily, having become accustomed to my dome home and the station's way of life. Also, not wanting to know what would happen to me on the other side of my grace period when I found myself amongst the turmoil of the treacherous Pavilion. Fortunately, Toni and I became fast friends and through her dad, she managed to hook me up with a decent assignment in the deliveries department. A job usually only available to Minions after six months of clean-up duty. Deliveries consisted of transporting food, post and other goods coming in and out of Brixton Station. The deliveries came from a collection point north of the river, as the LOE Society had simultaneously taken over a handful of stations on the Victoria Line as well as others, although I couldn't remember all the names. They now controlled Brixton in the south and Seven Sisters to Walthamstow Central in the north. In fact, The LOE had managed to get their claws on nearly every major station on the underground network, graciously leaving a fraction of certain stations open for public use at less desirable locations or for strategic purposes. All the government could do at the time was barricade the tube entrances to stop The LOE from infiltrating the entire London underground. Before arriving at Brixton, it had been years since I had even entered one.

'*Not a place for decent folk like we!*' My grandfather always used to say, '*full up of undesirables and vagrants up to no damn good!*' I could still hear his voice, his hint of an accent ringing inside my head.

'*The London underground network is to dangerous and unpredictable. It is only to be used as a mode of transport in extreme emergencies!*' That was the public opinion of the DMV. But look at me now, here I was living inside one! I even had vivid memories of watching the 21-day siege of the underground takeover on the VTV. I was young, but I don't recall how old I was, but I clearly remembered when Transport for London began to blot out parts of the tube map as if the captured stations had never even existed. That's when things really went downhill, as if the riots before I was born hadn't done enough damage to the country. The newly comprised BFP soon declared Martial law, passing The Anti-Domestic Terror Act of 2035. This new legislation gave the Recons the right to raid any property or use lethal force against anyone they deemed a vigilante, terrorist, or an illegal alien. Anybody caught associating with the LOE Society or any such organisation was to be immediately deported or much worse... I shuddered at the thought of it as I skimmed the walls down a tunnel on my way back to platform 1. I was ashamed that I hadn't known all this before. It had taken a savvy LOE born rebellious teenager to teach the true history of my own damn country. What had my 21 years even taught me? I had gullibly believed all the lies and government propaganda. I sighed as I eased to a stylish halt with a professionalism, I thought I'd never acquire. I was finally getting used to my sliders which were anti-gravity hover boots that enabled me to glide around the Brixton fast and efficiently. They were welcomed tools of the job, as was the plug and accompanying telekom that came along with the Minion status. It was a basic model with restricted abilities but it was good enough for a Minion and I was able to sync up to my dome which proved quite helpful. With these tools, I quickly learned my way around the station tunnels, and now liked to glide the scenic route to clear my mind. The whole station was a LOE safehouse so not only consisted of Brixton Tube Station itself, but also encompassed all the buildings surrounding its perimeter as well as the overground station. It was vast stronghold in South London, and the LOE Society kept the east part of the structure private for their living quarters and exclusive activities. It was rare to see a Loelife above a Junior rank in the market, or around the Pavilion and I could see why. Every day my mouth watered as I sniffed boxes of the fresh food I delivered to the east quarter while the rest of us had to heckle at the market for pigeon, rabbit, squirrel, or bone marrow stew. I shuddered and shook myself out of my daydream just as my handler Swifty came marching out of the delivery train and down the platform towards me.

'Ah, Raine... Just the person I wanted to see.' He said rubbing his hands together.

'What do you need Swifty?' I asked looking into his beady little eyes behind his mask. He was a short stout man with cheeky grin, visible through his mask. He rolled the elastic covering up onto is head and revealed his caramel complexion.

'This needs to get to Phoenix on platform 2 immediately,' he said shoving a small package into my hands.

'Come on Swifty...' I said holding my hands up and backing away. 'You know I prefer not to drop off high profile deliveries...' I continued, walking over to my usual sorting station on the third carriage. The truth was I hadn't seen Phoenix since I was in the infirmary and that was over two months ago. After he rented my dome at The Halfway, the last thing I wanted to do was deliver him a package. Not only did I need to thank him... I needed to ask for even more help, and I was dreading her possible answer. He had down more than enough...

'Where's Peanut anyway?' I called behind me, trying to walk away. 'Doesn't she usually do the Senior deliveries?' She would always swap jobs with me even when I was assigned them, she liked the that they tipped her with cred.

'She's already on one... and I'm not asking Peanut I'm asking you.' Swifty said assertively as he stepped back onto the train.

'But...' I said awkwardly as I looked over my

package quota for the rest of the day.

'Raine, you're a good girl, and I like you.' Swifty said after a few seconds of silence form inside the carriage. 'But the truth is I've got plenty of Minions ready to fill your spot in a heartbeat...'

'Fine,' I sighed loudly as I turned around and Swifty exited the train and dropped the package into my hands.

'Good girl.' he said smiling as I tapped my feet together to activate my sliders. He began to whistle as he moseyed away and I listened to his heavy footsteps shuffling down the platform. I hovered beside the train, inspecting the small box and wondering what was inside. I shook it before tucking it into my sack, and as soon as I reached the exposed track, I soared down the familiar intersection of tunnels towards platform 2. I went the long way arrive so I could use the stairwell, and I cautiously slid down the first couple of steps as I heard voices down below. I let my gliders gain a little momentum but stopped myself mid-glide as I heard distorted voices behind me. I felt a chill as I looked back over my shoulder and I didn't even see the figure push me down the remaining steps until I fell face first onto the platform floor below. I managed to save myself with my hands but groaned as I pulled my head up off the floor. I kissed my teeth loudly as I drew myself to my knees looking up into the face of the masked Loelife pointing a large blade at me.

'I've got a delivery for Phoenix...' I said through gritted teeth as I began to get up.

'Don't move!' The Loelife snapped as I began to

protest.

'But I just need to deliver this…'

'Who are you!' He hissed before I could say another word.

'Why's that matter, can't you see my uniform?' I said pointing at the winged LOE signet on my chest and hat.

'Why don't I know you?' he hissed, bringing the blade closer to my face.

'It's alright, let her through!' A computerised voice ordered, and I saw Phoenix with a small group of masked Juniors walking across the platform towards us. The lower ranked Loelife retracted his knife and stepped aside finally allowing me to stand up.

'She was sneaking around,' the Junior said sheathing his weapon as soon as Phoenix approached.

'Creeping and eavesdropping like a little spy.'

'I was doing my job, delivering packages.' I retorted narrowing my eyes at him.

'Yeah well… I ain't never seen you before,' He sneered as he looked me up and down through his generic colourless mask.

'Apologise…' Phoenix ordered coldly as I dusted myself off and retrieved his package. The Loelife paused.

'I'm sorry for pushing you over,' the Junior Loelife said obediently without looking me in the eye. Phoenix dismissed him with a wave of his hand and he quickly scurried away to join the other Loelifes standing a few feet away on the platform.

'You alright?' I nodded.

'You've got something for me, right?' he said staring into my eyes.

'Uh huh,' I said smiling stupidly as I watched turquois blue swirl around his mask.

'Thanks,' he answered without breaking eye contact as I handed him the box. My heart was beating erratically and I had to look away. I wanted to thank him for waving the rent at the at the Halfway. I wanted to ask him for even more help but the others were watching and this didn't seem like the time or the place.

'You need to print for it,' I said quickly plugging in and holding out my palm in front of him. Phoenix pressed his thumb into the centre of my telekom as he silently continued to stare at me.

'Well, aren't you a pretty little thing.' A robotic female voice said as a woman suddenly appeared on the platform beside us. I didn't even see her coming, nor did I hear her approach. She circled me like a vulture before staring at Phoenix. I noticed his demeanour changed slightly.

'So, she's the one then?' She said smirking as her mask suddenly turned a smoky grey. 'The girl who mysteriously made it out of Herm Hill all alone?' She chuckled loudly just as a train rumbled into the tunnel and screeched to a halt beside the platform. The train itself was only three carriages long and it was covered in graffiti inside and out with most of the windows either broken or blacked out.

'Let's go,' Phoenix shouted as soon as the carriage doors eased open and I watched the group of

Loelifes loudly climb aboard. The woman lingered for a second before scoffing loudly and leaving Phoenix alone on the platform. I could feel his eyes boring into mine so I broke away from his gaze and smiled awkwardly before skating away.

'When I get back, you'll let me scan your memories?' Phoenix yelled just as I reached the stairwell. I glanced back at him half hanging out of the carriage window with a huge grin plastered across his masked face. I nodded and he disappeared into the carriage just as the train slowly eased away.

7

RAT RACE

'**O**i, listen up!' A rather large Senior Loelife called Razorbill shouted to get our undivided attention. '*You lot* will follow me to the ground.' He pointed at the group nearest to him which included me, Toni and four others. 'We'll be patrolling the safehouse's exterior... and remember this is strictly a routine patrol exercise.' He said looking at each one of us in turn. 'You are volunteering to partake in the upkeep of security for everybody who resides in this safehouse so keep your eyes peeled and keep up!' He shouted as he marched off towards one of the tunnels with my group scurrying after him. I dragged my feet behind Toni who had just turned eighteen and had now officially pledged to join the LOE Society. The *rat run* was the only serious duty a Minion could partake in before becoming an Inferior, after you had completed three months on your work assignment. Toni's dad had pulled a few strings to prematurely get her on the night watch with me, since she hadn't completed her official work assignment yet. Although she kept on reminding me that working at the Halfway for most of her life definitely counted. I just wished that I could share in Toni's excitement. She idolised the LOE, but then again why wouldn't she? She practically grew up here, and I was pretty sure she had been mentally preparing to join the LOE Society for most of her life. I on the other hand was joining out of necessity. I hadn't even known half of this world existed before two months ago. All I cared about was getting my family out of Hermitage Hill. But to do that one needed power and allies so it seemed becoming a Loelife was my only way I could stay close to Pheonix.

I sighed as we quickly arrived at the blocked entrance to Brixton Station. The light was dim but I could finally see how The LOE had used vehicles to completely block the entire exit. Since I had been there, I had never been back to the front of the station, it being off-limits unless you were stationed there. Looking down from the tower I recalled the night I had first arrived. A stairway had been cleverly fashioned out of old vehicle parts and the only way out seemed to be through the same bus that blocked my entry the night the Recons first chased me right into the camouflaged scrap yard. Razorbill quickly lined us up and began to lift standard issue pulse guns out of his duffle bag. Soon he was handing one to Toni and then to me.

'Finally reached eighteen ay?' He asked as he smiled down at Toni and handed her a gun.

'Yep, and I bet I'm a Junior Loelife before I reach twenty,' she beamed proudly.

'You hear that, Minions? Now that's what you call confidence!' He chuckled bending down to grab another pulse gun out of the bag.

'Haven't seen you before,' he said as he stepped towards me and paused before handing me the weapon.'

'I'm Raine… I'm new…' I said shrugging nervously.

'Have you ever used a pulse gun?' He asked raising an eyebrow.'

'I've told her how to use it,' Toni quickly said on my behalf.

'Well, it's not rocket science, so you better learn quick.' Razorbill grunted as he squinted down at me and showed me the basic functions. After a minute or so he passed it to me along with a generic Minion mask and a pair of hybrid infrared night-vision contact lenses. Toni had to help me press them into my eyes and after blinking a few times I was immediately dazzled by the shimmering cerulean light. I looked around in awe as every inanimate object instantly radiated an electric blue, with every warm body around me emitting an orangey red heat signature. When everyone had geared up Razorbill led the way out of the tower and into the labyrinth of abandoned vehicles.

'Listen up Minions! We'll be running around the outer perimeter of the station and the entirety of the Brixton safehouse. We will be casing all LOE territory to check that there haven't been any security breaches.' Razorbill said as we silently followed in single file. 'We'll be taking the scenic route down Electric Avenue, Electric Lane and then onto Brixton over ground station on Atlantic Road.' He instructed as he pointed at the four Minions filed directly behind him. 'You lot will take the ramp on Electric Lane back over to the scrap yard in front of the station on the main road.' He said now pointing at me, Toni and two other Minions in line. 'Ready, set, stay LOE!' Razorbill shouted as he clicked on his sliders and zoomed off. We all followed suit, watching in awe as he ran and somersaulted into an expert glide. One by one we sprinted in line behind him. Our boots gradually lifting us off the ground as we weaved in between the maze of broken-down vehicles, splitting up only to go up, over or through the twisted pieces of metallic junk. By the time we got through the entire scrapyard and sailed into the road I was breathless. But it was overshadowed by sheer exhilaration, this being the time I had been gliding outside. The cold night air whipped around us as we carried on skating around the LOE's perimeter and onto Electric Avenue. Hover boots required kinetic energy, so speed made it possible to defy gravity and elevate higher into the air. I hadn't really been able to experience the gliding potential confined to the station's tunnels. But as excited as I was, I was still out of breath and struggling to keep up. My feet were slowly getting closer and closer to the ground and now I was seriously lagging. By the time I floated around the corner onto Electric Lane I was barely even gliding. I could hardly see Razorbill and the Minions following him in the distance as they separated from my group and continued onto Atlantic Road. A huge gate had opened ahead and pushed on, my feet pattering against the concrete until I got to a decent speed. I finally caught up to Toni just as she was just about to glide over a huge mountain of scrap. The other two had already skated over and disappeared.

'Raine! What happened to you? I turned around and you were gone!'

'Toni, I... can't keep up.' I said breathlessly, 'I'm not a raised glider like you lot.'

'Yes, you can Raine!' Toni called as she skated back towards me, 'you've got to keep moving.' She said skidding to a halt as the huge gate closed behind us. 'You almost got locked out!' I nodded taking a deep breath as I glanced back as the barrier was sealed shut.

'And we're gonna lose face now!' Toni moaned loudly.

'What? Razorbill never said it was a race' I said standing upright.

'No, but they left us behind!' Toni snapped as she pointed to the empty ramp with the outstretched palm of her hand. 'We'll lose rank for getting separated, and for being slow!' Toni whined sulkily.

'We'll catch up,' I said clicking on my sliders and smiling enthusiastically.

'We can try!' she huffed as she skated ahead of me and up the ramp. I rolled my eyes as I followed her to the top. She went straight over, but I paused to take in the view. It was eerily quiet and all I could see were the twinkling lights from the buildings beyond the junkyard for as far as the eye could see. I heard Toni shouting my name and I took a deep breath before quickly descending over the steep ramp. The icy wind whipped at my cheeks as I rapidly slid down and leap into the air, landing with a skid on the top of an up-turned lorry.

'Wooo, that's gliding 101 baby!' Toni sang from the ground as I teetered on the top of the lorry; my heart beating so fast that I couldn't even move.

'Raine, what the hell are you doing up there? Hurry up!' Toni screeched, 'We've still got to catch up to the others.'

'Alright!' I called back as I saw something moved out of the corner of my eye. I jumped down and looked in the movements direction as Toni continued to berate under her me.

'Come on!' She hissed, as I turned to follow her. But then my ears pricked up when I heard a peculiar sound.

'What was that?' I whispered, interrupting Toni's relentless mumbling. She didn't respond. I knew that this dummy mission meant a lot to her, so ignored her endless ranting until I heard the noise again.

'Toni shut up will you! Didn't you hear that?' I hissed again, reaching out and grabbing her arm. We had been gliding slowly with our feet only a few centi-metres off the ground. We stopped, hovering idly for a moment as we listened.

'Hear what?' She whined as she turned back to me. 'I don't hear anythi–'

'Shhh…' I snapped as I heard the noise again. It sounded like the clinking or clanking of metal banging together, and, and a voice. 'It's coming from over there…' I said as I instinctively began to glide in the opposite direction and directly towards it.

'Raine… Where are you going?' Toni asked as she trailed behind me.

'To check it out,' I said pointing towards the noise. 'I think someone's in trouble.'

'No Raine we'll be in trouble!' She hissed standing in front of me. 'We're meant to be on the rat run, and we should've gotten back to base by now!' Toni grumbled. I could hear the agitation in her voice but I dismissed it and moved around her.

'Razorbill won't like this; it's against the rules to deviate from the flight path!' Toni protested, as she sped up to glide beside me. I rolled my eyes and ignored her, moving closer towards the sound as it grew louder. I couldn't help but think, *what if was an escapee like me, what if they needed my help?* I slowed my pace down to a hover and Toni fell in line behind me as we got closer to the source of the noise.

'Listen… do you hear that? It sounds like crying.' I whispered glancing around. The look on Toni's face told me she had heard it too. *What if it was one of my sisters, maybe Sebastian had gotten them out too and they had found their way here*! I thought excitedly, unrealistically but excitedly none the less. I looked for the best route over or around the junk in the darkness.

'Raine please...' Toni whispered as she pulled out her pulse gun. 'I think we should go now... Razorbill's gonna be pissed!' *I could care less about Razorbill.*

'Come on Toni...' I egged her on encouragingly as we hovered in front of the last pile of rubbish blocking our way. 'What if someone needs our help?' She pondered this and I realised that she was probably scared, after all she spent most of her time underground. 'Ok wait here for me,' I said before quickly skating up a mound of tires and surfing over a pile of cars down to the other side. I landed at the edge of the scrap yard and skidded to a halt next to a broken single decker bus. I saw a something trapped in an old trolley cage on top of a mound of scrap metal at the edge of the road.

'Seriously Raine!' I turned to see Toni descending over the mountain of dismantled cars behind me as I moved in to get a closer look. 'Why did you leave me like that!' She hissed landing beside me.

'I told you to wait for me there.' I said shushing her dismissively.

'You're going to get us in so much trouble.'

'Look!' I said pointing at the little boy in the trolley cage.

'Raine...' Toni whispered as she activated her pulse gun. 'We need to retreat and report this to Razorbill right now.' She said looking around and backing away.

'But we need to see if he's ok,' I whispered looking at the helpless little boy.

'Raine, this is supposed to be a training exercise just to see if we can take instructions, and clearly *you cannot* take instructions!' She snapped erratically, 'Now come on, we have to go back… Please!'

'Ok…' I muttered quietly. But I was being drawn to him like a moth to a flame and I quickly drew closer as she turned to leave.

'Raine, what the hell?' Toni called as we drifted in opposite directions.

'But he's seen us now,' I declared as I hovered towards the trapped little boy. 'We can't just leave him here.

Toni groaned loudly.

'Raine we'll come back for him ok… *This* just doesn't feel right…' She griped, trailing behind me at a distance. 'I don't like it… something feels *wrong*… was this pile of mangled cages even here the first time we went around?'

'You're being paranoid,' I said sighing loudly. 'A little boy got trapped that's all, he's probably just lost.'

'How Raine! How? How did he get trapped in the cage like that?' She asked, shining the light of her gun on the heap of scrap metal.

'I don't know do I… but I'm about to find out.' I retorted as I cautiously hovered over the mound debris around the cage.

'I'm sorry Raine, you've left me no choice but to call this in.' *Snitch,* it thought to myself. 'Don't be a hero, Hero's get caught!' Toni yelled as I finally reached the boy.

'Hi...' I said smiling as I bent down to get a better look at him. He was a skinny little thing dressed in rags, with long tangled hair that had matted into dreadlocks. 'How did you get trapped in there?' I asked as I looked into his wide glassy eyes through my hybrid contact lenses. He stared back at me but he stayed silent.

'Raine my plug signal is blocked and I'm leaving now with or without you!' Toni shouted from the ground. I could hear the urgency in her tone and I finally relented. I supposed it couldn't hurt to get help.

'Okay!' I called back just as the little boy reached out of the cage and grabbed my hand.

'I'm coming back to get you out ok.' I said looking back at him, he opened his mouth as if he wanted to say something, but he just stared back at me with his big round eyes instead. He looked afraid, very afraid. I tried to remove my arm but he clutched my wrist tightly.

'Help me!' His whisper was barely audible and it broke my heart. He looked no older than five or six, and he reminded me of my little cousin Rico.

'I can't leave him!' I called out as I reached out for the cage's latch. 'I'll wait with him. Or let me see if I can open it.

'Raine don't!'

'Just one minute!' I called back as I grappled with the dented door.

'We don't know what we're dealing with!' Toni shouted as I tugged at the cage, there was a bit of give and I pulled harder but it would not budge. I quickly jumped and hovered above it as I pulled out my pulse gun. I turned down the voltage and then took a shot at the lock. There was a bright blast and the door immediately popped open. But not without shocking the little boy in the process and knocking him out completely.

'Recons!' Toni suddenly screamed, her shrill voice echoing through the darkness.

'What!' I screeched panicking as I quickly grabbed the boy's lifeless body and hovered over the ground.

'Where?'

'Behind you!' Toni yelled as she skated towards me with a look of horror on her face. She fired her pulse gun past me as I made my way towards her.

'They've got force shields!' She shouted hysterically as she flung the gun over her back. 'Glide Raine glide!' I held onto the little boy and frantically strode away. But something suddenly hit me. My body froze as I went hurtling towards the ground. The little boy went flying out of my arms and I was suddenly being dragged across the yard by something clamped around my foot.

'Go!' I screamed as Toni leapt forward and caught the boy in mid-air. She took off as I saw two Recons glide over my head. The frozen sensation rippled around my body. But thankfully Toni had just enough time to get away, and I sighed in relief as I watched her disappear over a pile of scrap. My body was coming around and I grabbed the pulse gun off my back and I tried to shoot at the cuff around my foot. But it was too little too late, the Recons had doubled back and quickly closed in on me. The first one stunned me again and the second one grabbed my weapon. He also pulled off my hooded mask and I was lifted off the ground and hauled up into one of the mangled cages. Only now did I realise that there were more than one.

'Well, well, well... What do we have here then?' The one that pulled off my mask said to the other as he scanned my head with his ID device. I studied them as the reader tried to analyse me, but they wore full hooded body suits making it impossible to see their faces.

'She's unreadable.' The first one said as the other one scoffed and leaned in to inspect me.

'Typical,' 'he said stepping away to follow his colleague around the pile of junk and out of sight. 'I'm not sure if she's a Loelife though, they aren't usually that stupid.'

'Well, I don't really care who the hell she is as long as she makes us enough profit to cover this week's dry spell.' The other one replied as I heard the vehicle doors slamming shut.

'Raine!' Toni yelled as she appeared on a pile of debris in the distance. 'We're coming!' she called as she quickly came flying towards me with a line of Loelifes sailing beside her. My heart skipped a beat, and I dared not to hope as I watched them gliding across the mountains of junk. They rapidly approached and I held my breath as I rattled the thick metal cage around me. It didn't budge, and my stomach dropped as I felt a sudden rumble beneath me. The twisted cages encased in a mound of scrap was some sort of vehicle, and its engine had just come to life. It had been camouflaged to looked like it belonged in the scrapyard. *How, could I have been so dumb!* I rattled the cage even more violently than before as I heard the voices continue from inside.

'Looks, like we got a little chase on our hands, she must be Loelife after all.'

'Yeah… wasn't expecting that… She must be a bit wet behind the ears.' A few chuckles followed and then the engine roared.

'Pity about little Danny though… I grew to like the little chap… Best bait we've had in a while.'

'Yeah… He always seemed to reel them in with those big sad eyes of his… It's a real shame, we lost a good one there…'

'Right, come on Terry put your foot down! Stop teasing em' you bloody wind-up merchant, even if they catch up to us, you know they won't get her out.'

'Yeah, but I like to see em squirm!' They both guffawed at that, then the vehicle quickly started to move as we rumbled away, just as Toni and the others reached the edge of the scrap yard.

'Raine we're coming!' Toni yelled as they gave chase. They followed us all the way into the intersection. But the vehicle picked up speed and I knew it wasn't much point in them to go much further. Tears began to stream down my face as I accepted the inevitable.

'Don't worry about me!' I called not knowing if I'd ever see Toni again. 'I'll be back!' I shouted sounding a lot more confident than I felt. I had no idea what would become of me, and I watched helplessly as Toni,

Razorbill and the calvary of gliding Loelifes gave up the chase, and finally disappeared into the distance.

***

My nostrils twitched as I groggily opened my eyes. A door had opened blinding me with a flash of light that ran astray into the pitch-black space around me. I groaned loudly and it took me a few seconds to realise that the blurry figure coming into focus was a guard standing at the foot of the mattress. He held a large round metal plate in one hand and a misshapen mug in the other. Both items were steaming.

'Good morning BF35372,' he hummed chirpily. He received a silent stare in response as I groggily sat up and rubbed my eyes. I looked up at the stout rosy cheeked guard standing at my feet and he seemed as vivid as a dream.

'What did you just call me?' I asked as I rubbed my face.

'BF35372... your number, it says so there on your tag,' he said eyeing me curiously. I looked down at the plastic tag hanging from a cord around my neck and he was right. 'The first two letters stand for Black female, then your date of birth and then– '

'Alright, I get the picture.' I said cutting him off as I shielded my face from the light. I had a splitting head ache and I squinted at him as he stood watching me for a moment.

'Here we are then,' he finally announced, smiling awkwardly. He cleared his throat as he stepped forward and carefully handed me a metal tray. I took it, eying the contents suspiciously as I lowered it onto my lap and placed the mug on the concrete floor beside me. I then gazed down at the steaming plate of food in front of me.

'Well go on then luv,' he said handing me some plastic cutlery. 'It's just a full English it ain't gonna hurt ya.' I didn't have to be told twice and I immediately discarded the flimsy knife and fork and expertly worked my way around the plate with my fingers.

'Where am I... how long have I been in here?' I asked in between mouthfuls as I looked around. I was confined in some sort of cell different from the one I remembered, for starters this one had a door. I swallowed a large mouthful of food as the guard stood smiling widely, watching me chew with my mouth open.

'Erm let me see,' he said looking up at the ceiling and tapping his chin. 'Hmm, this'll be your third day back at Hermitage Hill... no doubt you'll be groggy from the drugs they gave you during the interrogation.'

'Back?' I said nearly choking, caught off guard by the fact that he knew I'd been here before.

'So... how'd you like ya breakfast?' He asked ignoring my comment and quickly changing the subject. I held a thumb up as I swallowed another mouth full of food making the guard chuckle to himself. 'Yeah, thought you might. You've your baked beans, fried eggs, buttered toast, a real meat sausage and even a bit of bacon.' He said rubbing his large round belly. 'Mind you, the meals are the best part of the job!' He said covering his mouth as if somebody was listening. 'We get bubble and squeak on Mondays, pie and mash on Tuesday... fish and chips on Friday and if we're lucky an occasional roast dinner on a Sunday afternoon.' He said as if he was going into some sort of trance. I burped loudly and grimaced at the guard. He was making this hellhole sound like a flipping hotel. I wasn't about to complain though, and finished my last mouthful of beans, proceeding to lick the plate as he continued to chat. '*You're* not meant to get none mind you, being a *prisoner* and that you're meant the gruel... Which I think is quite cruel especially for the last meal.' He whispered as I finally discarded the metal plate.

'What do you mean last meal?' I asked looking up at him, but he carried on talking as if he never heard me.

'But me, I always get my meals and go back for seconds and thirds... and fourths.' He chuckled rubbing his protruding stomach again, it was so taut underneath his blue shirt it seemed as if it could burst at any moment. 'They never check you when you're on working the last row you know.' He smiled as he closed the cell door behind himself until it was barely ajar. 'Those bastard's all laugh at me behind my back as well,' His face suddenly displayed a bitter expression as he spoke. 'Calling me soft, fat, and clumsy, always leaving me down here alone. Nobody cares about big fat Bernard! So, whenever I can I like to have a natter with the inmates, nothing beats a friendly chinwag on you're on the way out.' He said coming a little closer and looking around as if someone was watching. 'They'd go nuts if they knew I give my third and fourth portions away to you lot!' He smiled proudly as I finally decided to interrupt again.

'So where am I?' I asked picking up the mug. I might have been in Hermitage Hill, but I had no idea which wing. I slurped clumsily from the hot mug of tea and repeatedly scalded my tongue as I waited for him to reply. The guard paused as he rocked back on his heels for a moment before bending down to retrieve my plate.

'Like I said, you're on the last row.' He said after a short pause.

'Last row?' I asked confused, not liking the sound of that. 'What do mean?'

'You're in a holding cell luv... sorry but you're on your way out...' The guard said finally, 'It's where they put you before you're... deported.'

'What!' I said dropping the mug and spilling its contents on the concrete floor. 'But... but I just got here!' I wailed as tears stung at my eyes.

'I know... but you've been fast tracked...'
I covered my face with my hands as I sobbed.

'Why!' I cried through my fingers, 'I'm a no-body! What did I do?'

'Well, my dear, unfortunately that information is way above my paygrade. The guard said groaning as he bent down to retrieve the plate and mug. I continued to cry for I don't know how long and the guard kindly stayed even though I wasn't sure I wanted. Then again anything was better than being alone.

'Do you mind me asking where you're off too?' The guard asked after he had waited for my cries to regress into periodic sniffles.

'What?' I said looking up at him standing awkwardly by the ajar cell door clutching the empty metal tray.

'Jamaica, I guess,' I said blankly, knowing that the place I would be deported to depended on my father's heritage, despite his British nationality.

'Oh well that's fortunate... nice weather ay... lovely beaches...' he said encouragingly. *Yeah, with a side of crime, death, and poverty if you were caught on the wrong side of the island,* I thought, I had heard various stories...

'Not like our putrid sea sides.' We were both silent again as I stared into space and tried to ignore my thumping headache. 'Well... I wish you all the best luv,' he smiled before he turned around to leave.

'Wait,' I said quickly, and he slowly turned back to me.

'Why do you even bother to help us? With the food I mean,' I asked making more conversation and secretly hoping that he wouldn't leave me alone in the dark cell without light. The guard pondered for a moment before he smiled.

'When I come in with the usual shite you lot don't even stir to eat it... Nothing better than a fry up to awaken the senses.' He licked his lips and fell silent as his voice trailed off. I fought to keep back the tears as he pulled the heavy door open.

'Well, take care of yourself sweetheart.' He said looking back once more before walking out of the cell and into the hallway. He had a sympathetic look on his warm round face.

'Thank you,' I called to his back, and he nodded as he slowly closed the cell door.

***

They came for me a few hours later. I had stopped crying by then but the snot from my nose and continuous stream of tears had dried onto my face. My eyes were swollen, puffy, and sore, and I felt frozen down to the bone. I had chewed my fingernails right down to the beds in terrified agitation, and I was now attacking my already bleeding cuticles. I was just sitting on my mattress staring into dark space when the cell door flew open. I covered my brow and blinked under the harsh light. Two guards stood intimidatingly in the doorway, and they were clearly of a totally different calibre to the guard that had bought me the secret breakfast just a few hours prior. I wiped my puffy eyes and jumped up as one guard entered the cell. I backed into the corner as he threw something at me. It hit my stomach and then landed on the mattress.

'Put it on.' The guard demanded as I looked down at the garment. I quickly retrieved it and opened it out into a cotton jumpsuit. I glanced at the two guards as I turned into the corner to change pulling off the tatty cotton dress and quickly stepping into the jumpsuit. 'Hurry up!' The guard ordered grabbing me

125

by the arms as soon as I had pulled my hands through the sleeves. The second guard entered the cell and clamped a set of metal cuffs around my wrists. He looped a chain around them and hooked it onto my neck. He then laughed as he yanked on it making me stumble forward. I was reluctant to follow the guards, and so they dragged me out of the cell by the chains and forced me into the long thin corridor where several other prisoners were already lined up. The guard then took the chain around my handcuffs and clasped it to the chain that hung from the inmate in front of me. I was suddenly pulled forward as we were led through several dark corridors and into a large hall with no windows. There were even more prisoners standing in assembled lines underneath the bright artificial lights, with an armoured guard standing in between each row. After just a few minutes we were taken outside and I felt the cold of a chilly winter's day whipping around me as I gazed up at the dull grey sky. I had no idea what time it was as we were frogmarched into the courtyard and promptly herded onto one of the awaiting buses. We weren't permitted to speak, but we all spoke with our eyes, exchanging looks of terror as the engine beneath us roared into life and carried us away. I felt numb as I craned my neck to gaze back at Hermitage Hill disappearing into the distance. I felt a pain in my chest as I wondered if any of the barred cell's I could see contained any members of my family, if the hands desperately reaching through the bars towards the sky were that of my kin. This was the closest I'd been to them in months, and a 20-minute drive through the countryside felt like an eternity as I got further and further away from them. I crucified myself for getting re-captured. *How could I have been so stupid to end up even worse off than I was to begin with? I was finally getting somewhere with Pheonix and I cocked it all up! Don't be a hero, don't be a hero, don't be a bloody hero, hero's get caught! What's wrong with me?* I thought as Toni's words went round and round in my head.

I could suddenly see Gatwick airport coming into view and my mouth dropped open as I saw how enormous an aeroplane looked up close in real life. My eyes then fleeted across the huge grey building with hundreds of windows as I took everything in. I had heard of this airport. It was where important people who were allowed to travel, like the CEO of the DRB Office often went to escape the country. Regularly journeying to exotic places, my colleagues and I could only dream of as we gossiped in the DRB staff kitchen over lunch and cups of tea.

We were driven right onto the runway as I began to feel nauseous. The full English breakfast I had eaten a few hours earlier began to bubble and churn inside my stomach. I leaned against the barred window and closed my eyes until I was being unshackled and ordered out of my seat. I followed the other deportees out of the bus and onto the hard black tarmac of a huge runway. I had to force myself to swallow a mouthful of bile as we were led to the nearest plane. One by one we were unshackled an ordered up onto the staircase. My chest began to tighten as soon as it was my turn to ascend and I couldn't hold it anymore. The full English made appearance, drenching the feet through my fabric jumpsuit. I was pulled out of line and allowed to empty by guts beside the stairs, the warm contents of my stomach soaking in between my toes. I heard the groans of the other prisoners who were forced to walk through it behind me, the cotton feet attached to the jumpsuit doing little to protect their soles. I looked around, finally able to stand upright. *Should I just end it all? I could just run away and be shot dead on the tarmac by one of these armed Recons… It's an option. Maybe that's better than what's coming…* The Recon at the foot of the staircase impatiently shoved me in the head with his rifle and forced me back in line. I was now the last to board.

'Hurry up!' he barked, and I flinched away from him as I stumbled up the first few steps and slowly climbed to the top. The Recon at the entrance to the plane threw a powder protein pack and a bottle of water into my hands before he too shoved me inside. I could see that the windows were blacked out as my eyes gradually adjusted to the dim light of the dark interior. The cabin was cold and musty with old dingy brown cloth seats and flickering overhead lights. Men and women of all ages filled the rows and I even passed a designated area for children as I was directed to the back of the plane. I was placed in the middle aisle in between two men who both stared blankly at the chairs in front of them.

'Oi! Listen up!' A Recon at the front of the cabin suddenly shouted, drawing everybody's attention away from the men being dragged through the red curtain at the back of the cabin. 'Mix up your protein packs and take them now.' We followed the order in silence ripping the packets then dumping the powdered contents into the bottles of water we had been given. I shook mine violently before downing the artificial flavoured liquid and discarding the bottle in the pocket of the seat in front of me. I felt slightly sick again

'Now place your hands in the arm rests.' The Recon shouted as some of his colleagues began to leave the cabin through the nearest exit behind him. I did as I was told, and metal restraints sprung out of the armrests and clamped over my wrists. A few Recons remained on the plane to wrestle down the rowdy deportees not willing to be strapped in. They quickly subdued the troublemakers before filing out one by one. The last Recon turned to salute us.

'*Bon voyage.*' He smiled before he swiftly shut the plane door behind himself. The crowd quickly began to murmur as a faint hissing suddenly filled the cabin. The sound got progressively louder and I could see people starting to panic.

'They're killing us!' a woman screamed as the misty gas settled around us.

'Hold your breath!' Another woman shouted, 'they've put us in a gas chamber!' I could hear children crying and see several people pointlessly struggling to get out of their seats. I was too tired to fight the inevitable and I closed my eyes, tilting my head back as I took a few long deep breaths. I could smell the toxic gas, but at that moment I welcomed the descent into nothingness even if it did mean death.

8

HEAT WAVE
KINGSTON, JAMAICA 2057

Dust flew in through the window as the rickety vehicle came to an abrupt halt in the dirt at the side of the road. The sun was viciously beating down on me as I jumped out of the hot metal truck and walked around to the driver side window.

'Is this…' I said slowly as I glanced around, 'Oliver Road?' I asked and the driver nodded his head as he held his hand out. 'I don't have any money, I told you that when you offered me a lift from the highway,' I said looking down at his open palm.

'Listen gyal, yuh affi pay mi.' The driver hissed as he suddenly reached out of the window and grabbed at one of my breasts.

'Get off me!' I screeched slapping his hand away and jumping back. He abruptly opened the driver side door to get out but changed his mind at the sound of another car impatiently beeping behind him. The driver kissed his teeth, slammed the door, and sped off leaving me in a cloud of dust. I coughed as I rubbed the grit out of my eyes. My skin was on fire and my stomach groaned painfully. I was starving and probably in danger of dehydration if I didn't get some water soon. I hadn't eaten anything since downing the protein pack on the plane, and that was over 48 hours ago. The flight had landed in Montego Bay early yesterday afternoon and as soon as I was manhandled through reimmigration, I got directions to a highway that led straight to Kingston, and I had been walking ever since. The journey had been treacherous, it was a major road so sometimes there was hardly any curb to walk on at all or the edge of the road just descended into a river, ravine, mountainous terrain, or perpetual jungle. The first day was ok as I had walked with a group of other deportees I met at the airport. But we had to separate so I couldn't continue to walk during the night because the drivers seemed to swerve their cars even crazier under the cover of darkness, and I was sure I would be knocked over, attacked, or I'd fall into a gulley beside the poorly lit highway and get eaten by a crocodile. I yawned exhausted as I looked around and tried to gather my bearings. I hadn't slept all night and I had already been walking for over ten hours by the time that driver had picked me up. He had pulled his truck into one of the very few clearings at the side of the road and when he had gotten out to piss. I think I accepted his offer of a lift out of pure exhaustion. Not just from walking but from being eaten alive by flying insects. I had covered my exposed skin in dirt attempting to keep them at bay, so when he approached me under the shine of his headlights as I sat in the darkness at the side of the road how could I refuse? Was it a smart decision? No, but he seemed decent at the time as we chatted for a few minutes before I reluctantly but gratefully accepted his offer to drive me the rest of the way to Kingston. So, at least I had gotten here in one piece. I now stood on a long concrete road, surrounded by houses with galvanised roofs and corrugated fencing. I sighed looking this way and that before deciding to walk downhill to get a better look at the houses. I didn't have a full address just a road name and a mental picture of my dad as a young boy sitting on a swing underneath a mango tree. The image in my head came from a photo that once stood on the mantlepiece long before my parents divorced, but I could see it as if it was yesterday. It was still early morning, but the sun only seemed to be getting hotter as I walked down the long concrete road. It took a while but I finally got to what looked like a dead end where the trees seemed to swallow up the concrete as the road descended into the bush. I crossed over to the other side of the road and walked in the opposite direction. My feet were hurting, the cotton feet of the jumpsuit having torn open because of the rough terrain. The concrete was hot and winced as I quickly plodded on, not daring to look up into any of the passing faces. I could hear people talking about me as they walked by, commenting on how dirty I was, and I must not live nowhere. I kept my head down trying to ignore them, and the feeling of wooziness slowly overtaking me. It was getting even hotter, I was dehydrated and felt like I was going to faint underneath the heat of the merciless sun. There was no way I could climb a coconut tree. I saw some other trees bearing fruit but I had no idea if they were even edible, and I didn't make it all the way to Kingston to then die eating some toxic pear. But there was no more saliva in my mouth. I was getting desperate, and just when I thought that I couldn't go on any longer I spotted a mango tree hanging over a metal fence a few houses in front of me. I traipsed up to it and looked around before tip toeing to pull on a cluster of ripening mangoes. The branch shook, releasing its fruit as I scrambled to catch them. I caught two and bit right into the larger riper one, using my teeth to rabidly tear through the skin. The fleshy fruit touched my tongue and gave me an instant sugar rush as the sweet pulp slipped down my throat. I was startled, hearing a barking dog as it suddenly hit the inside of the metal fence making the mango tree tremble. I jumped out of my skin and dropped one of my mangoes as I turned to run, almost knocking over an old lady in the process.

'Oh, I'm so sorry!' I cried, carefully bending down to pick up the bag of fallen groceries so as not to drop my other mango.

'Watch yuhself nuh!' The old woman snapped as I quickly stood up and handed her the bag. She was dressed in a baby blue blouse and knee length skirt with an extravagant hat on top of her head.

'of course...' I said sheepishly, even though I towered over her.

'Neva mind, jus tek time nuh,' the old woman replied as she looked me up and down. 'Wha happen? why yuh look soh?' She asked eyeballing for a few more seconds.

'It's a long story,' I said shuddering as the barking dog hit the fence again.

'Where yuh come from… England?' She mused as she ruffled around in her bag. 'So wha, dem deport yuh as well?' She tutted and shook her head as I gazed down at my dirty jumpsuit, scratching the enflamed skin that had been attacked by mosquitos during the night. I looked up as the old woman pulled out a bottle of water.

'Here,' she said pushing it up into my face, 'tek it, yuh mout look dry.' I grabbed the water gratefully and downed the contents in a few long gulps. My stomach was full of air and I let out a loud burp before continuing to eat my mango.

'Do you know Elroy Montrose by any chance?' I asked with my mouth full of mango strings. I ignored the fact that she was frowning at me and just hoped that she could at least help me find the right address.

'And yuh are?' The elderly lady asked as she continued to stare.

'His granddaughter…' I said as I retrieved the other mango I dropped earlier. 'Hmm' She huffed giving me the side-eye as I knelt down to pick it up out of the gutter. 'Me neva no him have anuda granddaughter, and from England at dat…' She said finally as she began to walk away.

'So, you know him?' I asked excitedly as I

skipped to catch up to her.

'Everybody no everybody round here,' she said as she stopped abruptly, turned to me and dumped the bag of groceries back into my hands. I sighed and thanked God that I had almost made it.

'Can you please tell me where he lives?' I asked as she pulled out a bunch of keys and began unlocking the gate in front of her.

'No need.' She murmured as the sound of cackling suddenly caught my attention. I turned to see two young women coming out of a gate two houses down. They were chatting excitedly as they jumped into a waiting car which then sped off down the road. The old woman pushed open the gate and retrieved her bag of shopping from me. I quickly turned back to the old woman who was already closing her gate.

'See yuh people dem deh,' she said nodding her chin towards the disappearing car. 'And dat deh is yuh grandfarda's yard.' She said pointing to the house a little further down the road. I could only see a small portion of it but it wasn't overshadowed by a large tree like in the old photo of my dad.

'Thanks,' I said turning back to her, but the old woman had already shut the gate and disappeared. Slowly, I down the road towards the house. The gate had been left open and I quickly slipped in-side. The house seemed smaller than the one I remembered in the picture; it was wooden at the front but as I craned my neck, I could see a concrete extension to the back. I walked up onto the veranda. *Could this really, be it?* I thought apprehensively as I walked up to the front door. I stood in front of it for a few seconds with my right fist raised before I knocked. I gently rapped my knuckles against the wood, holding my breath as I waited. I stepped back as I heard footsteps slowly approaching the door, my heart thumping anxiously as the front door eased open. Then, for the first time in my life I was gazing at the man who I hoped was my paternal grandfather. His eyes met mine as he leaned against a tall wooden staff. He was short and frail looking with smooth dark skin and grey dreadlocks down to his waist. He looked me up and down before he spoke making me even more aware of how dirty I was.

'Patrice and dem gaan already.' He said after a few seconds as he slowly began closing the door.

'Erm... actually, I'm looking for you...' I said quickly. He held the door ajar as he narrowed his eyes at me, eyes that reminded me of my father.

'Mi yuh ah look fah?' He asked suspiciously.

'Are you Elroy Montrose,' I said nervously looking for any signs of a reaction behind his intense stare.

'Me no yuh?' He asked as he reopened the door and I let out a huge sigh.

'Erm, I'm your granddaughter Raine... Michael's daughter,' I said quickly as his eyes widened. 'Rainey! Is dat yuh?' he exclaimed launching forward and embracing me into a firm hug. 'Blood-fire! mi neva tink mi wud see de day wen my likkle Rainey wud tun up pon mi doorstep.' He said stepping back to take a good look at me. 'Yuh alone come? Where yuh farda?' He asked suddenly glancing around the veranda behind me. I could see the alarm on his face as I nodded and looked away.

'I'm alone,' I choked, holding back my tears.

'Come chile,' my grandfather said quickly beckoning me inside the house.

'Tell mi everyting,' he instructed as soon as he brought me a glass of water. I was now sitting at a large wooden table in front of a steaming bowl of soup and he placed the tall glass of water beside it. My grandfather settled in an armchair opposite me and leaned his staff against it. He looked over at me as I swallowed the lump in my throat.

'Well, wha happen chile?' He asked as he picked up the challis on the small table beside the chair and lit it. Tears began to blur my vision and I tried not to blink as I picked up the glass and gulped at the water.

'I got deported,' I said finally.

'Bloodfire!' My grandfather said slowly as he looked off into the distance. 'And... de rest of de family?'

'I'm not sure,' I said as he exhaled a large of cloud of opaque smoke. He had a troubled look on his face as he watched me blink away my tears. I felt unable to speak without releasing the explosive ball of emotion building up inside me. My hands were now visibly shaking as I grabbed the glass and swallowed more water. I abruptly put it down and raised my hands to my face to cover my sobs and to stop myself from heaving. I failed miserably and my grandfather got up to comfort me.

'Don't worry,' my grandfather said after a few

minutes of sobbing as he placed a large wad of tissues in my hand and replenished my glass of water.

'You're safe now.' My grandfather said as he kissed me gently on the forehead. 'Tell me wha happen when yuh reddy, mi nuh wan see you ball.' He said as he hobbled back over to his chair. I blew my nose into a ball of tissue as I watched him settle down and relight his challis. My rumbling stomach soon bought my attention back to the bowl of chicken foot soup in front of me. It was still steaming as I grabbed the spoon on the table and began to tuck in. It was just cool enough for me to eat and I savoured every delicious bite. I finished the whole bowl within a few minutes, sucking the bony feet and using the side of hardo bread to scrap the bowl. I wiped my mouth on the sleeve of my jumpsuit before getting up from the table and walking across the room. I sat in the chair beside my grandfather. My head was thumping and eyes were still stinging but I was determined not to cry again for his sake. He looked up from the large ancient bible in his lap as he waited for me to speak.

'It all started when we were waiting on dad to bring Ryan home.' I said after taking a deep breath, 'It was the night after the *apparent* end of World War 3.'

'Oh yes, mi did see dat pon de news.' My grandfather said as I nodded and let out a helpless sigh. 'Well...dad couldn't wait... he said he was going to the barracks to meet Ryan himself, after all the false announcements we'd had over the years.' I said looking down as I wiped a single tear away from my eye. 'We waited... but... Dad never bought Ryan home; in fact, he never even came back... that night, Recons came instead.'

***

I stood under the warm water until it slowly began to run cold. I went over everything I had told my grandfather the night before, and every time I thought no more tears could fall, I proved myself wrong. I had no money or papers to get myself back to England even if there was a way. I knew I would never ever see the rest of my family again and I sobbed until my body shuddered under the cold water, breaking my train of thought. I stepped out of the shower and wrapping myself in a towel, before tiptoeing to one of my cousin's bedrooms across the dark hallway. I sat at the end of the bed and creamed my skin with the castor oil I found on the dressing table. I then helped myself to a pair of leggings and a t-shirt I had found at the bottom of the crowded wardrobe. I wasn't sure what time it was but the scent of something frying made my belly rumble. I left the bedroom and followed the aroma down the narrow corridor until it opened out into the spacious living room area. The clock above the front door revealed it was lunchtime and I could see my grandfather cooking through the cubby hole to the kitchen.

'Mawning,' my grandfather called as soon as he heard me come in.

'Morning,' I replied as I leant against the kitchen door frame. I was already sweating under the heat of the day, and the thick and heavy castor oil which left a shiny slick on top of my skin. Even though the back door was open, the temperature in the kitchen was almost unbearable.

'Yuh sleep good?' My grandfather asked as he turned around to look at me properly.

'Better than I have in a long time actually.' I said smiling at him as I looked around the kitchen.

'Can I help with anything?' I asked hungrily scanning the prepared food on the countertop.

'Just put dem tings pon de table fi mi.' My grandfather said gesturing to the steaming dishes with his free hand. I did as I was asked covering the bowls of salt fish and steamed cabbage, plantain, and fried breadfruit with mesh protectors to keep the flies out. I also set the plates and cutlery onto the already laid place mats and bought in the jugs of freshly squeezed guava juice and coconut water. I sat down at the table and poured myself a drink just as the front door flew open and the two young women from the day before abruptly entered the house. They suddenly stopped conversing as they spotted me sitting quietly at the table, drink in hand. I slowly put the glass down and smiled nervously as our eyes met across the room.

'Unno cum jus in time,' my grandfather announced suddenly appearing from the kitchen and taking his seat at the head of the table. 'Dis here is Raine, yuh Uncle Michael's dawta,' he said proudly. 'She will be staying here from now on,' he smiled as he clasped his hands together and waited for a response. He didn't get one and he cleared his throat before speaking again. 'Patrice is your older cousin,' he said pointing to the slimmer one of the two with long black tresses, slanted eyes, and caramel skin. 'And dat one deh is Corrine, her likkle sista.' Corrine was shorter, browner, and plumper with a fiery red bob that framed a pretty round face. Her eyes were friendlier than her sister's and she smiled at me when our eyes met for the second time.

'Wha gwan cuz,' Corrine said as she walked across the room and pulled out the chair opposite me. She kissed my grandfather on the forehead and placed a wad of Jamaican dollars on the table before she sat down.

'Patrice, find your manners nuh gyal!' My grandfather bellowed as he banged his staff on the floor. Patrice just stood there for a moment rolling her eyes as she unfolded her crossed arms.

'Hello.' She said through pursed lips as she walked towards the table and placed another wad of bills next to Corrine's before she sat down. I looked up but didn't bother to smile at her as she studied me closely. After my grandfather had blessed the food, Corrine served up his plate before we each took our share. The atmosphere was tense as we began to eat in silence but thankfully the sound of music drifted in through the window from somewhere outside. After a few minutes of silent eating, I cleared my throat uncomfortably as I tried to concentrate on the heavy bassline making the old wooden house vibrate. I could feel Patrice's eyes boring into me from across the table as I slowly ate my food.

'So... Raine.' Patrice announced, breaking the awkward silence as she used her fork to push food around her plate. 'How's England?' I slowly lifted my head narrowing my eyes at her as I chewed on a slice of plantain.

'Fine.' I said coldly as I swallowed the fried fruit.

'So... how long yuh plan pon staying?' She then asked looking me dead in the eye as I shovelled more food into my mouth. *Forever!*

'I... don't know,' I said slowly as I swallowed and grabbed my glass to take a drink.

'Huh.' She hummed sceptically as she picked her nails and stretched her perfectly rouged lips.

'So, how yuh plan fi mek money?' She probed as my grandfather shot her a glance from across the table.

'I... don't... know,' I mumbled slowly as I began to play with my food. 'I... I just got here,' I said quickly looking around the table at the staring faces, 'so I haven't really thought about it.'

'Well, nuttin in dis life cum fi free,' Patrice said snidely, 'remember, mi tell yuh dat...'

'Patrice, hush your mout nuh!' My grandfather said angrily kissing his teeth.

'Raine is our guest!' He said loudly as he threw his cutlery down.

'Yes, Dadda but yuh no how tings stay ahreddy,' Patrice shot back across the table.

'Yes well... never mind dat, yuh ah gwan like seh you no mek enuff money fi all ah we.' My grandfather hissed as he shot her a side glance. 'Raine can help mi work de likle land mi have out de back deh, since unno too busy nowadays.' Patrice laughed cynically as she slapped the table.

'And how dat fi help we pay de bills dem... and your debts?'

'Watch yuhself gyal.' My grandfather snapped eyeing her. 'Rememba who raise unno afta your mudda run way...' He stopped himself as he glanced over at me.

'Lies mi ah talk?' Patrice retorted as she rolled her eyes over to Corrine.

'Just watch it yuh hear mi?' my granddad hissed coldly as he leaned on the table to stand up to his feet. 'Coz unno ah gwan like seh me nuh no, wha gwan round here!' My grandfather barked as he picked up a wad of cash and dashed it at Patrice. Most of the notes hit her in the face or floated on to the table in front of her and all over the floor. 'Mi neva ask unno fi pay my debts.' He muttered as Patrice kissed her teeth loudly and mumbled something to herself as she began to snatch up the money. 'Wha yuh seh gyal?' My grandfather hissed as he cradled his ear condescendingly. 'Yuh wan seh sutton? Yuh best tek dat money, an go look fi de pickney yuh dash weh! him farda did bring him fi see mi de odda day!' My grandfather snorted as he pointed an accusatory finger in her face. 'Sometimes mi wonda if De'shawn even no him have a damn mudda!' He baited and I wished I could just disappear as a ferocious argument suddenly ensued. They were now talking so fast that I couldn't understand the patois, and I stared down at my plate gladly being ignored.

'Raine!' My grandfather suddenly, and I jumped before looking up at him startled. Patrice was already halfway across the room waving the wad of money around as she cussed.

'Don't follow dat dutty likkle gyal inna nuttin, yuh understan mi? nuttin!' My grandfather shouted as he stood up and waved his staff in the air. I nodded obediently as Corrine gave me a sheepish look from across the table.

'Come out a mi house dutty gyal!' My grandfather shouted as he turned back to Patrice.

'Wid pleasure!' Patrice hissed as she strutted towards the front door. My grandfather watched her leave and then sighed as he slowly sat back down.

'Corrine!' We heard Patrice scream from the veranda and she rolled her eyes before she downed the rest of her drink.

'Noh mind her Dadda,' she said getting up and kissing him on the forehead, 'she loves yuh really.' My grandfather turned away from her and shook his head.

'Yuh tink yuh is any better?' He asked her, but Corrine just sighed and swiftly left the house as Patrice screamed her name again. I jumped again as the front door suddenly slammed shut and the room fell silent. The sound of soft reggae re-entered my consciousness, still playing in the background from somewhere outside. I listened to the melody and gazed out of the window at the leaves of the rustling trees.

'Dat Patrice will be de death a mi.' My grandfather said, drawing my gaze back into the living room. 'Ever since she was a pickney she was too damn fast and facety...' My grandfather sighed as he took a sip of his drink. 'And now she a drag Corrine behind her too...' He rubbed his forehead and angrily kissed his teeth as he violently swiped Corrine's pile of cash off the table. He thumped the table with his fist, and I looked over at him solemnly as the notes floated gracefully down onto the floor. Silence for what seemed like a long time and I didn't know what to say to him. So, I just got up and fetched him his chalice instead.

9

ILLUSIONS

This can't be it! I thought as I wrapped myself in the sheet and sunk into Corrine's old bed. *It just can't be,* I sighed as the metal springs groaned under the weight of me trying to get comfortable. '*The likkle piece a land*' Granddad had out back turned out to be a neglected plot of earth behind the house that he ferociously tried to work himself; and now he had me digging in the dirt for yams and sweet potato like a bloody mule. Day after day my knees were grazed, my hands blistered, and my muscles worked until they burned. Even my skin was sore after baking in the sun day in day out for months on end. I sighed exhausted but satisfied with my full belly, before yawning and slipping off to sleep.

'Raine… Raine?' I wiped the dribble off my cheek and turned over to see a figure standing in the doorway. The light suddenly came on and I squinted,

shielding my eyes as Corrine's silhouette came into focus.

'Raine... wake up nuh!' she sang again as she
walked into the room.

'Whyyy!' I groaned, squinting up at her confused.

'It's only 9 o'clock inna de evening.' I covered
my head with the sheet and sighed loudly, I had only
been asleep for an hour or so.

'And?' I said annoyed.

'And... It's too early fi sleep,' Corrine said pulling down the sheet and energetically moving around
the room.

'So, what!' I groaned loudly turning away from
the light and pulling the sheet back over my head.

'SOOO... time to cum out wid mi.' Corrine
chimed as she suddenly shook my body through the
sheet. I batted her away and kissed my teeth as she
pulled the sheet off me again.

'*With you*?' I said finally as I squinted up at her.
I had only seen Corrine a handful of times, and I hadn't
seen Patrice since the argument with my grandfather
almost three months ago.

'Well... yuh wan get back home don't yuh?' My
ears pricked up at that as I shot my cousin a suspicious
glance.

'Dadda told mi wha happen to de rest a de family.' Corinne said as she broke eye contact.

'Is that right.' I sighed staring up at the ceiling
as Corrine sat down at the end of her bed.

'Look Raine, mi sorry fi wha yuh went tru... But round here we have it much worse dan yuh.'

'What's your point,' I snapped cutting her off as she met my gaze.

'Well... wha mi a seh is... where deh is a will deh is a way...' She smirked and I squinted at her as I sat up in bed.

'So, what exactly are you saying?' I asked curiously looking her dead in the eye.

'Listen... deh are ways a woman can get anyting she wants in dis world, especially inna Jamaica–'

'Can I really get *out*... Is that possible?' I interjected as my heart jumped into my throat. Corrine chuckled mischievously and my eyes widened at the very thought of getting back home to my family.

'Nuttin is impossible... But everyting has a price.' Corrine said slyly as she rose to her feet. My eyes followed her sceptically as she walked over to her wardrobe and began to sift through the rail. After a minute or so she pulled out a black jumpsuit and placed it neatly on the bed. My eyes traced the halter necked outfit as I thought about everything she had said.

'So yuh a come out or wha?' Corrine asked again eyeing me closely. 'Or wud yuh rahda continue to dig inna de dirt like a slave?' I shuddered as I looked down at the mud caked underneath my nails.

'What about Granddad?' I asked hesitantly.

'Him fast asleep in front a de VTV,' Corrine said crossing her arms.

'So yuh a come or wha?' Corrine asked again as she placed her hands on her hips. I glanced back down at my dirty fingernails and then over at the outfit Corrine had picked out for me.

'Ok,' I said yawning loudly. 'Just give me like half an hour.' I sighed and stretched my arms as I looked up at her.

'Jah knows we need longer dan dat.' Corrine mumbled, as she grabbed my face by the chin and used her other hand to pull her long fingernails through my natty hair.

***

It was something past midnight by the time we rolled up to a deserted beach. The taxi came to an abrupt halt at the edge of the sand and I stepped out. I was wearing a pair of Patrice's platformed heels since Corrine's were too small and my feet immediately sunk into the sand. I looked around as the warm sea breeze caressed my face and I admired the hovering fireflies illuminating the palm trees at the edge of the road. Corrine paid the driver as I gazed out at the sea. The rolling waves mirrored the dark purple sky and the moon light danced on its shimmering waters for as far as the eye could see.

'Raine come nuh!' Corrine called from behind me. I shook the sand off my feet and turned around to see a large plantation estate just up ahead. It was set back off the beach by a large garden lined with tall coconut trees. I followed Corrine along a path lined with colourful flowers, The trees encircling us lit up as we walked underneath them.

'Why the hell did he drop us so far?' I complained, my feet already starting to burn.

'Him have to pay a premium to come up here, now hurry up and stop whining!' Corrine snapped as she slowed down to wait up for me.

The path led us up to an extravagant fountain surrounded a floodlit pool filled with tropical fish. There was a huge holographic sign spinning high above its spouting centrepiece. The bright purple illuminous letters read; '*Palace of Illusions, making every fantasy your Reality.*' The fancy fountain itself was encircled by lavish gardens, which stood in front of a three-storey mansion with two large stone staircases leading up to the grand entrance. Huge majestic arches went around and underneath the building and I stood hypnotized by the dancing women who seemed to be floating inside the mansion's glowing windows.

'Raine!' Corrine hissed knocking me out of my daze. I buckled as I shimmied over to her and she looked back at me with disdain. 'Jus relax an nuh mek a fool outta mi.' I nodded as I carefully began to follow her up the stone steps and passed the large queue of people giving us dirty looks. The bouncers on the door let us straight through and I noticed that Corrine didn't pay anything for us to get inside. I followed her into a grand foyer with rich purple walls and several doors on either side of the large reception. A short, round Blackinese woman with thick dreadlocks wrapped into a bun was cussing a girl sitting behind the stylish marble desk. She looked up without acknowledging us and continued to berate the poor girl as we walked by.

I followed Corrine across the large lobby and watched as she pressed a code into a hidden keypad on the wall.

'Where yuh ah go?' a voice said out of nowhere and we both turned around to see the short, stout Blackinese woman now standing directly behind us. Corrine rolled her eyes before she answered the question

'To see de king,' she said flatly as the little Blackinese woman looked me up and down.

'An who is dat?' She demanded eyeing me suspiciously, 'mi nuh no her.'

'Dat's becar she's new.' Corrine said derisively as the lift doors suddenly pinged open.

'Well, she nuh sign in...' The Blackinese woman huffed crossing her arms over her large bust. 'And yuh no unno afi tell *mi* if yuh a bring a strange...'

'Relax nuh Ms. Dumpling.' Corrine interrupted as she pulled me into the lift and hastily pressed the button for the 1st floor. 'Check wid Bambi, I already booked de appointment,' she smiled indicating to the girl sitting behind the large marble desk. 'So, de king will be expecting us.'

Appointment, I thought as the lift doors swiftly closed on a sour faced Ms. Dumpling before she could say another word. The doors slid open a few moments later and we were met by another bouncer on the other side. Corrine smiled at him and he nodded in response, quickly moving his burly frame aside and allowing us to step into a majestic corridor. The walls were a deep luxurious red with a gold lampshade hanging beside each one of the fifteen mahogany doors on either side of the hall. The door at the opposite end of the corridor was the most significant. The wood was ingrained with gold leaf, and it had a fancy golden handle instead of a brass doorknob like the others.

'Who's the king?' I asked my cousin as we walked towards it.

'Yuh soon see.' Corrine said as she sashayed ahead.

'Unno late!' Patrice exclaimed startling me as she burst out of the next room.

'Betta late dan neva.' Corrine said winking at me, and I smiled sheepishly. Corrine practically gave me a makeover before she would allow me to leave my grandfather's house. She had dyed my hair blonde and trimmed down the misshapen afro when I refused to wear one of her unbearably hot wigs. She then insisted on doing my makeup and nails as well. Patrice looked me up and down as my heart pounded in my chest. She was making me nervous. But I thought I looked good, and for the first time in forever I felt like some-one who could possibly have some fun, or a strong drink at the very least. But Patrice's face gave me the impression that Patrice didn't approve of my new look.

'Wait... a my shoes she have on?' Patrice hissed looking down at my feet.

'Listen, yuh tell mi fi bring her,' Corrine snapped as she strutted on ahead, 'so nuh bodda start nuttin wid mi, chuh, a my fault both a unno have big feet?' Patrice cut her eye at me before she followed her sister down the hall. I sighed, trailing behind them as they began to bicker. We were about halfway down the corridor, and they continued to bicker all the way to the door with the elegant gold handle, suddenly stopping as if on cue. I could now see that an emblem of a lion with a crown was etched into the door.

'Gud evening ladies.' The bouncer standing next to the door smiled a mouth full of gold teeth. I gazed at the line of girls queued up along the short adjacent hallway up to the door.

'Ice.' Patrice said sweetly as she smiled and nodded her head towards me. 'Raine has an appointment to see de king.' *This* Ice looked me up and down as the next girl in line kissed her teeth and screwed up her face. 'She's a likkle late but de king *is* expecting her.' Patrice said as she gave the girl that had kissed her teeth the death stare. Just then the door behind Ice flew open and a woman came flying past us as she hurried down the hall.

'Next.' A deep voice boomed, and I hesitated as Ice directed us into the smoky room. Patrice nudged me impatiently and I crept forward into what seemed to be a very stylish office. I looked around apprehensively, fidgeting under the gaze of the man who sat behind a large marble desk. He didn't say anything until I finally met his gaze.

'Yuh know who I am?' He asked as he looked me up and down while playing with one of his dreadlocks. He had a light toffee complexion and he stared back at me with almond shaped eyes. I glanced back at Corrine and she quickly gestured for me to look back towards the king.

'Gyal!' He shouted and I quickly turned around to face him. 'When mi ask yuh a question yuh must answer mi.' He said calmly. 'Nuh bodda look pon dem.'

'I know who you are.' I said quietly.

'Oh, yuh do?' He said as he rose from his chair and slowly made his way around the desk. I kept my eyes on the large cane he held, it was black with a large golden lion head on the top. I swallowed as he stood directly in front of me, stroking the metallic lion head in his hand.

'Who am I den?' He asked again and I took a deep breath before I spoke.

'You're the king.' I mumbled without lifting my head.

'Dat's right, I am de king…' he said as he gently used his cane to lift my chin. 'Yuh no why mi associates dem call me dat?'

'No' I answered blankly looking up at him and he smiled revealing a mouthful of platinum teeth.

'Well mi a de king of de jungle around here yuh understand?' He said suddenly running two fingers down the nape of my neck making me wince uncomfortably. 'But now dat we've been formerly introduced, yuh can call mi Lion.' He chuckled as he traced my cleavage with one of the offending fingers. He was at least a foot taller than me and I just stared at the diamond encrusted lion hanging around his neck. 'So, Raine…' He said as he stroked the freshly shaved hairline around my ear. 'Mi hear seh yuh wan work fi mi? I glanced back at my cousins again barely moving my head. 'Wha mi seh jus a likkle while ago?' Lion hissed as he grabbed my chin and pulled my face up to meet his.

'Not to look at them.' I mumbled averting my eyes.

'Leave us.' He said suddenly dismissing Corrine and Patrice with a wave of his hand. I closed my eyes as I heard the door shut behind me a few moments later and immediately, Lion began to cup one of my breasts. 'Hmmm.' He said slapping my arse with his other hand before letting me go. 'Diamond did seh she had a nice likkle cousin from England staying wid her grandfarda.' He sighed thoughtfully as he rubbed his hands together. 'Look Raine, yuh jus reach back ah yard so mi no seh yuh fresh.' Lion said as he sat back down behind his desk and retrieved a half-smoked cigar from a large glass ashtray. 'Jamaica can be a treacherous place, *and* dat pretty likkle accent of yours could bring yuh a lot of trouble or… mek yuh *and mi* a whole lot a money. He grinned mischievously as he lit the cigar and blew smoke in my direction. I coughed and waved away the toxic fumes. He then grabbed the bottle of white rum sitting on his desk and poured himself a large measure. I watched him as he took a large gulp of the rum and sucked air through his teeth. 'So, hear wha mi a do fi yuh,' he said as he took another puff on his cigar. 'Yuh are now an entry level gyal at Wonderland.' I stared back at him for a moment not really knowing what exactly that meant.

'*Thank you.*' I said hesitantly as he finished the rest of his drink. Lion nodded as he put the empty glass down.

156

'Now listen, nuff gyal wud kill fi dis opportunity. He said staring me dead in the eye. 'So don't bring mi no fuckery, yuh zimmi?'

'Yes,' I said nodding my head submissively as I watched him pour himself another drink.

'Good,' he said as he sipped at it. 'Yuh can party tonight but come back tomorrow fi induction and yuh cousins dem will show yuh wha to do.' I nodded again and quickly turned to leave the room before he changed his mind. Ice opened Lion's office door as if he knew I was there, and I smiled at him nervously as I walked into the hallway.

'Next.' Lion called from his office and Ice nodded for the next girl to enter just as my cousins burst out of a room further along the hallway.

'Well, wha happen?' Corrine asked as she pulled me into the very nice boudoir styled bedroom Patrice had appeared from earlier, 'Yuh get tru?'

'Nuh bodda ask her chupid questions,' Patrice said scolding her sister. 'Of course, she got tru, the question is where?' I looked at them both blankly as they questioned me with their eyes. 'Well?' Patrice snapped impatiently, 'Him put yuh in Passion or Desire?'

'Er...' I uttered hesitating for a moment, 'he said something about a *wonderland*...' I said slightly confused.

'Yuh lie!' Corrine gasped as she and Patrice looked at one another then back towards me. 'Yuh mussi mistaken,' Patrice said quickly, 'yuh sure him seh dat?'

'Hush Patrice, dat's good news!' Corrine said quickly and Patrice kissed her teeth.

'It is?' I asked looking at them both in turn.

'Well, *yuh* very lucky, let's just she dat.' Patrice said snidely as she flopped herself down onto the fancy four poster bed in the middle of the room.

'Most gyal affi work dem all de way up to Wonderland,' she hissed looking up at me.

'But she'll be wid us straight away!' Corrine said excitedly.

'Lion shudda put her pon the ground floor like all de new gyal dem.' She said laying back and staring up at the ceiling. 'Better still, de dungeon.' She chuckled to herself as she picked up a spliff from the astray on the bedside table and examined it.

'Patrice! Don't be a bitch.' Corrine retorted as she shot her a sideward glance.

'Nuh mind her, *she's jus hatin*.' She whispered to me.

'Hatin pon wha?' Patrice shot back as she sat up, jumped off the bed and abruptly opened the bedroom door.

'She affi learn how tings work fi real, not get ah damn easy ride!' She lit her spliff as she waited for us to leave.

'Come Raine, mek mi show yuh around.' Corrine said rolling her eyes. I nodded and I quickly followed her out of the room as Patrice haughtily slammed the door shut behind us.

***

I quickly discovered that the Palace of Illusions wasn't just any random nightclub. It was a huge pleasure complex, set across three floors of a mansion and located on the grounds of a former plantation with its own stretch of private beach. The night of my interview Corrine took me into Wonderland, the luxurious gentlemen's club on the first floor where I'd soon be working. She pointed out the bar area and gave me a rundown of what an entry level position involved. I was hardly listening though; the club was busy, and I had been mesmerized as soon as I had followed Corrine through the extravagantly bejewelled double doors. I gazed at the large elaborate stage that completely covered the entire back wall of the club. It was lined with ceiling to floor golden poles that stood in front of an everchanging backdrop. There were fifteen poles in total, it seemed each catering to a different section of the club. There was also a catwalk that extended out from the stage and into the centre of the room. It had a circular platform on the end of it and one more pole in the middle. When we arrived, I saw that every pole was occupied by a shimmying half naked dancer being ogled at by an audience of hungry men. Four more girls twirled their bodies around glittery hula hoops tied to cords that hung from the ceiling. My mouth was agape as I watched overexcited punters using shiny golden guns to shoot money at the women and all over the stage. I hadn't seen anything like this in my entire life. Corrine had also shown me around the rest of the Illusions complex and it was just as luxurious. She had taken me to Passion, one of the two clubs on the ground floor. Then onto Desire, which opened out into poolside raving area, located at the back of the mansion in the surrounding gardens. I also found out there was a proletarian brothel located in the basement, but Corrine didn't bother to take me down there because *Wonderland girls were not to show faces in such places.* Nor did she take me up into *The Lion's Den*, an exclusive roof top bar located on the second floor. Apparently being a *Wonderland girl* didn't automatically grant me access up there either.

'Rainey?'

'What?' I grumbled after hearing my name for the fifth time. I could hear my grandfather's feet shuffling into the room, the tap of his staff on concrete floor and jarring sound of his sharp voice as he mumbled under his breath. I blinked a few times as my head immediately began to thump.

'Get up, it's time fi work!' My grandfather announced flinging open the dark sheet currently being used as a curtain.

'Granddad I'm tired.' I whined as I pulled the spread over my head and turned away from the light.

'Tired! Tired from wha... mi nah work yuh yet?' His shrill voice rang in my ears and I groaned loudly.

'I've... just got a headache,' I yawned as the dull thumping began to increase its beating above my eyes.

'I'm not well...' I coughed. 'I can't work today.' My grandfather kissed his teeth loudly as he shuffled towards the bed.

'Yuh tink mi nuh hear yuh sneak inna de yard dis mawning?' I shuddered and swallowed air as my eyes darted open. 'And sneak out de night before dat.' He said to my back and still I didn't respond. 'Wha mi tell yuh Raine?' He huffed, 'mi seh don't follow dem gyal inna no fuckery, and as soon as mi back tun yuh run an gaan wid dem!' I was silent for a long moment as I turned over to face him.

'Granddad I...'

'Mi dun talk.' He snapped cutting me off.

'Only Jah no wha fi do wid unno...' He sighed as he quickly left the room and I winced as the door slammed shut behind him.

10

SAPPHIRE

It was late and the club was busy, but I could still feel Ms. Dumpling staring at me from behind the bar as I emptied my tray of drinks.

'Did you want something?' I asked as I set down my tray and handed the empty glasses to Brandy who was on the bar. I had quickly learned that it was better to approach Ms. Dumpling rather than to wonder why she was boring holes into my soul from across the room.

'De king wan see yuh,' she said swishing the liquid around in her glass, from her position propped up on the bar.

'What, right now?' I asked as I fingered the lion head pendant that hung on a chain around my neck. It vibrated whenever a customer flicked on the call lamp at one of my VIP tables. I turned back to Ms. Dumpling who was looking at me with a raised eyebrow.

'Wha u tink?' She snapped sarcastically before gulping the rest of her drink and slamming the glass down on the bar. I rolled my eyes as I collected the fresh tray of drinks Brandy had prepared for me and went to drop them off to my table. On my way out of the club I asked Sugar to cover my section for a few minutes and then headed off to see what Lion wanted. I now knew that all the doors along the corridor that led to his office were themed ensuite bedrooms for the *wonder girls* who danced and worked at Wonderland. Just having access to one was a status symbol and competition was fierce. I wondered if I'd ever get one as quickly strode down the corridor towards Lions office. I had been working at Wonderland for just over six months now and I wondered on how long it would take me to get a room. Ice greeted me at Lion's door with a cheeky smile and a nod of his head before he promptly let me through.

'Gud evening,' Lion said smoothly as soon as I had entered the room, 'long time mi nuh see yuh.' He said frowning and I smiled politely as I adjusted my skimpy burlesque uniform under his gaze. 'Yuh miss me?' He smirked and I giggled like a little girl, I had learned how to stroke his enormous ego.

'Of course…' I said smiling insincerely. We did this little dance every now and then, and sighing I wondered what he wanted this time as he leant back in his chair.

'Yuh dancing yet?' He enquired as he took a sip of his drink.

'A little bit,' I answered making a face, and he chuckled as he lit a chalice and took a long drag.

'Show mi,' he croaked as he exhaled a large grey plume of smoke. I sighed, silently glancing at the silver pole behind him. It stood a few feet away from the desk on a furry black rug in front of a plush sofa in the corner of the room.

I took a deep breath and closed my eyes as Lion clapped his hands to start the music. After visualizing my routine, I strutted over to the pole in my high platinum heels and gyrated in front of it before launching into a spinning chair position, followed by a few more intermediate moves I had learned. Corrine had been giving me lessons every week and I often hung around and practiced after my shift on the bar, especially when I didn't want to go home and face my grandfather.

'Dat's enuff.' Lion said after a few minutes of watching me and slowly, I got up from my split position on the floor. 'Not bad,' he smiled as I straightened up. He stroked the mane of his lion headed cane like a pet as he tilted his head and squinted at me.

'Keep practicing, dere have been requests to see you pon de pole.'

'Really, who from?' I asked curiously wondering if I had been endorsed by any of the returning clients in the VIP section who had often asked me for a private dance.

'Nuh worry who from...' Lion said pursing his lips. 'Yuh ask too much damn questions, and when mi first meet yuh, it come like yuh fraid fi open yuh mout.' I nodded subserviently and looked down at my feet.

Wonderland was an exclusive club and most of its membership consisted of travelling businessmen and tycoons who had purchased their own little slice of paradise on the right side of the island. I knew requests came in when customers acquired favourites. But I also knew that I wasn't ready for the pole, let alone prime time! And even though dancing could lead to me becoming an *inhouse girl* and eventually getting my own luxurious bedroom, I was still filled with an anxious dread.

'Soo...' Lion said interrupting my thoughts. 'Yuh ready fi de pole?' I smiled and nodded as I looked up from my pretty platinum stilettos.

'Good!' Lion said proudly, 'yuh can start pon de early bird shift tomorrow... see how yuh do...' He said as his concentration shifted to the flashing telekom screen on his desk. He waved his hand across it and a hologram popped up. He glanced up at me. 'Yuh can go,' he said flicking his hand at me dismissively and I quickly excused myself from the room.

I had been ignoring the vibrating pendant around my neck, and it now began to flash meaning I had a new occupied table in my section. Ice opened Lion's door for me and I quickly rushed down the corridor back to Wonderland. I was feeling a little conflicted. I was making good money now, especially since moving up to VIP and giving private dances. But I knew I needed to start dancing on the pole to make even more, since the Jamaican currency was so weak. I needed to get as much money as possible to be able to buy a seat on a container cargo ship and back out of the country.

It took me no time at all to get back into the club and I quickly noticed that it was much busier than when I had left not even fifteen minutes before. I walked straight over to my area of the VIP section and scanned the tables. I could see that a premier side room had been opened for what seemed to be a large group of well-dressed businessmen. Sugar was so occupied with her section that she hadn't even managed to serve them yet. Despite that they seemed to be waiting patiently while enjoying the prime view of the stage and taking advantage of the free bottle of champagne, and luxury confectionery available in the VIP side rooms. I put my game face on as I sashayed towards them and stopped dramatically in front of the entrance. I stood with a hand on my hip and pouted as I made eye contact. The whole party stopped conversing and hungrily watched me hit the switch on the side of the booth to make the pendant around my neck stop flashing. I smiled at them seductively looking at each one in turn. They looked young, excitable, and smelled of easy money.

'Good evening gentlemen.' I said playfully as I watched them exchange wide eyed glances. 'Welcome to Wonderland, where everything you see *may* become your reality.' I smiled, recognizing one of them from sitting in one of the VIP booths only the night before. I had given him a short private dance and he had returned with friends. I winked at him mischievously as I stepped even closer to the table to collect the empty bottle of champagne, deliberately exposing my ample cleavage. They watched me silently until I had collected all the empty glasses and placed them on my tray. One of the men pressed the button on the cluttered table and a curtain automatically drew itself across the large glass window facing the stage. The door behind me shut simultaneously, and I smiled, knowing exactly what they wanted.

'Good evening boys.' I sang as I bent down to set the tray down on a side table, and I watched them whisper amongst themselves as I clicked my lion pendant around my neck to request some music. The speakers in the upper corners of the room began to vibrate as the men gave each other ecstatic glances. 'My name is Sapphire.' I smiled, and they pulled out their wallets as soon as I began to whine to the beat.

'I will be taking care of your every need tonight,' I chanted, gyrating out of the see-through dress, and exposing my lacy lingerie. The men began to jostle with excitement as they simultaneously pulled out wads of cash. I smirked as I waited for the crisp notes to start raining down on me. 'Ok boys, time to make all of your dreams come true...'

***

I sat down on the four-poster bed to prepare myself for work. I had to push my roommate Ruby's legs aside. She was sprawled across the bed having crashed after finishing her shift a few of hours ago. She suddenly flipped onto her back and began snoring softly as I laid out my chosen outfit.

I took a swig of rum before finally putting on my bikini, a halter neck and thong plastered with multiple red and white St. George's flags. I hated the gimmick; it reminded me too much of home, but I didn't really have a choice in the matter. Every time I turned up to work in attire unrelated to the UK, Ms Dumpling sent me right back to my room to change. So, I finally stopped fighting against it, every girl had a gimmick and this was mine. After all I was nothing now but an advertised commodity, merchandise being sold off to the highest bidder, a piece of meat to be eaten and regurgitated every night. Various drugs had helped me to make peace with my present existence. Despite that, I had to admit that Ms Dumpling knew how to market me. As soon as she dressed me up in this patriotic garb, I seemed attract most of the European tourists as well as the big British spenders.

I applied my make-up and then put on a sheer white kimono with fur lined sleeves before checking myself in the mirror. I looked cute enough, the bob length hair extensions framing my face nicely, and the thigh high kimono showing off my slender legs.

I twirled in front of the mirror and took in my surroundings; I couldn't believe that I had finally made it. I was finally an inhouse girl, and even though I had to share a room, it was better than travelling halfway across the island to go home and face my grandfather's wrath every night.

It had been a whole month since I had last gone home to see him, ever since I had stormed out of the house when he forbade me from every coming back here. I

just couldn't face him right now. I couldn't even answer the messages he had left for me at the front desk.
How could I call him back when he had cursed me out
for following Patrice and Corrine into their debauchery? I had no way to justify myself, and when he had
told me that he was ashamed of what I had become. I
was silent because I was ashamed too. But what choice
did I have?

Lion had been very gracious letting me move in with
Ruby after I had quickly outstayed my welcome in
Corrine's room. The old school inhouse girls were
above sharing their space, and upon the rear opportunity of a bed vacancy on the *top floor* Corrine readily
sort to fill it. I just was grateful that she convinced Lion
to give it to me, and that I ended up in a room with
Ruby. She was much nicer than some of the other inhouse girls, probably not yet having been poisoned by
their toxic hierarchal attitude.

Becoming an inhouse girl was an *earned* privilege, and
with limited space somebody had to get kicked out or
disappear before you could be allowed in. There were
many rumours about what happened to my predecessor, but I tried not to dwell on the gossip too much
knowing I couldn't pass up this rare opportunity. On
average it took a girl three who years to get access to
one of the exclusive rooms on the luxurious *top floor*,
and even though I was happy about my premature inhouse status, this undeserved advantage had undoubt-
edly affected my dwindling popularity with the other
girls. Especially those who were already on the waiting

list long before me. I had come along and had unwittingly upset the hierarchy, and for that I would have to pay, *or so I had been told.*

I was making more than five times the money I was making on VIP section, But I was still no closer to buying my safe passage on a freighter home. Even though I made more cash, Lion took half my wages instead of a third he took while I was waitressing, despite that being an inhouse girl still worked out much better for me. But I couldn't help but think how much quicker I could reach my goal if I as allowed to keep most of it.

I was daydreaming and the small lion shaped pendant around my neck began to vibrate. Every Wonderland girl had one and now I was an inhouse girl I was required to wear it all the time. In fact, it had been welded shut and I couldn't take it off even if I wanted too. It tracked my every move and informed anyone that cared to look that I was owned by Lion. The pendant flashed as it buzzed again.

I was being summoned. It was time to start my shift. I took another swig of rum and a few pulls off Ruby's spliff to calm my nerves before slipping my feet into my open back stilettos. I was a little nervous like I always was before going to work.

You never knew what to expect so you had to be ready for everything.

Tonight, I was on the twilight, as I had been since moving in. Apparently an inhouse girl dancing on the early bird shift was practically unheard of. Twilight was a step up from the early bird shows and if I did well it would guarantee me a spot on the primetime roster.

I sprayed some perfume as my pendant buzzed for a third time, more vigorously, and a heavy-handed knock, at the door made me jump.

'What?' I called as Ruby briefly stirred in the bed.

'Yuh late, Ms Dump–'

'I'm coming!' I called as I sprayed my mouth with freshener and checked myself once more in the mirror. I recognised the gruff voice of Titan, one of the century guards who stood at the entrance to the top floor to keep watch over the inhouse girls living quarters.

'Well Ms Dumpling tell mi fi bring yuh be–'

'No need,' I called as I ran towards the door and flung it open. Titan was the size of a grizzly bear and he smiled down at me, scanning my body with his shifty eyes before he stepped aside and allowed me to walk into the hallway. We walked together briefly before he stationed himself in his usual spot next to the lift at the end of the corridor as I turned right on my way to the club.

I went the long way around to walk in through the back way, not wanting to bump into Ms Dumpling and have her berate me in front of potential clients.

When I got into the dressing room most of the girls were ready to go on stage. I was still new to the twilight group. It consisted of Amethyst, Venus, Vixen, Desire, and Honey amongst others. As soon as I walked through the curtained partition separating the dressing room cubicles from the rest of back stage area they

171

stopped their whispering and stared at me. I immediately knew then that I had been the topic of their conversation, as per usual. I walked down the line and squeezed in between Emerald and Candy so I would end up on my rightly assigned pole.

'Shouldn't yuh be pon primetime?' I heard Venus say from behind me.

'Look like she nah mek it yet!' Desire's shrill laugh cut through me as ignored them and refused to turn around. *Here we go again,* I thought. Of course, if it was up to me, I would have jumped straight onto primetime but I needed to earn that position, and quickly because I was sick of all the drama.

'She tink she betta dan we,' Amethyst added, 'Just like Diamond and onyx,' she said referring to Patrice and Corrine. Something suddenly hit me in the back of my head and I turned around to face them angrily. I glanced down at the floor and saw that someone had thrown a dirty flip flop. They glared back me, the ringleaders Venus, Amethyst, and Desire seemed ready to get physical as they stepped out of line. I balled my fists ready to fight, every night of the last month had been the same and I was sick of it. I stepped out of line as they strode towards me but they were suddenly stopped by Star, Ms Dumpling's daughter who was in charge back stage.

'Wha gwan?' She asked as she strode down the line and stepped in between us.

'Nuttin nah gwan,' Venus offered but Star was having none of it.

'It look like suttin a gwan to me!' She said eyeing us all in turn. 'Venus? Amethyst? Desire?' She said looking at each one of them. 'Sapphire? Care to enlighten me?' I shrugged my shoulders and stared straight ahead as I stepped back in line. Venus and Amethyst and Desire followed suit and backed away as Star walked up and down the line to inspect each one of us.

'Unno no de rules!' she barked loudly. 'No politics backstage, why?'

'Because, dancing and drama nah mix.' All the dancers grumbled in unison.

'Right! now does everyone here understand de rules?' We all nodded as she stepped back and glared at us. 'Gud!' Star said seemingly satisfied, 'now go out dere and have a good damn show!'

Star walked to the curtain and gave the DJ the signal to announce the start of the twilight entertainment. I wiped the nervous layer of sweat from my brow as the girls in front of me began to disappear out onto the stage. I was determined to perform well tonight, and finally get off the twilight shift and away from these hostile females. I sighed to myself; I was on next so plastered the best fake smile across my face as I was introduced. The crowd cheered as the sound of my stage name rang in my ears. I ignored my elevated heart beat and stuck my batty out as I sashayed onto the stage. It was showtime.

***

I posed under the spotlight next to my pole with my hands on my hips as the DJ introduced me. It was another Sexy Saturday and the customers were bidding for the chance to win a private performance from their favourite girl. I had only been working primetime shows for a couple of months so I used to it. Primetime was much more demanding than doing the early bird shows or the twilight shifts, but you had the chance to make much more money. I snapped out of my daze as Amber, the last girl coming on tonight sashayed onto the stage and posed beside her pole. After she was introduced, a heavy baseline started to play and each girl began to dance to the rhythm of the music. I snaked my way up my pole until I was high enough to quickly scan the room. I slowly slid back down into a spread-eagle position as I took in the club's atmosphere. I could see Sugar ushering a group of businessmen into one of the booths in Crystal's VIP section. I swivelled around the pole taking full advantage of my position on the of the podium that extended out from the centre of the stage. I was still fresh meat, so for the most part was stuck dancing for the regulars who congregated in the middle of the club. Wonderland had a pole hierarchy, each pole being positioned in front of one of the twelve expensive VIP booths situated along the front of the stage, except for the three poles that ran along the podium. The more experienced well-known girls

174

pulled in the most cash, so they always got the best positions. The newer girls like myself were dumped on the pole numbered 7, 8 and 9, where throngs of leering men surrounded the catwalk and shot at you with novelty guns loaded full of one-dollar bills. Even though my pole wasn't directly in front of any VIP tables, I could clearly see the men sitting in the booths. I posed low on the pole allowing prying fingers to stuff dollar bills in the crevices of my bikini as I watched Sugar escort a group of men across the club. I noticed that she was being very giggly with one of them and that she was carrying a bottle of our very best champagne. One of the customers in front of me suddenly yanked my leg and I lost my grip on the pole. Startled, I fell onto my arse and kicked the culprit in the face with my free leg as he tried to drag me off the stage and into the crowd. The heel of my shoe slashed him in the face and he immediately let me go, but then lunged at me as I retreated towards the pole. Security flew across the club and grabbed him before his feet could even touch the stage. I watched the customer being violently removed as I bent down to pick up the blood speckled money. I cursed myself for not paying attention. I vaguely recognised the guy that had lunged at me, and I felt no sympathy knowing that he would be beaten up outside. I smoothed down my orange bikini as regained my composure and exchanged a look with Vixen, a former twilight girl behind me on pole number 7 before I slowly began to continue my dance. I did a few spins and then swivelled back down as my eyes darted around the audience like a sonic radar. There was a good crowd in tonight and the VIP booth in Amber's section had just been opened. I slowly lowered myself into the splits as I looked over at the newly seated table and caught someone's eye. After an hour or so the lights dimmed for the show's interval, and as soon as I left the stage, I grabbed a drink and hovered around the edges of the VIP tables like a stray dog looking for handouts. During competitions each booth was catered to by the girl that danced on the pole directly in front of it, and since pole number 7, 8 and 9 had no VIP tables, I was supposed to mingle amongst the regular crowd. What I was doing was called skimming, but I had to be careful. It was a little trick Ruby had taught me until I could get more established and demand a pole with a VIP section. It was disrespectful to invade another girl's jurisdiction but I had caught the eye of a gentleman sitting in booth number 10 in the section right next to the podium. Crystal was dancing on pole number 10 which gave her equal access to Amber's tables whenever she finished on stage. But the audience had been given the chance to add to their blind bids during the second performance, and so I sneakily shimmied around Amber's VIP section while she was seducing a customer at the other end of the table. I concentrated on the rich businessman who had caught my attention during my last dance, hoping that he would put in a bid for me. I quickly introduced myself, flirting with him for a few minutes until I felt Amber giving me the evil eye from across the table. I flashed him a quick smile and abruptly made my exit before she called Crystal and made a scene. Since I had to skim, I often broke etiquette and so I had to be mindful. If I wasn't cautious, I could end up getting jumped by the other girls. For the rest of the interlude, I mingled with the 'ordinary' men on the tables around the catwalk, and before I knew it, I was being summoned back to the stage.

'Listen up!' DJ Redz shouted as each girl took her place back beside her pole.

'All votes have been counted and it's now time to announce tonight's Queen a Wonderland!' He said theatrically as he lowered the music. 'Will Crystal, de reigning queen please step forward.' DJ Redz dimmed the spotlights on everybody's pole except Crystal's and she waved at the audience as she strutted down the catwalk that extended out from the middle of the stage. She barged past me, a single spotlight following her all the way down to the end of the catwalk making the glistening tiara on her head sparkle. Coco, the girl on pole number 9 moved aside as Crystal did a little spin around the pole and twerked her arse at the cheering audience. 'Will Crystal lose her crown tonight… or will she remain queen fi de fourth week in a row?' DJ Redz teased as the music faded into a drum roll. A spotlight suddenly appeared above Sugar as she walked across the Club waving the golden envelope. The crowd whooped and hollered as she pranced in between the tables and up the steps to the stage. She gave the envelope to DJ Redz and the crowd jostled impatiently waiting for him to open it. 'And tonight, de Queen ah Wonderland is...' A drumroll played out as he ripped the envelope open and pulled out a glittery piece of paper. 'Sapphire!' He boomed into the mike as he threw the envelope into the air. I jumped as I heard my name, a cloud of silver and gold confetti exploded behind me. My eyes widened as I instantly felt sick from the rampant butterflies fluttering around in my stomach.

'What?' I said my mouth dropping open as a spotlight suddenly shone on me. Not expecting it, I froze like a deer in headlights. This was the first time I had won anything. The crowd was chanting my name and I took a deep breath before I walked out onto the end of the catwalk. Crystal gave me a dirty look as I walked past her. She stood with her arms crossed just watching as I waved to the cheering crowd. I felt light headed as another ripple of nerves gurgled in my stomach. I had to blink a few times as I watched Sugar take the tiara off Crystal's head and place it on mine. Our eyes locked for a moment and Crystal looked at me like she wanted to slice my throat. I ignored her, smiling at Sugar, who approached the platform with a bottle of champagne, a red rose, and my prize money. I smiled as I took the golden envelope knowing it contained the money from the winning bid placed for me. The crowd was still cheering as Crystal marched down the catwalk and off the stage.

'Crystal's rule is over...' DJ Redz announced, dimming all stage lights as the other girls left the stage. 'And now a new reign has begun.' The only spotlight left on the stage was shining down on me as I stood at the end of the catwalk on the podium where men could get a 360-degree view of my solo performance. 'Please

welcome Queen Sapphire... De new Queen of Wonderland!' DJ Redz bellowed into the mike and I swallowed hard praying I wouldn't fall after the three large
glasses of champagne I'd had during the interval. The
beat started and I leaned back against the pole as I
rocked my hips from one side to the other seductively.
I bent over shaking my arse and whining my waist before I lowered my body into the splits. Money was
raining down on me as the men closest to the podium
enjoyed the view. I confidently snaked upwards and
held the pole between my thighs as I swivelled around
it. I then unlocked my legs and slid down in a suspended seated position with both legs at opposite
ninety-degree angles. The crowd went wild as I unfas-
tened my Union Jack bikini top and threw it into the
audience. I slid down the pole and danced topless
amongst the floating money as it fell gracefully onto
the podium. I shimmied up the pole again, locking my
limbs in various positions to anchor myself against the
slippery metal. I leaned back as the spinning column
spun me around over the gawking audience. I then
grabbed the pole with one hand over the other, my legs
curled as I suspended my body in mid-air to create a
graceful carousel. I expertly undid my side-stringed
thong and threw it into the crowd just before I gracefully touched the podium floor. I leaned backwards to
end my routine in an elegant hook and then sunk into
the splits. The audience erupted as I stood up and
bowed. I then began to scrape up the money on the catwalk before leaving the stage. It was mostly small
change but every little helped. I was completely naked

and went to grab my bikini but it was snatched up by the crowd. I could hear wolf whistling as I bent over to collect the last of the money before I quickly hurried backstage. I grabbed a robe from my small dressing station and stuffed the pockets full of scrunched up money. I took a swig of the rum I had left on my dressing table before retrieving my prize money and flowers from behind the DJ booth. I retreated to my room to freshen up and then retreated to one of the hideaway boudoirs at the back of the club. I could still see the main club area through the wall with one-way mirrored glass and I waited patiently in my lacy underwear and satin kimono. After waiting for a few minutes or so, I cracked open the bottle of complimentary champagne to keep me company. A rapid *Knock, knock, knock* startled me, and I quickly positioned myself on the plush sofa. I pressed the button in the middle of the coffee table and a one-way mirrored window in the door lit up revealing his face. I wasn't surprised to see the very same businessman I had poached from Amber's VIP booth and smiling, I pressed another button on the table to unlock the door.

'Come in...' I called seductively just before the door slid open and I watched him hesitate before he walked into the room. 'Hi...' I said sipping at my glass of bubbly before setting it down on the side table. He smiled bashfully and I noticed that he was already sweating. 'Drink?' I asked getting up to take the jacket from his arm.

'Whisky please,' he said in an impeccable English accent as I took his belongings. 'Straight.' he said as I hung his suit jacket on the coat stand. I retrieved his drink from the barely stocked mini bar, draining the last of the whisky into a tumbler, it was a good thing he didn't ask for ice. I then passed it to him as I sashayed over to the plush sofa. He downed it in one gulp and sighed before tentatively placing the glass on top of the side table. I patted the space beside me as I sat down with my champagne and slowly, he took a seat.

'So, what do I call you?' I asked moving closer to him as I ran my fingers through his sandy coloured hair.

'Oh, of course, excuse my manners,' he said nervously wiping the sweat off his brow. 'Please… call me Harry,' he mumbled looking at me sheepishly. I smiled at him as I put my glass down on the table. 'Well Harry… *You* made the winning bid for me.' I said standing up as I undid my robe to reveal my chocolate brown lacy underwear. 'So, if there's anything I can do to thank you… All you need to do is ask…' I said invitingly as I stood over him. I let my robe fall to the floor and began to dance to the soft rhythm drifting into the booth from an overhead speaker. He watched me silently, his eyes rapidly searching every crevice of my body as I moved in time to the music. I gazed at him teasingly, and after a few minutes of gyrating in front of him he had loosened his tie, grabbed his crotch several times and licked his lips repeatedly. I slowly removed my bra as I began softly sliding my body onto his lap. I felt him shudder beneath me as I paid special attention to the stiff bulge in his trousers. I carefully circled my body on top of him, whining my waist to the slightly faster tempo of a new song floating in through the overhead speaker. Harry startled me as he suddenly grabbed my waist as I continued to twirl on top of him. He grabbed one of my breasts and jolted beneath me as he let out a muffled groan. After a few heavy breaths he abruptly let go of me and I smiled as I got up off his lap to retrieve my bra and kimono.

'It's usually extra for touching…' I said turning back to him.

'Oh my… I'm incredibly sorry!' Harry said apologetically, 'Money is of no object,' he mumbled slowly. He seemed very embarrassed as I watched him dab at the crutch of his cream trousers. 'Don't worry about it,' I said smiling, and he blushed as I studied the angles of his face. He had a straight Roman nose, a strong chin, and eyes that were the most startling shade of blue. 'I'm glad that you enjoyed my little dance.' I said tying up my robe.

'Will I ever see you again?' Harry asked suddenly as he gently grabbed my wrist.

'Oh, were not finished yet… I'm just getting you another drink.' I said chuckling as I eased his hand away. 'Don't worry,' I smiled, winking at him before I turned towards the door. 'I promise *you'll* get your money's worth…'

***

My blood was still hot from having a shower as I stretched my aching body across the bed. I just lay there for a few minutes feeling the rum creeping up on me as I closed my eyes. I flipped over onto my back and lay against the luxury pillows to clear my mind. It was my sixth month of being an inhouse girl living and I had been crowned queen two more times thanks to Harry. Every time he travelled to the island, he came to see me and thanks to him things were looking up, *slightly*. Thanks to Harry's frequent visits I was suddenly making much more money, having been given the opportunity to exclusively cater to his requests, and his latest holiday had been his longest time on the island to date. Most girls weren't so lucky. But I still had no friends except for my roommate Ruby, who had been working at Wonderland for a year longer than I had. We were mostly always dancing on different shifts so I had sole use of the room and vice versa, and we only really seemed to bump into each other when our rest days clashed. I had just clocked off, and after pouring another generous measure of rum I downed it in one gulp, savouring the burning sensation as it slid down my throat. It was becoming apparent that I needed some sort of substance to numb my intrusive thoughts. I took a few more pulls on my chalice and decided to play some music as I tried to force the images of my family out of my head. I wondered if they were dead, alive, or even deported as I got up to switch on the overhead surround sound to tune into the club. The DJ would be playing a set and maybe that would distract me. I emptied the last of my crim, a powered drug into the weed the weed laced chalice.

Tap, tap, tap... The faint knock at the door startled me and I jumped up as I glanced at the clock on the bed-side table. It was going up to 11pm and I almost forgot that I was entertaining tonight. *Shit!* I thought as I frantically opened the window and quickly scooped my paraphernalia off the bed. I exhaled a red cloud of smoke and waved it away until it dispelled in the air.

'Just a minute.' I coughed as I checked myself in the full-length mirror. I grabbed a stick of gum and furiously began chewing on it as I flew around the room spraying air freshener. 'Hi Harry.' I said innocently leaning against the bedroom door frame.

'Good evening, Miss Sapphire,' he said smiling and I rolled my eyes.

'Harry, what did I tell you about this *Miss* business?' He shrugged innocently as he lifted his hand to reveal a little red bag swinging from his finger. I squealed as I snatched it and skipped over towards the bed. Harry followed me inside the room and shut the door behind us as I pulled a little black box out of the bag. I opened it and gasped as I lifted out a gold neck-lace with a beautiful blue sapphire dangling gracefully from the end of it.

'Harry, I... I don't know what to say.' I whis-pered looking up at him as I sat down.

'A thank you would suffice.' Harry said chuck-ling from above me.

'Oh yes of course. Sorry where are my man-ners... Thank you.' I said shaking my head. Harry al-ways bought out the proper English accent in me.

'Here, let me help you.' He smiled coming over to fasten the necklace around my neck. 'There we are.' He said adjusting the gem which nestled nicely in between my ample cleavage. I got up and went to the full-length mirror to admire my new piece of jewellery. I touched the stone in awe as Harry slid up behind me and began kissing my neck. Harry had already bought me perfume, chocolates, and lingerie on several occasions but nothing as extravagant as this. I moaned as Harry rubbed my nipples through the negligee's thin material and continued to nibble on my ear. I spun around and began to slowly undress myself as he moved towards the bed. He watched me dance along to the music as he began to undress himself and lie down. I watched his little pink manhood stand to attention as he quickly covered it with the anti-infection spray sitting on the bedside table. I slowly approached the bed, sliding myself down on top of him. Harry let out a loud groan as he began to scatter my breasts with hungry little kisses. His lips moved rapidly towards my face as his cumbersome hands clumsily explored my body. He kissed me awkwardly as he ungracefully flipped me over and tried to re-enter me from the missionary position. His legs were pinching the skin in between my thighs and I winced, adjusting my body accordingly. Harry wasn't exactly in shape and his bulk was heavy but still, I moaned appropriately and closed my eyes thankful that he was a gentle lover that often came prematurely. Tonight, was no different, and after he tired of the missionary position he came loudly and shuddered as he flopped down on top of me. I slid out from beneath him rolled over onto the bed. I lay back and smiled as I watched him get up and walk to the bathroom to wash off the film from the anti-infection spray. He left the door ajar and I waited until I heard the water running before rolling across the bed to search through his belongings. It was a nasty habit I had quickly acquired whenever a client went to the bathroom; *another one I couldn't seem to kick*. It only started with a few customers that had pissed me off, but soon I couldn't help myself. It was too easy, a cheap little adrenalin rush, and just a little extra change for my get home fund. up until now I had refrained from violating Harry. But my high was making me curious so I expertly found his wallet by snaking my fingers into his discarded jacket. I flipped it open and took 1 measly 100-dollar bill as I shook off a pang of guilt, knowing that Harry would tip me, and that I still had to collect my wages from Ms. Dumpling. There was so much money in his wallet he wouldn't even notice. I pulled out a few of his cards and studied them, but one caught my eye. I blinked as I realised that it was a Parliament I.D pass.

Harold J. Winchester MP, House of Lords, United Liberals Party. I heard Harry flush the toilet and I scrambled to shove the cards back into his wallet and into his jacket. I dropped the clothes beside the bed and quickly rolled away. My heart was beating wildly as he re-entered the room and went to retrieve his clothes. *So, he's an MP, and a member of The House of Lords…* I thought to myself as I watched him pull on his underpants.

186

'Where do you think you're going?' I cooed as I tugged at his briefs suggestively. He smiled at me meekly and I smirked naughtily. 'Your time's not up yet.' I said seductively, patting the space beside me on the bed, feeling relieved that I had never seen any sign of a wedding ring. Harry complied and sat back down as I took another fiery gulp of rum straight from the bottle before falling back onto the bed beside him. I watched him pull his boxers down around his ankles and re-cover his groin in anti-infection spray. I just needed enough money to get a passport and buy my passage off the island and after over a year's hard work I was a quarter of the way there. *Or maybe,* I thought smiling mischievously as I got up and walked around the bed … *I could get Harry to take me home.*

***

Something moving in the darkness startled me out of my sleep as I felt a shiver go down my spine. I opened my eyes and through the darkness I could see a figure standing at the end of the bed.

'Harry?' I whispered as I sat up and rubbed my eyes. I glanced up at the digital clock on the dresser fully aware that Harry had already left. I was still high, maybe I was imagining it. But I gasped as the figure suddenly moved closer. 'Who are you,' I said quickly as I drew my knees into my chest. The figure ignored me as it silently moved around the bed. 'What do you want?' I asked my heart beating erratically. 'Come any closer and I'll scream.' It was a man; I could tell by the height and stature. I stretched my hand across the bed, it was empty so Ruby was still at work.

'TITAN HEL–'

'Don't mek a bloodclart sound!' The man growled as he flew towards me and climbed onto the bed. He quickly produced a knife pressing the cold metal against my throat. I could feel his hot breath against my face as he leaned over me and pressed a large blade against my lips.

'What do you want!' I hissed again through gritted teeth. 'Mi wan wha you owe mi,' the man said as slowly removed knife. I watched it glint in the moonlight as he whipped back the covers and pulled my legs straight.

'Wha mi owe *yuh*?' I said trembling in confusion as he ran the knife lightly over my stomach. He was still for a moment as he stopped and looked down at me, I could barely see his face in the moonlit darkness.

'Yuh memba mi?' He asked as he started to touch my breasts. I shuddered silently keeping my eye on the knife. 'Well!' He barked making me shudder.

'No, mi nuh no yuh!' I cried as he suddenly cut through the slip I was wearing with the serrated knife.

'Well... mi no yuh.' He said aggressively as he grabbed my hand and pulled it towards his face. He ran my fingers over his skin, and I felt the outline of a large scab just beside his eye. *Shit!* I thought as I snatched my hand away. It was that guy from the audience who had tried to pull me off stage, I thought I recognised the voice. He threw a light orb into the air and it floated above us and it stay suspended over the bed indiscriminately shining down on us.

'Yuh memba mi now?' He said clambering on top of me as I had a flash back of kicking him in the face a few months ago. *What now?* I thought panicking. I could scream for help, but I'd be dead by the time Ice or Titan made it to the room. *How did he even get in here anyway? And past Titan or whoever was working security tonight?* I thought, my mind racing a hundred miles a minute. 'Eh gyal?' He said grabbing my chin, 'Answer de question.' I could see his bright teeth as he smiled in the under the shining orb of light.

'Yes... I remember.' I whispered finally as I felt the cold metal knife drifting down below my belly button. Tears ran out of my eyes as he moved the blade lower still, grazing the manicured pubic hair just below my bikini line. 'Please don't...' I pleaded shivering as he pressed the knife into my skin. 'I'm sorry... about your face... It was an accident... I didn't mean to scar.'

'Shhh!' He said harshly pressing a heavy finger over my lips. 'Hush yuh bloodclart,' He grunted as he fiddled with his trousers. 'I can give you money...' I whispered, thinking about my stash of money hidden in my wardrobe. 'Or what about drugs, mi have crim, loads of crim, it's the best purest stuff you'll find.' I whispered desperately.

'Shut up!' he spat as if I was interrupting some sort of sadistic ritual. 'Lion will give you anything you want... Just, just please don't hurt me, I prom−' He hushed me by raising the knife back up to my lips.

'You tink Lion give a rass bout yuh gyal?' he

chuckled as he removed the blade from my mouth and placed it back down on my stomach. He didn't let go of the handle as he quickly positioned himself in between my legs. He grunted and I held my breath as he forced himself inside of me. I was bone dry, and it was as if he was rubbing my vaginal walls with sandpaper. I tried to inch away from him, but I could still feel the cold knife pressed against my stomach as he forced himself deeper. I cried out as he cut me, the sharp knife easily piercing my flesh. 'Nuh bodda try run from mi.' He said as he used one of my legs to pull my body back down towards him.

'You're hurting me!' I cried as I writhed in agony. He chuckled as he grabbed my arms and anchored them above my head to stop me squirming. I cried out again as he began to thrust even harder, manoeuvring my legs so that he could secure his body against mine. I began to scream as he pushed a pillow over my face to muffle my cries. I couldn't breathe, the soft material of the pillow smothering me as he pressed it against my face. I lost most of the air in my lungs as he got even more excited and pushed down even harder. I frantically struggled to free my arms and was able to pull one out of his grip. I desperately reached out and felt for his face and dug my fingers into the semi healed gash under his eye. He grunted loudly and cut me in the stomach again before pulling his face out of my reach. I was choking and I reached out in vain trying to grab or scratch something else so he would set me free. He leaned away from me and that's when I suddenly felt the coldness of the knife pressed against my side. He was moaning in excitement and I felt for the knife as he groaned and shuddered above me. As soon as he orgasmed, I grabbed the handle and thrust the blade into his belly. I could suddenly breathe again as his weight rapidly lifted off me and I quickly flung the pillow away from my face. I sat up coughing trying to catch my breath. The light orb had disappeared and I switched on the bedside lamp. I gasped as my eyes focused on the blood-soaked white sheets. He looked down at his bloodstained hands. I could see the nasty gash under his eye was now bleeding from where I had scratched it and blood was rapidly seeping through his light blue t-shirt. I winced as he slowly pulled the knife out of his midsection. I stood up as he groaned loudly, his eyes zeroing in on it as he tried to steady himself.

'Yuh try kill mi gyal?' He spat, spluttering even more blood over the sheets. 'You mussi bloodclart mad!' he heaved as he tried to lunge towards me with the knife in hand. He stumbled forward and I quickly jumped over the bed before he could reach me. He caught one of the tall bed posts to steady himself, dropping the knife onto the mattress. I lunged for it and then held the large serrated blade out in front of me as he struggled to stand back up. He looked me dead in the eye as he leaned against the fourposter bed heaving. 'Yuh dead gyal,' he hissed as he tried to take a few steps. 'Yuh hear mi? dead!' He murmured before collapsing face down on the bed. I dropped the knife as he fell on the mattress and began to convulse. I could see the blood soaking through the sheets underneath him and slowly dripping onto the tiled floor. I began to panic as I paced up and down stealing pained glances at the twitching body. I burst into tears as I watched his chest rise and fall for the last time… *What was I supposed to do now?*

***

'A wha de bombaclart Raine!' Ruby shrieked as she entered the room a few hours later.

'Wait nuh! I can explain!' I said quickly jumping up from my seat on the bed. I had been anxiously waiting for Ruby to finish her shift, rocking back and forth as I nursed almost empty bottle of rum. I had finished all my crim and I dared not leave to buy some more.

'No, actually, whateva did is, mi nuh wan fi no!' She said turning around. I ran behind her, blocking the door as I poked my head into the hall before slamming it shut.'

'It wasn't my fault...' I said taking another swig of rum straight from the bottle. My eyes were blood-shot from hours of spontaneous crying fits, and I was covered in blood from wrapping the body and cleaning up the floor.

'Mi nuh see nuttin, mi nuh hear nuttin!' Ruby said holding her hands up as she tried to retreat around me towards the door. 'It was self-defence I swear! I don't even know how him get in!' I exclaimed still blocking the entrance and forcing her to retreat towards the bathroom. 'Ruby please, just listen to me nuh!' I ranted as I forced the bathroom door open behind her. 'I was set up.' I blurted as I burst into an un-stoppable tangent recalling the whole incident. I had already managed to clumsily wrap the body up in all the sheets I could find, scrubbed the mattress, flipped it over and made the bed. But the body still lay there in the middle of the floor and I had no way to get it out of the room, Or out of building.

'How can I move the body without Ms. Dump-ling or Lion finding out about this?' I said erratically pacing around the bathroom. 'I need your help.' I said sheepishly as I glanced at the swaddled mass in the middle of the bedroom floor then back at Ruby, who sat opposite me on the closed toilet seat. She had been silent the whole time and I felt another uncontrollable crying fit coming on.

'What about Onyx? Maybe she can help.' Ruby suggested, and I kissed my teeth.

'Corrine?' I made a face, 'Uh uh!'

'Diamond?'

'No way Ruby, you know what Patrice is like!'

'But dey yuh cousins doh!'

'I can't trust them!' I said grimacing.

'Well den get changed.' Ruby said after a moment of silence. I slowly wiped my eyes as I looked up at her inquisitively.

'Why... what for?' I asked warily.

'Mi affi tele-call Ice.' She said calmly as she got up off the toilet seat and strolled out of the bathroom.

'But Ice will go straight to Lion!' I wailed franti-cally as I trailed behind her, 'won't he?'

'Maybe...' she said thoughtfully. 'But him help mi before, and mi nah bodda wid de rest ah security so mi affi try him... dere's no one else.' Her pupils dilated as her plug flashed from inside her ear, before I could even stop her.

'I don't know about this Ruby,' I said as my eyes began to well with tears.

'Yuh have a betta idea?' She said flippantly as she glanced over at the body. I sighed as I shook my head. 'Ok, suh gwan, mek yuhself pretty.' She said looking me up and down.

'Why?' I asked anxiously, and Ruby rolled her eyes as if it was obvious. 'So, when Ice reach, he can see wha yuh have fi bargain wid!'

***

'The sound of my telekom vibrating on the bed-side table forced me to reach for my ear pod and pop into my ear.

'Hello' I answered croakily.

'Sapphire, it's me... Harry.'

'Hi,' I said trying to perk up but failing at sounding energetic. 'Where have you been?' I asked slightly miffed that I hadn't seen him for nearly two weeks.

'I told you that I would be Offshore... On business.' He said cautiously as I yawned loudly. 'I did that thing you asked me to do...' He said changing the subject. 'And it seems that none of your family has come through any of Jamaica's national airports.' That was

194

too much information for my exhausted brain to take in.

'What?' I asked suddenly awake. 'Did you try my mother's maiden name?' I said sitting upright in bed as the early morning sun stung at my eyes.

'Yes, I did, and she hasn't arrived on the island either.'

'Are you sure?' I asked reaching for the bottle of tequila on my bedside table.

'What about my sisters and the rest of my family, did you try to trace all the names on the list I gave you?'

'Yes of course… but none of their names were found on the deportation index. *That must mean they're still at Hermitage Hill!*' I thought in relief. I squeezed the bridge of my nose trying to think clearly.

'Thanks Harry,' I said with a sigh. 'When did you find out?'

'My source made contact on Monday.'

'Monday?' I repeated as my ears pricked up. It was Saturday, eleven days since Ruby had called Ice to help me get rid of a body. 'And you're just telling me now!' I said heatedly.

'I've been trying to get hold of you for a whole week!' Harry exclaimed as I rolled my eyes up to the ceiling. *Yes, I had been laying low since the incident and was getting shitfaced at every given opportunity. Ruby had practically saved my life by calling Ice, who had sorted my problem and gotten me out of my sticky predicament for regular payment in kind.*

'What the hell is that supposed to mean?' I said trying to keep calm.

'Sapphire, I've left you countless messages and you haven't returned any of my calls...'

'Then why didn't you come to the club to see me?' I countered.

'I've only got back yesterday,' Harry said sheepishly.

'You should've been here!' I said heatedly, my anxiety making me more erratic than normal. 'But you're always so damn busy doing God knows what!' I whined as Ruby groaned loudly and rolled over in the king-sized bed beside me. I didn't hear her come in.

Harry was silent for a few long seconds and I squeezed my eyelids to stop the tears of frustration welling up in my already swollen eyes. I waited for him to say something... anything. But what did I expect him to say? I knew I was acting like a spoilt child. It wasn't Harry's fault a rapist had turned me into a killer. Harry had just done me a huge favour and here I was being hostile. I wasn't even sure if he was still on the line until I heard the familiar sound of his heavy breathing.

'Sapphire... I have to travel offshore again for another few days,' He mumbled finally. This revelation pissed me off even more, so I just stayed silent. I was too hard-headed to apologize for my ungrateful attitude, but I told myself to remember what side my bread was buttered on in future. Harry could easily drop me like a rotten mango and pluck another one off any tree.

'Let's do dinner as soon as I'm back.' Harry said light heartedly after another long pause. I smiled at his attempt to brighten the conversation.

'Ok,' I said yawning. I was on the early bird shift, so I was looking forward to going back to sleep for another few hours. 'I'll see you when you get back.'

'Excellent!' Harry chirped chippier than ever. 'I'll call you as soon as I land.'

11

YOU REAP WHAT YOU SOW

I didn't feel like shopping today even though it was my 21st birthday, and Harry was gingerly walking beside me offering to pay for everything. I let him buy me three new stage outfits with matching heels. A bracelet and a pair of Sapphire earrings to go with the necklace he had already bought me before I really got fed up. I let out a loud pitiful sigh as he pushed a piece of rum cake towards my face and enticed me to take a bite. I pushed it away as I shook my head. Being lavished with expensive gifts was wearing a little thin, and could no longer fill the empty void growing inside of me.

'Cheer up Sapphy.' I rolled my eyes at Harry's new little pet name for me as he smiled exposing a mouthful of sparkling white privileged teeth. 'What a beautiful day for your birthday.' *Don't remind me* I thought, noticing that his face had flushed pink from the sun. 'Don't you like the gifts I bought you?'

'Of course,' I said feigning a smile as I looked back towards him. I turned away before sighing again and wiping a stray tear from my eye. I was trying not to seem ungrateful, but my mind was preoccupied. My 21st birthday was supposed to be special, a day to remember... a day spent with family. Instead, here I was, stuck on this godforsaken Island a million miles away from home. I was supposed to sharing this special milestone with my twin brother, not my portly fifty something year old sugar daddy. I was sick and tired of being stuck on a revolving hamster wheel, and even though it had been nearly a month since the homicidal incident, I was paranoid as hell! Something didn't feel right. Ice hadn't turned up for his weekly appointment and I had a feeling that Lion knew something. Corrine had also been fishing for information last night, grilling me before my shift so I knew that there was some sort of gossip or rumours going around. All I could think about was escaping the island and getting away from the toxicity of Wonderland, but I had nowhere near enough money to escape yet. I took another deep sigh remembering that I needed to be back in the next couple of hours, so Harry took me to a quaint little beach restaurant not far from the club. I had been deathly silent for most of the afternoon and I think I was starting to get on his nerves. Just like the scraping of my fork across my plate as I searched the snapper fish I had ordered for bones. Harry kept glancing at my hands as I played with my food after I was done eating. I knew my table manners bothered him and on one of our numerous dinners he once told me that a gentle-woman never scraped. *Pompous bastard*, I thought as I screwed up my face remembering the comment. I drew the fork against my plate on purpose to aggravate him even more. Harry looked up at me, his blue eyes finally meeting mine. I knew he knew why I was acting like this; we had already discussed it. So instead of reacting he just smiled politely, looked back down at his plate, and continued eating. *Pussy*, I almost mumbled. Always running away from confrontation. I looked out to sea and watched a high wave roll into shore before I turned back to Harry, who was now staring at me, his strawberry blonde hair being gently tussled by the ocean breeze.

'Warm evening, isn't it?' Harry said finally clutching at conversation. I looked at him coldly as I grabbed my glass and sipped at my wine. I had to give it to him, he'd been at it all day and I was being a total bitch. I couldn't help it.

'We're in the Caribbean Harry, it's always warm.' I said indifferently looking back out to sea. He was right though, and despite the soothing sea breeze rushing in with every wave it was a particularly warm evening. I immediately felt guilty about battering his attempt at small talk. I turned to smile at him, but he was trying open his lobster claw. I saw the concentration on his face as the breeze rustled through his light wavy hair, Harry was a good man and I had developed genuine feelings for him. Not... Love but it was something... And I knew he felt something for me too. I continued to push the cold food around my plate as a waiter came over to our table for the third time that evening. He offered us more wine and we sat silently as he filled our glasses and walked away. I sighed again and Harry suddenly slammed his knife and fork onto the table making a few other diners turn around. My eyes widened, we had been sitting in near silence for almost an hour and this was the most exciting thing to happen all day.

'Why won't you let me take care of you?' Harry demanded slamming his fist down on the table so hard he made the cutlery jingle. I rolled my eyes up to the sky knowing exactly where this conversation was going. Harry had repeatedly offered to put me up in his private villa in Montego Bay. But I always refused knowing that Lion would never let me leave. Harry seemed to think that Montego Bay was far enough for me to escape, it being on the other side of the island, but I knew better, and as long as I remained in Jamaica, I belonged to Lion and to him only.

'I don't need anybody to take care of me.' I said flatly, sipping at my wine as he pulled the napkin from around his neck and dusted off his light cream shirt. 'I can take care of myself.' Harry wrinkled his forehead and stared at me with his piercing blue eyes, his skin was a reddish hue from spending so much time in the sun.

'So, you'd rather be a whore and continue to sell that overpriced *pum pum* of yours?' He spat viciously. *Overpriced, how dare he!*

'Harry calm down.' I said through clenched teeth as I smiled politely at the staring diners.

'Why should I?' he retorted. 'When you're content to sell your punani to any Tom, Dick and Harry in possession of a 1000-dollar bill!' I couldn't believe what he was saying and if I wasn't so shocked by his outburst, I probably would've laughed myself off my chair. But still, we were out in public and I knew there was only one way to handle this situation. I gently put my right hand over his palm still resting on the table.

'Harry, people are staring,' I said softly as I caressed his fingers. 'For once, I do not care!' He said defiantly, 'let them stare.' He huffed as he stubbornly faced the ocean like a five-year old child.

'Harry please...' I said again firmly squeezing his hand. 'You're making a scene.' The tables had turned, it was usually me making a scene. He sighed loudly and finally looked around at all the other couples watching us. A waiter was rapidly approaching but Harry shoved a bunch of dollars into his hand and sent him on his way.

'You're right... Please forgive me, I really don't know what came over me...' He looked away embarrassed staring out to sea again. I sat back in my chair giving the couple sat behind Harry the evil eye until they looked away. I followed his gaze as I cleared my throat.

'Harry...' I said breaking the silence. 'Why haven't you ever asked me how I ended up here?' I already could see he was uncomfortable with my chosen topic of conversation. He pulled his hand from underneath mine and looked down at his lap.

'I...' he hesitated as he looked up to meet my

gaze. 'I... just couldn't, I thought... well I assumed that you just wouldn't want to talk about it.' His shoulders sunk as I huffed loudly at his excuse.

'I thought you didn't care about me enough to ask.' I mumbled and Harry suddenly sat forward taking both my hands and enclosing them in his.

'Sapphy, of course, I care you know I do.' He said caressing my hands and guiding me up to a stand. He pulled me in for a hug and then hastily paid the bill before leading me onto the restaurant's private stretch of beach.

'Sapphire, I care more for you than I have for anyone else in a very long time... You know I would do anything for you.' I looked up into his face with watery eyes as I pulled away from his grasp. I yanked off my heels and walked towards the sea. I dipped my toes in the rippling waters as the light from the setting sun danced on the rolling waves. I suddenly felt Harry's arms around my waist, and I sighed excepting his embrace.

'Sapphy, you don't have to sell your body anymore, I will take care of you.' Harry said as we swayed in time to the soft music coming from the restaurant. 'If you move into my villa, you could rent out the guest house and charge what you want for it...' He twirled me around and reeled me back into his chest as I giggled. 'I'll come and visit you as often as I can...' I pulled away from him. 'I know I know...' He said quickly as I turned around to face him. 'Lion will never let you leave, but... I could even hire security; you'll be safe I promise you that.'

'Thank you for the generous offer, Harry but that's not what I want.' I sighed and he puffed loudly and shook his head. Harry was getting frustrated; I could tell by the way his cheeks flushed under the golden light of the fire-flies.

'Then what do you want?' He asked impatiently. I smiled innocently as I silently slipped out of my dress and I ran into the sea. I let the waves run over my body, soaking through my underwear and into my skin. I stayed there for a few minutes jumping with the waves and gazing up into the star littered sky. When I came out of the water Harry was waiting for me with my dress folded over one arm and my strappy shoes hanging from an index finger. I savoured the moment knowing this would be one of the last times I would see him. Harry's latest three-month hiatus was over, and he was going home in the next few days. I wished he could stay longer but he had already extended his trip for an extra fourteen days just to be with me. He had business to tend to back home and he couldn't even tell me when he'd be able to take another vacation. My skin dried as we strolled along the beach and back to his chauffeur driven car.

'Do you need money or erm, anything to keep you going for a while, I could send something on a regular basis.' I looked at him feigning offence, knowing deep down I would take whatever he offered. 'I'm sorry,' he said quickly catching the expression on my face. 'I'm just not happy about leaving you like this. I wish I could stay even longer.'

'Then don't leave me!' I said looking up into his

eyes.

'You know I wish I didn't have to.' He said looking down at me confused, 'but I'm needed back in the UK.

'Then marry me and take me back with you!' 'I said abruptly as I stared up at him anticipating a reaction.

'What! Are you completely mad?' he said shaking me off and pacing away from me. 'How would I? It would never work!' He said turning back to me after he'd taken a few steps.

'I thought you said you'd do anything for me! You think I don't know who you are or what you're doing in Jamaica?' I bluffed. I only knew his name and that he was probably a corrupt politician.

'I'm sorry,' he said sadly, 'I can't marry you Sappy, it's just not possible.' The tears came then, partly on purpose and partly because it was my last chance to get out of Jamaica without being dangerously smuggled off the island like a piece of illicit cargo. Harry was wrong! It was possible. I knew it was because I had thought about it extensively. We could easily be married at the Registry office in Spanish Town and be back in the UK by the weekend, before Lion was any the wiser. I knew I had enough to buy fake immigration papers from a well-known seedy customer at the club, Harry could pay for my passport and safe passage.

'Please Harry, I can't stay here,' I said squeezing his hands. 'Lion will kill me if I try to leave the club and stay in Jamaica, *you know that*' I said pondering on the fact that Lion might kill me a lot sooner rather than later. 'Wherever I go he'll find me... I'll never be safe.' Harry seemed horribly disturbed by my revelation and I quickly kissed him on the lips as I pressed my body against his.

'You can have me every... single... day.' I whispered into his ear as I used his hands to trace the outline of my body. 'All I have to do is pack a bag... and you can have me forever... as your beloved wife.' I said as I tiptoed to whisper into his ear. He was silent as he held me tight and ran his fingers over my smooth damp skin. I looked into his eyes as he stared back into mine 'Please marry me Harry,' I implored again. 'Marry me... and take me back home.'

***

It had been almost a month since Harry had abandoned me, and I lay sprawled across my bed completely oblivious to my surroundings. I spent most of the money he sent on drugs and I was so high that my body felt completely numb. Now that Harry had gone without telling when he would return forced me to take on new clients, and for that I needed to be emotionally detached. I had no idea how long it had been since my last client had rolled off me. I was so out of it that when one of Lion's henchmen charged into my room and ordered me to get up, I didn't even stir.

'Get up!'

'Why?' I groaned loudly, barely able to lift my head.

'Just move yuh rass!' He said pulling me off the bed by my legs. I was jilted out of my crim-induced trance as my body hit the hard tiled floor. He began to drag me out of my room and suddenly alert, I grabbed the door frame and held on as hard as I could.

'Eh bwoi! Wha yuh ah do?' I screamed as I looked up into the face of Spider, as he began to hoist me up. 'Let me go!' I squealed as I pushed him away.

'Yuh smoke too rahtid much!' Spider said kissing his teeth as he dropped me. I landed with a heavy thud. 'Move yuh bombahole! Lion wan fi see yuh...'

'I can't!' I groaned loudly as I writhed around on the floor.

'Dutty crimhead gyal' He grunted impatiently as he towered over me. 'Yuh want mi drag yuh?' I kissed my teeth as I groggily got to my feet. As I did so I saw a few of the other girls poking their heads out into the hallway. Embarrassed, I jumped out of the corridor and darted back into my room.

'Behave gyal!' Spider snapped grabbing my wrist as I tried to retreat behind my bedroom door and slam it in his face.

'I'm naked!' I whined as he pulled me back out into the hallway.

'So wha? yuh had a chance fi get up.' He smirked, looking me up and down.

'Come Spider... lemme get dressed nuh? You expect me to go in front of Lion indecent soh?' I snapped as I tried to twist my arm out of his tight grip. He kissed his teeth, some of the girls were still watching from the corridor.

'Don't unno have nuttin better fi do?' I snapped.

'Gwan, hurry up!' Spider hissed finally letting me go. He watched me closely from the open doorway as I quickly slid my naked body into a satin slip and dressing gown, another gift from Harry. I then re-trieved a pair of flip flops before hesitantly walking to-wards him. My heartbeat quickened as soon as I en-tered the hallway and I tried to shake off my high as I closed my door. My mind was foggy, and my stomach began to turn as I slowly followed Spider's huge frame down the corridor. My legs felt like dead weight so I had to drag my feet along the worn carpet. I shivered as I wondered if Lion had found out about the incident. What else would he have summoned me for? I had to swallow the bile rising in my throat. My body began to quiver, and I wiped my sweaty palms on the front of my slip as my blood ran cold. I began to panic as we finally reached the outside of Lion's Office. Convinced that Ice must have grassed me up. My heart jumped into my throat as my head tried to figure out what would happen next. I wiped my sweaty brown as I no-ticed Spider watching me. I looked away as Titan opened the door to Lion's office. He smiled at me sheepishly, he knew something and I couldn't bring myself to smile back. I hesitated before stepping inside and Spider frowned at me, making the huge tattooed arachnid on his face move along with his expression. He probably knew what I was in for and before I could even think about making a run for it, he grabbed me and shoved me inside. I stumbled into the middle room, my high state making me unsteady on my feet. I nervously raised my head to see Lion where he usually was, sitting behind his desk smoking a cigar. I froze as my eyes met his gaze. I could see that we weren't alone, and I glanced around uneasily, quickly studying the three strange men sitting on the sofa in the corner. I could see Ice, skulking on the far side of the room. His faced turned to the wall as if he was in a time out, and Spider stood behind me blocking the door.

'Sapphire...' Lion said drawing my attention back to him.

'Yes Lion.' I answered obediently as I glanced down at my feet.

'Yuh have any ting yuh wan fi tell mi?' I swallowed a gulp of air and wiped my sweaty palms on my thighs. *This was it; my terrible murderous deed had caught up to me.*

'No... No Lion.' I stuttered shaking my head a little too vigorously. The room was silent as Lion took another puff on his cigar and slowly exhaled expanding rings of smoke. I nervously watched a spreading ring smoke swirl in my direction before is dissolved into the air.

'Enuff ah dis bombaclart foolishness!' The large man sitting in the middle of the sofa suddenly announced jumping up. 'Is dis de guilty likkle bitch eeh?' I gasped stepping back as I looked at the man accusing me. He eerily resembled the man I had killed, and an image of the body lying in a pool of blood flickered before my eyes.' Spider and Ice stepped forward and the men on either side of the sofa jumped up defensively. My high was rapidly diminishing as I watched the scene unfolding in front of me. I began to feel sick as more bile encroached on my neck. I reluctantly swallowed.

'Everybody sekkle!' Lion said loudly as he poured two equal measures of rum into a pair of empty glasses on top of his desk. 'Listen mi, if we cyan reason like men den there will be no negotiation, yuh understand?' He said as he got up and handed a glass to this Bishop. After a few strained seconds of intense staring, Bishop slowly reached out for the rum, and then reluctantly took his seat. His henchmen followed suit. Ice and Spider slowly returned to their former positions, leaving me once again exposed in the middle of the room. I hadn't failed to notice the deep gash that Ice had a gash on his face as if someone had cut a line from his ear to his mouth. I feel like he tried to hide it from me by turning his head to avoid my gaze. My eyes followed him as I swallowed the lump in my throat, trying to stop myself from heaving and bursting into tears. Everyone in the room was watching me, and I quickly wiped my glassy eyes as Lion sauntered towards me, rum glass and lion headed cane in hand. My stomach refused to stop turning, and my body was visibly shaking as he suddenly struck me in the face with his cane. 'Don't yuh ever bloodclart lie to mi again!' He shouted as I lost my balance and fell onto my knees. I cowered beneath him, holding my mouth as it throbbed painfully and began to bleed. I could have sworn that he loosened a tooth. 'Get up!' He barked from above me and I quickly rose to my feet. 'Now tell mi de rahtid truth.' Lion demanded as he sat on the edge of his desk and sipped at his rum.

My mind went blank. I mean what could I say? Yes Lion, him did rape me, soh mi kill him dead, dead as a damn doornail and mi would do it again!'

'It wasn't my fault... It, it was an accident. Mi never mean fi kill him.' I mumbled instead.

'Liar!' Bishop bellowed lurching forward in his seat. 'Mi hear sum dutty skettle get him dash out of dis club and since den he was on a rampage!'

'He dragged me off stage!' I cried through my falling tears as I turned to look Bishop right in the eye.

'So wha? Just fi dat, yuh get a man fi kill him?' Bishop accused me angrily, 'fi dat stupid likkle reason!'

'Hold on nuh Bishop, becar you no seh dat nuh mek sense.' Lion interjected.

'Well, mek it mek sense nuh Lion, becar de last time mi see Regan alive, him tell mi him ah come look fi Crystal...'

Crystal, what did that two faced sket have to do with any of this? 'After dat mi neva see him again, not until a box a fingers tun up pon mi mudda doorstep!' Bishop shouted hysterically as he lurched forward again. H was now barely sitting on the chair. 'A long wid ah ransom letter demanding 20 million dollar to keep de rest ah him in one bloodclart piece!' Lion held his hand up to silence him without taking his eyes off me.

'That wasn't me!' I said confused. 'I don't know what the hell you're talking about!' I cried frantically. 'Regan, your brother raped me... and I had de right to defend myself... So, I... did what I had to do...' I mumbled.

211

'Yuh did what eeh! wha yuh ah do?' Bishop heckled loudly as he snorted and narrowed his eyes at me. 'Yuh expect mi to believe yuh alone kill him?' He snorted as if the very notion was ridiculous. 'Listen mi bitch, yuh betta tell mi who kidnapped Regan right bloodclart now!' He shouted angrily. 'And further-more, where de rass is my money!'

'Lion, I swear, I have no idea what he's on about!' I cried glancing over at Ice who was still avoid-ing my gaze. 'I just stabbed him… in self-defence, that's all! It all happened so fast… I was just protecting myself–' Lion waved me to silence as he glanced over at Ice and then back towards me. 'Please Lion, you have to believe me!' I sobbed falling to my knees in front of him as an uncontrollable barrage of tears flooded my face. 'I had nothing to do with any kidnap-ping! I couldn't, I… I wouldn't!'

'Stand up straight!' Lion said abruptly as he turned back to Bishop. 'How much yuh wan fi sekkle dis disagreement?' He asked as poured himself an-other drink.' Bishop was perched so far on the edge of his seat that he might as well have been kneeling on thin air. Lion went to fill up his glass but Bishop waved the bottle away.

'Disagreement?' Bishop said it as if it was a dirty word. 'Yuh dare insult mi by offering money fi Regan's life?' He asked venomously.

'More like compensation.' Lion said smoothly. 'Would 30 million, plus de 20 million you lost suffice?' He was met by stony silence as Bishop exchanged glances with his henchmen.

'Yuh mussi mad Lion! Mi wan dat bitch DEAD! She affi suffer! Plus, mi wan de head a every pussy-clart man involved in my bredda's disappearance.'

'Look mi understand de pain yuh going thru, but it's time to move wid de times Bishop.' Lion said calmly raising his glass to his lips. 'I'm sure we can find an alternative solution all this death.'

Bishop narrowed his eyes.

'Why mess wid tradition?' Bishop sneered, 'Afterall de crocodile dem still affi nyam, and yuh will watch dem nyam whoever helped yuh kill my bredda before dem nyam yuh!' He said pointing his stubby finger right at me. I shuddered and looked back down at the floor as Lion chuckled cynically.

'No disrespect to yuh or de family Bishop, but everybody no Regan was nuttin but trouble. Everywhere him went he bring a whole heap of fuckery.' Lion's remark surprised me and I looked up. 'In fact, he had a notorious reputation fi troubling young gyal... alie?' I looked up at Bishop and he silently stared me down with cold vengeful eyes. 'Just a likkle while back mi coulda swear he was wanted dead or alive ova de kidnapping of Prince's dawta.'

'Rassclart lies dem ah tell!' Bishop snapped. His eyes were almost popping out of his head and I could see a large twitching vein pulsing on the side of his neck.

'Well, it look to mi like Regan had quite a few enemies alie?' Lion said scathingly as he paused to pour himself yet another drink. 'And in despite of dese unfortunate rumours I tink we can still reach some sort of agreement.'

'Bout wha?' Bishop spat heatedly as he jumped up. 'Lion, mi done talk! becar it come like seh unno tek Regan's life fi joke and nah tek mi serious. When mi she she affi die den she a go dead tonight!' He growled as he pulled out a gun and pointed it directly at me.' Everybody else in the room quickly drew their weapons and I ducked suddenly standing in the middle of a Mexican standoff.

'Mi wan de bredda name… now!' He shouted at me and I closed my eyes. 'Yuh have three seconds or yuh dead!' He cocked his weapon and I held my breath. My heart was on the verge of exploding and I suddenly felt the sensation of hot urine running down my legs as he inched towards me.

'Yuh dare pull a gun in my presence!' Lion said loudly as he got up from his desk and stepped in front of me. 'Just mek anuda step and see!' Bishop paused as he lowered his gun.

'Mi own dis gyal yuh understand!' Lion said gripping me tightly around my neck and pulling me upright. 'Ah my property dis! and mi no bizniz bout Regan, yuh, or any udda bomboclart. Nobody plays wid my revenue!'

The atmosphere in the room was so tense you could have cut I with a butter knife. Everybody silently stared at each other, eyes shifting, trigger fingers ready to apply fatal pressure. Nobody seemed to be backing down until Lion spoke, sighing loudly as he let go of me. 'Mi have a likkle respect for yuh family still Bishop, but right now yuh ah play wid bloodclart fire.'

Lion hissed as if in disappointment. 'Look, mi no seh yuh angry, but dis situation will only go one way. I told I would get to de bottom of Regan's death, and I have, so now yuh have closure.' Bishop was still pointing his gun at me. His hands were shaking, and I could see large beads of sweat collecting on his indented forehead. His facial expression made me notice just much he resembled his brother. They had the same wide set jaw, heavy brow, chocolate brown skin and demonic anger behind a pair of crazed eyes. His whole face twisted into an expression consumed with the notion of killing me. But Lion was right, and Bishop knew it. he and his men had three guns while Spider and Ice had four between them, not to mention the men out in the corridor, and all over the building. They wouldn't make it off the landing alive.

'So, wha want... Bishop?' Lion said taking a sip of his drink and opening a wooden box full of Cuban cigars. 'Yuh can have yuh way wid her and forget dis whole ting ever happened...' Lion said downing the rest of his drink as then clipping his cigar. 'Or I can leave yuh mudda an farda widout any pickney at all...' Bishop's men looked at each other nervously as Lion casually moved in between their lines of fire. 'No heir to carry on the family business...' Lion teased as he confidently placed his arm around Bishops unsteady shoulder as he ordered me to strip. I looked at my feet as I slowly pulled my dressing gown off my shoulders and let my slip fall to the floor, crying silently. 'Yuh can have her any way yuh like...' Lion said enticingly as he came up behind me and began to fondle my breasts. I winced as he squeezed them between his long fingers. I could see the demonic thirst to violate me growing in Bishops lustful eyes.

'Tink smart now bwoi.' Lion smiled exposing his platinum teeth. 'Don't let yuh emotions get de better of yuh.'

Bishop licked his blackened lips, and after a few more tense seconds, his big shaky hand was lowering the gun. 'Good choice.' Lion said as he let go of my breasts and smacked me on the arse.

'Wha... What about de money...' Bishop asked hesitantly after clearing his throat, 'and de rest ah de deal?' he added quickly. I continued looking at the floor as I slowly pulled the straps of my slip down over my arms and stepped out of it. My jaw was still hurting and I resisted the urge to cover myself with my hands in case Lion hit me again. I looked up slightly hearing him chuckle loudly as he returned to his seat behind his desk.

'Money still affi mek Bishop, so respect de merchandise.' Lion smiled as he lit his fresh cigar.

'Come nuh Lion, yuh no wha mi ah talk. De deal, de one yuh offer mi earlier! Is it still pon de table?'

'Afta such outright disrespect, yuh still have de audacity to ask fi money when just now pull a rassclart gun in my presence?' Lion sniggered sinisterly as he put his feet up onto his desk. 'Now, she is de deal...' He said leaning back in his chair as he exhaled smoke. 'Take it or leave it.'

Bishop mumbled something under his breath as he marched towards me and grabbed me by the arm. He dragged me behind him but before he could leave the office with me in tow, Spider who was standing in front of the door crossed his arms over his puffed up his chest.

'So wha no privacy?' He asked dropping my arm and looking back at Lion.

'Tek her right deh soh, where mi cyan see yuh before mi mind change my mind.' Lion said pointing towards the large round shaggy rug on the floor surrounding the pole. Bishop kissed his teeth as he trudged over.

'Wha kinda joke ting is dis!' Bishop protested as he slammed his fist on Lion's desk.

'Eh bwoi, noh bodda chat no fuckery afta yuh disrespect mi soh. True Regan gone and mi a tek responsibility, but yuh try violate de king memba? Now don't waste de last of mi good favour. Do wha yuh affi do or come from in front ah mi, yuh understand!'

'Come nuh gyal.' Bishop demanded aggressively taking out his anger on me. His beady eyes roamed over my body as he began to touch himself through his trousers. I didn't move, looking down at my feet defiantly. 'Bitch mi seh cum ere now!' He bellowed making me shudder.

'Move!' Lion barked after I had defied Bishop's order for the second time, and quickly I began to step closer. As soon as was I within arm's reach bishop grabbed me by the throat and began to dig his fingers into my neck.

'Yuh dutty likkle skettle!' He hissed as he pushed my back into the pole. Tears escaped my eyes as I placed my clammy hands around the metal pole. I used it to anchor myself and then instinctively kicked him in the groin as hard as I could. The sound of laughter erupted around the room as Bishop abruptly let go of me and fell to his knees. I desperately caught my breath as Bishop groaned and squirmed in anguish. But he soon recovered and then lunged at me throwing his fist towards my face. Luckily, I was quicker than he was, and I was able to move out of the way so that he hit the pole instead. He groaned loudly as he cradled his hand and I took the opportunity to swivel around the pole and kick him in the stomach. My high had dissipated due to the rush of adrenalin coursing through my body. He fell back onto Lions desk making Ice and Spider fall about laughing as I frantically climbed all the way to the top of the pole. I was so high on adrenalin that I wasn't thinking straight. Even so, I doubted that I would get the better of Bishop again and I climbed the pole up to the ceiling which was just high enough to get completely out of reach.

'Hol her still!' Bishop ordered and his men hid their snickers as they jumped to attention. Ice and Spider suddenly stopped laughing and drew their weapons as they tried to retrieve me.

'Ah wha gwan Lion?' Bishop said breathlessly, noticing that the guns were directly pointed at all three of them.

'Jus yuh alone.' Lion said leaning back in his chair seemingly entertained.

'Then control her nuh,' Bishop whined as he threw his hands up in the air and kissed his teeth.

'Yuh fi control her.' Lion said flatly, 'What kinda pussy cyan control a bitch?' He chuckled snidely.

'Him ah fish man!' Spider grimaced as they watched Bishop aggressively try to shake me off the pole. I had already climbed as high as possible, but he continued to shake the chrome cylinder until I began to lose my grip. My leg slipped and he grabbed me by the foot, violently dragging me off the pole and abruptly throwing me onto the floor. I groaned as my body hit the carpeted surface. I managed to take the brunt of the fall on my arms and frantically tried to kick him away as he jumped on top of me. When he failed to grab my flaying legs, he punched me in the stomach and used all his weight to hold me down and prise my legs apart. I lashed out and scratched at anything I could reach so he grabbed both my arms with one of his hands while using the other to keep my legs open. The spectators hissed and cackled as if they were watching a boxing match. I could hardly breathe with the bulk of his weight on top on my chest and he struggled to get his bottoms undone while wrestling with me underneath him.

'Yuh mussi sorry now.' He smiled from on top of me as he wrenched my thighs open.

'Fuck you!' I hissed squirming as he wedged his wide body into my crutch.

'Yuh about too.' He laughed and I hawked spit in his face. He knocked my head against the floor subduing me as he grabbed me around the neck. 'Lion, she too wild man.' Bishop whined as he gripped my neck and struggled to hold me down.

'Give her a shot nuh?

'No!' I cried loudly still a little dazed. 'I'll be good!' I rasped as he began to crush my throat. I watched as Lion paused for a moment, but my heart sank as I caught sight of the gun shaped injector, he was slowly pulling out of his desk draw. 'Lion, please don't!' I begged as he handed it to Ice, who then began to cross the room. 'I don't need a shot… I promise I'll be good!' I pleaded manically as Ice approached me with the little steel gun. My eyes widened, 'Ice please…' I whispered as he got closer. He could easily just pretend to inject me and empty the small glass cylinder of liquid into the air. But he wouldn't even look me in the eye, and I blinked away my tears as I writhed around trying to make it more difficult to inject me. 'Shots' were only used down in Wonderland on the bad girls, the ones that broke the rules or tried to run away. It was a highly addictive cocktail that made you docile, half paralyzed but still completely awake so you'd do whatever the customer desired without issue or complaint. Bishop pulled my head up and Ice quickly pressed the injector gun into the back of my neck and pulled the trigger. I continued to squirm as I felt a cold rush of liquid spread around my throat and up into my head, before it ran all the way down to my fingers, down my spine and into the tips of my toes. It chilled my veins and made my body feel stiff and heavy. I tried to speak but my face locked into position and wouldn't move on my command. My body froze and I lost the ability to blink. I couldn't even cry out when he finally forced himself inside of me, not that I wanted to give him the satisfaction. He quickly went deeper and the pain was almost unbearable, but I couldn't even move, or make an audible sound.

'Yuh wish yuh dead yet?' Bishop grunted loudly as he drew his pelvis back and plunged into me so viciously, I almost blacked out, I wished I would black out. My vision was going hazy and everybody in the room began to melt into blobs and form one big blur. Bishop had me completely pinned down and I felt like my chest was collapsing, *was I losing the ability to breathe?* I couldn't feel him thrusting anymore and I felt like I was drifting away into nothingness. I began to see vivid colours and the images of my family suddenly flashing before my eyes began to fade into blotches of bright white light. I felt lightheaded as a rush of impending doom washed over me. My body felt weightless, and soon I was floating away. There was nothingness for a while which I was thankful for, and I had no idea how much time had passed when I opened my eyes. I felt like my consciousness had floated out of my body was now hovering over the commotion in Lions office. I watched Spider and Ice dragging Bishop off my limp body as more security rushed into the room hauled them away. *What on earth!* I thought frantically looking down at the scene. This isn't really happening. There's no way this could be happening! I told myself as I watched Ice and Spider hoist me up and carry my lifeless body into the hallway. *Am I... dead?*

***

'Where... am I?' I asked coughing uncontrollably. I felt something obstructing my throat and my eyes flickered as they adjusted to the bright light.

'Rainey, calm down, yuh alright' My grandfather said as the blurry images around me came into focus. I was confused but after a few seconds I could see that I lay in a bed surrounded by beeping equipment in a small white room.

'What's... going on?' I asked gagging on the clear plastic tube coming out of my mouth. I quickly ripped it out of my throat and spluttered violently, almost choking on it.

'Stop dat!' My grandfather hissed as he slapped my hand away from the canula coming out of my arm.

'Behave nuh, Yuh in de hospital.' He said gently, just as Ruby and Corrine breezed into the room. Ruby had an armful of snacks and she quickly ran towards the bed and dumped them onto the food tray.

'Yuh finally wake up!' She exclaimed giving me a hug.

'Ow!' I croaked, feeling bruised all over. Corrine stepped forward and stood behind our grandfather as she placed a hand on his shoulder.

'Yuh lucky to be alive....' She said flatly, half smiling, half frowning at me.

'And who fault is dat?' My grandfather snapped shaking her hand off.

'She neva call mi!' Corrine protested, 'how mi fi know she get herself mix up inna all dat fuckery?'

'Unno fi look out fi each other!' My grandad

retorted as he craned his neck to give her a dirty look.

'Wha mi woulda seh to yuh farda eeh?' My grandad continued as he turned back to me. 'If him ever did show up one day looking fi him Pickney?'

'Grandad, I don't even remember what happened,' I whined groggily as I watched Ruby and Corrine exchange side glances.

'Yuh nuh member nuttin?' He asked raising an eyebrow, and I slowly shook my head.

'Wha drugs yuh tek hmm?' He asked with a disapproving look on his face. 'Coz all mi no is, de doctor seh dem affi pump yuh belly hard!' He said accusingly as he narrowed his piercing brown eyes at me. 'Since wen yuh turn crimhead? Mi no yuh know betta dan dat!'

'Come Dadda… Let we go fi ah walk.' Corrine said kicking up the break on his wheelchair.

'Walk fi wha? yuh nuh see mi in a wheel chair!' My grandfather snapped as he scraped his cane against the floor to stop Corrine moving it.

'We a go walk just down deh suh.' Corrine said rolling her eyes 'Yuh need some fresh air, and de walk wud do you good.

'But she just wake up!' My grandfather protested as he tried to hit her with his wooden staff. 'Lef mi alone, yuh chupid fool fool gyal, mi nuh need no air!'

'Elroy, stop yuh noise!' Corrine said as she snatched his staff away and leaned it against the bed. 'We'll be right back, and she nuh go nowhere.' She mumbled and my grandfather kissed his teeth as Ruby jumped up to get the door.

'Raine, mi soon come, yuh hear?'

'Yes grandad,' I said sitting up a little too quickly. My body felt bruised and I winced as a sharp pain ricocheted down my limbs and spine.

'Yuh sure yuh nuh rememba nuttin?' Ruby asked quickly as soon as the door closed behind them.

'All I remember is getting high, lying down... and... den... nothing...' I said shaking my head. Ruby frowned as she dug around in her bag and pulled out a container half full of little red pills. She slammed them down onto the food tray next to the snacks as if she was playing a game of dominoes.

'Suh wha, yuh ah tek crim now?' Ruby asked as she narrowed her eyes at me and pointed to the clear plastic cylinder. 'Dis is wha yuh ah get high pon?' I crossed my arms and shrugged in response. Crim was short for crimson, on account of the drug's dark red colour. I had been taking in secret for a while now. 'Where yuh get it from?' She asked dubiously and I looked away from her. 'I can't remember,' I lied. I knew I had gotten them from a customer a few days ago, depending on how long I had been in the hospital.

'Yuh been in here three days already... and what a way yuh mek yuh grandfarda fret.' Ruby said frowning as if she had read my mind.

'If mi deya three days, then why do I still feel like I've been hit by a bloody lorry?' I said forcing a smile.

'Mi hear seh Lion give yuh ah shot de udda night...' Ruby said shaking her head in disgust as she glanced at the container of pills. 'So, all de drugs dem mix up in yuh system and mash yuh up gud and proper! But at least yuh still here to tell the tale, unlike some…' She said sinisterly. *What did she mean by that?* I suddenly clutched my neck searching for the lion necklace but it was bare.

'Nah bodda worry!' Ruby said clutching my wrist, 'it's been taken care of, Lion won't find yuh.'

'But what about yours?' I said eying the golden tracker, 'and, and Corrine's?' I stuttered picturing Lion's goons on their way to drag all three of us back to Wonderland. Ruby fingered the lion head pendant around her neck. 'Relax, like me just say it's been handled!'

'How?'

'Me have ah fren,' she smiled cryptically.

'Who?' I asked curiously.

'Seriously, you nuh memba nuttin at all?' She asked swiftly changing the subject, and I was silent for a moment as I tried to search my head for answers. Ruby's eyes bore into me as I scoured my fuzzy memory. Until Spider bursting into my room and dragging me of the bed hit me like a slap in the face.

'Bishop!' I gasped as my memory suddenly came flooding back to me.

'Umm hmm,' Ruby said eyeing me closely. 'When mi see dem drag yuh body thru de hallway… Mi did tink yuh was dead! dead like Crystal…'

'Wha?' I asked confused, 'Wha yuh mean, dead like Crystal?'

'I mean Crystal dead, dead, as in she a par wid

duppy now.' Ruby said widening her eyes. 'Lucky Ice find out it was she who set yuh up and let Regan into de room dat night...'

'Yuh lie!' I said rubbing my forehead in astonishment. My mouth was dry, and I quickly grabbed the half full glass of water off the tray beside my bed.

'Jealousy is one hell of ah ting!' Ruby sighed shaking her head vigorously.' 'If Ice neva find dat out, yuh and him woulda dead too!' She said as I sat there in bewilderment. 'And tru mi nuh like speak ill of de dead but serve her right! Mi glad Lion kill her after de likkle sket set yuh up fi taking her crown! So wha if yuh find ah man in her VIP section!' Ruby rambled on, and I zoned out as my mind went over every single detail I could remember. She was still cussing a few minutes later, when the door abruptly flew open. The appearance of a nurse finally startling Ruby into silence.

'Oh, yuh wake up now.' The nurse said seemingly surprised. 'How yuh feeling?' she asked as she walked over to my bed and checked the chart hanging on the rail.

'Okay... I suppose,' I said avoiding her gaze as she came closer.

'Well wen mi dun mi will call de doctor,' she said as she proceeded to take my vitals and update my chart before exchanging my jug of water for a fresh one. We both watched her silently until she went to leave.

'Well, mi no Lion neva pay fi dis,' I scoffed noticing how fancy the nurse's uniform was as she left the room. Ruby chuckled awkwardly, just as the door swung open again.

'Hello Sapphy...' I slowly looked up and gasped as I saw Harry standing in the open doorway. My eyes welled up with tears, and I rubbed them away in disbelief, wondering if he'd still be there when I removed my hands. He was and I was speechless as I covered my gaping mouth and watched him step inside the room. He paused for a moment before coming towards me, and my heartbeat matched the sound of his deafening footsteps as he strode across the floor. He hesitated before planting a kiss on my forehead as Ruby quickly excused herself and slipped out of the room.

'When did you get back?' I asked my voice cracking with emotion.

'That doesn't matter,' he responded as he smiled down at me.

'You paid for all of this didn't you?' I sighed looking around, and he nodded as he took my hands in his. They were soft and warm like he'd never done a day of hard labour in his life.

'I couldn't have you recovering in that place, how could I allow you to be kept there after what that monster did to you!' He grimaced as he searched my glassy eyes for some sort of explanation. I didn't oblige.

'How did you even find out that I was hurt, who... who told you?' I asked changing the subject.

'Ruby tele-called me...' he mumbled. 'In the middle of the night I might add.' He chuckled slightly, revealing a pained smile. I gave a small nod; Ruby must have found Harry's business card in my bedside table.

'I just can't believe you came back for me.' I rasped, swallowing the lump in my throat.

'Well, didn't I say I'd do anything for you?' Harry replied cupping my face in his hands as my tears finally fell.

'But... You said it was impossible?' I uttered as I searched Harry's watery blue eyes for answers. 'You said you had important business to attend– '

'Shhhh,' Harry hushed me as he placed a soft finger over my swollen lips. 'Don't you worry about all that now.' He whispered as he gently wiped away my tears with a white handkerchief. 'I've taken care of everything.' He sat on the edge of the bed and my face sank into his chest. There was silent for a moment and all I could hear was the faint hum of the machine beside my bed and the occasional beep

'Sapphire, will you marry me?' I could hear my heartbeat over his words, and for a moment I wasn't sure if I was dreaming, had he actually said what I thought he had said?

'Pardon?' I said looking up at him. He smiled down at me as he quickly produced a ring from out of his suit jacket pocket. It was gold with a neatly set sparkly yellow stone in the middle.

'Sapphire... Will you marry me?' He repeated slowly, and my heart almost stopped as we stared into each other's eyes.

'Yes... of course I– '

'And who dis white bwoi now?' My grandfather said as the door swung open. I ignored his loud interruption as Corrine pushed him back into the room.

'Yes Harry, of course I will!' I repeated them as more tears streamed down my cheeks.

'Well!' Corrine scoffed as she pushed the wheelchair right up to the end of my bed and shushed my confused grandfather. 'Dada,' she said bending over him to see the huge stone set ring. 'It looks like de white bwoi is her one-way ticket back home...'

12

MY FAIR LADY
ESSEX, GREATER LONDON 2058

'**M**rs Winchester, Mr Winchester has asked that you please come away from the window and come down to dinner.' I sighed as I slowly got up from the fancy chaise longue situated underneath the bedroom window and closed the curtains. The flashing from the dwindling paparazzi cameras was still evident through the crack in the heavy velvet where the curtains didn't quite meet.

'Maria please, for the last time just call me Raine.' I said for the umpteenth time as I turned around to face her. She spoke well enough, but I could still hear the remnants of a cockney accent.

'Very well Miss *Raine*... dinner has been served, now come on then before it gets cold.' I rolled my eyes as I followed the aging maid through the stately Essex mansion that had recently become my home. Nearly a month had gone by, since Harry and I eloped in Spanish Town and embarked on a ten-hour journey back to the UK aboard his private jet. Thankfully, due to Harry's VIP status, I was able to avoid the customs holding centre upon arrival and was allowed through the VIP terminal. However, somehow the media had gotten wind of our *union* and after some political pressure, I was interrogated at Harry's home, tagged, and placed on house arrest while my conditional residency application was being processed. I was deemed an illegal alien and it was as if I hadn't even been born in Great Britain. My first few weeks back in the UK seemed so surreal after nearly two years out of the country. Now that I was back, I knew I was closer to my family but yet, I still felt so far away. Leaving the grounds of the mansion was out of the question with a security tag on my foot and the last of the paparazzi on standby outside the front door. Video footage of me being rushed into Harry's mansion still plagued the VTV, and as if my return to the UK wasn't controversial enough, the sordid details of my occupation in Jamaica and my previous links to the LOE Society had been leaked to the press. My marriage of convenience had become a public sensation, a spectacle, a source of entertainment to a nation in turmoil. I had been dubbed a diplomatic prostitute, a concubine, a distraction for the rich, and poster girl for underclass. Nothing more than a pawn for Harry's party to use in the political struggle against the BFP. Protests still raged outside the mansion walls, campaigners with placards

marched back and forth, throwing projectiles at passing vehicles whenever they got the chance. Why
should I be allowed back in the country just because I
had married a lord? What about the countless others
who hadn't been so fortunate. After all, cases like mine
were practically unheard of. Why should the rich and
powerful be allowed to do what they want when the
poor could barely feed themselves. Why should Harry
be allowed to bring a common whore into the country
for his own pleasure without scrutiny? It didn't matter
the fact that I was born here, as far as anyone was concerned, I was a refugee, a Jamaican prostitute, a deportee never to be allowed back into the country ever
again. So once again I felt like a prisoner, hemmed in
by circumstances beyond my control. But fortunately
for me that prison happened to be Harry's Grade II
listed mansion surrounded by four acres of farmland.
All the rooms were beautifully decorated with high
ceilings, extravagant fixings, and grand mahogany furniture. Rich tones of red, blue, and green ran throughout the house along with magnificent floors of marble,
wood, luxury carpet and antique tile. Besides the two
dining rooms, the drawing room, living room and six
ensuite bedrooms, there was a ballroom, games room,
library and gym with sauna and steam room that led
to an inside pool and jacuzzi. There were also stables,
a tennis court, a barn, and a small farmhouse on the
grounds. Each of the bedrooms had a quaint little
French balcony and a four-poster bed. The master bedroom had a his & hers conjoined bathroom and double
doors that led to an open roof terrace that overlooked

Harry's farmland and Epping Forest in the distance. Some would call it a dream.

I sat down next to Harry at the head of the table, and opposite his mother and daughter. Harry's daughter Millie was staring at me as she twiddled her long thick curls around an index finger. Harry squeezed my hand reassuringly as I sat down. He had kept the existence of his immediate family and his old money fortune swept firmly underneath the carpet, until the car ride home from the airport. His mother Blanche and daughter Millie were just as surprised to meet me as I was to meet them in the foyer of the house just a few weeks ago. Today we were eating a traditional Sunday roast in the informal dining room at the back of the house so we could get the best view of the sun setting over Epping Forest. After eating my Yorkshire pudding and most of the under seasoned chicken, I pushed the carrots and parsnips around my plate in deep thought.

'Is something the matter dear?' I looked up at Blanche, Harry's tight-lipped mother gracefully chewing on a baby carrot as her watery blue eyes met mine.

'I'm fine,' I said looking down at my cold roast potatoes. I could see Millie still eyeing me across the table. I sighed again and Blanche gave me another look as I continued to push food around my plate.

'Are you sure dear?' I nodded and Blanche smiled thinly as she turned towards Millie and told her to stop playing with her hair and eat her food. I wondered if Blanche really cared or if she was just being polite. I suspected that she maybe just didn't like my table manners. She was probably secretly livid that

Harry had bought another black woman into *their* lives, and I was in no way trying to replace Millie's mother. Even so, it troubled me that there was no sign of her mother anywhere. Not even a picture, and it was clear from Millie's honey complexion, freckle flushed cheeks and thick curly afro that her mother was black. I stared out at the purple orange sky as the sun began to disappear behind the trees.

'Millie, table manners!' Blanche snapped as Millie continued to watch me while she chewed a coil of her hair. 'Young ladies do not gawp or chew their hair at the table!'

'Well, I'm just looking at what doesn't belong here. I can't help if she's the odd *thing* out.' Millie sneered as she screwed up her freckled face in disgust. 'Daddy brought her home like a stray dog, and you expect me to just sit here and play happy families?' Harry dropped his cutlery and gave his daughter the death stare. 'He even gave *it* mum's ring!' She whined glaring at me. I had since stopped wearing *said ring* due to the added tension it had caused when we had arrived.

'Don't ever presume that you're old enough to forget your place young lady. Since that ring is a family heirloom, it belongs to me!' Blanche said coldly looking at her granddaughter with disdain. She glanced over at Harry, as did I, and I could see a large vein pulsing from within his prominent forehead.

'*Me?* Forget my place!' Millie exclaimed as she wrinkled her button nose. '*I'm* not the gold digger who just turned up on *our* doorstep!'

'Here we go again.' I huffed angrily to myself as I eyeballed Harry. He glanced up at me and met my stare, his face slowly turning red.

'And now she's living in our house, eating our food, and banging *my* dad to get whatever she wants!

'Millie, that's enough!' Harry roared as he slammed his fist down on the table.

'What the hell have I told you about your attitude!' He said scolding her as he furiously wiped his hands in his serviette.

'Sapphi... *Raine,* has been through a great ordeal and you *will* show her some respect!' He continued as he angrily threw the napkin down onto his half-eaten plate of food.

'Oh really?' Millie said crossing her arms. 'Then why marry her, if she's damaged goods? And I'm confused... is it Raine or Sapphire? I mean which one was the prostitute?' She eyed me closely along with her grandmother who continued to chew on her food daintily as if nothing was happening.

'I am warning you young lady!' Harry growled, his face reddening even further.

'Whatever, I bet she's like all the others, and I don't know what's so special about this one that you had to give her mummy's ring! I hope he throws you out like the rest of them!' She hissed over at me.

'Melina Rose Winchester!' Harry yelled slamming both hands down onto the table.

'Trust me, *my dad, will* get bored *of you.*' She sniggered looking me dead in the eye.

'That is enough!' Harry bellowed making Blanche almost choke on her food.

'You will apologise to Sap... I mean Raine, this instant, and then you will go to your room immediately!' He said throwing down his napkin and standing up. 'Raine is not just a guest in this house. This is her home, and you *will*, treat her and I with some damn respect!' Harry spat through gritted teeth.

'Ohh... she's a guest now?' Millie said patronizingly. 'I thought she was meant to be your *wife*?' She smirked. 'And my new latest mum.'

'That is, it young lady! There will be no VTV, no games, no horse riding, no swimming, no tennis, and *no ballet* for the rest of the month!' Millie groaned loudly and slumped back in her chair. 'Mark my words young lady, you will not leave your room let alone this house until you go back to school!'

'Harold, don't you think you're overreacting?' Blanche said sharply as she gracefully dabbed the corners of her mouth with her serviette.

'Stay out of this Mother!' Harry snapped as he and Millie embarked on a staring match in a battle for the requested apology.

'Melina, I'm waiting!' Harry said tapping his foot loudly as he stood over her. She crossed her arms and stared back up at him defiantly.

'It's ok Harry.' I said quickly, using the incident as an excuse to leave the table before he could stop me. After all, I didn't blame Millie. She *was* a spoilt, privileged teenaged brat, but that wasn't her fault... and she was completely right. I *had* intentionally invaded her life for my own personal gain.

I swiftly left the dining room after the sun was finally set, and I could still hear Harry reprimanding Millie as I fled into the hallway, bumping in Maria who was eavesdropping by the door. I entered the open planned kitchen, and quickly stole away from the house, running down the rear staircase and into the wine cellar. I punched a code into the hidden keypad on the wall and a trap door slid open. I then flicked on the lights before stepping into the dimly lit tunnel. I hurried past the emergency underground bunker, and I kept on going until I heard the muffled neighs from above. I pressed the same code into another keypad and a trap door popped open in front of me. The braying horses sensed my presence as I ascended the stone steps to the barn stables above. They jostled in their pens until I got close enough to comfort them in the darkness. The light closest to the stables weren't working so I walked over to the pens and stroked Storm, my favourite horse. I retrieved the horse brush from a hook on the wall as I proceeded to stroke his dark grey coat. Harry had been teaching me how to ride and after unsuccessfully trying to learn on a few mares, Storm and I had hit it off like a house on fire. Storm continued to neigh as I brushed him, and I wondered why he was so agitated tonight. I looked into his eyes under the speckled moonlight intruding through the stable's weathered roof. I told him that I was going to brush his mane and after a defiant snort, he bowed his head obediently. I sighed and looked out into the evening through the open stable doors. The stars twin-kled in the sky, as did the yellow lights from the house shining in the near distance. I could see the thick trees of Epping Forest behind the fields in the opposite di-rection and I wondered what they were hiding. Storm suddenly shook his mane aggressively knocking the brush out of my hand.

'Storm!' I huffed as I bent down to retrieve it, but I couldn't see the brush on dark hay layered floor. I jumped up as I suddenly heard a noise from out-side... I listened closely and held my breath.

'Harry?' I called into the darkness. Storm jostled restlessly making me step away from him as he kicked the back of his pen. He was getting the other horses excited and I tried to calm him but he wouldn't settle.

'Hullo Miss.' I jumped at the sight of the tall dark figure suddenly standing in the stable doorway.

'Flipping hell!' I screamed jumping back.

'Sorry... it's just me Miss... Jose!' Jose said as a light orb appeared above his hand. 'Jaime's brother.'

'I know who the hell you are!' I said clutching my chest.

'Sorry Miss, I didn't mean to scare you.'

'Well, that's what generally tends to happen when you sneak up on people!' I snapped as my heart-beat slowed to its normal pace.

'Oh... Well, erm... I've just come to fix that faulty light and then I'll be out of your hair.' He mumbled meekly.

'That's fine Jose.' I said as he walked away. 'I didn't mean to snap... You just scared me that's all,' I muttered to his back as he disappeared into the darkness.

Jose and his brother Jaime took care of Harry's farm and lived a cottage on the grounds. They also did a few odd jobs around the house and took care of securing the perimeter. I didn't really mind Jaime but for some reason Jose gave me the creeps, not to mention that he was always being followed by a mangy old dog. He replaced the light within seconds allowing me to finally find the brush on the hay covered stable floor.

'All done now,' Jose yelled, and I continue to brush Storm as he walked out of the stable. I turned around and jumped at the site of his mangy old sheep dog panting loudly a few feet away from me.

'Shoo!' I said waving my hand at him, but he began to growl.

'Come on Nigel,' Jose called from outside, and thankfully the musty mutt scurried off. Storm bucked his head and knocked the brush out of my hand once again.

'What is up with you today?' I asked as I looked him in the eye and patted him firmly. He let out a hearty neigh as the stable light began to flicker off and on again before going out completely. I rolled my eyes and sighed, but then held my breath as I suddenly heard a noise from somewhere in the Darkness. *Jose must be coming back to fix the faulty light;* I thought as my ears pricked up. 'Jose... is that you again?' I waited for a few seconds but got no answer. I heard another noise and Storm suddenly kicked the back of his pen making me jump out of my skin. 'Jose?' I hissed looking around. 'What did I just tell you about creeping up on me!' Something grabbed me before I could finish my sentence and I tried to scream but my mouth was covered. All I could do was flay my legs wildly as I was dragged away from the horses.

'Raine, calm down... I'm not going to hurt you...' The intruder said as he spun my body around to face him. I recognised the voice, it was a voice from my distant past, a voice I thought I would never hear again. 'It's me...Phoenix...Remember?' I stepped back and looked at him under the light as it flickered back on.

'Phoenix!' I said in shock as I pushed him away and caught my breath. 'Of course, I remember!' I hissed as we just stared at each other in silence as my breathing returned to normal.

'You're a long way from Brixton.' I said finally as I studied his mask under the dim lights of the stables.

'Why are you here?' I asked crossing my arms.

'I... I just had to see you...' He said peeling back his mask to reveal his face. 'When I saw you all over the VTV, I just had to find you...'

'Why?' I asked, tilting my head in bemusement.

'The little boy you saved that night, the bait...' Phoenix said after hesitating. 'Nobody's ever done anything that brave...' He stuttered stepping towards me. *Or that stupid* I thought.

'I've pondered it ever since, and even thought it was stupid... it was also brave.' I rolled my eyes at his obvious analysis. 'And I just wanted to say that I'm sorry that that happened to you...' I chuckled in disbelief.

'Phoenix, it wasn't your fault, so you don't owe me anything,' I said thinking back to what seemed like another lifetime. 'So much... *worse*... has happened since then...' I sighed looking away from him.

'Well... I just wish I could've done something to change all that.' Phoenix said as he stepped towards me.

'You expect me to believe you came all the way here just to apologise for something that wasn't even your fault?' I asked crossing my arms after a few seconds of silence. He just stared at me silently, and before I could conjure up another sentence, Phoenix's lips were caressing mine. He kissed me gently, and I eagerly reciprocated. Our tongues snaked around each other hungrily until my whole body was tingling with excitement. We only parted lips to quickly undress each other. I gasped in pleasure as he pushed his hand into my underwear and slid his fingers inside me. We continued to kiss, Phoenix hoisting me up onto his hips and carried me into an empty pen in a corner of the stables. He lay me down on a stack of hay and began to caress my body. He kissed me all the way down my neck and collarbone until he was sucking my nipples and slowly sliding his fingers in and out of me. I gasped as he continued to plant little kisses me all the way passed my belly button until he was massaging my insides with his tongue. I was trying my best not to make any noise, but he licked me gently I shuddered uncontrollably and let out a little scream. He entered me quickly and he teased me with short shallow strokes, kissing me to muffle my moans. He eased himself deeper inside me and I wrapped my legs around his back as we continued to kiss. I was in ecstasy and my body tingled from head to toe as my mind turned to mush. I couldn't think about anything let alone Harry or the risk I was taking; all I could do is experience the waves of pleasure rippling throughout my body. We changed positions as he quickly picked me up and held me against the side of the pen. He kissed me roughly and squeezed my breasts as he began to thrust harder and deeper. His tongue muffled my moans and he clutched my thighs as he came a few minutes later. He held me there for a few seconds as we both caught our breath. He then gently put me down and hauled his trousers up around his waist. I quickly pulled down my bra and jumper and shoved my legs into my leggings.

'Sorry... I didn't mean to jump you.' Phoenix said after we had scrambled around in silence for a few minutes. 'I just couldn't help myself; I've been hiding out for two days and almost gave up on seeing you.' He said guiltily and I suddenly felt guilty too. I didn't respond, having to shake the thought of Harry out of my mind as I dusted itchy hay out of my leggings. 'I have to go now.' I mumbled. 'Me too, I should have been gone already.' Phoenix said quietly. He was plugged in to his telekom and looking down at his hand as if he was seeing something important.

'Oh, ok…' I said looking down at the ground, not sure how to feel about what had just happened. All I knew was that was the first time I had enjoyed any form sexual contact in as long as I could remember.

'Come with me!' Phoenix exclaimed suddenly, enthusiastically grabbing my hands, and gently leading me towards the stable doors.

'What! Where? Back to Brixton?' I looked up at him surprised as I slipped my hands out of his grasp.

'I can't…' I said quietly glancing back at the house as Phoenix gently pulled my face back to meet his.

'Why?' he asked as I gazed at him under the light of the full moon. I thought about Harry and the mess his life was in because of me. I couldn't just leave him like this… I had to let the dust settle; I owed Harry that much at least.

'You don't love that white man,' Phoenix hissed as if he had just read my mind. 'Just come with me,' he pleaded, 'you know you don't belong here.'

'So where do I belong, with you?' I snapped and he looked down at his encrypted hologram. 'I can't leave… not yet, it wouldn't be right.' I said looking back at the house again.

'I've got to go…' Phoenix sighed quietly as he followed my gaze out of the stable doors. He tucked his telekom into his pocket 'I've been gone too long already.' He mumbled as he clicked on his sliders and meandered in front of me. 'I'll be back in a few weeks, ok.' He said finally and we stood there in awkward silence before he leaned in to kiss me. 'When you see the stable light flickering, I'll be here.' He said and with that he ran off into the night. My eyes tried to follow him, but his camo suit made him impossible to see as he skated off into the gloom. The stable light suddenly stopped flicking and I stood at the door listening to the low hum of his gliding hover boots until his tracks disappeared into the night. A sinking feeling suddenly washed over me, and I looked up at the stars and sighed. I decided to take the long way back to the house, trudging through the field in complete darkness. Even though I was alone I felt safe, far away from the snapping cameras of the press and protestors at the front gates. I was shivering slightly by the time I got back to the house and I slipped in through the large rear conservatory. I walked down the main corridor and snuck past the front room. The door was ajar, and Blanche was sitting in front of the VTV with a glass of sherry in hand. She was talking to one of her old cronies whose hologram was nodding attentively above the coffee table. I flew up the staircase and ran straight into Maria carrying a bundle of clothes.

'I'm so sorry,' I said as I helped her to pick them all up.

'Oh, there you are!' Maria said unfazed. 'Master Harold is looking for you.'

'He is?' I said my face dropping into an uncontrollable frown. 'Where is he?' Maria nodded towards the master bedroom with her head as we both bent down to retrieve the fallen clothes

'Thanks Maria.' I said as I headed towards the east wing of the house.

At the end of the corridor was a dainty room with a deep blue and silver leaf embossed wallpaper, grand oak furniture, and a four-poster bed. The room was at the back of the house, overlooking the forest, and this is where I retreated when I wanted to be alone. After a long shower I wrapped myself in my silk dressing gown and decided it was time to face the music.

I opened the master bedroom door and stepped into a dimly lit atmosphere. Harry was on his side of the bed reading under the light of his bedside lamp, with scented candles burning on the mantle. I silently oiled my skin and slipped on the negligee already laid out for me. Harry's eyes came to life behind his glasses as he watched me quietly prepare for bed.

'Darling, where have you been?' he asked finally as I pulled back the covers on my side of the bed. My throat was dry, and I had to swallow saliva before I spoke.

'Tending to the horses.' I said as I got into bed.

'For so long... and it's dark out...' he frowned as I covered myself with the duvet.

'I just needed some space.' I said as he placed his book down on the bedside table.

'Were you not cold?' I shook my head as he placed his reading glasses down next to his book.

'I had a jumper on.' I mumbled without giving him eye contact.

'I see...' He murmured as he slid across the queen-sized bed.

'I thought Millie might have upset you at dinner,' he frowned touching my shoulder, and I scoffed loudly as I shook my head.

'It'll take more than a hormonal teenaged girl to upset me.' I said smiling as he sceptically narrowed his eyes.

'I'm fine Harry, really.' I said patting his knee reassuringly.

'Good.' He smiled as he leaned over and began to kiss my neck. 'Do you like what I picked out for you?' he asked pulling down the duvet to reveal the lingerie's lace trim. 'The yellow compliments your skin beautifully.' He whispered while using one finger to trace my nipples through the light material. He reached out to pull down the straps, but my body froze as he tried to touch me. 'Are you alright...' Harry asked as he gently pulled my face towards his.

'I'm fine...' I lied, as he began to kiss me.

'Good.' Harry said as he planted a trail of kisses along my neck, all over my breasts and down my stomach. 'But please... don't ever be afraid to tell me anything.' He whispered and I instantly felt guilty, knowing it had barely been a few hours since Phoenix had come inside me. I tried not to think about it as Harry clumsily hitched up my slip, and I quickly turned onto my side to avoid the missionary position.

'What's this?' Harry questioned from behind me.

'What?' I asked flinching as he touched the small of my back.

'That...' He said gently rubbing the large sore patch of skin. I thought about Phoenix. How had pushed me up against the side of the horse pen, and how my bare back had rubbed against the wood, as well as bales of hay.

'It's just a rash...' I said quickly, 'must be all the fancy new skin products I've been using,' I chuckled as he gently kissed me on the shoulder.

'Funny looking rash... Do see that Maria gets you something for it.' He whispered into my ear and I gasped as he suddenly entered me. My body automatically tensed up and I locked my legs together as he grunted and groaned into my ear. I wanted to scream for him to get off me, but I just lay there as he worked himself into an irregular rhythm, thinking about Phoenix as I cried into a fluffy pillow. 'I love you!' Harry panted as he clutched my hips and plunged into me even deeper. I wished I could say the same, but for me this interaction was just another day at the office. I was still a prostitute, masquerading as the loving wife Harry longed for me to be. 'Your mine, you hear me, mine forever!' Harry groaned loudly, and as my head annoyingly began to bang against the padded headboard, I couldn't help but wish that I had just run off into the night with Phoenix.

13

THE CALM BEFORE THE STORM

It was late, and I anxiously paced back and forth behind the closed curtains. The huge bay windows were covered in heavy velvet, making it impossible to see into the lounge from the outside. The press had disintegrated over the past couple of weeks, but a small group of protesters still loitered outside the estate, harassing any vehicle that came inside.

I kept peeking through the gap in the curtains, and I let out a huge sigh as I saw Maria shuffling up the driveway, her short body partially covered by Harry's huge black umbrella. It was raining heavily outside, the raindrops resembling thin shards of glass that shattered into puddles as soon as they hit the ground. I ran to open the front door as soon as Maria approached the porch. She greeted me with a swift nod before she waddled into the house. I swiftly shut the door behind her and anxiously followed her through the foyer, down the main corridor and straight into the kitchen.

'Did you get it?' I asked impatiently as she tugged at her fingertips to remove her leather gloves. She unbuttoned her coat as she put her hand into her inside pocket, pulling out a small brown paper bag. She handed it to me, and I quickly opened it and ripped at a corner of the packet inside with my teeth. Maria went to hang her coat in the hall and returned just as I pulled out a small metal cylinder. She sat down opposite me as I read the instructions, pulled off the cap and popped the sterile end of the contraption into my mouth. I looked up at Maria nervously. *How could I have been so stupid!* I thought as my heart began to quicken. If I didn't get the right result in a few minutes, I would be in breach of my conditional residency application and unable to pass my last interview. Maria grabbed my hand and smiled at me from across the table as if she had read my mind.

'You'll be alright luv.' She cooed reassuringly as she squeezed my hand a little tighter.

'I'm so sorry for putting you in this position.' I mumbled as I glanced up at her. 'I just thought that since you have blue papers, it would be easier for you to get your hands on one...' I said trailing off as Maria looked at the floor.

'I don't have blue papers... they're yellow. I haven't been outside of the district of Essex in over a decade. I have to report to my local DRB office every week.' I knew the drill Maria was here on a work permit. I should have known better than to assume her status, that was DRB training 101. 'If I don't show up to my appointment my papers automatically turn orange, and you know once you're issued with orange papers, it's only a matter of time before they turn red.'

'I know.' I said nodding understandably. I didn't have the heart to tell her that I already knew the biased system inside out.

'My job, well Master Harry is the only reason I'm allowed to stay here... I don't know where my boy and I would be without him.' My stomach dropped as I thought about Maria's teenaged son Luca asleep upstairs. He was a shy boy, a bit older than Millie, and he and Maria lived in a small apartment on the third floor.

'I'm so sorry, I didn't know.' I said quietly. *I should have known... was I that out of touch? Had I been away for so long that I couldn't tell a blue carrier from yellow?* At the DRB Bureau you were told never to judge your clients, but it was the first thing you did when they were assigned to you. Figuring out if they were a blue, yellow, or orange paper carrier could save you a lot of time and effort.

'Don't worry about it,' Maria shrugged. 'You don't get to be a tough old bird like me, without learning a few tricks.' she chuckling, and we both suddenly jumped as the small device beeped loudly informing us that the timer was up. I took the small cylinder out of my mouth and set it down on the table in front of me. It vibrated gently as it began to glow. My eyes widened as a florescent blue light flashed in front of me. Blue meant pregnant.

'*Your test is positive... You are Pregnant...*' A robotic voice announced as if to just make sure that I got the message. I fumbled to turn it off, paranoid that somebody somewhere in the house might hear, even though it was the small hours of the morning. I grunted loudly and swiped the test of the table. The metal cylinder hit the tiled floor with a subtle clatter. 'Don't you worry luv.' Maria said as she rushed to retrieve it.

'Master Harry will make sure that you're allowed to keep your baby... despite the restrictions.'

'Great...' I scoffed loudly as I shook my head vigorously. Pregnancy was a major inconvenience, especially when I'd been having periodic sex with two different men. Maria watched me with a bemused expression on her face and I quickly feigned a smile as our eyes met across the table. Just one more gigantic problem stood to add to my list. *How would I figure out who the father was...*

***

I hadn't slept a wink all night, and I waited patiently under the covers until Harry had left for work. It had been a few weeks since I had found out that I was pregnant but I still hadn't told him. My stomach was getting firmer by day and it was getting impossible to explain away the morning sickness. I had a feeling Blanche was onto me, her endless questions and underhand comments over the dinner table leaving me with heart palpitations. Harry knew something was going on, and the other night he had received a tipoff from an *unknown friend* informing him that Recons would turn up any day now on an unannounced visit. That was all I needed as if I wasn't already running out of time. If the Recons found out I was pregnant they could arrest me for breach of papery conditions. That was almost a week ago so, they could turn up any minute, and I was becoming more paranoid by the hour. Harry had promised me that he would work from home more often. But of course, there was always something that called him away. We had argued about it last night because he just couldn't understand why I was suddenly so clingy. He knew that I would crumble if I was interviewed alone, and in a sulk, I refused to kiss him goodbye this morning. I sighed as I rolled over on my back and lay in the middle of the huge mattress. A wave of nausea suddenly washed over me and I jumped out of bed to be sick. I was heaving over the toilet bowl for at least half an hour before I felt well enough to take a shower. My mind ran as fast as the hot water was hitting my body.

What would happen to me when the Recons found out that I was pregnant? Would Harry have enough power to protect me? Would they take me away? Dump me in a breeding farm? No, Harry would never allow that! But could he stop then from chucking me back into Hermitage Hill? I dragged myself out of the shower as my mind continued to race.

'I have to telecall Phoenix!' I announced as I paced into the bedroom. It was nearly two months since I'd last seen him and I hadn't told him I was pregnant either. 'I need to clear my head,' I muttered as I stopped pacing and looked out of the window. My eyes scanned the fields and rolling hills in the distance until my gaze settled on the barn. I felt suffocated and I needed to get out of the house. The sky was a threatening shade of grey so I went to the walk-in wardrobe to retrieve my weatherproof riding suit. I slipped it on and grabbed my thick puffer jacket for extra protection before pulling open the bedroom door. I ran down the hall towards the back stairs and through the kitchen towards the cellar. My nose stopped me in the pantry and I backtracked to quickly stuffed my face with a couple of Maria's freshly baked scones.

'You off riding?' Maria asked as she came in from the conservatory holding a mop and bucket.

'Flipping hell!' I spat nearly choking on a mouthful of freshly baked doughy goodness.'

'Sorry, I didn't mean to scare you.' She said putting the mop and bucket down.

'No, it's me,' I said swallowing, 'I'm just a bit jumpy this morning.' We hadn't spoken about the pregnancy since the night I had found out and I knew she was wondering why I hadn't told Harry yet.

'You off riding?' She repeated.
I bit into another warm scone as I nodded.

'Do you think that's safe?' She mumbled and I shrugged, I hadn't really thought about it. The front door bell suddenly rang startling the both of us, and I used the interruption as an excuse to get away from her questioning gaze.

'I'll see you later,' I said as I glanced away from her and headed into the pantry. Her eyes followed me but the door rang again, followed by a series of loud knocks.

'Alright, alright I'm coming!' Maria called as she marched towards it. My heart began to race as I glanced back at the clock on the kitchen wall. It was 9:30am in the morning.

'Raine...' Maria said stopping me before I reached the cellar door.

'I'll be going out to the shops soon,' She called from the hall. 'Do you need anything?'
Yeah, unconditional blue papers.

'No thanks,' I called as I continued down to the cellar, trying not to think about who was knocking on the front door with such authority. It couldn't be *them*, could it? I knew it very well could be, whoever it was had been buzzed in through the gate by Jose or Jaime. If it was the Recons what the hell was, I going to do? Storm neighed excitedly when I entered the barn and walked towards the stables. He sensed me before he saw me but I didn't stop to stroke him like I usually did. Instead, heading straight outside to telecall Phoenix. I walked around to the back of the stables and faced the fields. It had been raining all night, and the air was damp and foggy, with a heavy mist settling over the near distant hills and Epping Forest. I thought it looked more foreboding than usual as I drove my hand into my inside breast pocket to retrieve the telekom Phoenix had given me. It was only supposed to be used for emergencies, hence the reason I had resisted the strong urge to contact him up until now.
I popped the plug into my ear and cleared my mind to activate it. I concentrated on who I wanted to contact

and as soon as I was locked onto a frequency I tele-called Phoenix. I concentrated on him as hard as I could but he didn't *or he wouldn't* respond. Wherever his whereabouts, he should have been able to sense that I was calling him unless he was detached from his plug. After redialling and staring hopelessly into the distance for a minute or so, I left a message for him to call me as I marched back around to the front of the stables. Little droplets of rain began to fall as I noticed that almost every single light was on in the house. I gasped heard a loud horn and turned to see a large black vehicle beeping erratically at the front gate. I knew a gas van when I saw one, and my stomach flipped upside down as the blood in my veins ran cold. *It must have been Recons at the door!* I thought panic stricken. *They must have called for backup!* My heart almost burst through my chest as I realised that they must be searching for me. The sky suddenly lit up and thunder rolled overhead making me jump. No doubt Maria had covered for me but it would only be a few minutes before they hunted me down, despite the bad weather possibly interfering with their tracking equipment. I quickly ran into the stables to hide as I tried to pluck a single tangible thought out of my frazzled head. The mares seemed a little spooked but Storm seemed to neigh sympathetically as I began to pace up and down. *What am I going to do?* I thought pacing one way. *If I don't leave now, they're going to take me away!* I mulled as I turned abruptly to pace in the opposite direction. *But where can I go?* 'I've got nowhere to run to!'

'Pheonix where are you!' I cried as I walked over to the stable doors to peak back at the house. *'Harry's not home… so maybe Maria will send them away,* I thought trying to reassure myself as I saw several suited individuals getting out of the big black vehicle now in the drive. *Why did they send so many?*
I knew that they wouldn't leave without seeing me in person, and I knew that only Harry could possibly get them to go away and return another day. There was absolutely nothing that Maria could do to protect me, and in that moment, I absolutely hated Harry for leaving me alone. I started to cry but then Storm neighed loudly jolting me out of my pitiful thoughts. I reluctantly dried my eyes.

'Ok think!' I said as the pitter patter of the rain against the roof grew heavier. It began to leak as another roll of thunder echoed overhead. 'Maybe… I could try to find the safe house Phoenix spoke about in Epping Forest.' I said walking back over to Storm who tossed his mane and swished his tail as if he understood my intentions. 'Phoenix *had* mentioned it once or twice…' I said to Storm as I peered into his big round eyes. Another thunderous rumble a few seconds later startled me into making up my mind. I entered Storm's stable and quickly and expertly saddled him under the watchful gaze of all the mares in the neighbouring pens. I knew trying to find the Epping hideout was risky, and I paused before I undid the hatch to let Storm out of his pen. Not only did I not know where I was going. I'd only been riding for a few months, albeit every day, and even if I did manage to find the safehouse without breaking my neck first, whoever ran the place could just as easily break it for me. I shook off my doubt. If I stayed, I ran a very high change of being sent back to Hermitage Hill for an illegal pregnancy, especially in Harry's absence.

That notion alone forced me to open Storm's pen and he came jostling out as if he knew he had been chosen for my special little mission. He bowed his head obediently as I quickly applied his bridle and climbed onto his back. I had become a decent horse rider, but prancing around a grassy field at a steady trot was one thing, galloping through Epping Forest on uneven hilly terrain was another. I turned my plug up to its maximum connectivity in case Phoenix called me back, and I promised myself that I would only ride straight in one direction in case I got lost. I gently pulled on Storm's reins and squeezed my legs around his back.

Shit! I thought looking down as I felt the security tag rub pinch my ankle. I had overlooked the tracking device attached to me, and they could potentially follow me. I had no idea how to take it off safely, nor did I have the time. Plus, I had no idea what would happen once I breached the permitted perimeter. I wiped my face as I got ready for what I was about to do, running away on tagged yellow papers was the ultimate defiance and it would ruin Harry's dwindling political integrity. But I couldn't think about that now.

I took a deep breath and gave the command for Storm to move off and he gingerly trotted toward the entrance, neighing at the mares as we went by. I knew there was no turning back now and I pulled his reins a little harder until he galloped through the stable doors and out onto the windy field. It was still raining outside and the sky was even darker than it had been a few minutes before. At least the fog had begun to clear, but bitter wind suddenly began to whip the rain into my face as we rode towards the end of the meadow. I held my breath as we neared the hedging that separated Harry's field from the next. I steadied myself as Storm leapt and we landed evenly on the other side.

I silently congratulated myself, and patted Storm's neck gratefully. After all I was a very inexperienced jumper. But thankfully even though he was immature, Storm was such a good strong horse, having supported a young Millie until she was a proficient rider, who then demanded a Shetland pony.

The security anklet suddenly started to beep and I quickly glanced back. We weren't that far from the house and only one more field away from Epping Forest. It was soon time to jump again and before I could even think about it Storm had elegantly leaped into the last field. It suddenly began to rain even harder and the beeping anklet started to constrict as I caught a flash of lightning in the distance. I slowed Storm down to a trot and he neighed disorientated by a herd of grazing cows. I patted his side to calm him as I reached down to feel my ankle. I groaned as it continued to tighten, restricting the blood supply to my foot, but another streak of lightening and a subsequent booming thunder brought my attention back to the matter at hand.

It was louder than ever, and it spooked Storm who neighed frantically and instantly took off galloping across the field, dispersing the confused mooing cows as we went. The rain was getting harder still, and I pulled on his reigns to try to slow him down but the brightening sky and instantaneous rolls of deafening thunder made him gallop even faster. I couldn't stop him now, and the rain was now viciously lashing at my face as we galloped towards the ocean of trees on the outskirts of the forest.

'Storm, stop!' I screamed as I pulled on his reins as hard as I could and thankfully, he halted abruptly just before we reached the brush. *What the hell was I thinking!* I thought catching my breath. I knew I still had time to get back to Harry's and do some damage control. *I could just say that Storm took off because he was freaked out by the weather.* I thought gritting my teeth under the agonising grip around my ankle. I gently tugged on Storm's inside rein to turn him around while he was still calm, knowing a large cluster of trees was the worse place to be in a lightning storm. But Storm had other ideas as the sky flashed again, etching a bolt of lightning right across the sky and striking a large tree just a few feet away from us. It split in two and half the trunk fell to the ground as the closing thunder roared like it was the end of the world. Storm neighed as he kicked up his front legs and immediately took off galloping wildly into the forest. I tried to use my body language cues to make him stop, but he wouldn't slow down. Panicking, I pulled on his reins as he recklessly hurtled deep into the undergrowth. I shouted for him to stop but he ran deeper into the forest still, the sporadic lighting illuminating us for a few seconds as it struck nearby trees. I tried to take in my surroundings but it was still raining heavily and the forest was so dark underneath the canopy. I glanced over my back, and although we had only entered the woods a minute ago, I couldn't even see the light from where we rode in. The trees were already too dense and frightened, I yanked Storm's mane in desperation. What use was escaping if I ended up dead!

This time Storm suddenly stopped making me fall forward onto his neck.

'It's ok Storm,' I said wincing as I sat upright. I patted him reassuringly. I could still feel the tag tightening around my foot and my ankle had started to throb. I quickly attempted to turn Storm around again but it was of no use as another flash of lighting lit up the trees around us. Thunder roared relentlessly as Storm neighed and kicked the earth with his hooves, moving sideways agitatedly as I tried to get my bearings. I pulled out my telekom and threw a holographic light orb into the air. Looking down, I could just about see like we had come to the edge of some sort of sloped ditch which Storm did not want to cross. The rainwater was making the earth shift underneath us as storm trotted from side to side. He neighed erratically as I tried to make him back up and turn around. I stopped moving for a second, suddenly hearing something through the pitter patter of the rain. Storm began to buck and stamp his hooves. I had to hold onto him as he jostled, and kicked his hind legs. I could've sworn that he hit something but I didn't see what it was as he took off down the embankment and galloped into a stream. He continued his sprint through the forest and as the trees, and the light orb followed us as we were illuminated by yet another flash of lightning. I could suddenly see dark blurs moving beside us. Too quick for me to make them out in the heavy rain. We kept moving and I believed that we must have gotten turned around somewhere because I could now see an open clearing up ahead leading back out to the fields. We quickly drew nearer and I prayed it would be close to the fields behind Harry's mansion. Storm quickly galloped through the thinning trees and straight out into the open. But the apparent field was nothing more than a large bushy glade surrounded by more encircling trees. *Shit!* I thought hysterically, *we must be going deeper into the forest!* Suddenly, a large white wolf came running through the trees opposite us illuminated by blanket of lightning across the sky. Storm skidded to a halt right in the middle of the glade. The wolf howled loudly and the rest of the pack, all black finally broke through the trees all around us. They were huge, bigger than any dogs I'd ever seen, and Storm neighed frantically as they began to circle. They were getting closer and without warning the white wolf suddenly leapt at us, yelping loudly as Storm kicked struck it with his front legs. He bucked and struck another one with his hind legs as it growled and flew towards me. Then Storm tried to escaped, running, and jumped clean over another wolf but the rest of the pack quickly reformed the circle. He then began to buck back and forth uncontrollably neighing and rearing up like a wild stallion as they surrounded us again. I tried to hold on but he stood upright on his hind legs as the wolves closed in and I lost my balance. I fell off his back and onto the ground awkwardly hitting my head. I lay there dazed for a moment looking up into the sky as the rain beat down on my face. I tried to look around for Storm but my head was too heavy for me to lift, I turned to the side and all I could see was Storm moving around my body trying to protect me. 'Go home Storm!' I yelled as I heard him neighing in distress, and I prayed that he would find his way back to Harry's as another bolt of lightning lit up the sky.

***

I was no longer lying on my back in the middle of a forest glade underneath a stormy sky. My head was pounding, and I had no idea where I was, or how long I'd been lying there. The last thing I remembered was falling from Storm's back. I tried to move but my arms and legs were bound together. I stopped struggling and held my breath as I heard something move across the room. I was being watched. My body stiffened as footsteps trudged towards me.

'Who's there?' I asked as I tried to shift my body into a more comfortable position.

'Get up.' Someone said as they suddenly cut away at the material binding my limbs. I was still blindfolded, and I heard a door open as I pulled upright.

'Where am I?' I got no answer as I put my feet searched out the ground. I winced when my right foot hit the cold hard concrete. 'What's going on?' I asked as I forced up onto my feet.

'You're being collected.' The man finally replied.

'By who?' I hissed trying to balance my weight unevenly on my swollen foot.

'No more questions!' He grunted as he dragged me along by the arm forcing me to limp blindfolded across the room. I could feel the breeze, and hear the rustling of trees all around us as I was led outside. The person leading me abruptly let me go and left me listening to his footsteps as they got further away.

'Hello?' I said shivering as I heard voices approaching. I got no answer but several twigs snapped as footsteps squelched towards me. I recoiled as the blindfold was roughly pulled off my face, nearly losing my footing. I rubbed my eyes as they came into focus and adjusted to the glow of the light orbs suspended in between the trees. I did not recognise the strange man holding the blindfold beside me. But I breathed a huge sigh of relief when I saw Phoenix standing a few in front of me. My eyes welled up with tears of joy, but I noticed that Pheonix's face was stern and emotionless as he stepped towards me.

'You alright?' He asked unnervingly as he studied my face. I smiled meekly as he turned to the strange man now standing beside him.

'Is she clean?' He asked and the hooded man slowly nodded his head. 'She had better be...' Phoenix said as he narrowed his eyes and looked down at my bandaged foot.

'Give it a rest P, I've done *you* a favour remember!' The hooded man said as he held up both his hands innocently.

'Yeah, and what's that gonna cost me?' Phoenix asked rolling his eyes.

'Well, you know how it is...' The hooded man chuckled. 'There's the labour for the tag removal, plus the finder's fee...' He said clearing his throat when he realised Phoenix was not chuckling along.

'Spit it out Vinny,' Phoenix hissed impatiently. I ain't got all day.'

'Whoa... what's with all the hostility?' Vinny asked putting his hands up again. 'You're as right as rain ain't ya luv?' He said winking at me before turning back to Phoenix. 'Look, as soon as I found out she was yours... Well let's just say I took extra good care of her...' He said covering his mouth as if I couldn't hear him. I watched their exchange curiously as Phoenix rubbed his chin.

'I'll give you a bag and a half,' he said finally.

'Come on mate, you know I can't go back in there with that! Everyone needs to get there cut... and with the cost of living these days were looking at about...' Vinny mumbled looking around. 'Tell you what, throw in another monkey and a favour, then she's all yours.' He said smiling at Phoenix with a glint in his eye. Phoenix stared back at Vinny as he held his hand out.

'What kind of favour?' Phoenix asked wrinkling his forehead.

'I'll know when I need it...' Vinny said chuck-ling, 'But it's either that or due to inflation I'll have to charge a percentage on quid so then you'll be looking at–'

'Alright, deal,' Pharoah barked cutting him off. I watched curiously as Phoenix kissed his teeth before he finally shook on it. He then reached into his pocket and pulled out an envelope. He plucked out several bills and handed them to Vinny one by one, who then began to flip them through his fingers. I hadn't seen proper old money in years, not since the government outlawed it and instituted the mainstream quid sys-tem. It was mostly useless now, but I had heard that it was still a rare and valuable commodity on the under-world black market.

'Good doing business with ya,' Vinny sang as he walked away. Phoenix grunted in response and we both watched Vinny saunter away before he plugged in. His ear lit up and within seconds I could see the lights of a large vehicle creeping towards us. I glanced over at Phoenix hoping that he would say something.

'What day is it? I asked as the jeep finally came to a halt in front of us.

'It's Friday morning.' He said as the doors auto-matically popped open. He helped me inside, carefully lifting my injured foot in after me.
The clock on the dashboard said 3:35am, and that meant I had been missing for almost two days. Phoenix marched around the car and jumped into the driver's seat without saying another word. He didn't even look in my direction before taking off abruptly and driving

recklessly through the trees. He turned on the muted dashboard VTV, and several minutes went by in absolute silence until he finally broke the ice.

'Why did you run? Was you in trouble?' Phoenix asked at last over the roar of the engine. I nodded silently as I looked away from the holographic images on the dash VTV and out of the window. 'Was it that bad that you couldn't wait for me to come back for you?' I choked as I glanced at his profile not knowing what to say. I was on the verge of tears. He didn't even look happy to see me.

I swallowed the lump in my throat as he turned onto out of the forest and onto a dirt road. I wanted to tell him that I was pregnant but what if he rejected me? I silently looked back out of the window and wiped my tears away. 'Raine, don't you realise how dangerous Epping Forest is? What if it wasn't the Beefeaters that found you! Do you think they're the only ones lurking in there?' I ignored him as I continued to look out of the window. 'Their wolves could've eaten you alive!' I could feel his eyes boring into the side of my face. 'Raine, answer me!' Phoenix hissed as he slapped the steering wheel making the horn beep loudly.

'I just panicked!' I snapped, 'and then I ran.' I muttered quietly looking back out of the window.

'Why?' Phoenix pressed just as we turned onto a gravel slip road.

'The Recons were coming for me they would've taken me away. I, I had no choice. I had to run.' Phoenix's face contorted into a scowl.

'I thought your sugar daddy was untouchable?' he hissed, quickly switching the car into auto drive as we entered a concrete motorway. He turned to face me.

'He is, but...'

'But what?' Phoenix pressed as I took a long deep sigh.

'I'm pregnant!' I said quickly looking away from him and concentrating on the VTV screen. He slammed it shut and looked me square in the eye.

'You're pregnant?' I nodded and refusing to look at him, I faced the window. It had started to rain, and the windscreen wipers automatically clicked on.

'Is it... mine?' Phoenix asked after a few seconds.

'Of course, it is.' I said shifting uncomfortably in my seat.

'How can, you be sure?' Phoenix quizzed, making a tight knot form in the pit of my stomach.

'I just know!' I said as I turned to look back at him.

'Were you sleeping with him?' he asked distantly.

'No...I couldn't bear too, after we'd... not after you came to see me.' I lied as I glanced at my fidgeting fingers. Phoenix didn't respond, he just stared straight ahead. Right through the windscreen window as he silently switched the car off auto-drive and took control of the wheel. We didn't speak for the rest of the journey, and I closed my eyes trying to ignore the tense atmosphere inside the car. I had no idea if he believed me, but I pushed the negative thoughts to the back of my mind, relieved that he hadn't kicked me out of the vehicle in the middle of nowhere.

I blinked away my tears restlessly gazing at the burnt-out buildings and dilapidated streets rolling by. Barricades made up of abandoned cars and industrial waste containers blocked most of the roads. Which were impossible to navigate unless you had an ever-shifting map of London. I fell asleep for an hour or so until were stopped in front of a large tollgate that was blocking the entrance to a steep hill. I came too to the sound of blaring horns as a light shone down onto the windscreen and awoke me. My eyes flickered under the bright light, adjusting just as the huge gate swung open allowing us to drive through. The fortified gate closed loudly behind us and two heavily armoured men saluted Phoenix and waved us by. We began to drive uphill on the bumpy winding road lined with thick trees. I could just about see the tops of buildings rising in the near distance as my stomach began to turn. The rain had eased up a little but not enough for me to clearly see where I was. I wiped the steam off the passenger window.

'Where are we?' I asked as I peered through the glass and looked around.

'You know where we are.' Phoenix said ominously as I we reached the top of the hill. I looked at the dark buildings cascading down the hillside, and my stomach sank as I finally realised where we were. The grey apartment blocks went on for as far as the eye could see, dissolving into the bright smoky lights of the rest of London beyond it. How could I not know where we were?

Everyone knew this place. I had seen the same backdrop in the headlines and on the VTV on countless occasions.

'Where are we going?' I mumbled quietly as I took in the entirety of the infamous graffitied Alexandra Palace as it came into full view.

'Home.' Phoenix said stopping the car abruptly as we were met by loitering crowds scattering into the road. He beeped his horn loudly as they moseyed across street without looking.

'What about Brixton?' I asked quietly.

'What about it?' Phoenix snapped as he suddenly took a sharp turn off the main road into a narrower street. We drove downhill for a few more minutes, winding deeper and deeper into a grey bricked ghetto cascading all the way into the valley until Phoenix parked in front of a low-rise tower block set into the hillside.

'I just thought that we'd go back...' I muttered, my hopes of seeing Toni again completely dashed.

'Well, you thought wrong,' Phoenix said flatly as I looked around at the imposing structures jutting out of the elevated highland. 'This is your home now so you better get used to it.'

***

'You'll be alright for a few hours...' Phoenix said as he handed me a takeaway bag and switched on the VTV. I was lying in the living room of his 3rd floor flat, on the sofa under a blanket with my injured ankle propped up.

'Where are you going?' I asked, staring at the back of his head as he walked away. He pulled on his mask.

'I' won't be long.' He answered dismissively as he walked out of the room. The front door slammed a few seconds later as I hungrily ripped open the bag of food and stuffed chips into my mouth. I couldn't remember the last time I had eaten, and my stomach was so empty that the food hurt going down. I gobbled down the oily concoction meat and chips, sucking the pigeon wings down to the bone. I finished the meal and slurped down the fizzy drink, burping loudly as I rubbed my stomach in satisfaction. I sighed, laying back on the sofa and discarded the takeaway box on the coffee table in front of me. I was tired, but as soon as I closed my eyes and began to nod off a familiar beep coming from the VTV jolted me awake.

'This is an important announcement... I repeat this is an important announcement... Viewing... will continue in due course. Please pay full attention to this Twilight News Flash.' Another long beep reminiscent of white noise followed, drawing my attention to the BFP logo hovering in front of the screen. The usual red-faced chauvinistic newsreader addressed the nation as I tilted my head towards the VTV.

'This morning, on Twilight News,' he said with a menacing smile. Recons still on hunt for dangerous fugitive Raine Montrose, after she absconded from a luxurious house arrest, leaving behind her guardian and alleged husband, MP Harry Winchester. My eyes widened as I sat up to get a closer look at the holographic screen. I began to feel sick, and I quickly grabbed the soda on the coffee table as I saw Harry's puffy, grief-stricken holographic figure staring at me through the VTV.

'Raine, you're not in any trouble and whoever has you will pay!' He said pleadingly as he stood in the rain under his huge black umbrella wearing a dark navy coat. I reached out to touch the hologram and it disintegrated in between my fingers before the pixels flickered back into a recognisable picture. 'I know you wouldn't have left me voluntarily. So please... Whoever has my beloved Raine, if you're watching this... quid is no issue, just please bring her home....'

14

IN THE EYE OF THE STORM
WOOD GREEN, NORTH LONDON 2059

*A*lexandra Heights… Or the slums, as it was more commonly known was a lawless, dilapidated ghetto and the last place I wanted to be. The vast area was broken up into 4 districts, Alexandra Rise, Alexandra Mews, The Mount, and The Valley. It was once a luxurious housing estate built into the hillside of Alexandra Palace in the mid-2020s. North London was still an affluent area back then, and this state-of-the-art complex was an architectural masterpiece. Built on top of historic land surrounding a Grade II listed building famous worldwide for being the first place to broadcast TV, the archaic predecessor of virtual Television. Built under the guise of affordable housing for the next generation and rapidly constructed in a bid to soothe the country's ever spiralling housing crisis. The government backed initiative, located in a prestigious part of North London with luxury facilities and discounted mortgages quickly attracted many first-time buyers desperate to get a foot on the property ladder. Unfortunately for them, the poorly managed cheaply built properties deteriorated quickly, and it seemed as if their pretty little labyrinth of hillside properties were predisposed to become one of the most dangerous ghettos in the country.

But it was only after the 2030 General Election was won by The National Sovereign Party that the two yearlong Liberation Riots began, enabling the siege of the League of Equality, more commonly known as LOE Society to really start to take hold. The LOE quickly overthrew several tube stations around London, taking advantage of the civil unrest, vigilante violence and the lack of resources at the government's disposal. They seized London bridge and Tower Bridge allowing them to control major movements across the river Thames. This put pressure on the Prime Minster and his party, forcing them into a coalition government with the Anglican People's Party during the probably corrupt 2034 general election. Thus, the Conformed British Fundamentalist Party, or BFP as it is more commonly known was born. This didn't stop the LOE Society who managed to seize Alexandra Palace in the January of 2035, quickly making it their southern England headquarters. The BFP enforced Martial Law in a desperate bid to get control of the capital's streets when the world was on the brink of World War 3.

'Raine, are you listening to me?' Phoenix was staring at me from across the table. I nodded even though I wasn't really listening to what he was saying. This was the first time I had been out in a couple months, and I had gotten so used to sitting at home all alone pondering on my own thoughts. Phoenix would disappear for days on end without telling me where he was going or when he'd be back, and now after two months of practically ignoring me, he had surprised me with a trip to Pandemonium. The LOE Society's exclusive bar and restaurant located in a secluded part of Alexandra Palace. The guest list was strictly limited to Loelifes, their family, and their links or side chicks, which I came to learn made up most of the staff.

'I'll be back in a minute,' Phoenix said as he abruptly pushed his chair out and stood up unexpectedly.

'Please don't leave me, people are staring!' I said grabbing his hand as he went to leave the table.

'Stop being paranoid It's just because you're with me.' Phoenix said playfully flashing his best smile as he caressed my wrist.

'This isn't funny!' I said through gritted teeth. 'What if it's because there's a price on my head?' I panicked. 'You know the reward Harry promised for me,' I whispered.

'Didn't I tell you that you're under my protection?' Phoenix said frowning. I nodded as he slid his hand away from mine. 'Then stop being silly,' he snapped impatiently as he quickly walked away. I kissed my teeth loudly, not even noticing the waitress standing by the table until she began to clear the empty plates.

'Anything else to go with your main course?'
She asked politely as she piled the dishes onto her arm.
My mouth felt dry, so I asked for a large glass of red
wine to calm my nerves. I handed her the closed menu,
and she shimmied away just as Phoenix reappeared
and slunk into his seat.

'Look babe… something's come up.' He said
quietly as soon as he sat down.

'What does that mean?' I snapped as the waitress reappeared with our food and delicately placed
the dishes on the table. I stared down at my steaming
plate of duck as Phoenix impatiently waited for the
waitress to leave.

'We have to go straight after dinner…'

'But we just got here,' I said as I watched him
forcefully cut into his steak.

'I'll make it up to you.' He mumbled with a
mouth full of meat.'

'But this is the first time you've ever taken me
out anywhere!' I whined. 'You said we could go to the
lake, or the old ice rink!'

'It's business!' Phoenix barked as he stared me
down.

'It's always business!' I retorted loudly as I
dropped my fork and crossed my arms over my chest.
Now I was sure that people were staring.

'Hurry up and eat!' Phoenix hissed as our waitress returned with the wine. 'We didn't order that.' He
grunted dismissively waving her away.

'I, ordered it.' I said coldly as I beckoned her
over.

'Take it back!' Phoenix snarled as soon as she came closer.

'No!' I almost shouted as I leant forward and snatched the glass out of her hand. People were now staring and whispering, and so reluctantly Phoenix relented as the waitress tentatively backed away from our table.

'Eat your food.' Phoenix demanded, eyeing me closely as I put the glass of wine to my lips. I met his gaze as I sipped at the smooth liquid. I hadn't had a drink since going cold turkey at Harry's behest when I had first arrived in the country.

No more alcohol, no more weed, and definitely no more crim! That had been his mantra when he locked me up in the bedroom at the back his mansion, the same room that I had taken as my very own. It took over a fortnight of severe withdrawal symptoms, and nothing but the VTV for company and Maria bringing three square meals a day before I could even function without some sort of foreign substance in my blood stream.

I swallowed the smooth red vino, treasuring every sip at it as if it was the nectar of the gods. I sighed savouring it's warmth as it went down my throat, and our eyes met across the table as I swirled the remaining liquid in the glass. Phoenix watched me with what I could only describe as disgust, and after another unnecessarily loud sip, I smiled to myself and set the glass down. I slowly picked up my knife and fork and started to eat.

'So, you're a wino now yea?' He sneered as he finally looked back down at his food. I shrugged, taking a long loud slurp of my wine just to annoy him. He kissed his teeth, then ate quickly, not saying another word or giving me any eye contact until he had completely emptied his plate. I was beginning to think that he hated me.

He then summoned a waitress with the click of a finger. 'You ready?' He asked looking over at me impatiently. I ignored him as the waitress cleared our plates and handed us each a dessert menu.

'We won't be having dessert,' he said waving her away.

'I want dessert,' I said casually as held my hand out for the menu. The waitress glanced at Phoenix before handing it to me.

'Then get it to take away or something so we can go,' he said through gritted teeth as I studied the menu.

'I don't want it to take away,' I retorted as Phoenix glared at me in silence.

I was sick of being at home alone with no one to talk to. '*If you need to go* then just go, I'm sure I can find my own way home.' I shrugged indifferently as I sipped at my wine, not knowing when I'd get the chance to go out again.

'Nah, not happening.' Phoenix said shaking his head. 'Pick up your shit and let's go now!'

'Why can't I stay?' I whined. 'If I'm under your protection *like you say*, then there's nothing to worry about... is there?' I narrowed my eyes at him as he stared back at me silently. 'Who would dare mess with me when they know that I'm connected to the *Superior Loelife Phoenix*.' I said sarcastically as I drained the dregs of my glass to the very last drop.

'I said no.' Phoenix snapped cutting me off. 'Five minutes ago, you were crying about the price on your head and now your miss independent? I don't think so Raine, let's go.' He demanded as he pushed his chair out and stood up. I stared at him defiantly as he walked around the table and grabbed one of my arms. 'Get up!' He demanded and I kissed my teeth as I snatched my arm away.

'The only way I'm leaving is if you drag my pregnant body out of here kicking and screaming.' I replied rebelliously. He squinted down at me for a moment, then looked around at the other tables of Loelife couples watching us.

'Here!' He sneered as he threw a wad of quid down onto the table in front of me. 'Get dessert and go straight home, you understand?' He ordered as he leaned over me. I nodded and I beckoned the waitress over as I watched him turn and walked away without even saying goodbye.

'What can I get you?' She said smiling, clearly more relaxed in Phoenix's absence.

'Can I get the candied bacon cookies with the bone marrow ice cream please.'

'Anything else?' She asked nodding.

'Erm… could you also bring me some more of that lovely red wine?' I said closing the menu.

'No problem.' She replied as she retrieved it from the table and walked away. I picked up the quid as soon as she had left. Phoenix had left me with an assortment of blue and yellow serial marked notes. But there was a bit of old money mixed in amongst the stack. I pulled out the ancient currency. It was a pinky, the infamous brightly coloured £50 note, the most valuable bill you could trade on the black market. It was, thin, worn, and papery as opposed to the quid's rigid metallic and plasticky texture. I held the pinky up the light to study it, after all it was the first time, I had touched old money. It shimmered under the light but I quickly pulled it out of the air as I noticed many eyes were still watching me. I popped the old note into my bra for safe keeping and put the stack of quid back down onto the table.

'Here you are…' The waitress chirped as she promptly returned with my order. She placed the fancily dressed plate in front of me, and then proceeded to pour me another large glass of wine. 'Do you need anything else?' She asked before turning to leave.

'No thank you, I'm fine,' I said happily as I smiled up at her. 'Just leave the bottle…'

***

I crossed my arms as a chilly gust of wind rushed off the foggy lake and sent a shiver down my spine. The alcohol in the large glass of wine I had had at dinner was starting to wear off and I was finally feeling the cold. I turned away from the water after what felt like an eternity and decided to head home. It was after midnight by the time I had walked back up to the palace, and I could see a crowd of masked Loelifes leaving through an exit at the back of the building. I guessed that there must have been some sort of *secret society* meeting or something, which would explain why Phoenix ditched me at dinner.

By the time I had reached the palace entrance most of the Loelifes had already dispersed into the slums. I stopped to catch my breath as a group of masked stragglers walked behind me whispering amongst themselves. A few of them glanced back as they descended into the slums below, eyeing me up as if I was some sort of spy. I took a deep breath and followed cautiously dropping back, not trying to garner any unwanted attention. There were more Loelifes behind me but I opted against the use of my sliders as I tentatively walked down the large steep concrete steps until I reached the cracked slabs of pavement before the main road. As I slowly moved towards the curb as I heard more voices closing in behind me. My ears pricked up as I recognised one, and I turned around to see Phoenix. He was with a masked woman standing at the top of the concrete embroiled in some sort of conversation. I quickly ducked behind the large stone staircase as they swiftly made their way to the bottom. I crouched down and crept over to a small crowd of beggars warming themselves by a barrel fire as Phoenix and the masked woman stopped abruptly on the pavement. I pulled my hood up and pretended to warm myself by the open flames. The smell of body odour was pungent under the intense heat of the barrel fire, and the beggars who were mumbling amongst themselves barely noticed me. I didn't have to strain my ears for long to hear Phoenix's conversation.

'The pregnancy *is* a problem, and you know it!

'A problem for who?' Phoenix snapped loudly.

'Come on Phoenix, don't be stupid; you know that we *can't* afford a liability like *her* at a time like this!'

'Liability!' I thought angrily as I zeroed in on the masked woman who was obviously talking about me. Her mask was intricate and it covered three quarters of her face meaning she was also a high ranking Loelife. I couldn't help feeling that it looked vaguely familiar.

'I know how to handle my business Widow!' Phoenix snarled.

'Oh really?' Widow said laughing cynically, loud enough to make a few of the beggars turn around at the sound of her cackle. Her voice was shrill but real enough, so I assumed that the voice disguising function of her mask was currently turned off. 'I saw you tonight… playing happy families at Pandemonium…' She said snidely in her high-pitched tone. 'You're a mess! and Rex would have a fit if he knew what was really going on.'

'What the hell does that mean Widow!' Phoenix barked, 'what I do with my life isn't any of yours or Rex's business. Do you understand?'

'Well… it is actually. It becomes our business when you're using LOE resources to track down members of her estranged family.' She scoffed. 'That girl is playing you like a fucking fiddle and you can't even see it!'

'SOOO, I sent *some of my* Inferior's on a couple of errands, so bloody what?' Phoenix said shrugging dismissively.

'Well, *those couple of* errands turned into enough of a wild bloody goose chase to land two of those Inferiors up shit creek without a flipping paddle.' Widow hissed. Phoenix groaned loudly as he sparked up a spliff and blew a large cloud of smoke into the air. Several beggars' noses twitched as they turned towards the smell. 'What were you thinking?' Widow pressed.

'I sorted it didn't I!' Phoenix grunted after kissing his teeth.

'Well, that doesn't excuse the fact that they were caught in places that they had no business being in!' Widow said crossing her arms.

'Whatever!' Phoenix said stubbornly and Widow sighed as she shook her head and placed her hands on her hips.

'Look Phoenix this is serious, not only were they caught outside of our jurisdiction, everyone knows that you had to pay the owner of that territory an extensive ransom to get them back... which *you* took out of our expenses I might add. How do you think that makes us look?'

'What are you? like the LOE's new accountant now or something?' Phoenix hissed as he casually blew smoke into her face. 'Did a little birdie whisper something into your ear... telling you to come and have a nice little friendly chat with me after the meeting?' He said mocking her high-pitched voice as he chuckled to himself.

'The answer is bad Phoenix! It makes us look bad! And I'm warning you, if you do anything else to jeopardise the LOEs objectives… well I'll simply have to take matters into my own hands.' She stuck her nose into the air s Phoenix's demeanour suddenly darkened.

'That sounds like a threat Widow?' He said callously as he quickly snatched her by the throat and held her out at arms-length. She struggled to speak as she grasped at his hands around her neck. I gasped, having never seen this side of him.

'Come on don't be stupid Phoenix, you're putting us all in jeopardy. Remember I vouched for you once upon a time! Or have you forgotten?' Widow rasped as he loosened his grip and backed away from her as if he had suddenly come to his senses. 'So, consider this a warning…' she said as she smoothed down her clothes. 'And I'm only warning you because we go way back. but *you* would do well to remember your place and the people who brought you into the league.'

'I'm done with the mid games Widow, enough is enough!' Phoenix snapped as he pushed her into the shadows of the concrete steps to escape the now leering group of beggars.

'Ok look, there's no need to get excited, 'she protested from the darkness. 'There's been a lot of talk amongst the other Loelifes, and I'm only getting involved because I care… It's better me than someone else, *right?*' Her voice was clearer so I presumed that Phoenix was no longer strangling her.

'What talk are to talking about? Who's been chatting?' Phoenix demanded loudly.

'Multiple people, different ranks. Everyone is saying that the baby's not yours.' I put my hand over my mouth to stop myself from cursing out loud.

'I want names!' Phoenix roared.

'Their names don't matter, and you know it.' Widow countered quietly. I could hear the apprehension in her voice. 'Anyway, you shouldn't be surprised.' She said snidely. 'I mean first, she was nabbed by the Recons in Brixton, on your watch, and then she popped up after falling off the face of the earth for a couple of years! And to top it all off, now she's the bloody wife of a flipping MP! I'm sorry but I don't buy it.'

'She was deported to Jamaica, and he brought her back home simple! She told me what happened, and she did what she had to do to survive, she did what anyone would do.' Phoenix hissed and I smiled proudly at his defence of me.

'Yeah, yeah, yeah, I've heard all the stories! Come on Phoenix, use your big damn head… and I'm talking about *the one above your neck* not between your legs!' I waited for Phoenix's response but none came.

'Who are you trying to fool huh? The girl was a *nobody, a ghost, a common deportee*, and then she becomes front-page news overnight? Something smells fishy!'

'Just shut up Widow, and keep your flipping mug out of my damn business!' Phoenix grunted.

'I will. Once you get your bloody house in order. Now get the hell out of my way!' There was silence for a few seconds before Widow stormed out of the shadows.

'Why are you always watching me anyway? You've got too much time on your hands you know that?' Phoenix jibed as he sauntered out of the darkness after her. 'It's coming like you want a slice or something...' He laughed; his body language puffed up and full of bravado.

'I wouldn't touch you with a shitty barge pole!' Widow's spat as she put her hands on her hips.

'That's not what you said once upon a time.' he chuckled slyly, 'Don't worry, you're too old for me anyway.'

'Watch it, Phoenix!' She hissed as he slapped her arse on his way towards the road. I raised an eyebrow as I stepped away from the circle of baggers almost choking on the apparent toxic sexual tension.

'This isn't over!' She shouted at his back. Phoenix laughed and held his middle finger up as he sauntered across the road. 'Don't blame me when you find yourself face down in Alexandra Lake!' She snorted. 'And don't say I didn't bloody warn you!' She continued, mumbling to herself as he disappeared out of site. 'What the hell are you all looking at?' She screeched zeroing in on her homeless audience as she began to pace up and down on the cracked pavement. I pulled my hood further over my head and faced the fire just as a car rolled up to the curb. I could still feel Widow eyes shooting daggers into my back as she got into the vehicle. I didn't turn around until the car finally sped off. I then hurriedly slipped away from the barrel fire taking only a few minutes to walk the short distance downhill to my block. I nervously anticipated the look on Phoenix's face when he got home to an empty flat, considering that he had left me at dinner over two hours ago. I turned the key in the lock and immediately saw that Phoenix hadn't come home yet. The house was completely black, and I burned with anger. Not only had he dumped me at dinner, but he couldn't even be bothered to come home and at least check on me. I slammed the door without going inside and clicked on my sliders. Taking long strides down the corridor I zoomed down the stairs out of the building and all the way to the end of the long winding road. The weather was slightly bitter, and the sharp breeze nipped at my cheeks as I continued to glide towards an unknown destination. My feet kept on moving as my mind went around and around in circles matching the pace off my persistent strides. Before long the backroads began to get busier, making them trickier to navigate in gliding boots, and I lost my momentum weaving in and out of the thickening crowds. I was now out of breath, and it was only then that I realised how far I'd come. I had never been to this part of the slums before. I clicked off my sliders as the flashing neon signs lit up the pavement in front of me. I had naively sailed right into *The Valley*, the ghetto's allocated red-light district. I must have made a wrong turn somewhere. Worst still my legs were exhausted, and with all my adrenalin used up, I had no more energy to glide back home. I turned back and tried to retrace my steps, but only ended up walking around in circles for longer than I cared to remember. Reluctantly I decided to hitchhike, hoping that a kind soul would stop for a pregnant woman lost in the wrong part of town. I teetered on the curb and I held my thumb out, praying that I could catch a ride back to my side of the slums. Noone seemed be taking notice of me and after a few minutes of endless passing traffic, I leaned back against a lamppost to take the weight off my throbbing feet. Maybe I'd have more luck on the other side of the road. I heaved myself forward and waited for a gap in the traffic before attempting to cross. But I was suddenly startled by a large vehicle cutting off my route as it mounted the curb in front of me. My heart was beating erratically, *did that car just try to knock me down?* I thought breathing heavily as I peered into the tinted windows of the large jeep. The rear window slowly began to wind down, and my stomach dropped as I saw Widow staring back at me from the back seat. Her mask shimmered scarlet lighting up the darkness around her face.

'Hello *Raine.*' she said finally, fashioning her plump red pout into a little insincere smile. I took a deep breath before answering.

'Do I know you?' I asked narrowing my eyes.

'You should...' She said smugly. 'But then again... I don't believe that we've ever been introduced. 'I'm Widow,' she said, her eyes boring into mine. I smiled wanly in response, and she met my silence with a stony stare.

'You lost? Get in, I'll give you a lift home.' Widow smiled and the sudden reappearance of her masked smile sent a shiver down my spine.

'No... I'm ok thanks.' I said turning away.

'Nonsense!' she said impatiently. 'I saw your thumb sticking out, clearly you need a lift so let me give you a ride.'

'I'm fine, really,' I insisted.

'Well–' she paused eyeing me up and down. 'You shouldn't really be out here alone at this time of night.' Widow tutted shaking her head. 'Don't you know there are people out here who would cut you open, sell your baby on the black market without a second thought?' She leaned out of the window as she said it, and smiled again showing off her pearly white teeth. 'So, I would suggest that you jump in.'

'Thanks for the warning, but I'm perfectly fine!' I snapped as I began to walk away.

'Don't be silly,' Widow called to my back as I sped up into a brisk march. 'Besides... what kind of woman would I be if I left you out here and something happened to you.' She trailed off as the door on the opposite side of the vehicle popped open and two Inferiors jumped out. My heart dropped as I nervously looked over my shoulder to see the Inferiors creeping around the vehicle towards me. My mouth dried up as I began to panic, and quickening my pace across the pavement, I weighed up the slim possibility of reaching the crowd of people loitering outside a building a few feet up ahead. I clutched my stomach as the Inferiors suddenly blocked my path.

'Don't touch me!' I spat as they reached out to grab me.

'Well, go on then! what the hell are you waiting for?' Widow snapped as I tried to sidestep them. 'Just *take* her!'

'HELP!' I cried as the Inferiors suddenly seized me by the arms. 'Let me go!' I shrieked trying to shake them off.

'Quietly!' Widow called from the back seat as they dragged me across the pavement yelling and screaming. One of the Inferiors attempted to cover my mouth and I bit at his fingers.

'What the hell are you doing out there?' Widow yelled impatiently. 'Stop messing around and put the bloody bitch in the car!' She barked from the back seat.

'Well, well, what on earth is going on here then?'

'Rook! what are you doing here?' Widow said seemingly startled as she stuck her head out of the open door. She eyed her Inferiors standing a few feet away from me with their heads bowed like repri-manded children. I stood beside this *Rook* character for my own safety.

'So, what's all this malarkey then?' Rook asked suspiciously as he stooped to peer inside the vehicle.

'I don't know what you mean.' Widow said flatly as she leapt out. She slammed the car door and took a step towards us.

'Widow, I ain't gonna ask you again,' Rook said sternly, 'what are you up too?'

'What I'm up too is *none* of your bloody business *Rook*… and since you're new to this rank.' She narrowed her eyes as she stepped up to his tall frame. 'I suggest you take it down a notch and remember who you're talking too.'

Rook rolled his neck and chuckled loudly.

'Well, it does concern me when whatever you're up too is happening on my patch, and is possibly affecting *my* business.' He replied as a large smirk stretched the material of his mask.

'Whatever?' Widow laughed. 'This is Merlin's turf,' she scoffed dismissively as she snapped her fingers giving her Inferiors permission to move.

'Not since he lost it in a bet two weeks ago.' Rook sniggered as he stepped in front of them blocking their route towards me. 'And unlike Merlin,' he said smugly looking down at her, 'I'm not going to let *you* take the piss in *my territory*.'

'Is that right…' Widow said scornfully. 'And what do you think Rex would have to say about you and Merlin gambling with the districts?'

'Hmmm, I don't know Widow… What do you think Rex *and the rest of court* would say about you kidnapping innocent pregnant women? Surely the constituents of our fair little city will want restitution for such a heinous act…'

'Kidnapping?' Widow said kissing her teeth. 'That's preposterous!' She scoffed. 'I was merely helping out a sister in need.'

'Oh ok… So, I, and about 30 witnesses standing outside of my club over there, must have just heard screams of thanks and appreciation then?' Rook jibed.

'I don't know what you mean.' Phoenix said haughtily sticking her nose into the air. 'Raine my dear,' Widow said, having the audacity to address me by name in a sickly-sweet tone. 'Could you kindly tell my friend *Rook* here that I was only offering you a lift home.' I stared at her in disbelief, I was so angry that I was almost visibly shaking.

'Look sweetie,' she said when I didn't answer. 'Let's not make this any more problematic than it has to be, ok? Just tell Rook everything is fine!' she said through clenched lips and gritted teeth.

'Any *more* problematic?' I snapped.

'Your Inferiors just physically violated me.' I grunted angrily as I crossed my arms across my protruding stomach.

'Violated! Now that's a very strong word don't you think?' She chuckled awkwardly, trying to play it down. 'They were merely assisting you– '

'Well Widow, it looks like you've been saved from making an unnecessary trip.' Rook announced cutting her off, 'and I'm sure you have somewhere very important to be,' he said sarcastically as he gestured for Widow to get back into her car. She snapped her fingers at her Inferiors before she reluctantly got inside. Rook slammed the door shut behind her as the Inferiors clambered inside the vehicle behind her. She glared at me through her open window, only looking away as the car sped off.

'What's Widow got against you?' Rook asked as we both watched the car violently speed off down the road and around a corner. I shrugged my shoulders, ignoring the funny feeling inside my stomach. It was suddenly tying itself up into tight knots as I looked up at his tall frame. He seemed familiar and that made me feel safe. 'What are you doing around here all alone at this time of night anyway?' He asked in his disguised voice and I didn't respond. 'Does Phoenix know you're out here?' I looked into his eyes, but he looked away as he scolded me, gazing off into the distance.

'I just needed to walk.' I sighed feeling slightly obligated to give him some sort of explanation. Since he had just practically rescued me from the clutches of Widow and company.

'Well, you definitely wandered into the wrong part of the slums.' Rook said glancing down at my belly.

'So, there's a right part?' I huffed as I put my hand on my hips.'

'Oh, so you got jokes yeah,' Rook smiled as his mask flashed a streak of gold. 'But jokes aside, trust me it's not safe out here.' He said as a black car slowly ground to a halt in front of us. The passenger window rolled down and Rook greeted the driver before opening the rear passenger side door. 'This is my guy, Blue' he said nodding towards the driver and throwing up the LOE hand sign. 'He'll take you home,' he said avoiding my gaze as he opened the car door. I stepped inside the vehicle and sunk down into the plush back seat,

'Thank you,' I said gratefully.

'Don't mention it.' Rook said as he shut the door behind me and turned back to the diver. 'Blue, take her straight home and then meet me back here, we got urgent business to attend too.'

***

'I'll deal with it.' I was confused by Phoenix's lack of reaction.

'That crazy bitch just tried to kidnap me, and that's all you have to say?' I cried angrily as I sat on the end of my bed in my dressing gown staring up at Phoenix in disbelief. He stood opposite me in a towel leaning back against the dressing table.

'What were you doing in the Valley anyway?' He asked coldly.

'Didn't you hear what I *just* said?' I screamed in frustration. 'Widow just tried to have me thrown in the back of her flipping car and you're acting like you don't even care!' I stood up putting my hands on my widening hips. 'Have you slept with her?' I snapped thinking about their weird interaction the night before. He stopped what he was doing for a moment and glared down at me.

'Don't be stupid!' He said staring into my puffy eyes.

'Then why aren't you bothered by what she tried to do to me?'

'Well, it looks like Rook was conveniently there to save you, wasn't he? So, no harm no foul.' He said spitefully. I couldn't believe what he was saying, he knew that I'd never even met Rook before.

'*No harm no foul*? Are you flipping serious!' I snapped walking towards him. 'I can't believe you're actually jealous right now! What about Widow? You have to do something!' I cried hysterically, 'how can you let that bitch get away with this!'

'Raine, get out of my face!' He barked loudly as he kicked the dresser. 'I said I'll deal with it!' I shrunk for a second as he bellowed at me, half jumping out of my skin, and also remembering how he had grabbed Widow by the throat last night. I leapt out of his way as Phoenix stomped away in frustration. I sighed and sulkily threw myself down on the bed. I lay on my back and gazed up at the ceiling as I pulled my right hand across my stomach to where the baby had just delivered a flurry of kicks. The combo took my breath away and I lay still for moment, trying to listen and sense the baby's presence inside me.

'And you're still going to leave after everything I've just told you?' I asked as soon as Phoenix came back into the room fully dressed. He turned his head and glanced at me blankly as he continued to pack. 'You just got back,' I said sitting up.

'I already told you that I wasn't staying.' He said without turning around to face me.

'But that was before I told you what happened last night.' I whined; not wanting to be alone.

'I don't feel safe by myself.' I mumbled feeling a little emotional.

'Why don't you telecall Rook, I'm sure he'll come over and keep you warm.' He retorted shrugging his shoulders. I mumbled obscenities under my breath as tears began to sting my eyes.

'When are you coming back?' I muttered as he buckled up his belt.

'I'll be gone for one night,' he replied as he pulled on his shoes. 'Two nights max.' I heaved myself towards the end of the bed until my legs were hanging over the end as he walked around the bed to kiss me on the forehead. I turned my face away and he kissed his teeth before walking straight out of the front door without uttering goodbye.

15

SHADOWS

Knock, knock... My eyes darted open as I subconsciously heard a knock at the door. The VTV was still one and I stared at it for a moment until I heard it again. I waited for a third knock before I sat upright and clutched my stomach. *Who is that at this time of night?* I thought as I scooted to the edge of the bed. My feet delicately touched the carpet, and felt out my slippers in the dark as another knock cut through the silence. Panicking, I heaved myself up and tiptoed towards the hallway, pulling on my dressing gown as I went. I listened intently as I carefully crept up to the front door. I could hear voices as I put my face against the peep hole, and saw shadows in the dark hallway.

'We know that you're in there, so you might as well open the door.' I clutched my chest catching the sight of three masked Loelifes standing in the corridor.

'What do you want?' I asked nervously, stumbling backwards in the darkness.

'You have been summoned to court. You have five minutes to come out voluntarily.'

'What!' I exclaimed in confusion as I flicked on the light and pressed my face against the door.

'Raine Montrose, Rex has summoned you to court,' the Loelife in the middle repeated.

'This must be a mistake! What would the leader of the LOE Society want with me?' I said anxiously.

'That's on a need-to-know basis, and all you need to know is that Rex has requested your presence.' The same Loelife remarked with an air of authority. She flashed a hologram in front of the peephole, and I saw that it was a summons with my name on it demanded that I appear in court immediately. I rubbed my forehead as my mind tried to think of a way out of this situation.

'And... If I refuse to attend?' I asked nervously, making the two other Loelifes behind the one in charge exchange glances.

'Well… we've been sent to retrieve you by any means necessary.' The Loelife in the middle said as she stepped forward and looked straight into the peephole. Her eye met mine and I backed away from the door. 'By the way,' She called as she rapped a rhythm on the door with her fingernails, 'you've got three minutes left before we break this door down.'

***

I was escorted to Alexandra Palace and delivered to a holding area deep within the building. I could hear echoing voices on the other side of a large door, and I was left alone for a moment as that strange feeling began to build up in the pit of my stomach. Then without warning one of the Loelifes returned, opened the large door in front of me and violently shoved me through it. I was suddenly standing at the back of a large wooden stage, and I froze as I looked around at the mass of masked Loelifes that filled the room. They murmured amongst themselves, exchanging questioning glances as they watched me closely. A thin layer of sweat quickly covered my entire body and my stomach was now twisting so much that I felt physically sick. Rex sat elevated above the crowd on a large wooden throne on a raised platform in the middle of the stage. This first time I had seen him in the flesh and I only dared to steal glances at his imposing full-faced mask as her glared down at me. To the right of him, there seemed to be what could only be described as a jury of Superior Loelifes. They were seated slightly beneath him, each one of their faces covered with an extravagant mask of a different design. I saw Widow and Rook sitting among them but not Phoenix. I jumped anxiously as Rex banged a staff on the wooden floor of the stage to settle the murmuring crowd.

'You!' he bellowed making a chill run down my spine. His voice was robotic as I had expected, typical of the voice changing tech that higher ranking Loelifes often used. 'You *may* proceed to the dock,' he said imposingly, and I gulped taking my time to walk across the stage. I paused before cautiously stepping into the small wooden enclosure.

'Now to the next order of business,' Rex said turning back to me as I took my seat. His mask gave off a green glow as did the special contact lenses covering his eyes. 'You,' he said again point at me with his long wooden staff. 'State your name for the court.'

'Erm… Raine Montrose,' I said nervously as I cast my eyes over at the audience. A sea of shadowy masked faces peered back at me, their contact lenses flashing an array of different colours.

'Raine Montrose,' Rex stated drawing my attention back to him. 'You have been accused of sedition and conspiracy to commit high treason. How do you plead?' I gasped as the crowd began to mutter.

'High treason!' I blurted out as Rex watched me intently. 'Accused by who?' I asked in alarm.
Rex banged his staff on the platform and held up a palm to quieten the watching crowd.

'How… do… you… plead?' Rex repeated with a hint of impatience in his synthetic voice. Silence settled over the audience as the room waited with bated breath for me my answer.

'Not guilty!' I said finally after taking a deep breath.

'Hmm,' Rex said as he squinted at me.

'Is that your final plea?' he pressed as whispers drifted in from the Audience.

'*Yes!*' I said breathlessly as the whispering grew louder.

'Are you not the same Raine Montrose that was detained at the Hermitage Hill Detention Facility?'

'I am...' I replied firmly trying to sound confident.

'The very same Raine Montrose who then escaped and found refuge at the Brixton safehouse?'

'Yes, but what's that got to do with any—'

'Only to be recaptured and deported to Jamaica a few months later?'

'Yes but I...'

'The one and very same fugitive now known for seducing a MP, *a former member of The House of Lords* no less, into providing you with safe passage back to the UK?'

'Yes, but I only…'

'A simple yes or no will suffice.' Rex said cutting me off again as he glared down from his throne. 'Not only are you *not* a member of the LOE society, or in any way affiliated with the League of Equality, apart from your dubious links to one of my Senior Loelifes.' He paused as he glanced over at his jury. 'The authorities seem to believe that *you* can give *them* information about *me* and *my* organization.' He paused again as he looked down at the Senior Loelifes beneath him. 'Therein lies the problem,' he said finally. 'Besides the fact that some members of my inner circle find your turbulent history suspicious at best, you've gotten one of my most loyal officers to compromise himself in the futile search for you incarcerated relatives.'

'It wasn't like that—,' 'So,' Rex said loudly over me, 'what do you have to say for yourself?' I took a deep breath unable to escape the stare of a thousand pairs of eyes.

'What do you want me to say?' I said boldly, 'I'm not ashamed of anything I had to do to stay alive!' I added loudly determined to show that I had nothing wrong. 'My past doesn't prove me guilty of anything, except relentless survival.'

'Ah...But can a relentless survivor be trusted? Since you'll do anything to survive, what would you do if you were caught, say in a Recon raid for instance.' Rex mused as the crowd began to murmur again. 'What were to happen if they tortured you, flayed your family in front of you hmm? Totally hypothetically of course.' I sighed loudly. I knew that a Recon raid hadn't happened since the beginning of the resistance and was very unlikely to occur again.

'I don't even know anything, and I haven't done anything wrong!' I pleaded. 'How can you punish me for a crime I haven't even committed yet!' I turned my face to the audience to garner some sympathy. 'Is this what you call justice?'

'Rex, this is ridiculous!' Widow spat, suddenly jumping to her feet. 'Come on... I mean it is obvious the girl is a dirty little spy!'

'Remember your place!' Rex snapped viciously, 'how dare you speak out of turn in my courtroom!'

'My apologies Rex,' Widow said nervously as she cleared her throat. 'Please may I address the court?' She waited patiently for Rex to nod his permission before she spoke again. 'The woman sitting before you is a spy!' She said pointing right at me. 'She is an unnecessary liability and a threat to the entire LOE Society!' Widow spoke eloquently addressing the room as she gracefully moved across the stage in her black catsuit. 'Do not buy into her little act of innocence and naivety, believe you me she's been well trained,' she hissed with vim and disdain in her voice as she turned to face me. 'Not only can she *not* be trusted, but she also puts everything we stand for as an organisation at risk!' I watched as her mask swirled red matching her obvious anger. 'Rex, I beg that you deal with this *situation* before it gets out of hand! We just cannot not allow any outside infiltration. As you all know we need to weed any spies out by the root and cut off their blood supply.' I had to defend myself, surely this was defamation of character!

'And when you say deal with the situation, do you mean by way of kidnapping before the appropriate intel is gathered, and a conclusion established?' Rook said in a smooth robotic tone as he rose from his seat before I had a chance to speak. He now stood tall amongst the small, seated group of Loelifes as he addressed the court.

'Explain yourself!' Rex said turning to face him.

'Rex, forgive me for speaking out of turn but I couldn't stand by and say nothing when I have–'

'Widow tried to kidnap me,' I blurted suddenly standing inside my wooden box.

'Liar!' she screamed furiously as she spun around to face me. She was standing at the front of the stage in between Rex's throne and the jury. Rex picked up his engraved staff and banged it loudly on the stage floor.

'Enough!' He bellowed in his deep synthetic voice.

'Rook, what is the meaning of this!' Rex demanded as the crowd continued muttering amongst themselves.

'Well… I believe that I witnessed the attempted kidnapping of the defendant.' Rook said calmly sitting back down in his chair as a few gasps erupted from the crowd. 'So, it seems to me that Widow attempted to deal with this matter outside of the court, without making you privy first Rex.'

'This is absolutely ludicrous!' Widow protested, 'It's… it's Sabotage!' She screeched hysterically, 'Sacrilege!'

'Widow, explain yourself!' Rex demanded but for once Widow seemed speechless, and she silently looked around as we all stared back at her waiting for a response.

'It was nothing Rex, just a minor misunderstanding that's all.' She said nervously.

'Are you trying to make a fool out of me in front of the entire court?' Rex grunted as he leaned forward and glared down at her.

'No, no, no, of course not!' She said as she backed away.

'Then fucking Elaborate!' Rex bellowed, his altered voice echoing around the grand hall. Widow sighed loudly as she took her seat at the front of the jury. 'Get up!' Rex barked as he flicked his finger at her.

'Well...' Widow said quietly as she jumped to a stand. 'Raine here was in the valley the other night... and I merely offered her a lift home that was erm, slightly misconstrued... and that's all it was, completely nothing untoward.'

'Are you calling me a liar?' Rook said provokingly.

'Stay out of this, it has nothing to do with you!' Widow retorted bitterly through gritted teeth as both their masks swirled with random flashes of colour. 'Do I have to remind you of where your loyalties lie Rook?' She hissed maliciously.

'Enough!' Rex growled striking his wooden staff onto the stage one more time. 'I will deal with you later!' he hissed pointing the staff towards Widow as she skulked back down into her seat. Rook also sat back down as Rex turned to address me. The audience was engulfed in a flurry of whispers 'As for you Raine Montrose,' he said as if he was tired of saying and hearing my name. 'You will no longer be allowed to exist in the limbo of the slums. With a entangled history such as yours, I cannot allow you to live as an ordinary citizen.'

My stomach churned uncomfortably as I wondered where he was going with this, *maybe he would send me back to Brixton!* I thought excitedly. 'However, you will be given the opportunity to prove your loyalty to us, and this will be your one and only chance to establish your trustworthiness. At the next court session, I will officially initiate you into the LOE Society as an menial

Loelife.' I swallowed hard to keep the sudden rise of bile down.

'I...I can't...!' I said glancing down at my swollen belly as my vision began to blur. The crowd gasped at my inappropriate outburst and immediately began to heckle me. Several people threw random objects that hit the glass on the outside of the wooden box. I flinched under the unexpected assault.

'You dare to defy me, after such a gracious opportunity!' Rex grunted as I wiped the tears freefalling down my face. 'My proposition was not a request! But if you rather I withdraw the offer, there are other ways I will deal with you.' Rex said squinting down at me as the audience began to jostle in excitement.

'Rex, if I may address the court?' Rook said standing up again with his L-shaped hand sign held in the air above his head. Rex sighed as he rolled his eyes towards him before giving him a stiff nod. 'Shouldn't the defendant be given some time to process your generous offer given the condition she's in?' I looked up at Rook as he gave me a ray of hope. 'It's only right considering this trial has conveniently occurred in Phoenix's absence.' He said glancing down at Widow. 'Plus, the defendant is emotional, and heavily pregnant with whom we can only assume is Phoenix's progeny.' I glanced over at Rook to thank him but he wouldn't even look in my direction.

Rex tapped his fingers on the arm of his throne and tilted his head backwards in contemplation.

'Very well!' he announced after a moment of thought as he dismissed Rook with a wave of his hand.

'Upon Phoenix's return, *you*, Raine Montrose will immediately be sworn into the LOE.'

***

I opened my front door and heaved my heavy bulk inside. It had been one hell of a night and I groaned loudly as I unbuttoned my coat over my taut stomach. I hung it up, slipped off my shoes and walked straight towards the kitchen, wincing as a brighter light automatically lit up the room. My head was hurting, my stomach was twinging, and my mouth was incredibly dry. I sluggishly dragged my swollen feet across the smooth linoleum floor and grabbed a bottle of water out of the fridge. I sighed loudly as I retrieved a clean glass out of the cupboard and hastily poured myself a drink. I put the glass to my lips but almost choked as I caught the sight of a shimmering mask in the reflection of the kitchen window. My blood ran cold, and the glass slipped as I scrambled to grab a knife off the draining board. I whipped around just as the glass smashed loudly on the tiled floor.

'What do you want!' I spluttered loudly, clutching my chest with one hand and the knife in the other.

'I'm sorry, I didn't mean to scare you.' I lowered the knife slightly as I realised the mask belonged to Rook. He stood in the dim light of the hallway, the material of his mask reflecting off the artificial kitchen light.

'I thought you were Widow!' I snapped leaning back onto the counter as he walked into the brighter light of the kitchen. 'What the hell do you want?' I demanded still in a state of shock.

'And what are you doing in my flat? how did you even get in?' I ranted keeping a firm grip on the blade. 'Did you follow me home?'

'Is this any way to treat the *only* person that had your back tonight?' He let out what seemed like a nervous chuckle as he leaned against the fridge and swung the door open, turning his back on me as if I didn't have a weapon.

'Don't play games with me Rook!' I hissed agitatedly still pointing the knife at him. I watched him bend down to scan the empty shelves. 'What do you want?' I demanded impatiently staring at his back as he made himself at home. Rook slowly shut the fridge door and turned around to face me.

'Raine… we need to talk...' He said standing upright.

'We?' I said looking at him suspiciously. 'What in the world could *we* have to talk about?' He was avoiding eye contact, like he always did. 'Is this about Phoenix? Well? Hello… why are you here?' I spat jabbing the knife into the thin air between us as I spoke. He seemed distant, like he was carrying the whole world on his shoulders.

'Look, I need to tell you something but please just put the knife down first.'

'Now why would I want to do that?' I said still firmly gripping the blade in my hand.

'Because...' he took a long deep sigh as he rubbed his face and stepped towards me.

'That's close enough...' I said as he closed the space between us. The baby chose that exact moment to kick and I staggered backwards, bumping into the counter.

'Raine, be careful there's broken glass every-where. Just calm down, you must know that I'm not a threat by now.' Rook said as he continued to come closer.

'I can't trust anyone,' I hissed through clenched teeth as the baby kicked again. 'Let alone you. Now. Just. Stop. Moving!' I panted waving the knife around until he stopped just out of my reach.

'Ok ok, just listen...' He said with his hands raised.

'What for?' I hissed still brandishing the knife.

'I'm... It's just... look, I'm here to help you ok... I can get you out of the slums...tonight.' He said turning away from me and looking out of the kitchen win-dow.

'Why! Why would you do that for me?' I asked in bewilderment as he let out an exasperated sigh.

'Look, it's not safe to tell you now, someone could be watching.'

'What? Who's watching?' I asked confused as I glanced around.

'Look, it doesn't matter, I just know you're not happy here, so let me get you out!'

'And how would you know that?' I said nar-rowing my eyes. 'Have you been spying on me?'

'Course not!' He said shaking his head innocently.

'Then how would you know that I'm unhappy?' He attempted to respond but I wouldn't let him. 'You need to leave.' I said without taking another breath. 'Now!'

'Raine, if you would just listen to me for one minute…'

'I said GET OUT!' I screamed swiping the knife at him.

'Ray Ray please!' He shouted grabbing my arm. 'I will tell you everything when we leave...' He sighed as he looked deep into my eyes, and my stomach lurched, almost leaving me breathless. It was the first time I had seen him up close without contact lenses and my head began to spin.

'What did you just call me?' I asked my heart beat increasing rapidly as I began to shake.

'I'm sorry, I just couldn't risk telling you before.' He said as he slowly lifted his arm and pulled off his mask.

'Ryan!' I said breathlessly as the knife slipped out of my hand and clattered loudly onto the floor.

'I'm so sorry!' He mumbled, 'I couldn't tell you, I, I have enemies, I had to protect you… I'm sorry'

'You're sorry!' I screeched as tears of anger, confusion and shock streamed down my face.

'Ryan, I thought you were dead! and you mean to tell me that you've been here under my bloody nose this entire time?' I shouted furiously, not knowing whether to hug him or slap him around the face.

'I know…' he said sheepishly. 'I should have… I should have taken you away from all this madness already,' he muttered tearing up.

This new information was too much for my tired brain to process, and my stomach twitched violently as if to say *I told you so*. As I knew deep down somehow. The day I met him in the valley, He walk, his stance, his frame was all so familiar I should have known. But I thought he was dead.

He put a hand on my shoulder and I shook him off.

'Don't touch me!' I cried turning my back on him. Tears blurred my vision as a crippling pain suddenly shot through my lower stomach. I stumbled, cutting my foot on a piece of broken glass and I lost my footing. But Ryan was close enough to catch me before I hit the ground. I fell, like a heap into his embrace and broke down weeping uncontrollably. I grunted into his shoulder, and he held me upright as another cramp ripped through my abdomen making my legs buckle. A slimy liquid suddenly gushed down my thighs and splashed onto my feet. My waters had broken,

'It's too early!' I cried before the next contraction crippled me into silence. It took my breath away as Ryan carried me over to the kitchen table and hoisted me up on top of it as I began to scream.

16

SECRETS

I woke up groggy and woozy from the painkillers, but I could no longer sleep. I slowly rolled over onto my side as my eyes focused on the tall dark figure standing over my baby's cot.

'What are you still doing here?' I said croakily as I cleared my throat. My voice was horse from screaming, and I slowly reached out for the jug of water on the bedside cabinet. Ryan grabbed the jug before I could get to it and poured me a glass of water.

'I needed to make sure you were ok... plus we still need to talk,' he said quietly, and I winced as I sat up in bed properly and took the glass.

'I'm not talking to you with that mask on.' I said coldly as I took a sip. I watched him draw the circular curtain around the cubicle and then stand at the end of my bed. He pulled the mask up letting it rest on the tip of his forehead.

'And the contact lenses…' I said as I put the glass down and crossed my arms. Ryan sighed as he removed his LOE issue lenses and placed them in a little tube he retrieved from his pocket.

'Raine I'm sorry,' he said looking up at me as he walked around the bed.

'Ryan, don't ok just don't,' I said looking away from him. The unmeasured joy I had initially felt when he had removed my mask had instantly transformed into anger and disdain. 'Do you have any idea what I've been through?' I croaked. 'And what happened to our entire family? How could you look me in the eye and lie to my face? For so long!' I said as my already tired eyes began to burn. 'I thought I'd lost you… But you were here the whole time, playing flipping vigilantes with the bloody LOE Society while our entire family is locked up in Hermitage Hill!' Tears suddenly came flooding down my cheeks. 'Ry, Dad went to pick you up and he never came back! He's probably dead for all I know!' I hissed as I tried to sit up. 'The bloody psychotic Recons killed Maxwell, and Granddad died in the back of a fucking snuff van!' I sniffled, wiping my nose on my forearm. 'He died Ryan! And God knows what's happened to Deja and Skye! And what about mum huh? Rico, Aunty Pam, Grandma, Uncle Kenny!' I rubbed my forehead remembering the distress that I had buried deep down within me for such a long time. 'How long have you even been hiding out here anyway?' I demanded as Ryan silently met my gaze. He looked ashamed, as he should be.

'I already said that it's not safe to talk about this here.' he said under his breath.

'Ok,' I whispered wiping my eyes. 'So… what is it you want to talk about then huh? Because I'd really love to know why the *hell* you didn't come home!'

'Keep your voice down!' Ryan snapped agitatedly.

'No, not until I get an answer!' 'I said angrily as my eyes bored into his.

'It's complicated ok.' He hissed a hushed voice looking away from me, 'right now we need to discuss getting you out of here before Phoenix comes–'

'Complicated!' I cried, sobbing uncontrollably.

'Yes, complicated!' Ryan replied loudly. 'Don't you think I wanted… that I tried to get home before they–' he trailed off, 'but by the time I got a chance to… It was already too late, the house was wrecked, and you were gone.' He began to pace up and down as he cracked his knuckles, something he always did when he was anxious.

'It just feels like you don't care!' I cried.

'Don't be stupid, of course, I care!' Ryan said as he stopped pacing and turned to face me. 'I just think you're too emotional to take all of this on right now…' He sighed as I suddenly lurched forward in pain. I took a deep breath and groaned loudly as the sharp pain grew in my lower stomach.

'What is it?' Ryan asked as he rushed to my bedside, realizing that something was wrong. I grabbed his hand as the pain reached its peak before it quickly subsided.

'It's nothing, just an aftershock,' I breathed as I let go of his hand. 'We need to get our family out of that God forsaken place Ryan, it's been years!' I panted loudly as Ryan circled the confined space of the cubicle watching me closely.

'Enough Raine, like I said we can't talk about this here!' Ryan declared, quickly pulling his mask down over his face as if we were being watched. He peaked through the curtain before turning around to face me.

'Right now, I need to figure out how to get *you* out of the slums before Phoenix gets back.' I grunted loudly as the searing pain ripped across my lower belly like a tidal wave.

'Raine, what's wrong, tell me!' Ryan demanded rushing back over to me as I doubled over in pain again. I tried to breathe through it, but the pain rolled across my stomach like a riptide until I cried out in agony. 'We need a doctor in here now!' Ryan shouted as the white bed sheets suddenly turned a bright shade red underneath me. 'Where's the doctor!' I watched Ryan's disappear as he flew through the cubicle curtain and returned with a nurse and a doctor in tow. My eyes rolled back as another sharp pain shot threw my uterus. *Maybe something went wrong with the birth,* I thought horrified. I suddenly heard my newborn baby cry as I continued to writhe around unable to reach her.

'I don't want to die!' I sobbed as I suddenly felt myself being examined. More staff rushed into the cubicle and they held down my flaying limbs. I could hear Ryan's voice through the chaos telling me that I was going to be ok.

'Calm down Raine you're going to be fine,' a doctor said sternly over the baby's cries. 'You're not dying! Just listen to the sound of my voice and on the count of three... I need you to push!'

'Push! Push what?' I cried hysterically.

'Listen to me Raine, there's another baby coming ok, so you need to get ready to push!'

'Another what! I screamed frantically.

'Just relax and take a deep breath... Are you ready?'

'No!' I screamed in distress.

'Ok good girl... On my count. 1... 2... 3... Push!'

***

'Raine, are you listening to me?' I sighed loudly... after two days in the palace clinic, I was too tired to cater to Phoenix's jealousy and insecurities. So, I ignored him as I looked out at the dark morning sky through the large window opposite my cubicle. There were other women around, some heavily pregnant, some with occupied cribs by their bed. No doubt they were connected to Loelifes being admitted to the Alexandra clinic. Ordinary citizens were forced to pay for subpar care at infirmary located in the mews. 'What the hell was Rook doing here?' He asked again. I continued to ignore him as I listened to the sound of the ward stirring to life around us. I tried to use the sound of a baby crying in the corner to drown out his irritating voice. 'Raine, answer the damn question!'

Phoenix barked as he paced towards me with my first-born daughter Tia in his arms. I didn't respond as I settled down on the bed with my youngest daughter Mya. She was a bonus, but born a few hours after Tia she didn't favour Phoenix at all. I stroked her little face as I got ready to feed her.

'Raine!' Phoenix hissed angrily, jolting me out of my daze just as a female doctor waltzed into the cubicle and silently drew the curtains around the bed. We both stared at her and when she was done, she stood idly at the end of my bed. She must have felt the tension between us because she just smiled awkwardly before grabbing my chart and looking down at it for a long time. She looked professional and I wondered if she had been a doctor on the *outside* before ending up in the slums.

'So, how are mother and babies doing?' She asked as she hung my chart back onto the bedrail and finally looked up. 'The second birth was a little stressful huh?'

'And unexpected!' I snorted 'but I'm ok considering...' I glanced up at the doctor who was gazing down at Mya cradled in my arms.

'What about dad?' The doctor asked enthusiastically gazing over at Phoenix in the corner of the cubicle. 'Well, I'm just *fucking dandy!*' Phoenix said sarcastically in a phony voice as he flashed an over exaggerated fake smile. The doctor grimaced but kept her professional poise as she turned back to me.

'Now Raine, I know you're probably still a little groggy and sore but I'm going to have to give you a little examination before I can let you go.' She smiled again as she pulled on a pair of white latex gloves from out of a cubby on the wall. 'Sorry dad but you're going to have to step outside for just a moment.' She chirped as she glanced over at Phoenix. He nodded and turned to leave the cubicle with Tia still cradled in his arms.

'Phoenix, put her down.' I said abruptly sitting upright in bed.

'I'm just taking my daughter outside of the cubicle Raine,' he said coldly.

'Sorry dad,' the doctor said feigning a frown. 'I'm afraid you're going to have to leave your little ones with us for just a few minutes. The doctor said grimacing politely, 'they need to be examined too.' Phoenix gave me a dirty look as he put Tia back into her cot and left the cubicle. Both the doctor and I silently waited for him to leave before speaking again.

'May I?' She asked gesturing towards Mya who was asleep in my arms. I handed her over and watched as the doctor gently placed her inside the cot beside her sister before making her way back over to my bed. She smiled at me wanly probably sensing that my mind was burning with a thousand questions. I watched as she breathed onto the stethoscope, polished it with her doctor's coat and then gently placed it on my chest.

'Raine, are you feeling, ok?' I nodded aware of the fact that she could probably hear my heart beating a hundred times a minute.

'Are you sure, do you usually suffer from heart palpitations?' she asked removing the stethoscope. I shook my heard my and she placed a comforting hand on my arm. 'You're shaking like a leaf.' I opened my mouth to speak but I was too aware that Phoenix must be listening, and nothing came out. She paused for a second before proceeding to wrap the thick Velcro strap around my arm to take my blood pressure. 'I know you must be a little confused,' she said quietly.

'I... I don't understand. How could this happen?' I whispered desperately, my eyes telling her everything she needed to know. The doctor nodded instinctively before leaning in to flash a tiny torch across my eyes. She then stood upright as she dropped the torch into her pocket and retrieved my chart from the bed rail. She began to scribble something down making me feel a little uneasy.

'Should I presume that you're talking about the disparity in your children's physical attributes?' she asked in a hushed voice. I nodded; my heartbeat still slightly elevated way above normal. 'Is the man outside the only possible father?' She asked quietly and I shook my head as she scribbled something else down.

'What are you writing?' I hissed irritably.

'Just a few notes,' she said glancing up.

'Notes about what?' I asked getting annoyed.

'Is the other possible father also...erm.'

'*Black*?' I snapped with an agitated roll of my eyes.

'No, he's white.' I whispered before she could say anything else, aware that Phoenix was probably straining to hear our conversation from behind the curtain.

318

'Apologies I just had to be sure this was a case of Superfecundation.' She said calmly replacing my chart.

'Super what?' I asked confused.

'It simply means you have fraternal twins... by two different fathers,' she said quietly as she examined my stomach through the gown. 'It tends to happen when you have unprotected sex with two partners in close proximity to one another–,'

'Yes, I think I get the picture!' I hissed as she flicked off her latex gloves and finally undid the Velcro strap around my arm. '50 years ago, it would've been something of a phenomenon, but it's quite common these days,' she continued in a faint whisper. 'Funnily enough it usually goes undetected in cases where the fathers are of a *similar* phenotype.' She said furrowing her eyebrows as she pulled on another pair of latex gloves before making her way over to Tia and Mya's cot.

'What exactly is taking so long?' Phoenix demanded as he marched back into the cubicle through the drawn curtain.

'Just wrapping up now dad,' the doctor said cheerfully as if our secret conversation had never occurred. I closed my eyes and took a deep breath as I tried to calm my racing heartbeat. No doubt Phoenix had heard everything, and it was clear that Tia was his child. But it was obvious to anyone with eyes that Mya didn't belong to him. I tried to push it to the back of my mind, thinking that maybe Phoenix might come around somehow.

I thought wrong. By the time we got home we were barely speaking to each other, and I knew that I couldn't keep ignoring his questions like I had been doing for the last few days.

'Please, just let me sleep!' I groaned wearily as he cornered me not allowing me to get onto the bed.

'Not until you tell me the truth about Mya to my face!' Phoenix hissed grabbing my chin and forcing my face up to meet his. 'Did you really think that I was just going to except the fact that she's not mine?' He squeezed my cheeks together as he furiously searched my eyes for an answer, I could see how hurt he was as I stared back at him. 'Answer me!' He growled as his piercing stare infiltrated my soul.

'I'm... sorry,' I whimpered quietly.'

'Sorry!' He grunted shaking me aggressively, 'Is that all you've got to say?' I closed my eyes as tears began to stream down my face. *'You lied to me.* You told me you weren't bloody sleeping with him!' He hissed squeezing my jaw until I opened my eyes. 'I didn't have a choice Phoenix, I, I had too... he's, my husband.' I mumbled.

'Your husband!' he hissed as he stared back at me with eyes as black as coal. 'And what the hell am I then?' He barked crazily. 'Widow was right about you,' he muttered coldly as he pushed my face away. 'And *now* I finally see you for the lying little whore you are.' He looked down at me with unblinking eyes. 'And then there's Rook,' he said with disdain as I retreated to the bed and sat down with my back facing him. 'Did you two– '

320

'Of course not!' I snapped craning my neck to face him.

'Don't lie to me!' he spat angrily as I groaned loudly and cradled my head in my hands.

'Phoenix, please stop,' I pleaded feeling a headache coming on. 'I'm not going over this again!'

'Oh yes you are!' he barked as he marched around the bed and stood over me imposingly.

'Explain to me again how *Rook* just happened to be around when you went into labour!'

'I don't know, he just was!' I snapped looking up into his angry face.

'I don't believe you!' He roared as he kicked the bedframe making me shudder. 'You expect me to believe that after you lied to me about sleeping with that pathetic old sap!' I ignored him and tried to lie down but he forced me to sit upright.

'You're hurting me!' I whined shaking him off.

'So, you're telling me that you weren't with Rook in my yard, in my bed all them nights I left you alone?'

'No!' I yelled jumping him up.

'How I can I even be sure that Tia's my baby!'

'What the *hell* is wrong with you!' I snapped pushing passed him and marching out of the bedroom, 'be quiet, you're going to wake up the twins!' Phoenix kissed his teeth as he followed me out into the hall.

'Twins usually have the same damn father!' He said coldly, and we stood in a silent stalemate for a long moment as I closed the door.

'Just admit it,' Phoenix said calmly trying to change tactics.

'Admit what?' I groaned tiredly putting my hands on my hips as I squinted at him.

'That not only were you sleeping with that gullible old idiot, but you and Rook have been *doing a ting* behind my back!'

'Phoenix, enough!' I cried in disgust as the thumping intensified above my eyes.

'Just tell the truth!' He grunted towering over me as I leaned back against the door.

'No, I'm done with this all I want to do is get a bit of frigging sleep!' I hissed exhausted.

'Well, I'm not done!' Phoenix said through gritted teeth as he put his hands against the door to block me in. 'First Rook turns up when Widow *apparently* tried to kidnap you... Then I hear that he stood up for you in front of Rex and the entire court.' He said angrily, counting the incidents on the fingers he held in front of my face. 'Then he miraculously shows up to be your bloody birthing partner, and then the next thing I know, I come back to find him *still* with you and holding *my* new-born daughter!' He barked standing over me. 'And you expect me to believe it was all some sort of coincidence?'

I sighed loudly as he glared at me.

'You're taking me for a prick!'

'Look Phoenix, I already told you that it wasn't like that!' I sighed feeling completely drained.

'Well come on then, tell me what was it like?' He spat agitatedly.

'I don't know what to tell you Phoenix. He was just there ok, he turned up at the right place at the right time.' I paused as I narrowed my eyes at him. 'And *you* weren't!' I hissed viciously. 'You never are, so maybe you're the one who's cheating on me!' Phoenix looked me dead in the eye for a moment before he slapped me hard across the face. 'You really are taking me for some sort of dickhead!' He hissed as he thumped the door making me flinch. I held my face in shock as he began to pace up and down the hallway. When had almost reached the front door, I rushed into the bedroom and locked the door behind me.

'We're not done!' Phoenix growled as he immediately started banging on the other side.

'Leave me alone!' I cried as I let myself sink down onto the floor.

'Raine open this door!' Phoenix ordered as he continued to pound on it heavily.

'Why!' I sniffled getting to my feet as I wiped the tears from my eyes. 'So, you can hit me again?' I said coldly through the door. The banging suddenly stopped.

'I'm sorry about that, I didn't mean to hurt you... I was just so angry... Let me apologise properly. I, I promised I'll never hit you again.'

'Damn right you won't!' I retorted through the door.

'Come on Raine, just open the door and we can talk properly.'

'I don't want to talk!' I said defiantly as a loud boom made me jump back from the door.

'Raine, I swear to God if you don't open this flipping door, I'll kick it down!'

In that moment I was so grateful for the security feature on each door, so I knew there was no way he was getting in. All went silent as I heard him stamp away. He was probably going to try and override the system at the electric box, little did he know I had changed the codes weeks ago. I listened through the door until I could no longer hear his movements before I walked across the room to check on the twins. Miraculously, they hadn't even stirred and after watching their little chests rise and fall for a few seconds, I made my way to the ensuite to run myself a bath. I was so tired but my mind was racing after what just happened and I retrieved some painkillers from the bathroom cabinet to relieve my headache. I paused in front of the mirror to take a good look at myself. My eyes were red and puffy and one of my brows was swollen from Phoenix's back handed slap. There was a small cut where my skin had burst upon contact with the LOE ring he wore on his index finger. I sighed, sitting down on the edge of the bath in a daze as I listened to the water run into the tub. I closed the tap when it was nearly full and allowed myself to sink into the piping hot water. I dunked my head, wetting my braided hair as I massaged the hot water in between my messy cane rows. I exhaled in relief, finally allowing myself to relax as I closed my eyes.

I was awoken a while later. The water had turned lukewarm, and my head was nearly underneath the water. Half my face was covered and I lurched forward heaving as I spluttered loudly. The twins were crying hysterically, but I was almost delirious from lack of sleep and it took a minute to remember where I was.

'Mummy's coming...' I coughed as I pulled out the plug and hoisted myself out of the bath. I wrapped myself in a towel and rushed into the bedroom, lifting both babies out of the cot one by one. I placed them on the bed before settling in between them and hoisting them up onto pillows to breastfeed. I changed then and rocked them back to sleep before I crept to the bedroom door and peaked into the hall. I was met by silence. But when I finally emerged from the bedroom, I saw Phoenix lying on the sofa in the living room as I walked into the hallway. The VTV was off, and his plug flashed inconspicuously in his ear, so I wondered who he was tele-talking too. I could tell from the expression on his face that he was in the middle of an important conversation, and ignored me when he noticed me standing in the doorway. I quickly averted my gaze and carried on towards the kitchen, but my heart sank as I noticed a black envelope leaning against the front door with my name on it. My stomach turned as I retrieved it and I cautiously ripped it open. It was a summons ordering me to appear at court tomorrow night. My mouth went dry and I marched into the front room and waved the notice in front of Phoenix's face.

'Did you tell them I was home?' I demanded, not caring that I was interrupting his telepathic conversation.

'I have a duty to the court.' He said barely glancing at me, 'Anyway the LOE knows all, they don't need me to keep tabs on you.'

I kissed my teeth annoyed as I stormed back into the bedroom. I began to rifle through the contents of my meagre hospital bag and before impatiently dumping it out bits onto the bed. I sighed in relief as I spotted my plug Ryan had given me at the clinic amongst the debris. I grabbed it and popped it into my ear to activate it. Once I was got a sensing tone I channelled Ryan, but his line was busy. I tried again and again but only got through his mind mail so I left an urgent message. An urgent message would interrupt whatever he was doing. I kissed my teeth and tapped my knees in frustration. I was just about to try him again when he suddenly tele-called me back.

'*You've got to get me out of here now!*' I thought, not even giving Ryan a moment to think.

'*I need another day or so, before I can get you out.*'

'*I ain't got that long,*' I thought frantically as I sat bolt upright on the edge of the bed. '*I thought you could get me out now!*'

'*Things have changed Raine, now Phoenix's back, and in the way we've got to be extra careful. Theres just a few more variables I've got to consider*'

'*But I need to leave now Ry!*' I yelled telepathically.

326

'*Why! what's happened?*' Ryan thought back, I could immediately feel his growing concern.

'*I can't wait, I hate it here!*' I screamed inside my head as I tried to hold back my tears.

'*Rain, calm down and tell me what'd happened!*' Ryan demanded; I could hear that he was getting agitated as my tears soaked my face.

'*My summons came for tomorrow night and–*' I said anxiously trying not to blub out loud.

'*Ok... And?*' Ryan questioned impatiently, '*Raine, what is it*'

'*Phoenix hit me, and... I, I don't know what else he might do.*'

'*He did what!*' Ryan thought furiously, his ferocious anger hitting me like a surge of electricity right in the middle of my forehead.

'He thinks we're in some sort of twisted relationship!' I hissed out loud, unable to contain all my thoughts inside my head.

'*Ok, I'm going to kill him?*' Ryan ranted indignantly, '*I'm coming over there to get you and the twins right now! I'll take him out and make it look like an accident.*'

'*No! Ryan, that'll make everything worse! Somehow the LOE will find a way to blame it on me!*' I thought sternly trying to block his transferring energy. '*All you need to do is discreetly get me and the girls out of here ASAP!*' I thought firmly as I felt myself starting to feed on his anger. I sniffled as I waited for his response.

'*Okay,*' He thought after a long pause, '*I'll sort something out, Blue will pick you up, just be ready tomorrow night by 11.*'

'*Why can't you come get me?*' I asked concerned.

'*Raine, I have court duties before the twilight session. So, it's either tomorrow night or I come for you now, and deal with Phoenix in my own way!*' Ryan thought coldly, and I could sense his violent intentions intensifying.

'*No, do not come here!*' I said harshly, '*The mere sight of you will make everything 10 times worse!*'

'*Ok, then we'll do it right before your initiation. Phoenix will be summoned to a pre-ceremony to vouch for you, so he will have to leave you alone for at least a little while. That's our chance.*'

***

The twins were all packed and ready to go but I was getting antsy. It had been over an hour since Phoenix had left me and it was already past 11pm. I stood shivering on the balcony as a vehicle suddenly swerved into the secluded grove and pulled to a halt in front of my block. *About time.* I thought as a dark figure got out and walked up to the communal door. I could only see the top of his head in the gloom and I jumped as the intercom rang. I rushed inside and answered it anxiously.

'Hello,' I said nervously 'Blue is that you?'

'You ready?' A ruff voice responded. I tapped the camera on the intercom monitor but it didn't seem to be working.

'You ready?' he repeated.

'Yeah, sorry,' I said trying the front door but it was locked. I tried the code again before I ran over to the electric box but it was also locked. I began to panic; Phoenix must have overridden the system and had now locked me inside the flat.

'Hello?' The voice on the intercom called.

'I'm here,' I said choking back tears, 'I can't get out. There was a silent pause.

'Hang on,' he said before I heard him trudge away and then return a minute later.

'Stand back,' he said and I obeyed as I walked over to check on the twins who were both sleeping silently in their Moses baskets. By the time I had reached them the front door beeped green as he swung open.

'Who are you?' I asked, as I looked at the man standing on the other side.

'You're not Blue,' I said studying him closely.

'Yeah, Blue got caught up so I was sent instead.' The stranger smiled a mouth of gold teeth. Cheap gold teeth, no doubt purchased and installed in the valley. I turned around and tried to tele-call Ryan, but for some reason I couldn't get a sensing tone, I couldn't even get through to mind mail.

'So, you ready or what?' The stranger asked as he walked inside the hallway without my permission. I hesitated for a few seconds before I turned around.

'Who are you?' I asked again.

'The name's Goose,' he said leaning against the nearest wall.

'Goose?' I asked raising an eyebrow.

'Yeah Goose,' he repeated as he flashed his golden smile. 'I run cars with Blue, for Rook down in the valley.'

'How did you get through the security system?' I asked sceptically.

Goose shrugged and tapped his wide nose.

'That's top secret LOE intel,' he said smiling again as he looked me up and down.

'Look luv, with all due respect,' Goose said after a few seconds of awkward silence. 'I have my orders and I need to get back to the valley so, are you coming or what?' he said as if he was getting tired of me. I sighed in agitation, Ryan hadn't informed me about this change of plan, I was expecting Blue and I didn't like surprises. I was hesitant but I let Goose pick up one of the Moses baskets and help me down to the car. I strapped twins into the back of the large vehicle and got into the passenger seat. I felt anxious as I strapped myself in, aware of that familiar funny feeling building up in the pit of my stomach. I was apprehensive of what I had to do next.

Goose took off abruptly and drove recklessly through North London. It didn't take long to leave the slums behind and after a couple of hours of navigating through London's ever-changing labyrinth, we arrived at Harry's private estate under the cover of darkness. I instructed Goose to pass by the house and park further down the country lane. My heart was beating wildly as

I got out of the car and slung the baby bag over my shoulder. I couldn't believe I was back here. Ryan didn't like the idea of me returning to Harry's mansion, but it was better than hiding out in a mother and baby brothel like he had planned. I sighed, attempting to convince myself that I was doing the right thing while trying to ignore the echo of Ryan's sceptical voice. I knew that Harry loved me but still, I wondered if he would help me *again* after everything that had happened. I'd been missing for over six months and all I could do was pray that Harry wasn't still under government surveillance, and that he still felt the same way.

I walked around the car, listening to the gravel crunch loudly underneath my feet. I popped the boot open and groaned when I saw that it was empty, I was expecting to see a buggy to carry the twins.

'Where's the buggy?' I called loudly.

'What?' Goose replied from the front seat.

'You know a push chair, there's meant to a double buggy in here!' I yelled agitated, 'where is it?'

'Sorry luv, I just do the driving,' Goose yelled back, and I rolled my eyes as I slammed the boot shut. I walked around the car muttering to myself, how was I supposed to manage two Moses baskets and a hefty baby bag all by myself? The last thing I wanted was Goose helping me up to the front door. I sighed pulling on the rear door handle behind the driver's side, but it wouldn't open.

'Well open the door the door then!' I snapped tapping on the front window.

'My bad, the central locking's a bit dodgy,' Goose smiled apologetically as he turned the engine off and on. 'Try again,' he said confidently, so I tugged on the door once more but it still wouldn't budge.

'Seriously!' I groaned loudly throwing my arms up into the air.

'Try the other one...' Goose yelled over the spluttering engine. 'I've just got to fiddle with the controls for a minute.' I cursed under my breath as I walked around to the other side of the vehicle and pulled on the other door. It immediately popped open, and I leaned over to carefully unlatch the seatbelt around Mya. Tia was sleeping soundly on the other side of the car, and I quickly pulled the domed cover up over Mya and placed the Moses basket at the side of the dirt road. The car door closed automatically behind me, and I quickly walked around to the other side of the vehicle to retrieve Tia. I pulled on the handle and found that it was still locked. kissing my teeth, I headed back to the other side so I could pull her out across the seats. But as I was walking behind the car the engine suddenly came alive and started to move.

'Goose, what the hell are you doing?' I shouted running around and pounding on the glass of the passenger window. 'Tia is still in there!' I shouted panicking. 'Stop the car now!' I yelled in confusion, slapping the window, and trying to grab onto the front door handle. 'You've got my baby!' I screamed desperately. 'She's still in there!'

'I know luv, sorry but I've got my orders,' Goose said, as he cracked open the window. I forced my fingers into the gap as the car near enough dragged me along the ground. I couldn't understand what was happening.

'Orders? What flipping orders? Ryan would never order this!' I shrieked as I slipped and broke into a run after the moving vehicle. It was as if he was purposely driving slowly to cruelly tease me. 'Wait don't do this please I beg you, PLEASE!' I heard Goose laugh as I screamed and thumped on the glass. 'I can get you old money, or blue quid, anything!' I yelled frantically but he ignored me and finally accelerated, speeding off down the road and leaving me in the dust. 'Come back! You can't take my baby!' I cried breathlessly running until the car turned around the corner and disappeared out of sight. I stopped sprinting and tried to catch my breath. I felt physically sick and threw up on the side of the road. I didn't know what to do for a moment, and I just stood there heaving in confusion until headlights suddenly shone from behind me. I quickly came to my senses and turning back I made a dash for Mya's basket I had set down beside a tree. Still feeling sick, I helplessly watched the headlights go by as tears of hopelessness streamed down my face. Mya was crying hungrily but I was frozen, stunned by what had just happened. I sniffled as I wiped my face and took Mya out of her basket as she became more and more hysterical. *You need to be strong* I told myself as I cradled her in my arms, she was inconsolable, it was as if she knew that her sister was gone. I sat on a tree stump and tucked her into my coat to breastfeed, and then activated plug to telecall Ryan. His crazy Loelife had gone completely rogue and kidnapped my baby. Ryan needed to find her and quick before he sold her or did something unthinkable! I impatiently plugged in and finally detected a sensing tone, but I still couldn't get through to him. Instead, I heard Phoenix's voice in my head as a mind mail message flagged up. This surprised me because I didn't tell Phoenix about my new plug. I cautiously accepted the message and immediately, a pixelated hologram appeared in front of my eyes. I could see Phoenix holding Tia in his arms as he slowly looked at me with a smug look on his face.

'Say bye bye to mummy,' he smiled as he used Tia's arm to wave at me before the image of them disappeared into pixelated binary code. My body went completely numb as I watched the recording over and over again in my mind. I screamed loudly startling Mya in my arms. Tears streamed down my cheeks as I gently rocked her back to sleep before placing her back in her basket. I tried to call Ryan again but the plug had been killed remotely so it was dead. I took corrupted plug out of my ear and stamped on it as hard as I could. But I could still see the imprint of the hologram in my mind. I wanted to scream again, but I bit my lip silently in anger instead. Phoenix must have found the plug and planted a bug so he could spy on me. He had been listening to every single telecall since the hospital, and had used my own mind against me to kidnap Tia! I pushed the thoughts to the back of my mind as I hoisted the Mya's Moses basket and began to walk down the lane towards Harry's mansion. I had stalled for long enough and I was now freezing cold so I had to get moving. My tears had freeze dried to my face and I tried to stay out of sight as a few more cars drove passed. It didn't take me long to get back to Harry's mansion. But I began to get second thoughts as I drew nearer, having doubts about what I now knew I had to do next. Another change of plan that I hadn't prepared for.

I turned the corner and stepped behind the tall rose bushes on Harry's private country lane. I was able to keep out of sight until I reached the side gate just a few metres away from the main entrance. Two large cameras swivelled relentlessly as I stood motionless in the blind spot directly beneath them. The intercom for the gate was now just out of grasp in front of me. I waited for the cameras to go into dormant mode before dashing to the door and typing in the code which I hoped, was still Melina's date of birth. It was and I dashed back over to the blind spot to pick up Mya's basket as the CCTV zeroed in on me. I glanced into the camera lens now following my every movement, resigned to the fact that I couldn't completely avoid being seen. The keypad flashed green and beeped a few times as the gate creaked open. I picked up Mya's Moses basket and quickly slipped through, scurrying across the huge driveway, and dashing onto the large veranda just as it started to snow. Mya was still fast asleep, and I placed her basket in front of the front door along with the essentials in her baby bag. *At least now she'll have two of everything,* I thought sadly as I opened the basket and looked at her one last time. I kissed her on the forehead and watched her for a few minutes as the snow started to get heavier. I hadn't planned to leave her. I had expected to stay and hideout for a while until Ryan could sort everything out. But now Tia was gone how could I?

I sighed loudly as I stroked her face, I was running a huge risk loitering on the porch like a sitting duck. Thick white flakes had begun to settle on everything from the leafless trees to the plant pots full of evergreens planted along the path up to the house. There was a strange vehicle parked in the driveway that I suspected wasn't Harry's. It was a militant like jeep similar the one Goose had been driving, and wasn't dapper enough for Harry's taste, besides if it was his I was sure it would've been parked inside the ample garage at the side of the house. I wondered who it belonged too as I looked through the frosty window in the front door. But couldn't see anything through the translucent glass. Rubbing my freezing hands together vigorously, I thought about how warm it must be inside, Blanche would most likely be in her room watching her wall sized VTV, and Maria was probably pottering about in the kitchen at the back of the house preparing dinner for the following day. I fondly remembered the nightcaps we shared on various occasions, sipping at her homemade wine while she expertly prepared artisan bread. I wasn't ashamed to say that I didn't miss Millie one bit, and I guessed that she was probably in her room sulking about something irrelevant, and Harry, I deduced that he was probably in the drawing room entertaining the owner of the vehicle parked in the driveway. I shivered as a cold breeze brought me right back to reality, and I reluctantly bent down to give Mya one more kiss. I tucked her in to make sure she was comfy before I took off the priceless blue sapphire Harry had given to me in what seemed like a lifetime ago. I had managed to keep it hidden from Phoenix for all these months, and I was surprised that the Beefeaters hadn't found it hidden in the inside pocket of my riding suit when they had found me in Epping Forest. I gently placed the necklace on top of her blankets as I softly stroked her face.

'I'm so sorry I have to leave you.' I whispered as a tear rolled down my cheek. 'But I have to go and find your sister.' I said as I wiped my face and closed the hooded cover over her basket. 'I'll come back for you.' My voice trembled as slowly pushed her Moses basket right up to the front door. 'I promise!' I stood there sniffling for a few more minutes but I was running out of excuses for not leaving. I sighed loudly and my hand shook violently as I reached out to ring the doorbell. My finger hovered over the button, and I took a deep breath forcing myself to press it. The doorbell chimed loudly, and I stumbled backwards down the steps trying to get away as fast as possible. The driveway was too large and open to clear in one sprint, so I quickly slid behind the large parked car just as the front door slowly eased open. I saw Maria's head as she peaked through the crack in the door, and called out into the silence. She opened the door a little wider and only then did the light from the hallway fall on Mya's Moses basket. Maria quickly threw the door wide open, and I knew then that she had seen her. She crouched down cautiously leaning over the Moses basket as if she was unsure of what could be lurking inside. Finally, she tentatively opened the hood and stood upright covering her mouth with both hands.

'Master Harry!' Maria yelled as she peered back into the house. 'MASTER HARRY!' she called again, and in the minute or so that it took Harry to appear in the doorway she looked around the driveway as if she was searching for me. Her gaze lingered on my hiding spot until Harry's sudden appearance in the hallway behind her seemed to startle her.

'What is it, Maria?' He asked loudly. 'I told you that I wasn't to be disturbed!'

'My apologies Master Harry... But look!' She exclaimed pointing down at Mya in her Moses basket. Harry stared down at her for a long moment before he turned back to Maria. He then slowly bent down and when he stood up, the blue Sapphire necklace was dangling from his hand. He studied it for a long time before looking out into the darkness, and I slid further underneath the car as he peered in my direction. 'I'll just take the baby into the warmth then, shall I?' Maria said as she bent down to pick up the Moses basket. Harry nodded silently as he took of his glasses and rubbed his eyes.

'Yes of course!' He said finally as he replaced his spectacles onto the tip of his nose. He then looked out into the darkness scanning my hiding place again before slowly picking up the baby bag and following Maria into the house. I was left with an empty void inside me as the yellow light from the hallway disappeared leaving me alone in the darkness. I felt numb, not from the cold as such, but from the fact that I had lost both my children in the space of half an hour. *It's just temporary, I will get them back!* I told myself as my teeth began to chatter. The snow was still falling, and I crawled out from underneath the vehicle. Staying low, I snuck back over to the gate and hastily punched in the code before rushing through as it clicked open. I glanced back at the house and noticed that the curtains in the drawing room were no longer drawn shut. Standing on the other side and peering through the gate, I could see that the curtains were indeed wide open, and behind the bay window stood the silhouette of a woman staring in my direction as if she had seen me scarper across the drive. I tore myself away from her intense glare and darted out of the view of the camera's swivelling above me. I began to walk down the country lane, trudging through slushy mud beneath my feet. After marching for about a mile in the cold, I managed to hitch a ride back to the city. It was an old white couple that had picked me up, when they had spotted me walking along that secluded country lane alone. I held my thumb out, but they didn't stop immediately. However, they must have felt pity because they came to an abrupt halt about few metres up the road ahead of me.

'Well, you know what it's like these days,' John had said, immediately addressing his hesitation to stop for me as soon as I had gotten into the car. 'But we just couldn't leave a young girl like you to walk alone to God knows where at this kind of hour.'

'Especially not out here!' His wife Margaret shivered as she looked out of the window and into the black, 'Right on the edge of Epping Forest!'
John nodded his head in agreement as he finally turned onto the main road.

'Too right luv… get lost in there, and you'll probably never see the light of day again.'

You might… I thought to myself as I had a flash back of riding Storm through the groves on my great escape.

'So… Where are you off too deary?' Margaret asked turning her head towards me.

'Erm, Ally Pally, I mean Alexandra Palace….' I said realizing that they were probably from a gated community like I once was. *Although probably somewhere much nicer than Islington,* I thought as Margaret silently looked over at John. 'But… anywhere north of the river is fine and I can erm… make my own way from there.' I quickly interjected and Margaret nodded as she turned back around in her seat. They hardly said anything else to me after that and the car was almost completely silent for the rest of the journey. They both had blue papers allowing us to go through the busy London check point and down one of the guarded high streets, one of the few safe routes that avoided the renegade barricades plastered on the unmanned outskirts of greater London. They ordered me to hide inside of a small compartment underneath the back seat and only let me out when they dropped me off at Stoke Newington, on the northern border of Hackney.

'Thank you so much!' I said as I climbed out of the car and shut the door behind myself. Margaret smiled thinly, avoiding any eye contact and John sped off without looking back.

17

LOE LIVE FOREVER

After walking for well over an hour, I was able to follow various given directions and finally made my way back to the Slums. I could almost smell it from a distance as I made my way up to its busy summit. I crossed the pedestrian bridge over the abandoned train station, watching the watchmen inspect various vehicles before they were given access through the huge entry gates. There were clusters of minor crews demanding tribute from strangers and newcomers along the way on the way but luckily was generally recognised and thankfully left alone. I headed straight up to the Alexandra palace with one mission in mind. I fought my way through the night market crowds and loiterers outside, marching vigorously towards the great hall. Restless hordes that couldn't get into the crowded courtroom congested the hallway. I pushed my way to the front and mentally prepared myself to do anything to get my daughter back. I made it to the great hall's entrance and demanded entry, but a large Loelife used his staff to block my way.

'The meeting is closed!' he grunted looking down at me.

'I know but I need to be in there I'm meant to be getting sworn in tonight.'

'And you dare to arrive late for your own swearing in ceremony?' The Loelife scoffed in disgust.

'Then you're not even worthy of the LOE!'

'But you don't understand, I need to see Phoenix urgently!' I countered loudly, 'he's vouching for me!'

'Let her through?' The smaller Loelife standing on the other side of the door doors said suddenly. 'That's Raine Montrose, you know the one that-' he covered his mouth as he whispered something inaudible to his colleague. The Loelife blocking my way mumbled something back as his eyes darted in my direction. He looked me up and down as he silently pushed the huge wooden doors open and stepped aside. I took a deep breath before I stepped inside. The great hall was overcrowded and I shuddered as the large doors slammed shut behind me. The loud thump echoed around the public gallery, and I was quickly met with a hundred pairs of eyes as the masked crowd turned around to look at me. They began to murmur amongst themselves as they gradually separated, creating an open pathway up to the stage. My heart was pounding wildly, and I stood frozen as my eyes suddenly met Rex's mask. He leaned forward as he banged his staff to calm the crowd.

'Raine Montrose!' Rex barked, 'You dare arrive late to your own summons!' My mouth was dry as I quickly walked towards the stage.

'I apologize for my tardiness...' I said bowing my head as I got to the foot of Rex's throne. 'I didn't mean to disrespect you or your court room of loyal subjects.' I said meekly, my heart still beating uncontrollably as I looked up at Phoenix indignantly.
I knew that I was the last person that he was expecting to see, and the look on his masked face gave me a tiny bit of satisfaction for, just a second. It soon dissipated and I had to fight back the urge to lunge onto the stage and attack him in front of the entire court.

'You may proceed to the dock.' Rex declared finally, as he glanced over at Phoenix. I could hear him tapping the arm of his throne as I slowly climbed the stage steps towards that claustrophobic wooden box. I caught Ryan's eye as I passed the jury of Superior Loelifes and even through the mask, I could tell that he was furious. The rest of the Superior's eyes bored into me and as I finally reached the dock, I noticed that Widow wasn't amongst them. 'Raine Montrose,' Rex announced as soon as I took a seat. 'This is the last chance I'm going to give you to prove your loyalty to the League of Equality!' Whispers rippled across the audience as Rex got to his feet and lifted his staff. He waved it at the crowd before pointing it in my direction. 'Will you or will you not willingly join the LOE

Society?' Rex demanded loudly. 'Phoenix has vouched for you and the motion was seconded by Rook. I glanced over at Phoenix and Ryan who were both watching me intently. 'All Superiors in favour say aye.'

'Aye,' they responded in unison and Rex nodded as he turned towards the audience.

'What does the flock say?'
I swallowed hard and nervous beads of sweat began form on my forehead.

'Aye!' the mob answered as one and Rex sat back down.

'Very well,' he said after clearing his throat. 'Are there *any* objections?' He looked around as he said it, and apart from a few mumbles a stiff silence settled over the room. 'Raine Montrose will you now accept your duty and prove your loyalty by pledging yourself to the LOE?' he pressed as he zeroed in on me.
I looked around anxiously

'Yes!' I said abruptly.

'Yes what!' Rex bellowed.

'Yes, I am ready to pledge myself to the LOE,' I lied looking Phoenix dead in the eye. 'Then raise your insignia,' Rex declared victoriously.
I raised my right arm and held up the most basic LOE hand sign, my thumb and forefinger forming the shape of an L.
Rex cleared his throat.

'Do you agree to put loyalty over everything?'
'I do,' I nodded.

'Do you agree that the L.O.E will live forever?'
This I doubted but again I agreed.

'I do,' I replied nodding.

'Do you agree that you will always fly with the flock, where ever our destination?

'I do.'

'Do you agree to complete every assigned mission, with or without wings.'

I wasn't sure what this meant but I knew I had to comply.

'I do,' I said slowly.

'Do you agree to sacrifice your life for the wider cause, and to take our secrets with you to the grave?' *Sacrifice my life* I thought uneasily.

'I, I… do…' I stuttered fretfully.

'Then you may now recite the sacred oath,' Rex ordered. I took a deep breath as the holographic words appeared in the air in front of me and floated above the watching audience.

'I, Raine Montrose, willingly pledge my allegiance to the LOE Society, and I say these words in your presence for you all to witness. I vow to fight as a Loelife until the deed is done. I vow to fight as a Loelife until the war is won. I vow to never abandon the cause in this life or the next, and to sacrifice my life as loyalty's ultimate test. There is no room for weakness, together we reign strong, there is no room for outsiders, together we belong. There is no peace for the wicked, and no perch for the crow, but may The LOE last forever, and forever live LOE.' I lowered my hand and loud cheers immediately erupted around the room as Rex repeatedly whacked his staff against the wooden stage. The crowd began to chant L.O.E, stamping their feet in accord with the rhythmic beat of Rex's repetitive tapping against the stage. I listened to the sound of their drumming feet, their smiles stretching their masked faces. It was a lively welcoming party but after a short while Rex suddenly waved the crowd into an immediate silence.

'For the next six months you will be *a Minion,* the absolute lowest of the LOE.' Rex said finally turning back to me. 'You will have to earn the title of Inferior... and it will not be easy,' he said eyeing me. 'There is no room for weakness and *we*, your brothers and sisters in arms welcome you into the fold!' He smiled as he addressed the crowd who jostled excitedly at their mention. 'L.O.E!' he yelled saluting them with a double handed sign which mimicked the wings of a bird.

'Loyalty over everything!' The crowd shouted back, holding alternate hand gestures high above their heads depending on their rank. Rex stood up again followed by the Superior Loelifes sat below him as they repeatedly began to chant. 'LOE live forever, forever Live LOE!'
I jumped up abruptly, it seemed a bit cult-like but not wanting to seem out of place I quickly joined in.

'LOE live forever,' I shouted raising my hand into the air, 'forever Live LOE!'

***

I was suddenly falling. Everything went back as gravity forced my bum into the hard wooden chair. I landed with a loud thud, a large cloud of dust rising to choke me. I had a minor coughing fit and breathed heavily as I clutched my chest and tried to figure out what had just happened. I banged on the glass with my other hand as my eyes adjusted to the dim light. Wherever I had landed was dark and empty and I peered into the gloom confused. I tried the door but it was jammed. The dock, or the claustrophobic wooden box as I liked to call it had suddenly fallen through the stage in the middle of our chanting.

'Help!' I called looking up to see nothing but the top of the wooden dock. I suddenly heard the echo of footsteps, and I looked up to see someone approaching. It was an Inferior and I soon learned that the dock's door was locked not jammed shut from the fall. I sneezed as she opened it and looked up to see the Inferior staring down at me. I was expecting some sort of explanation as to what had just happened but she didn't offer one.

'Come on then,' she said instructing me to follow her, and I immediately saw that we were underneath the stage inside some sort of basement. I could see the light streaming through the trap door from high above, and the hydraulic contraction that had sucked the down the dock under the stage. I could hear a faint rumble from the great hall as the Inferior escorted into a long dimly lit corridor. I joined a long queue of dust covered women who I assumed had pledged before me and were also unwittingly dropped through the stage's trapdoor. There was something going on up ahead but I couldn't quite see what it was.

The line moved quickly and I was soon met by another Inferior with a contraption in her hand. She grabbed my hand tightly as she ran the device over my wrist. I winced as a laser burned something into my skin, and snatching my arm away as soon as she was done.

'Your infrared brand,' she said flatly as she shone a light over the same spot. I stared down at the encircled '*LOE*' as the letters faded away before my eyes when she removed the light source. I was sent into an adjoining room to join the others. I was the last one so no sooner than I had entered we were suddenly being frogmarched through many corridors and up several flights of stairs. Finally, we were lined up against the wall of a wide hallway somewhere deep within the palace. A long line of men stood opposite us in the dingy corridor as we were each handed a large bag. We were then filed into a large, dilapidated dormitory segregated by sex. I covered my nose to ward off the damp smell lingering in the air from the adjoining communal shower positioned at the far end of the room. The large yellow bulbs hanging from the high ceiling were extremely dull and did little to illuminate the room, barely giving off enough light to find your own bed in the darkness. I was directed to bed number 28, the same number on the front of my bag. It was in the corner of the dorm and way too close to the showers for my liking, but at least I had access to a window.

It was late and we were instructed to settle down for the night as we had an early start in the morning. Lights out was announced a few minutes later and the main lights were switched off leaving us in almost total darkness. I placed the bag I'd been given in little cabinet next to the bed as a chorus of whispers arose in the darkness. A few streaks of moonlight lit up the large spooky dorm. I could hear a commotion outside, and so I leaned over my mangled headboard to stare out of the large window behind my bed. My eyes zeroed in on the Loelifes now emerging from the twilight court meeting, chattering amongst themselves as they made their way back to their various districts. I could now see that the dorm was situated right at the back of the palace, and the Loelifes walked right underneath my window as they exited the building. Some using suspended orbs of light to illuminate their path. I only noticed the most intricated masks amidst the sea of generic black hoods. The higher ranked masks glistening flecks of colour in the scattered moonlight, making them easy to spot among the Inferiors. I watched them disappear around the building as I listened the other women already making alliances in the darkness behind me. After a few minutes the crowd started to thin out and that's when I suddenly spotted Phoenix, his elaborate mask shimmering just enough for me to notice the unique design in between his peers. I quickly pushed the ancient window open as far as it could go and forced my face into the narrow gap. It creaked dangerously as if it was about to slide shut and crush my jaw, but I held it steady as I called out Phoenix's name, just as he walked underneath the window. His body language showed no sign of acknowledgement but he must have heard me.

'Phoenix, I know you hear me!' I shouted, making some of the passing Loelifes look up and heckle me. 'You better answer me!' I yelled again, ignoring them.

'Be quiet!' I whipped my head around to scan the dorm room but I couldn't see the person who had shushed me, and as I turned back, Phoenix had almost disappeared around the corner.

'Phoenix!' I called again, but still, he didn't respond.

'Why don't you shut the hell up before you get all of us in trouble!' The woman griped again, and I pulled my face away from the window and let it drop down with a soft thud. I slipped on my shoes and jumped out of bed as I stood up and I scanned the room. Before I quickly snuck towards the open doorway and slipped into the corridor. I could hear some noise coming from the men's dormitory across the hall as I sunk into the shadow cast against the wall. There was an empty chair but I couldn't see any Loelifes stationed nearby so made a run for it, hoping to catch Phoenix before he disappeared into the slums. When I got to the end of the corridor, I sharply turned the corner and bumped right into a Junior Loelife probably returning to his post.

'Well, what do we have here?' He said looking over my shoulder as if he expected me to have an accomplice.

'Let go of me!' I hissed as he grabbed me by my forearm as I tried to get away.

'Whoa! And where you off to in such a hurry?" He asked suspiciously as he continued to periodically glance behind me.

'Look, I know it's lights out…' I sighed looking up into his generic mask, it was slightly different from the Inferior masks but still quite rudimentary compared to the higher ranks. 'But I just need like, five minutes to talk to somebody… Well not anybody, it's Phoenix, I really need to speak to Phoenix urgently!'

'Ok,' he replied with a sly grin, 'but what's in it for me?' He asked mischievously as he pressed me up against the wall.

'Urgh, take your hands off me!' I hissed as he pinned me against the concrete.

'You can scream if you like,' he said as he covered my mouth, 'Nobody who gives a damn will hear you anyway,' he chuckled and I could smell his pungent breath as he licked my cheek leaving a trail of saliva behind. I kicked him in the groin as I tried to slip out of his grasp but his thick Loelife uniform deflected the blow. He laughed at my attempt to injure him.

'LOE live forever!' A sudden camouflaged voice surprised both of us, and I sighed in relief as the startled Inferior hastily let go of me and stood to attention.

'Forever live LOE,' he replied seemingly nervous as he stood in front of me blocking my view.

'Why are you not at your post?'

'I, I needed a break and we're short-staffed tonight.' He answered lowering his head.

352

'Ok, so would you like to explain exactly what you're doing?' My attacker stuttered clearly caught in a debaucherous act by a higher ranked Loelife.

'Well answer me!' The higher-up demanded making the Inferior shudder pathetically.

'Move!' The high-ranking Loelife ordered as he shoved him aside. Our eyes met as I recognised Ryan's mask which immediately began to glow a bright red in darkness of the surrounding hallway. His anger was instantaneous and as soon as he saw my face, he grabbed the Inferior by the neck and pushed him up against the wall right beside me. 'I asked you a question Junior…' I jumped behind Ryan as he began to squeeze the Inferior's neck.

'She was pulling a runner!' he choked as Ryan continued to apply pressure.

'So, you thought you'd violate her to teach her a lesson huh?' He grunted, his synthetic voice sounding even angrier as the Junior shook his head vigorously. His mask began to change colour and I saw the terror in bulging his eyes as the material began to turn a greyish blue.

'Ryan, you're killing him!' I protested as I stared into the Junior's protruding eyeballs, but he carried on as if he hadn't even heard me. 'Ryan, stop this, now before he dies!' I pleaded putting my hand on his shoulder and finally he let go. We both silently watched the Junior drop to his knees and gasp for air to catch his breath. Ryan glanced at me for a second and sighed before grabbing the Inferior by the scruff of

353

his neck and dragging him up to a stand. He dragged his mask off his head.

'What's your name?'

'Fi, Finch,' he coughed, wheezing loudly.

'Who's your Senior?' Ryan hissed into his face.

'Ra, Ra... Raven,' he spluttered.

'Well, you've been marked Finch,' Ryan spat sinisterly as he narrowed his eyes, 'and now you owe me drudgery, do you understand?' Finch nodded vigorously.

'Do you know who I am?'

Finch nodded again without raising his head to make eye contact.

'Good.' Ryan said as he squeezed his shoulder menacingly. 'Tell you Senior to telecall me asap, and after this shift don't ever let me hear that you're on dorm duty again, or I'll move to demote you to Inferior duties. Do you get me?' Finch nodded again. 'Use your flipping words!' Ryan growled as he slammed him back into the wall and put his arm over his throat.

'I get it!' the Inferior coughed, and Ryan let him go, slapping him in the head as he scurried away.

We didn't speak until he had disappeared around the corner and the sound of his echoing footsteps were no longer audible.

'I need you to take me to Phoenix right now Rya–' Before I could even finish my sentence Ryan grabbed me by the arm and shoved me into a nearby room. 'Ryan stop manhandling me!' I protested as I stumbled inside.

'Are you dumb!' Ryan asked angrily as he slammed the door and flicked on the light. 'What the hell are you doing back here Raine?' He demanded crossing his arms. 'And pledging your allegiance to the flipping LOE?' He snapped glaring at me. 'Have you gone completely nuts? How was this any part of the plan!' I didn't respond, instead I silently hung my head, looking down at the lacquered floor. 'Do you have any idea of what you've just done?' He ranted while pacing back and forth in small space. 'You've just signed your entire life away! And for what?' He asked pounding his fist into a nearby shelf. He stopped in front of me waiting for an explanation. We were in some sort of storeroom and I tried to push passed him, but he blocked my path.

'Please... I beg you tell me that the girls are safe?' He probed as if he was afraid to ask. 'Where the hell are they?' I gasped for air as my chest suddenly became tight. My eyes grew blurry as I opened my mouth to speak but nothing came out. Ryan held me by my arms as a huge lump appeared in my throat making it hard to swallow. 'Raine, look at me!' Ryan barked shaking me as if I was some sort of rag doll. I shook him off violently as I turned away from him and began to cry. 'Raine!' He tried to say calmly, 'Tell me where the twins are right now!' I could hear the alarm in his voice as he pulled me around to face him. I suddenly couldn't control my sobs and I sank to my knees. 'Where are they!' He cried holding up right as my body went limp and I began to wail hysterically. 'Raine, you need to tell me where they are!'

'Mya is safe…' I blurted out, 'but….'

'But!' Ryan demanded as he shook me again, 'but what!'

'Phoenix took Tia…' I sobbed.

'What do you mean, *he took her*?' Ryan pressed.

'It means he kidnapped her!' I cried loudly. His eyes widened as he dropped me and ripped of his mask.

'And where the hell is Mya then!' He exclaimed as I slumped to the floor and wept.

'Where is she Rain?' He asked stooping down as he grabbed my chin to look me dead in the eye.

'I left her at Harry's….' I whimpered as I shoved his hand away. 'I know he'll look after her,' I snivelled wiping my eyes. Ryan went silent as he stood up and towered over me in the small room.

'How did this even happen? I sent Blue to take you… Did he betray–'

'It wasn't Blue.' I blubbed cutting him off, 'he didn't even show.' I whimpered quietly as Ryan's eyes searched mine for answers.

'What do you mean? He snapped, 'So who took you?'

'Some guy called *Goose*, told me that *you* sent him instead.' 'I sniffled as I wiped my nose in my sleeve. 'Said he worked with Blue down in the valley.'

'Shit!' Ryan shouted as he punched the wall beside me. 'Why did you get in the car?'

'I know!' I sobbed loudly, 'I'm an idiot, it's all my fault!' I said putting my head into my hands as I continued to bawl. 'I tried to call you but Phoenix bugged the plug you gave me. I didn't even know he knew about it; he must have searched my bag when he came to see me after the birth.' I blubbered uncontrollably.

'He's been listening to us since I left the clinic, scanning my thoughts, reading my mind mail, everything!' 'Ryan was quiet so I couldn't tell what he was thinking.

'How did he get her.' He asked distantly.

'It all just happened so quickly.' I whimpered trying to calm down. 'When we got to Harry's, he pretended that the back door locks were dodgy to make sure that I couldn't get Tia out first, and, and as soon as I was out of the car with Mya, he... he just drove off!' I sniffled wiping snot into my sleeve.

'I'm gonna kill him!' Ryan said roughly, and pulling me up by the arm, we headed for the door. 'This is war!' He barked suddenly stopping in front of it. 'He told Goose to tell you his real name to send me a message!'

'How do you figure that?' I whimpered as Ryan turned back to look at me.

'Because Phoenix could've told him to lie!' He hissed methodically. Ryan had that look in his eye, glazed over, crazed, the same one he usually had before he did something irrational.

'He's one of Phoenix's Junior deputies.' He continued coldly as he pulled on his mask and finally opened the door. 'Trust me, *he* told you his name because they wanted *me* to know.' He said closing the door behind me. His voice was even now, measured, but his eyes couldn't hide his burning rage as he led me down the now pitch-black hallway. A light orb appeared, and Ryan glared at the same Junior that had assaulted me as he sat on duty stationed at the end of the corridor. The Junior jumped up from his seat, and dispelled his light orb when he saw us, then disappearing into the men's dorm to leave us alone in the dark.

***

Two weeks after Ryan had escorted me back to my dorm, Goose's bloated body was found floating atop of Alexandra Lake. I decided against asking him about it, and I refused to attend the hearing with the other pledges, wherein Rex attempted to identify the alleged killer. It was just lip-service to make the regular *slummie* feel safer, after all if that could to a level 2 Loelife what hope was there for the rest of us? I didn't get involved in the gossip, but I listened to the stories though, even if I acted like I wasn't paying attention. I heard how the corpse was found without eyes, mauled, mangled, and distended after being pecked at by those jet-black ducks with red eyes until a Minion found it during stamina training. The factions were warring, and there was an invisible sense of tension that had settled over the whole slums. The rumours were rife as everybody knew a ghost couldn't get away with that sort of crime. It had to be an inside job and slummies who had a taste for that sort of thing betted on who would die next. It was one all now, in Ryan and Phoenix's silent war, seeing as Blue's body was dug up in the mount a week earlier by a Senior Loelife and GMA hounds out on patrol. He had been placed in a shallow grave; his decapitated head placed between his severed legs.

I currently had my own struggles to deal with, being forbidden from leaving the palace grounds for the first eight backbreaking weeks. Besides being trapped like an animal, I was barely fed anything except for fox soup and potato bread, and was expected to follow strict military exercise program. We were forced to train in hand-to-hand combat to within an inch of our daily lives, and then we were made to sit in front of endless holographic projections on the history and origin of the LOE Society. I didn't hate it, sitting in front of a VTV screen was much easier than learning the LOE's special form of martial art which contained elements of stick fighting, kick boxing, fencing, and gymnastics. I also learned a lot on those endless afternoons of being force fed information, I had no idea if it was totally accurate but I learned a lot more than I had in school. We were shown how The LOE Society evolved from an offshoot vigilante amalgamation into a national movement. I learned about the founders supreme, and their initial operations, practices, and philosophy. We studied their guerrilla warfare tactics in the plight for economic equality for the oppressed underclass. We went over the great recession of the late 2020s, the societal breakdown of the 2030s, and the subsequent civil war. We saw how The LOE took advantage of the crumbling government institution as the UK scrambled to import its lacking resources in the midst of international turmoil due to the emergence of World War 3. By the end of the 8 weeks integration, I was almost brainwashed into believing that The LOE Society *would* one day overturn the fascist, corrupt BFP government and take over the country. Finally putting a stop to their tyrannic rule and restoring peace to a broken nation. I almost bought it too, for a moment, I was almost a proper Minion. But after everything I'd been through, I was only concerned with one thing, and that finding Tia and seeing the rest of my family again.

***

I etched another line into the tally I had been scratching into my wooden headboard. It was another day; a bleak and dismal morning and I hadn't seen my children in over four months. *What if they'd forgotten me already?* I shuddered at the thought as I flicked the Swiss army knife closed. I fluffed my pillow and used it to cover the lines I had cut into the wood. A bird whistle sounded to call to attention and we formed a line at the end of our beds. I took a deep breath and tried to concentrate on pushing myself to the limit of my physical ability, the better my performance, the better I felt for the rest of the day since combat training had become my only solace and means of escape. After the first couple of months, I had begun to get used to the early morning drills around a gruelling obstacle course built into the palace grounds. Then onto combat training before gymnastics. We trained in a large gym equipped with ancient apparatus straight out the 20th century and this made up the first half of every day. Gymnastics came much easier to me than fighting. But fighting was the only thing that my numbness away. It was the only time I felt alive and welcomed the pain from every blow I received as punishment. Punishment for all my past mistakes, and possibly the ones I would make in the future. So, I put everything I had into learning how to fight. I experimented with all the weaponry available to us during sparring, and I practiced my combat techniques in the leaky showers during the middle of the night when sleep abandoned me.

I unleashed all my anger and frustration out on whoever my opponent was to be that day. I assumed that today would be no different, first the obstacle course, and then onto the gym. Except after I got to the end of my bed, I saw Phoenix standing to in the dormitory doorway. I wondered where Raven was, the Senior that usually accompanied us to morning training.

'Eyes straight!' Sasha shouted as she moved down the line and inspected us and our bunks. She was one of Loelifes little pets, a Minion who hadn't passed her 6-month initiation ceremony, and therefore had to join the next round of pledges. She had the best of everything, a better bed, better food, privileges that made her better than a Minion but still not yet an Inferior. It was of no wonder she took out her frustration on us, not being allowed to engage with those that had successfully passed the initiation ceremony she did not. I had also heard through the grapevine of her links to several superior Loelifes, including Phoenix, and Rook aka my brother.

My bed, number 28 was the last in the room, and I looked Sasha right in the eye as she stood in front of me. She looked me up and down before moseying back across the dorm to stand beside her bed, bed number 1.

'Your mentor Raven has been indisposed for a while so I'll be stepping in for today's exercise.' Phoenix announced after clearing his throat. 'Today's training will be done in pairs,' he continued, and I exchanged a look with the girl in the bed 26. This was different. After months of the same thing every day this was something new, it felt strange. 'You will *not* be able to complete the exercise without your partner.' He said as he walked the length of the dorm in between the beds. 'It will be a test of endurance, stamina and teamwork and the start of your level 3 training.' I listened to the sound of his footsteps as they echoed around the room. He paused beside me before walking back towards the door. 'Do you understand?'

'Aye,' the room said in unison.

'Good.' Phoenix replied as he stood in the doorway once again. 'Now follow me.'

***

'Come on, hurry up!' I snapped at Demi who was lagging behind. If I had the choice, I wouldn't have chosen anyone to be my partner let alone her. She just happened to occupy bed number 27. We had barely gotten halfway to the lake and she was already falling back.

'Wait up Raine, please!' She moaned loudly, slowing down and then stopping completely. I groaned, cursing the fact that I had been paired up with her. 'I feel sick!' She whined queasily. I tried to ignore her, gliding on for a few paces before sighing loudly and circling back. I had no choice; I couldn't finish the exercise without her.

'You sure you're not pregnant?' I sniped as I watched her double over and retch violently, thinking about all the times I had seen her and a few other girls sneaking over to the men's dormitory in the middle of night.

'You're one to talk with your history!' she retorted in between spitting up bile. *Touche,* I thought rolling my eyes, she had got me there. My eyes followed a pair of gliders as they zoomed past us.

'Great!' I said throwing my arms up in the air as I watched the other Minions disappear through the trees as I tried to ignore the sound of Demi's sudden projectile vomiting. 'Can you get it together please!' I said stepping back as even more pairs soared past, some laughing and heckling us as they went.

'I'm sorry!' Demi spluttered leaning against a tree, 'I'm ok, I just can't stomach these hover boots, when I'm too hung over, they're making me feel sick.'

'No, your hangover is making you feel sick!' I snapped glancing down at my humming sliders elevating me a few inches off the ground, they were quickly losing power. The boots used the wearers electro-kinetic energy to create an anti-magnetic field to propel you off the ground, and the faster you went the higher you could physically jump. But being stationery, I was running out of juice and I would have to use extra energy to charge them up again.

'Just leave me behind.' Demi sulked in between heaves.

'I would if I could,' I huffed as I studied my hover gloves which helped you to scale obstacles and prevent falling. 'But I can't leave you so, come on get up!' I said abruptly, looking up as her vomiting seemed to subside. 'Now!' I ordered pulling her up to a stand.

'Alright fine, I can get up myself!' she hissed snatching her arm away. Once on her feet, she took a few deep breaths, and reactivated her sliders, trying to regain her balance as another pair of gliding Minions shot past us.

'Ok good, let's go!' I said dragging her away from the tree by an arm, she wobbled a bit but found her balance. 'Just skate like you've done a thousand times before!' I instructed gliding off. 'Like we learned on the old ice rink, remember? The faster you go the easier it is to balance.'

'I know I know, but its different out here! It's all dark and bumpy.' She grumbled as I skated on ahead darting around the trees. Demi kept pace a few strides behind me and within minutes we were at Alexandra Lake. I skidded to a halt and had to grab Demi to slow her down.

'Where the hell is the bridge, and the vaulting pads?' She asked as we stood at the water's edge confused for a few seconds.

'Do you think this is the test Phoenix was talking about?' I shivered at the sound of his name. 'Do you think everyone got over the lake without falling in?' Demi continued hesitantly. I shrugged in response, looking at the island in the middle of the lake.

'We're gonna have to glide over the water.'

'Uh Raine! last time I checked, neither one of us was called Jesus ok.' She quipped. Can't we skip this part and just complete the rest of the course?' Demi asked slyly.

'What do you think? I snapped as I tilted my head towards the hovering drone humming softly above us. It had been watching us for a while now, lurking even closer ever since we approached the lake. If Phoenix was watching, I couldn't bear the thought of him seeing me fail.

'But I can't even swim!' Demi whined as another team of gliders suddenly burst through the trees on the island and expertly soared over the lake.

'See, its easy!' I exclaimed pointing at them as they skated by. I skipped about ten paces back. 'You've just got to do a *run up* and get enough drift...' I called enthusiastically, as Demi silently looked at me with a wide-eyed stare. 'Just follow me!' I yelled as I zoomed past her and confidently leapt out onto the water. I jumped as high as I could and landed a few inches above the lake creating a violent wave of ripples. I almost lost my balance and fell in, but was able to steady myself with the help of my hover gloves which stopped me from hitting the water's surface. I was on all fours, suspended in mid-air with my face about a foot above the lake. I tentatively pushed myself upright knowing I had seconds before I lost my drift and fell into the filthy lake. Quickly springing myself forward, I gingerly began to glide across the water until I reached the other side. I landed on the bank of the island with a thud and involuntarily rolled over in the soft dirt. I got up with a wide grin plastered across my face as I proudly dusted off my muddy clothes.

'What on earth was that!' Demi's shrill voice cut through the silence as she screamed at me from the other side of the lake. 'I told you that only Jesus could walk on water!'

'Well, at least I made it!' I yelled loudly, 'So shut up and come on!' Demi hesitated for a few seconds but then slowly backed up out of site and suddenly came skating frantically towards the open water. Her hover boots lit up as she seemed to glide effortlessly right over the lake, and without even a ripple, she skidded to a graceful halt right in front of me.

'Did you see that!' She shrieked excitedly. I rolled my eyes enviously.

'Just keep up!' I said bitterly, sailing off into the trees as more Minions passed us on their way back to base.

The morning sky was getting brighter, but it was still dark underneath the leafy island canopy of the island as we weaved through the undergrowth and snaked our way through the modified obstacle course. The drone was still on us and Demi managed to keep up until the end of the exercise. She was close behind me as I sailed straight over the lake on the way back to base. We followed the track religiously, tackling the last few obstacles on the other side with stubborn val-our, and by the time we had scaled the vertical wall, ran the tightrope through the tree tops and jumped on the 100-metre-long zip-line we were met by the daz-zling morning sun.

We were late, and as soon as we got back to base, we changed into our sparring gear, and quickly ran down to the gym in the basement of the palace. We scurried down the dark winding corridor in silence, listening to the muffled voices from the depths below. I knew we were most definitely the last pair back, and I could feel my heart beating loudly inside my chest as I contem-plated the possible penalty for our lateness. I let Demi overtake me as we barged into the windowless room, she had finally sobered up and seemed ready for ac-tion.

'Nice of you to join us.' Phoenix said sarcas-tically as the chatter in the room immediately died down upon our entry. My blood began to boil as he looked me right in the eye. He continued frolicking with Sasha, and I could still see the sly smirk behind his mask as he called the group to reassemble.

I had only seen Phoenix a handful of times in the last few months. Never once having the opportunity ap-proach him privately, and here he was again taunting me in public. I took a deep breath and balled my fists in frustration as we all lined up. Everyone in the room stopped warming up and stood to attention, and I reluctantly got in line beside Demi.

'What's wrong?' She whispered as my eyes welled up with tears. She knew about my relationship with Phoenix, everyone knew. It was then that I noticed Sasha was watching me, and I swore under my breath as Phoenix went over the rules of the first match. His disguised voice blurred into white noise as he described the combat techniques he wanted to see. I closed my eyes as I went over everything, I wanted to scream at him in my head.

'Choose your opponent Phoenix said finally.

'Raine, I challenge you.' I opened my eyes abruptly and I saw Sasha staring back at me. 'Well come on then,' Sasha jeered as she stepped closer. I paused for a moment glancing at Demi who still stood beside me. I think she was hoping that we would also spar after our enforced bonding exercise on the new obstacle course. 'Do you accept my challenge or what?' Sasha laughed, taunting me with a beckoning gesture. I nodded to accept and spotted Phoenix out of the corner of my eye who seemed to be watching our interaction.

'We'll spar next round,' I said smiling at Demi, and I watched Sasha's impatience grow exponentially as she marched off to pick a weapon.

'Are you sure about this?' Demi whispered, 'I heard she sometimes spars with the boys.'
I had heard that too, since Sasha had been at integration for six months longer than us, she didn't have to

repeat everything she'd already done and sometimes got to do things we hadn't experienced yet.

'I'll be alright,' I said confidently knowing that I couldn't refuse her challenge. Weakness was never permitted in the LOE. Demi nodded and went off to find a partner as I headed over to the weapons rack.

'Didn't you hear the rules!' Sasha snapped a bit too angrily for my liking as I ran my hand along an intricately decorated pair of nun chucks. I stopped what I was doing to look her dead in the eye. 'You're not allowed weapons for the first fight,' she snarled, circling me, 'because *you* didn't make it back before sunrise.' I kissed my teeth loudly as she twirled her weapon of choice in her hands. 'Latecomers penalty,' she chuckled as she walked away from me spinning a Bo-staff. I took a long deep breath and mentally prepared myself to take some degree of pain. I turned back to face her just as the drum sounded signalling us to start, and she was already standing within one of the many black rings painted on the gym floor. Multiple sparring matches began simultaneously, most of the sparrers had weapons besides me, Demi, and a few others. As soon as I stepped inside of the black ring Sasha immediately charged me, but I managed to painfully block her first blow with my forearms crossed in the figure of an X. She struck the same place again, trying to break my form but I firmed it just to be able to land a floor balanced side kick into her stomach. She lurched backwards and scowled at me, giving me the impression that I may not be able to hit her again. She landed another strike on my side but she left her whole body open, and I was able to counter attack again and land one more blow to her mid-section. I was starting to see why she hadn't passed her ceremonial bout as I shuffled and swivelled out of the way while she chased me around the ring. I could see that I was making her angry, and my limbs throbbed from where the staff had made contact several times. I knew I could only for so long before she landed a debilitating blow, and as she chased me around the confined space inside the black ring painted on the gym floor, I planned how to out manoeuvre her. I would need to get hold of the Bo-staff somehow and use it against her. I might have been prohibited from starting the match with a weapon but there was no rule against using my opponents. I was able to dodge a few more erratic swings, using the skills I had learned on the gymnastics equipment and on the pole to move around. But she finally caught me, swinging the Bo-staff as she spun around counter clockwise as I tried to leap out of the way of her initial swing. She caught me right in the ribs, and I doubled over giving her the opportunity to land a flurry blows to my back. I was too winded to get away and I suddenly went down as she hit me mercilessly. My training suit doing little to block the impact of the continuous blows. I could see Phoenix's feet coming closer as I curled up into a ball and Sasha screamed over me ordering me to submit. I flipped over as I refused adamantly, doing my best to block her continuous attack with my legs. *If only I could snatch the staff!*

'Submit!' She screamed as she delivered sporadic blows to my exposed limbs. I grunted through the pain and stupidly uncovered my head to spit at her.

'I will never submit to you!' I hissed, spitting up at her, but I left my head open and she quickly kicked me in the face. The tip of her foot awkwardly caught me in the jaw, giving me the opportunity, I needed to grab the Bo-staff. She was surprised when I seized it, and I smiled a mouth full of bloody teeth as she tried to yank it from me. But I held on tight as we began to wrestle for it, wrapping y body around it and refusing to let go. I was determined to not get hit by it again, and I continued to hold on even when she began to kick me in the side. I could see others gathering around our ring as I used one of my legs to kick her in the exposed leg she had planted onto the floor. She screeched in pain, grabbing her shin as she fell heavily. Still holding onto the staff, I struggled to stand up, using it to help me get up to my feet. I stood over her manically, raising the wooden pole high above my head ready to strike. I relished the terror in her eyes for a few seconds, spitting the blood in mouth down on her. But just as I was about to assault her with her very own weapon, the sound of the drum being struck repeatedly echoing throughout the gym. And just like that, the match was suddenly over, but I still landing a debilitating blow making Phoenix step into the ring and yank the staff from me. I glared at him as I held on insolently for a moment before letting go. He snatched it and I finally breathed out as I looked around, noticing that everybody was still staring at me. Sasha was still writhing on the floor and Phoenix pointed the Bo-staff at the closest spectators.

'Get her up.' he hissed looking around., 'And who told you lot to stop sparring?' There was silence as they continued to stare.

'What the flip are you all looking at?' I snapped as I spat out a mouth full of saliva thickened with blood.

'Enough!' Phoenix barked pointed the staff at my face, and holding it a few inches in front of my nose. 'Striking after the drum will cost you another penalty!' I narrowed my eyes angrily and kissed my teeth before wiping my mouth and tuning away shrugging.

'Now move it and switch opponents!' Phoenix growled looking around as he threw the staff across the ring. Everyone hastily averted their eyes as they began to look for a new sparring partner. 'Late comers, you may now pick a weapon.' He announced as he glanced back in my direction. 'You don't move, I will deal with you in a minute.' I rolled my eyes away from his gaze and crossed my arms over my chest.

'Are you ok?' Demi asked worriedly as she rushed over to me as soon as she thought Phoenix wasn't looking.

'I'm fine!' I snapped wiping the tears out of my eyes, and with that I left her there as I marched right out of the gym.

***

'I *know you* put her up to that?' I barked, instinctively knowing that the shadowy figure standing in the doorway belonged to Phoenix. His masked refracted a little of light in the dimly lit room as he silently approaching my bed. It was a dark grey cloudy day, and the grimy dormitory windows barely let in any daylight in.

'Actually, it was Sasha's idea,' he replied candidly. 'You're not exactly what I would call, well liked...' he remarked trailing off as his heavy boots echoed around the empty dorm room.

'Well, I'm not here to make friends,' I hissed as I stopped nursing my wounds and squinted at him as he drew closer. I was surprised to see him, thinking that he would have sent one of his Minions to apprehend me after storming out of the gym. Instead, I had gained his attention, but his jovial approach had me a little confused.

'What do you want?' I asked suspiciously as he stood next to my bed and leant against the same window, I had used to call to him months before. My mind was racing, here he was after avoiding me for so long, and I suddenly didn't know even what to say except.

'Where is she?' I asked in a measured tone, trying to keep my emotions in check. I knew screaming at him would get me nowhere so I needed to stay as calm as possible. I had planned this moment a thousand times over in my head, and now I was just completely overwhelmed. 'Where have you taken her?' I asked again but he just stood there, staring at me silently. 'Phoenix...' I said desperately, my breathing becoming erratic. 'Please… You need to tell me where Tia is.' I said, my voice cracking as tears blurred my vision. He continued to stare at me as I struggled to keep my composure.

'*Nala*, Is safe.' He said finally as he turned around to look out of the window.

'Nala?' I repeated in confusion. 'Who the hell is… wait, you, you changed her name?' I hissed in disbelief. 'How dare you!' I cried hysterically, swallowing the large lump in my throat.

Phoenix continued to stare at me coldly, antagonising me with his eyes. 'I'm her mother, she needs me!' I sobbed.

'She doesn't even remember you Raine,' he said as if he was disgusted. 'And now, *you* to belong to the LOE, you'll never be free to be a mother.'

'Please Phoenix… just let me see her… I need to see her. I need to know that she's ok.' I said getting up off my bed and standing up in front of him.

'Of course, she's ok, she's with her father!' He snapped viciously.

'You know what I mean!' I retorted.

'Do I?' Phoenix said coldly. 'After *everything* you've done to me!'

'So, if you didn't come up here to let me see her then why are you here!' I shouted as I wept. 'What the hell do you want? To gloat and rub the fact that you have her and I don't in my flipping face!' I spat pushing him away from me.

'I don't see you worrying this much about your *other* daughter?' He hissed callously with a smirk on his face.

'Don't you dare talk about her!' I screamed as I began to pound on his chest. 'You can't do this to me Phoenix, you have to let me see my child!'

'No... I don't!' he bellowed as he threw me down onto the bed. I lay there for a moment silently and motionlessly as my body recalled the blows from my fight barely an hour ago and began to throb. 'She's, *my* daughter!' He spat over me as I wiped away the tears and snot from my face.

'*But* there is something you can do to maybe change things...'

'What?' I barked as I sprang up and sat on the edge of the bed, 'I'll do it!' I said hastily wiping my face, 'I just need to see my Tia again!'

'Her name is Nala,' phoenix said coldly.

'Right. Nala of course.' I mumbled submissively.

'Good, but you have to do exactly what I say or trust me you will never *ever* see Nala again!'

'Name it! I'll do anything!' I exclaimed, clawing at the mattress with my fingernails as I began to rock back and forth.

'Ok, help me get rid of Rook,' he said venomously, 'and I'll let you see Nala again.'
The blood in my veins ran cold and my tongue felt as dry as a desert as I tried to respond, but I could hardly speak.

'You... mean kill him?' I asked for clarification and he nodded slowly, not taking his eyes off mine. 'I... I can't...' I mumbled, my mouth suddenly feeling gummy.

'I knew it! so, you chose him over me, and now you're choosing *him* over your own daughter!' He thundered as his ripped the mask off his face and glared down at me.

'No, you don't understand, it's not that, I...I just can't bec–'

'Because what!' he roared cutting me off.

'Because he's, he's, my brother!' I shouted, unable to keep the secret inside any longer.

'What?' Phoenix said, as he narrowed his eyes and scowled.

'Pathetic little LIAR!' he growled frenziedly as he balled his fists and turned his back on me.

'It's true!' I screamed desperately but he ignored me as he began to walk toward the dormitory door.

'I should have listened to widow, and Goose!' He hissed as he stamped away.

'What? Phoenix! Don't you walk away from me without telling me where my daughter is!' I shrieked as I lunged at him from behind, digging my nails into his face. 'You can't keep her from me!'

'If you want her back you know what you have to do!' Phoenix barked as he peeled me off his back with ease, and threw me onto the nearest bed, this time pinning me down. I continued to thrash about, lashing out and trying to bite him as if I was possessed, but he managed to hold me still.

'No more lies!' He grunted through gritted teeth as he sat on my legs, and put his hands around my throat. I could see the derangement in his eyes.

'Ok… I'm sorry, I lied, I, I am lying to you… but I'm done, and, and Rook isn't my brother, he nothing to me, I'll do it, ok It's done!' I wheezed as my eyes welled with salty tears; I was suddenly gasping for air as his grip tightened. I couldn't breathe and I quickly began to feel light headed as I dug my fingernails into his forearms trying to make him let go.

'It's too late for your apologies!' He hissed as I reached out and dug my nails into his face. 'This is *your fault* you know that? You always have to make things so difficult! I'll make sure that Nala turns out nothing like you!'

'Phoenix, please don't do this… you're right ok, it is all my fault, just think about what your about to do! I'm, I'm her mother.' I croaked as I tried to prise his fingers from around my neck but I was barely audible. I was blacking out, and the last bit of air was leaving my lungs when he unexpectantly loosened his grip and abruptly climbed off me. I heaved, spluttering as I forced air into my lungs. as Phoenix didn't say another word as he began to walk towards the door. He just left me lying there, staring at his back, and listening to the echo of his heavy footsteps disappear while I coughed and gasped for air.

18

FOREVER LIVE LOE

Ryan was standing on an elevated platform in front of the energetic crowd, dressed as Rook, his infamous alter ego. He looked down at the excited pledges in full battle disguise, an audience of newly masked Minions eagerly awaiting his instruction. The setting sun shone in through the huge glass window illuminating his shimmering mask as he began to speak.

'L.O.E Minions! are you ready to bring about the coming of a new dawn!' The crowd cheered hysterically, chanted L.O.E back at him in revering approval. 'We, The LOE Society, my brothers and sisters are going to make the BFP crumble and fall to their knees!' I looked around at the throng of dark grey hoods nodding their heads in agreement, and couldn't help my belly from tying itself into tight knots. 'This year's Libion Day will mark the end of our oppression!' He said as he stretched his hands over the admiring audience.

'We will no longer be hunted, tortured, chased or im-
prisoned!' The crowd roared again, stamping their feet
in excitement as my stomach flipped uncontrollably.
Libion Day was the annual celebration to commemo-
rate the creation of the Conformed British Fundamentalist Party, also known as the BFP. 'Once the prime
minister is assassinated the rest of the BFP will bow
down or die along with him!' The crowd cheered again
as Ryan's words rung over and over in my head. 'No
more recons!' Ryan yelled, riling up the crowd. 'No
more recovery, no more reconstitution, and no more
reconciliation!

'NO MORE!' The crowd chanted back in
unison.

'Only then, my brothers and sisters, will we
truly be free!' Ryan exclaimed as he raised his LOE
wings signal hi into the air above his head. His disguised voice echoed around the room and the crowd
descended into an excited frenzy, throwing up the
L.O.E 'L' and chanting LOE, LOE, LOE. I promptly decided that I had seen enough, and covering my ears
against the brainwashed white noise I hastily zig-
zagged through the cheering horde towards the door.
I took a deep breath once in the corridor. I could still
hear Ryan continuing his speech as I left the building
and the noise of the animated crowd behind. I tele-
called him and just as I knew it would, his plug forwarded me to mind mail where I proceeded to leave
him a message.

***

The cool evening breeze whipped around me as I anxiously awaited Ryan's arrival. I hadn't seen him for over a week, and he had missed our last late-night sparring session without explanation. I did not appreciate the fact that I had to infiltrate one of his stupid little meetings to get access to him. I was loitering around our usual meeting spot under the cover of darkness, and I cautiously took in my surroundings before squeezing through the gaping hole in the railings of the old abandoned playground. I manoeuvred around the mangled climbing frames and upturned tarmac toward a large set of swings underneath an ancient overgrown weeping willow. I lowered myself onto a seat veiled in the shadowy darkness of the trees overhanging leaves. The old swing squeaked under my weight, and I jumped as Ryan came bounding through the gaping hole in the broken gate.

'You're late!' I breathed startled, bringing the drifting swing to a gentle stop as he quickly approached me.

'Sorry, my meeting ran over.' He said breathlessly, sitting down on the swing beside me.

'Hmm, I'll bet.' I huffed 'how are killing of the prime minister going?' I asked disapprovingly.

'Didn't I tell you to stay out of my flipping meetings!' Ryan barked loudly suddenly turning on me. 'There not for you, and that better not be the reason why you summoned me out here!' He said accusingly, 'You're meant to be laying low and minding your own damn business!' he snapped eyeing me suspiciously. I kissed my teeth in response to his harsh rebuke.

'Well, it isn't actually!' I retorted, deciding to shelve that issue until we dealt with the matter at hand. 'I don't care about your stupid plans.' I lied crossing my arms.

'Well, what is it then?' Ryan sighed sounding annoyed as he got up and stood over me.

'First of all, where were you the other night? I was in the gym for ages, I had to practice alone! no call no message nothing, and you didn't even answer my hologra–'

'Raine!' Ryan grunted interrupting my rant. 'I don't have time for this, you know I get called away on LOE business without notice.'

'You sound just like Phoenix,' I muttered into the breeze.

'You what?' Ryan demanded as he walked around the swing to face me. I rolled my eyes towards him.

'I said… I spoke to Phoenix the other day…'

'And?' He asked grimacing as he gave me his full attention, 'did you get any useful info– '

'No, he erm wanted me to set you up.' I mumbled quickly standing up in front of him.

'What? '

'He wants me to help him kill you in exchange–
'

'For seeing Tia?' Ryan said finishing off my sentence. I nodded and he threw his head back and began to laugh loudly. This was far from the reaction I was expecting, and I watched him in bewilderment until he calmed down.

'I can't believe that he wants my own sister to honey trap me.' Ryan continued to chuckle until I thumped his forearm.

'Well, it's not bloody funny to me, he's planning to kill you and he wants my frigging help!'

'Of course... sorry,' he said frowning, 'so what did you say?'

'I said NO, obviously!' I replied as I crossed my arms over my chest.

'Well, you need to go back and tell him that you've changed your mind.' He announced as I stood there perplexed, still staring at him with my mouth agape.

'Are you nuts!' I shrieked, 'what, have you got a death wish or something?'

'Raine just trust me ok!' Ryan sighed as he placed his hands onto my shoulders reassuringly. He gave a look and knew that he was serious.

'No this is crazy, whatever your planning, it'll never work!' I said shaking him off.

'Yes, it will!' He said clutching my face and looking deep into my eyes. 'Look, we'll just trap him by making him think you are trapping me.' Ryan declared incessantly, his voice rising as he rubbed his hands together.'

'Nothing's ever that easy Ry... and besides I told him we're brother and sister...' I muttered breaking eye contact.

'Why the hell would you do that? Ryan groaned as he sat back down on the swing seemingly deflated.

'He was going to–' I trailed off knowing Ryan would lose his temper if he knew Phoenix had nearly strangled me to death. 'We were arguing and it just came out.' I said defending the fact that I had exposed the one and only secret I was supposed to keep to myself.

Ryan looked up at me disappointed. 'What else was I supposed to say? When I refused to help him *murder you*, he accused me of choosing you, over my baby!' I sat down on the swing beside him and sighed loudly.

'Did he believe you?' Ryan asked after giving me the silent treatment for a minute or so.

'Nope.' I said sighing again. 'Ironically, telling him the truth convinced him that I'm even more of a liar.' Ryan chuckled.

'Ok, good we can use that.' Ryan mused as he rubbed his chin.

'How?' I asked shrugging.

'If he didn't even believe you then we can stick to the original plan.'

'Wait what!' I exclaimed, shocked that he still thought this was a good idea. 'You can't be serious?' I huffed loudly. 'There must be another way around this,' I said shaking my head vigorously.

'I'm deadly serious.' Ryan said sternly as I jumped up and stood in front of him. 'Somehow you need to get his plug, I need to hack it.' He said more to himself than to me as he gazed up into the night sky.

'And how am I supposed to do that?' I grunted, crossing my arms.

'I don't know, seduce him innit.' Ryan casually replied and I slapped him in the chest as I kissed my teeth.

'I can't believe you just said that, Ryan!'

'Well, it's not like you're not used to– '

'What? Being a whore?' I spat angrily as I walked away.

'Raine, I didn't mean it like that.' Ryan called jumping up and grabbing my arm.

'Oh yeah, so how did you mean it?' I hissed snatching my arm away.

'Look,' Ryan sighed as he squeezed the bridge of his nose before looking down at me.

'You want to see your baby again, don't you?' He probed without breaking eye contact.

'Why would you ask me that!' I snapped. 'Of course, I do, you know I do!'

'Then getting on his good side is the only way. This isn't the time to be sensitive about your feelings. You're a Minion now, you have to play the game.' Ryan said staring into my eyes. 'You have to get him to trust you or you *will* lose your baby forever.'

'But but what if he doesn't buy it!' I cried worriedly. Ryan sighed, peering at me as he calmly sat me back down on the swing.

'Then make him buy it.'

***

The arena was filled to over maximum capacity, and I took a deep breath wiping my sweaty palms onto my fighting suit. The drum roll finally rang out as Rex re-took the microphone. The tenth fight had just finished and the whole arena waited with baited breath to see which numbers would appear on the holographic display above our heads. I knew Phoenix would be watching me, everyone would, but I felt as if I could feel his eyes on me already. He was out there somewhere watching from within the blurry darkness of the crowd. I had tried to get closer to him in the month since the night me and Ryan had devised a plan of entrapment in the abandoned park. But it was proving trickier than I thought. He didn't trust me and to be honest I couldn't exactly blame him.

'Next up is number 1 versus 28' The sound of my number rang in my ears as Rex's artificial voice echoed around the stadium. Two holographic digits flickered into focus and an image of my face materialized next to my floating number. 28 had been my identity for the last 6 months and hopefully tonight I would get to shed it for good. I took a deep breath as I slowly rose to my feet, not yet contemplating my obvious opponent. The time had come for me to prove my worth and earn the right to call myself an *Inferior*. I stood to attention as a light orb suddenly appeared above my head and over fighter number 1, Sasha who was standing just a few rows in front of me.

'You may now proceed to the ring.' Rex announced as I covered my brow squinting under the brightness of the spherical light. The drummers began to thump their skinned instruments in an animalistic rhythm as we made our way down to the centre of the arena, light orbs in tow. They followed our every move as we quickly descended to the raised platform. Sasha got to the elevated stage first and she watched me get into place on the opposite side of the ring. Once we were both in position, the drumming abruptly ended and the light orbs disintegrated, giving way to the huge spot lights that lit up the thick black circular line surrounding us. There was a lot riding on this fight, for both of us. I didn't have time to go through integration again but if Sasha didn't pass her second initiation ceremony, she would become an outcast. I had no idea how she had pulled of a public rematch but my extracurricular training with Ryan was about to be put to the test. She was bidding for a position in Phoenix's crew, she had to be, and I knew winning this match would give her the opportunity to join his faction and humiliate me in the process. I, naturally planned on joining my brother's crew, after I had won my initiation match of course. Another spotlight suddenly illumed the large array of weaponry displayed on the wooden rack just outside the black ring. Sasha chose quickly, and I silently watched her retrieve an engraved staff and confidently get back in position. *What was it with her and that Bo-staff?* I chuckled to myself as I shook my head. I preferred using both my hands chose a sleek pair of kali sticks before retaking my place back inside the ring. The platform began to rise into the air only stopping after elevating us several feet. The black ring around the perimeter flashed red meaning that a heat forcefield was now in play. If you were thrown through it, you would be severely burnt before breaking something when you landed on the ground below.

'You know the rules!' Rex declared as we sized each other up. '*Begging* for *mercy* is an automatic loss, pleading for time to *recover* is an automatic *loss,* and one *toe* outside of the red ring is also an automatic loss! You will fight until one of you goes down and submits. do you understand?' We both nodded as we locked eyes in an intense glare. The crowd whooped excitedly as assumed our starting positions. I squinted under the glare of the piercing spotlights. Because of the intense brightness, I could only see as far as the edge of the ring before the steep drop. I was ready as I zeroed in on Sasha's flushed face, her mouth twisted into a tight snarl as she clenched the Bo-staff with both hands. I could only hear the spectators surrounding the raised circular platform, elevated in the darkness of the ceremonial arena. It seemed as if the whole of the slums had turned out to watch the initiation ceremony and to bet on their favourite fighter. Those that could not fit inside the arena, lined the outside of the palace to watch it on a huge projected hologram in the night sky. A drum roll suddenly sounded drowning out the howling crowd.

'FIGHT!' Rex finally announced, his magnified voice thundering around the domed arena as the drumroll abruptly halted. The crowd was deathly silent as we danced around each other for a moment, swiping and ducking out of the reach of each other's blows. Until Sasha finally took the first definitive move. She couldn't help herself, and the crowd roared as she charged at me with her staff. She took a swipe at my head but I was able to side step, quickly deflecting her swing with one kali stick and then using the advantage to attack her rear side with a two-hit combination. She stumbled but rapidly recovered with a horizontal twist and a quick-fire strike to my lower stomach. I backed up, my suit taking most of the impact as she bombarded my abdomen with offensive blows. Our fighting suits were designed to take the brunt of any attack, but to also light up wherever they were struck, giving the opponent a short period of time to wreak havoc on the temporary weak spot until the area faded back to black. I skipped back and fought off her assault, kicking her in the shin and going low on my forearm to use my other leg to sweep her off her feet. She fell onto her back as the crowd gasped in anticipation. I jumped up and instantly delivered a melee of shots to her exposed limbs. I then attacked her midsection, continually blocking the Bo-staff with one hand until she rolled away to escape the flurry of blows. I let my guard down, chasing her tightly coiled body as she tumbled across the sprung floor. She kept her limbs tightly compact, and using the Bo-staff miraculously sprang back up to her feet just before she reached the edge of the glowing red ring. It was an impressive move, and the crowd booed me unforgivingly while chanting her number. I stood ready as she began to show off, twirling and throwing around the staff as she began to circle me. Finally, she stood still on the oppo-

site side of the ring, catching her breath as she glow-
ered at me. I baited her, going slightly closer and taking a few taunting swipes, but not getting near enough
for her to get a good strike. It didn't take long for her
to take the bait, and she lunged at me as soon as she
thought I was within range. She slid the staff through
her palms, shooting her weapon at me like a harpoon.
But I cartwheeled on my sticks and she missed. She
tried again, swinging the staff around her body to
catch me as I vaulted behind her. But I back flipped out
of reach as she leapt after me across the ring. It was my
turn to show off, much to her annoyance and to the appreciation of the crowd. She grunted in frustration as
the sound of my number being chanted began to
drown out hers. That seemed to encourage her into
launching another attack, and she came at me again. I
was done playing games, and my fighting sticks met
her staff ferociously, hers on the attack and mine
crossed in defence as we tussled violently. The crowd
spurred us on, our weapons locked together as we both
tried to dominate. I leapt away from the stalemate and
she caught me in the ribs but I spun around her and
was able to deliver a sneaky blow to her face. I watched
her spit blood out onto the floor and raised one of my
sticks into the ait triumphantly. The crowd cheered as
she glared at me, wildly exited at the first sight of
blood. Colourful holograms began to shine in the darkness as spectators visually showed their support for
their chosen fighter. My number repeatedly flashed in
the gloom.

'NUMBER 28 TAKES FIRST BLOOOD!' The commentator screamed, his voice rumbling around the arena through the amplified speakers. I jumped at the sound of his electrified tone, up until now it had been completely drowned out by the intensity of my own thoughts. But I knew that drawing first blood would get me major points, and I quickly collected myself to get ready to go in for an attack. It was time to change tactics and fighting style just like Ryan had coached me to do, and I didn't give Sasha any time to contemplate my next move. Nor did I give her a chance to strategize as I unexpectantly charged her, hoping to catch her off-guard and provoke an impromptu reaction. She went for me, as predicted, and I took the hit so I could use all my effort to sweep her off her feet. Her footing was weak, and she fell onto her back clumsily clinging to the Bo-staff. She looked up at me with disdain swiping at me wildly. I wasn't within her reach and dropping my fighting sticks, I took a few blows before I caught the end of her swinging Bo-staff. I jumped onto her legs and yanked it from her as she looked at me crazily.

'SUBMIT!' I screamed as the crowd booed me mercilessly for showing mercy and giving her a chance to verbally submit instead of beating her into staying down. Sasha looked at me defiantly and tried to kick out of her position as projectiles hit the stage. I dug the staff further into her stomach. 'Submit!' I repeated through gritted teeth as I put all my weight on it.

'Are you for real?' she spat looking at me angrily. 'And lose my chance of ever grading up to Inferior? Never bitch, you'll have to kill me right here!' Infuriated, I pushed the staff even harder into her ribs, forcing it upwards and onto her throat. But she suddenly shifted her weight sideways and swiped the staff from underneath me with her nearest hand. I stumbled and almost lost my footing as she regained control of her weapon. I had to retreat, grabbing my kali sticks as I backed up. Sasha sprang to her feet, and the crowd went crazy as she spun around to face me dead on. 'You should've finished it when you had the chance you stupid little whore!' Sasha shouted, backed up by the approving roars of the crowd. 'Who the hell do you think you are telling me to submit!' She yelled soaking up the excitement. 'I'm gonna make you wish you were still lying on your back in Jamaica!' The crowd began to heckle me, she was right I shouldn't have given her a chance. I would lose points now she was back on her feet, and it was clear that this match was as much as about the theatrical drama and entertainment as it was about the actual fight.

'We thought it was all over but it looks like the tables have unexpectantly turned!' the commentator shouted from somewhere in the dark arena. I could see Sasha's bravado building as the crowd chanted her number as they sent their holographic support into the air. A sea of flashing 1s lit up the shadows revealing the jostling audience supporting her. She began to move in a circular motion, giving me a wide birth as she pranced around the perimeter of the ring still soaking up the crowd's admiration.

'Number 1 has everything to lose if she doesn't win this fight, but number 28 also must also prove herself worthy of the LOE. So, who's it going to be folks, who will triumph? Who will be the winner of this fight?' I shook off the commentator's words as my eyes followed Sasha's strut around the ring. I *did* have to give it to her, she had surprised me twice now, so maybe she had learned a thing or two since our last encounter. But as the audience egged her on rambunctiously, I decided that I would not give her another chance to surprise me again. I had been training for this moment day in and day out for the last 6 months, and Ryan had taught me well. So, I was about to finish this and give Sasha exactly asked for by beating her into submission.

***

'You're late…Again.' I snapped as I watched Ryan approach the swings. 'We hardly meet, so the least you could do is be on time!' I said sulkily as I pulled of my Inferior mask.

'We shouldn't even be meeting outside of the faction rallies at all, people could be watching' Ryan replied, ignoring my moodiness as he sat down beside me and looked around. The abandoned park was often crawling with crimheads and other unsavoury activities.

'Anyway, how was the ceremony after party?' he sighed. 'If I remember correctly, mine was crazy!' he smiling, as he shoulder-bumped me excitedly. 'You deserved to celebrate after that beat down, and against a 2nd round Minion! Maybe I trained you a bit too well.' He laughed enthusiastically, but I shrugged my shoulders in response. The high of winning my initiation match and getting through the ceremony in one piece having already worn off. I was officially an inferior Loelife, but what did I have to show for it?

'I would have enjoyed the after party a lot more if my brother had stuck around to celebrate my victory after publicly accepting my pledge and announcing my entry into his faction.' I said irritably, nursing a lingering hangover. Demi had managed to get hold of a bit of crim last night, and I could already feel my body yearning for the drug after just a teeny-weeny taste. But still, I was determined to stay sober.

'Where did you disappear too?' I demanded turning to him. 'One minute you were handing me an inferior mask and next minute you were gone.'

'Raine don't start.' Ryan said side glancing me as he rubbed his face.

'You didn't even say goodbye,'
Ryan groaned loudly.

'You were busy with your friends!'

'I don't have any friends!' I retorted.

'Yes, you do, that girl Denise, you introduced me to-'

'*Demi*, is not my friend!'

'Ok...' Ryan sighed rolling his eyes, 'Anyway, how would that have looked to Phoenix if I stuck around all night?'

393

'It would have looked like I was doing exactly what I was supposed to be doing.' I snapped scornfully.

'So, you spoke to him then?' Ryan asked, still ignoring my grumpy disposition.

'You could say that…' I sighed as blurry memories of last night's sloppy intercourse flashed before my eyes.

'See if I stuck around how would that have worked?' I shot him a look and he rubbed a hand through his budding crazy dreads.

'So, what did the *almighty Phoenix* say?' Ryan asked sarcastically as my stomach turned. I was starting to feel physically sick.

'Well?' he pressed impatiently when I didn't immediately respond, 'Did you get any info.

'Not much,' I sighed looking away from him.

'What does that mean?' He asked watching me closely.

'Let's just say I don't think that he's holding Tia somewhere in the slums.'

'What makes you say that?' Ryan said squinting at me.

'I don't know,' I burped, holding my chest as bile gurgled at the back of my throat. 'I just have this feeling.' Ryan looked thoughtful as he looked off into the distance.

'But he did say that–' I was suddenly interrupted by an incoming call on Ryan's telekom.

'One sec...' He said as he pulled out the hand-held device slid it open. An encrypted hologram materialised above the palm held pad, and I watched Ryan scan it intently for a few seconds.

'I've got to go...' he said as soon as the blue lights flickered and disappeared.

'But you just got here.' I huffed.

'It's business.' He said indifferently as he stood up to leave.

'Libion Day business?' I quizzed as he clicked on his sliders to warm them up.

'Raine, what did I say?' He retorted; his eyes fixed on me. 'Just leave it alone.' He sighed shaking his head before turning to glide away.

'Well, how can you not expect me to get curious now that I have to attend all your faction assembles?'

'*You*, just worry about Phoenix and the plan, all that other stuff doesn't concern you.'

'Yeah, well the thing about that is...' I said running after him and bumping into his back as he stopped gliding mid stride.

'What?' He groaned loudly as he tipped his head back and let out an exasperated sigh.

'Erm well...' I squeaked, my voiced elevating in decibels. 'Phoenix wants your location on Libion Day.' Ryan spun around and glared down at me angrily.

'Raine, what the hell! I hope you told him you couldn't get it right? The plan was supposed to be executed before then, everything's been set up, once you get his plug, we can hack it and get rid of him!'

'Yes, I know. I did say I couldn't get it… at first but he kept pressuring me, Ryan! I thought he was onto me so I had to change tactics, and I said I would try.' I took a deep breath and quickly continued before he could cuss me. 'But that's not all he wants, not only does he want me to get your coordinates…' I sighed wincing. 'He has demanded that I join his faction and glide with him on the day instead of you.' I glanced down at my sliders recoiling in anticipation.'

'Did you plan this?' Ryan snapped belligerently, 'You do realise you were never actually meant to be going with me right!' I nodded timidly. 'He was just *meant to think you were going* with me RIGHT!' he barked loudly.

'Ry, I swear, it was all his idea.' I said quietly. Ryan looked like his blood was about to boil over.

'I… I… think he's trying to test my loyalty.' I stuttered. 'I mean, him calling the shots was to be expected, right?' I rambled, and Ryan looked around the park before he spoke again. 'I'm sure it'll all work out.

'Raine, are you really that naïve?' Ryan hissed. 'Phoenix wants to infiltrate the mission and take all the glory, kill me in the process, and probably *kill you too!*' I took a deep breath not really knowing what to say. The notion wasn't implausible, considering that he had almost killed me already.

'Talk about killing *three* birds with one stone,' I muttered, which seemed to infuriate Ryan even more.

'If I find out you've got anything to do with this!' He snarled, sticking his index finger in my face.

'Ryan, I swear, those were his terms, I had nothing to do with it!' I sighed slapping his hand away. 'What's the big deal any way, I'm ready for Libion day, I've been to the meetings...' I said after a few quiet seconds, 'We just need to make a new plan.'

'I don't want you there!' He roared loudly, making me jump out of my skin. 'I wanted *you*, as far away from Libion Day as physically possible!' He said heatedly as he slapped his puffed-up chest. 'I cannot do what I need to do and think about protecting you all the time.'

'I don't need your protection.' I huffed, putting my hands on my hips. 'You have no idea what you're talking about do you?' Ryan scoffed narrowing his eyes.

'Fill me in then!' I replied angrily crossing my arms, 'So, yuh wan duppy de Prime Minster, and den wha?' I spat; it had been a long time since I had spoken in patois but I was too pissed to contain it.

'Keep your flipping voice down!' Ryan grunted as he whipped his head around again, scanning the rustling bushes on the outskirts of the park.

'Gwan nuh, talk de ting den, spit it out!' I said irately, and Ryan took me by the arm and frogmarched me back underneath the weeping willow that covered the swings.

'All you need to know *is* once this is done it helps our family!' He whispered quietly, 'but I have to be the one to pull the trigger!'

'Ryan, what are you not telling me?'

'Don't worry about it?' He said coldly as he turned his back on me to look around again.

'I want to know what you're hiding?' I demanded ignoring him, 'Don't you think it's time that you told me everything?' I spat walking around to face him. 'I'm an Inferior now, I can handle it!'

'Just stop!' he hissed as he covered my mouth and pushed me down onto the swing. 'All this LOE stuff is going to your fucking head, and you just need to stay in your lane.' He groaned rubbing his face. 'You really think being an Inferior means anything? You're a nobody... A dogsbody, A flipping glorified ghost, an overrated Minion. You're nothing but a bloody number, do you understand?' He paused, lowering his voice which was echoing around the park. '*I*, just need you to concentrate on getting the twins back ok, and to be able to do that, you need to do exactly as I say until this whole damn thing is all over!' His words stung, and I watched the dust particles float around us in the scattered moonlight so I didn't have to make eye contact.

'Do you understand?' Ryan asked in a much calmer tone as he clicked his sliders back on. 'I said do you understand? He asked as if I was slow.

'*Yes!*' I mumbled finally, just as his telekom beeped again.

'Look... I've really gotta go.' he said sighing.

'Are you wearing a plug?' he asked trying to catch my eye.

'Don't be stupid! After everything that happened last time?' I snapped avoiding his gaze.

'Here,' he said chucking a box wrapped in brown paper at me.

'What is it?' I asked sceptically.

'Just open it, I was meant to give it to you last night at the after party but I didn't get the chance.' I tucked it under my arm stubbornly and continued to look out into the distance. 'I also left something in your dorm underneath the bed.' I didn't respond, and he sighed loudly as he skated away, leaving me alone with the crimheads to sulk in the park. After a few minutes alone I pulled the box out of my armpit and ripped off the brown paper. I opened it up to reveal a new sleek telekom set, and I popped the plug into my ear as I took the small telekom pad out of the box. A holographic image of Ryan immediately popped up and grinned back at me.

'Congratulations on your passing your initiation sis, I'm proud of you!' I smiled as the hologram quickly faded away in scattered pixels, and wondered what Ryan had left for me underneath my bed.

19

LIBION DAY
GREATER LONDON 2060

The scattered clouds danced across the bright blue sky as we fervently skated along the derelict tracks towards Finsbury Park Tube Station. It was the day we had all been waiting for, and I shook off my nauseous anxiety as a chilly breeze whipped around my face. I was wearing the dynamic sliders Ryan had left in a box under dormitory bed. Much better than the pair I had to earn during my training, and I didn't have to exert too much energy to kept up with the gliding group. In fact, I purposely trailed behind the faction of fellow inferior initiates as we sailed along the rails in a parallel formation, trying my best to stay out Phoenix's peripheral.

It was already mid-morning by the time we glided into the deserted tube station, and the warm stale air hit me as soon as we descended the broken escalators. We skated across a vacant platform and jumped onto the tracks, gliding into the darkness of the large subway tunnel. My contact lenses automatically activated in the darkness as we travelled in complete silence, my ears popping every now as we descended deeper and deeper into the depths of the underground. Suddenly, the radiant glow of florescent graffiti lit up the tunnel around us, transforming the atmosphere into a florescent blur of colour as we sailed by. We were gliding so fast that the never-ending tunnel felt psychedelic as the signature of the LOE Society seemed to fly off the walls. The notorious symbol, a feathered pair of eagle's wings with the Greek letters ΓθΣ sprawled in between them created a flapping optical illusion as we zoomed past.

'*Now remember Inferiors, all you have to do is create a diversion!*' Phoenix articulated subconsciously as he led the group past another platform at top speed. A rush of butterflies swirled inside my stomach as we hovered past the defaced sign for Highbury and Islington. This was the closest I had been to where I had grown up in years.

'*I have heard rumours of insolent talk rising through the ranks.*' Phoenix announced as he continued to communicate with us telepathically. '*The switching of objectives is strictly prohibited! Stick to the objective you have been assigned and carry out the orders you have been given. Your only other assignment is then to get the hell out of there... alive. Anyone caught deviating from the plan will be severely punished for their brazen insubordination!*' Phoenix asserted psychically, his mundane instructions interrupting the long-lost childhood memories flashing through my mind and bringing me back to my grim reality. *'Do not... I repeat, do not try to be a hero... Today is not that day!'* He declared as he led us through the dimly lit Kings Cross Station where we had to jump a platform and glide around a stationary train. *'Due to today's unique... situation...'* He continued as soon as we were back on the tracks. *'All surrounding tube tunnels within a mile radius of the event will be barricaded shut... Leaving them open would leave the sub community too vulnerable to outside infiltration.'*

'That wasn't the original plan!' A male voice yelled out shattering the serene silence.

'How dare you interrupt me when I'm tele-talking!' Phoenix barked shouting down the heckler. 'Remember you rank Inferior!' He asserted, his voice echoing around the dark tunnel. 'Today is no ordinary Libion Day and we are not going to jeopardize the *L.O.E* by leaving the access routes open so some, pathetic traitorous Inferior can lead the Recons right through our back door!' He paused for a few seconds before once again addressing us telepathically. *'The fact of the matter is that some of you will get caught today, and we cannot risk any of you leaking vital intel to the government.'* Disapproving mumbles arose from the troupe and bounced off the circular walls as we whooshed passed another vacant platform.

'Silence!' Phoenix ordered loudly, 'every one of you willingly pledged your allegiance to the LOE! You all fought to be here, remember that!' He let his words hang in the air for a moment as the finally murmurs simmered down. 'Today, you will learn and understand what pledging your life to The LOE actually means!' Phoenix yelled, obviously annoyed by the audacity of his inferior faction. 'Every *single* mission is a test, and only the worthy make it back alive…' A tense atmosphere settled over the group like a heavy smog as we drew closer to Central London. It was now clear to every Inferior present that we were nothing more than collateral damage, and silent contemplation prevailed for the next few minutes. Leaving us to listen to the faint whooshing sound of our sliders gliding a few inches above the metal tracks.

Finally, the sound of white noise drifted in through the tunnel walls and Phoenix addressed us again as we flew over the tracks of Warren Street.

'Listen up Inferiors! Make sure to sync your plug as soon as you get to the surface.' His telepathic voice was cold now, impatient, disconnected. *'All intel will be accessible through your plug for a maximum of 24 hours.'* My stomach dipped as I saw the florescent signpost for Oxford Circus coming into view. We kept on gliding for a few more minutes then began to slow down as we approached the illuminous signage sprawled across the tunnel ceiling. *'This is it… You all know what to do.'* Phoenix announced as he skidded to a halt underneath the glowing inscription. He stood watching us pull in as he clicked his sliders into walking mode. *'Get ready.'* He channelled as he led us through a doorway in the wall of the tunnel. *'And remember, LOE live forever, forever live LOE!'* We congregated along a narrow ledge on the other side of the doorway, standing in single file

with our backs against the wall as travelling beams of light penetrated through the thick darkness. *'Now!'* Phoenix channelled as a roaring train rolled in and eased to a squeaky halt in front of the platform. I could hear the pedestrians bustling inside as the train doors jolted open and we immediately spread out, climbing into different carriages to blend into the shifting crowd. We easily dispersed amongst the noisy mob of the underclass funnelling out onto the platform, into the stairwells and up to the streets above. They took no notice of us but their hostility was already evident as we quickly moved towards the surface. For some it was a family day out, a chance to spend expiring quid, or just an excuse to get out of the house and roam beyond the boundary of their usual districts. For others it presented an opportunity for criminal activity or freedom of speech. Libion Day being the only chance to protest the system in an overly oppressed society. Some people even held signs of protest high above their heads in defiant opposition of the BFP regime, chanting as they got ready to march around the perimeter of Hyde Park to obstruct the elite festivities.

The midday sun warmed my skin as I finally reached the streets above. I was sweating profusely, and I took a deep breath of fresh air as relief washed over me. Phoenix was nowhere to be seen, and I wiped my brow as I was involuntarily moved along by the shifting crowd. I scanned the faces around me before letting my guard down, but immediately froze when I felt a hand encircle my forearm.

'Thought you'd lost me, didn't you?' Phoenix asked smirking down at me as he tightened his grip. I looked up at him and forced myself to smile playfully. It took everything in me not to violently push him away and make a run for it, but I knew that would be futile.

'Of course not.' I said innocently shaking my head, unnerved at how fast he had found me within such a large crowd. *He must have followed me onto the train, either that or he's got me tagged.* I stopped my mind from panicking and distracted myself by syncing my plug.

The crowd had slowed right down, and was now moving stagnantly. It began to swell as the Recons tried to control the flow of people passing underneath a huge pair of identity scanners blocking the cross roads up ahead. Phoenix still had his hand clamped around my forearm and felt me shiver in anticipation. *'Don't worry, we'll be fully cloaked in a sec.'* He assured me telepathically. *'Once I connect the frequencies and get us online.'* The LOE had set up an intricate high-tech system on the airwaves, which would give us the ability to pass through the Recon security scanners completely undetected for 24 hours. But, only once our plugs were fully connected.

'Don't you think you need to hurry up with that?' I channelled back, trying to suppress my anxiety.

'Relax!' He thought brushing off my concern.

'Don't tell me to relax!' I snapped psychically, my mind racing.

'Just calm down, you do know that those scanners read agitation levels as well,' he snapped back. Phoenix was right, and I took a deep breath to calm my nerves. I didn't want to give the Recons any excuse to pull me out of line even if I was cloaked. 'We'll be live any minute now.' He said flatly, making no attempt to quell my anguish.

'We don't have a minute.' I hissed as we got closer and closer to the checkpoint.

The sudden faint sensation of my plug buzzing inside my ear meant that I was connected. In a flash the broadcast sent a feed to my mind. My contacts flashed and I saw the perimeter of the park, the location of my faction's objective, it's distance from my current position and the route I needed to take to get there. I took a deep breath just as the footage flickered. The frequency was weak and it quickly faded into jumbled binary code. I continued to walk, forced on by the horde around me. Phoenix was still holding my arm seemingly unconcerned about the *major* technical disruption. The crowd halted abruptly creating a crush. So, I stood on my tiptoes to see what was going on. There was some sort of commotion up ahead, and I could see that several people were being dragged into the middle of the road. Many of those holding rebellious placards were being cherrypicked out of the crowd and dragged across the concrete before they had even reached the scanners. Others were being pulled out right after going underneath the arch. The scanner was beeping loudly and flashing red beams of light onto the individuals that were being separated. My blood ran cold in my veins as I recognised some of the faces. Most of those being dragged away were the Inferiors from our faction.

'Phoenix, do something!' I yelped in my small inner voice as my eyes widened. *'It's too late for them.'* He said psychically, and I felt his heartless indifference wash over me as we moved closer still. I shivered, and shook off his channelled energy as I tried to stop my body trembling. *After everything I'd been through, I couldn't be caught like this!* I thought as I glanced over at the black tent the hostages were being herded into.

'You won't be.' Phoenix communicated as he heard my thoughts.

'How do you know!' I thought back, 'That'll be us in a minute if you don't hurry the hell up!' I spat; my plug was still scanning the airways for *his* lucid connection as the crowd began to inch forward again. I watched as the Recons used their genetically modified hybrid dogs to subdue the rowdier prisoners who tried to fight back. My heart was in overdrive as we got ever closer to the huge arched scanning device which continued to alarm periodically. More and more people were getting pulled out of line, and the crowd began to push back as droves tried to retreat in the opposite direction. Supplementary Recons on gliders now moved in pursuit making the throng splinter in panic. Recons were beating the trapped detainees as the multitudes dispersed, the dogs relentlessly attacking a few writhing bodies on the ground, and chasing down legions of runners like a flock of scurrying birds. I tried to flee but Phoenix held onto me tightly, leading me through the confusion and to the scanner still being manned by two

recons. I cringed as the underside of the arch came into full view.

'It's done!' Phoenix thought triumphantly as my plug automatically logged onto the frequency. But still I held my breath as we passed underneath the scanner… And just like Phoenix had promised, the light stayed green and absolutely nothing happened.

'See, all that worrying for nothing.' His psychical voice sounded smug and haughty.

'But what about the others?' I demanded indignantly after kissing my teeth at his arrogant pride.

'What about them?' He shrugged as he let out a derisive sigh… *'I did say some of them would get caught.'*

'You're unbelievable!' I snapped out loud as we left most of the commotion behind. I snatched my arm away as we walked amongst the scattering legion who had also made it through the scanner.

'Was letting them get caught a part of your plan too?' I hissed as the crowd thinned out. 'They were part of your faction; don't you even care that they got caught!' I pressed standing in front of him and crossing both of my arms over my chest. He silently watched a cluster of people circle around us as I stopped directly in their path. He then pushed his face right into mine and clenched his teeth.

'Get your head out of the flipping clouds and wake the hell up!' Phoenix snapped before he gripped my arm again. 'Now shut up and keep moving, you're making a scene!' I swallowed my repugnance as he aggressively pulled me along beside him. I turned my plug onto private mode, and now that he could no longer hear my thoughts, I decided to concentrate on the more complicated issue at hand. Something did not feel right, Phoenix was acting stranger than normal and I wondered why. Looking up I could see that there was more trouble up ahead. The Recons had now blocked off the middle of the street and were splitting the crowd into two groups on opposite sides of the pavement. I could see them forcing some of the public over to a few yellow tents that were pitched in the middle of the road. I took a deep breath and kept my head down as Phoenix pulled me out of the road and onto the pavement where a cluster of people lingered in front of a few fast-food take-away outlets. My eyes were fixed on the ground, as Phoenix unexpectantly pulled me into a grimy takeaway just a few feet away from the barricade. The smell of hot oil hit my nostrils as I gazed upon a greasy tiled floor. We approached the counter, pushing in front of several disgruntled customers, Phoenix yanking me along as I looked around confused. He then exchanged a look with the cashier who immediately left the counter as if at Phoenix's behest, aggravating the long line of consumers awaiting deep fried pigeon and sweet and sour fox. The cashier quickly returned with an oily fry cook who immediately let us behind the counter and led us into the back. We followed him through the dingy kitchen and towards a grimy larder. The cook ordered the other staff to take a break and then stepped away as he motioned for us to go inside.

'Ladies first.' The slimy cook said smirking as he wiped his nose on his rolled-up sleeve.

'What's going on?' I asked finally, my stomach beginning to churn uncomfortably as Phoenix shoved me in front of him. I have slightly afraid of being made into deep fried fast food.

'Just move,' Phoenix said impatiently thrusting me into the doorway and following me inside. The cook checked the empty kitchen again and stepped into the small space behind us, closing the door and locking us all inside. The cupboard was damp and musty, making me shudder in disgust as the smell invaded my nostrils. The cook quickly flicked on a light and scooted around us, brushing against me far too closely as he reached out to open a refrigerator. He poked his head inside and fiddled around noisily before beckoning us to come closer. As we approached, he pushed the door wide open to reveal a secret passageway.

'Voila,' The greasy chef said smirking as he wiped his sweaty brow and stepped back. Phoenix placed something into his hand and stepped inside. I hesitantly followed as the cook slammed the steel door behind us. It went pitch black for a moment until my contact lenses activated in the darkness. I shadowed Phoenix closely down a flight of steps and into a narrow hallway until we reached another door. Phoenix slowly opened it and we walked out onto an abandoned platform.

'Where are we?' I asked dumbfounded, 'what did you give him?'

'Don't worry, just stay close.' Phoenix said flatly as I noticed a weathered motif engraved in the tiled wall, revealing that we were inside the abandoned Down Street Tube Station. I obediently followed Phoenix across the deserted platform as he activated his sliders and jumped onto the tracks. I trailed behind silently as he skated off into the darkness, dropping back a little, as my mind raced uncontrollably.

I quickly came to the realisation that Phoenix didn't trust me at all. All the work I had done to gain it over the last two months was completely for nought. He had completely changed his plan without my knowledge or consent, and there was no way for me to figure out what he was up too. Feeling confused, I frantically tried to telecall Ryan but I then hung-up paranoid that Pheonix had somehow infiltrated my new plug without my knowledge. I held my breath as Phoenix turned back to look at me, as if he knew what I was doing. I sped up, erasing all record of the call to avoid his suspicion. I sighed as I saw a glimmer of light in the distance. Phoenix had stopped in front of a train carriage, the source of the yellow light that had lit up the tunnel. I paused in front of the steps, then cautiously followed him up inside, unsure of what would be waiting for me on the other side of that door. By the time I had walked up the stairs and entered the carriage he was already greeting several people, people I had never seen before. Five strangers, four men and one woman who all greeted me with suspicious stares.

'Phoenix, what's going on?' I said, interrupting their huddle. 'Who are all these people?' I asked looking at the female up and down.

'Relax, it's just my crew.' Phoenix, said dismissively before carrying on with his conversation. I kissed my teeth loudly and took a seat on the first bench, crossing my arms and turning my back on them. I had never met his crew and he hadn't told me about any of this. I began to wonder if the plan he had run by me previously, the one I had filled Ryan in on was just a lie, like bait he had set to lure me out. I began to bite my nails anxiously as I started to panic.

A few seconds later the train began to rumble as it started to move off. The old track lines squeaked underneath us as the rickety carriage violently jerked every few seconds. We had barely moved off when I felt a sharp tap on my shoulder. I groaned, instinctively knowing it wasn't Phoenix. I smelt a spicy perfume and turned around to see the strange woman standing behind me.

'Plug...' The woman said bluntly, holding her hand out in front of my face.

'Excuse me?' I asked squinting at her as I swivelled around completely.

'Your plug, in my hand now,' she repeated rudely, curling her fingers towards her open palm. 'I'm not going to ask you again.

'Swallow, play nice...' A man said as he came over and stood next to her. He held his hand out towards me. 'Did you even introduce yourself?' He asked turning to this Swallow, but she just rolled her eyes at him then continued to stare at me coldly. 'I'm Wren, he said as I reluctantly shook his hand. 'That's Frogmouth over there, Parus and Weaver.' He announced, pointing at the other three strange men giving me evils from the other side of the train. 'And unfortunately, you've already had the pleasure of meeting Swallow,' he smirked making a face at her. 'Don't worry, her bark's worse than her bite.'

'And how would you know? I ain't bitten you, *yet.*' Swallow hissed, flipping him off with her free hand.

'Well, I look forward to it.' Wren countered as Swallow rolled her eyes. 'And you must the famous Raine…' Wren chuckled as he turned back to me. I nodded warily.

'I wouldn't say famous.' I said cringing.

'Well, I've heard a lot about you…' He said squinting down at me.

'Hasn't everyone.' Swallow replied unimpressed as I looked them both up and down. I wasn't quite sure of what to make of either of them.

'I'm still waiting,' Swallow said turning back to me, still holding out an open palm.

'Phoenix, is this really necessary?' I asked loudly, tilting my body to look past her athletic figure.

'It's minor Raine, just a temporary precaution, do as she says.' He yelled back over the noise of the rickety carriage. I cursed him under my breath as I sat there stubbornly for a long moment, locked in a stare with this strange woman who was more attractive than I would like to admit. Her eyebrows were furrowed in the middle of her coffee brown forehead and her full lips were pursed as she waited.

'Fine,' I said finally, taking my new plug out of my ear and dropping it into her hand.

'Oh fancy,' she said studying the model between her thumb and forefinger before she popped it into her pocket

'What now?' I snapped noticing that she wasn't moving from in front of me.

'I need the whole telekom,' she said curtly.

'Is this a joke?' I shouted angrily staring into her almond eyes. She silently raised an eyebrow as she shook her head.

'Unbelievable!' I muttered as I pulled the telekom out of my pocket and dumped it into her open palm.

'There, that wasn't so hard was it.' Swallow said dryly before she sauntered off back to the front of the train. I sighed and rubbed my face; I was being treated like a criminal, a common spy. I looked up and caught Wren gazing at me sheepishly, his bearded face and wild afro reminiscent of a mad man. I cut my eye at him scornfully, and he looked away just as I felt the train slowing down. After another few minutes the train halted noisily and everyone jumped up. They pulled backpacks from underneath the seats and hoisted them onto their backs, I, of course was not given one. They paused before leaving the carriage, and I could tell that they were all tele-talking, most probably about me. Their facial expressions and the odd involuntary glance in my direction giving them away.

'Right, let's move out!' Phoenix said after rifling through his bag. 'Raine, you're up front with me.' The rest of the crew turned back to look at me as I walked through the middle aisle in between them. They whispered among themselves as I reluctantly followed Phoenix out the carriage and off the train.

20

THE HIGH LIFE

My eyes skimmed across the vast green space and focused on the large stage stationed in the centre of the park. A huge screen was situated behind a grand semicircle podium completed with St George's flags swaying on tall white poles at either side. The flags billowed in the wind, partly covering the grand orchestra playing a classical composition of *Rule Brittania* from a platform positioned slightly below the stage. I rolled my eyes; it pained me that I still remembered the words from every school assembly.

'Rule Brittania! Once again, we'll rule the waves! Britons will never ever, *ever*, EVER be slaves!' The crowd sang along swaying along with the instrumental melody. The abrupt halt of their garish singing drew my attention to Arthur Haywood, the Mayor of London who had just shuffled up onto the grand podium. He was a short portly man wearing a grey tuxedo. He seemed unnerved by the gathering crowds, wiping his sweaty brow repeatedly as he walked across the stage. He cleared his throat and tapped the mike abruptly before he spoke.

'Welcome everyone, and thank you for coming out to celebrate the 25th anniversary of our annual Libion Day celebration.' The crowd cheered as butterflies twisted in my stomach.

'Phoenix, can I have a word?' I called turning away from the window and walking to the doorway of the adjoining room. I peeked across the small hallway separating us before speaking again. 'Phoenix, I need to speak to you.' His back was facing me, and he ignored my request as he continued to confer with his crew. He was making me nervous; he hadn't made any eye contact with me since we had left the underground, and I had followed him up here like an obedient little mutt.

I sighed to myself as I turned back to the window. We were up on the 14th floor of a lavish hotel in a penthouse suite overlooking the park, as well as Ryan's position in another luxurious hotel across the road. From what I could gather, Phoenix was planning an ambush, and I knew Ryan wouldn't survive this unexpected change of plan. I had to do something, *but what could I do?* I thought panicking as I sat down to watch Phoenix and his crew from the large king-sized bed room. From this angle I could at least keep an eye on what they were doing. That didn't stop my mind from racing, and after a few minutes of thinking myself into a frenzy I stood up and marched across the plush carpet of the bedroom, over the lacquered floor of the small foyer and into the marbled lounge area. 'Phoenix, I said need to talk to you… in private!' I demanded, eyeing his crew while briskly tapping him on the shoulder. They stared back at me irately as I rudely interrupted their secret little huddle around the crystal coffee table.

'Not now!' phoenix grunted shaking me off as he continued to assemble the weapon he was intricately constructing. It looked like some sort of rocket launcher, and the various pieces awaiting assembly were laid out neatly on the coffee table.

'You're not allowed in here.' Swallow said firmly, stepping in front of me as she tried to block my view. But it was too late, I could see that she, Parus and Weaver were also piecing large artillery together. Wren and Frogmouth were looking out of the window, and my stomach dipped when I realised, that they were probably searching for Ryan's exact location. 'You were told to say in the bedroom,' she hissed as my eyes scanned the already assembled weaponry strewn across the plush velvet sofa behind them. 'Get out!' Swallow barked, snapping her fingers in my face to get my attention and stop my eyes from wondering. 'Oi!' I ignored her, continuing to watch Wren and Frogmouth exchange glances as they conferred amongst themselves. 'Move now!' She snarled loudly. Shoving me back towards the door by forcefully pushing the butt of her gun into the middle of my chest. I finally retreated, walking back into the bedroom and out onto the balcony to get some fresh air. The breeze rushed inside as soon as I opened the French doors. It was warm outside albeit a little windy, and I closed my eyes sighed loudly as the sun warmed my skin. After basking for a moment, I looked back towards the stage in the middle of the park. My contacts instinctively magnified, zooming in on the mayor who was just about rounding up his speech.

'I am honoured to introduce our honourable prime minister, Sir William Whitehart.' The crowd was quickly thickening, and they cheered as the PM walked into view holding the hand of a little boy dressed in an identical double-breasted suit. The mayor left the pulpit to join the rest of the British Fundamentalist Party who had already lined up at the back of the stage. They were uniformly dressed in the party colours of red and white, except for the PM who stood out in a rich blue.

'What a beautiful day for a Libion celebration, am I right?' The prime minister said chuckling as he covered his brow from the dazzling sunshine. The upper middle-class crowd clapped in agreement as he unbuttoned his navy suit jacket and looked out over the audience. 'The day of liberation and union, or Libion Day as it has come to be known started 25 long years ago making today a very special occasion! We have finally reached the quarter-century milestone of our revolutionary regime in despite of all the international naysayers, and the Scottish, Welsh, and Irish opposition!' The audience applauded his announcement as he emphatically waved his hands into the air. 'This day isn't just a celebration of *our* freedom... no, it's not just a commemoration of our unity, or just an unprecedented battle for the recognition of our English supremacy, and great British sovereignty around the world and amongst the former colonies. This day provides a stark reminder of the unified coalition between the Conservative Fundamentalists and the British Freedom Party, and what we went through to get here!' He paused as his party members clapped jovially, prompting more cheers of approval from the watching audience. 'This extraordinary union not only bought an end to the Liberation Riots, and threat of a foreign militia invading our shores but also marked the beginning of the BFP's international legacy!' Two members of the British Freedom Party stepped towards the front of the stage and began throwing wrapped items into the audience. The crowd scrambled forward for the gifts as a cage of black ravens were released along with a bag of red and white balloons. My eyes followed the ravens as they flew high into the sky. 'Today, we remember the moment we made unprecedented great British history!' The animated crowd roared with excitement as they tussled for the discarded freebies. 'Please calm down everyone, there's more where that came from.' He chuckled indicating for another two-party members to come forward with more sacks loaded with presents. 'I do hope you enjoy our donations, and today's family friendly festivities,' The PM continued as more wrapped parcels were thrown out to the grasping hands. 'Right,' he said as he lifted his son into his arms and the sack of handouts were emptied. 'Without further ado, please put your hands together for our holy sovereign, our great supreme leader… King George the 7th!' The crowd erupted again as the prime minister sauntered to the back of the stage to join the rest of the BFP party. The large screen behind them flickered with digitised colour for a moment before tuning in. Then a large 3D hologram began to pixelate in front of it.

'This entire event is sponsored by The House of Lords, and The Crown. In conjunction with Reconco, the National Department of Recovery, Reconstitution and Reconciliation. Keeping you safe every day, by keeping, ghosts, terrorists, and migrants at bay.' I pulled my eyes away from the propaganda filled advertisement and diverted my gaze towards the Black Gate at the far end of the park. The Black Gate was situated in an obscure corner of the huge park, where the underclass was routinely bottlenecked into an annex to be kept separate from the more affluent Libion Day attendees. The Black Gate never opened before evening, not until all the VIPs had had their fill of *fun* and left for the day. Then the underclass would then be allowed in to enjoy the attractions, spending what little they had on the zoo, funfair, and carnival games.

My contacts zeroed in on the gathered crowd outside the closed gate as I closely watched the underclass for signs of disruption. Trouble was brewing somewhere, it always was. In fact, disorder happened every year and I used to wonder why the lower classes were even allowed to attend. I knew now that it was a human rights tick box exercise of course, just *a distraction*. Or as we were told by my manager Karen at the Diminishing Rights Bureau on numerous occasions, *Libion*

Day presents the average commoner with the supposed opportunity to stand for something, have an impact, have a voice! Or simply escape their district and enjoy the rare commodity of 'fun' once a year. She always followed this statement with a hearty little chuckle insisting that it was the *new British carnival much better than the old one that was full of debauchery, and where the underclass used vigorously copulate all over the street of Notting Hill.*

I hated her, and I had to shake her pasty-faced smile out of my mind. I was getting distracted, and taking a deep breath I focused back on the surroundings of the Black Gate. This was where the Inferiors had been assigned to carry out their objective, and for a split second, I was glad to be high up in a hotel and far away from the chaos that was about to ensue. Afterall I was supposed to be down there, but then again, I was in no better position trapped inside a stifling hotel room full of potential hostiles.

My gaze was drawn back to the stage as the advertisements ceased and the orchestra played the national anthem, *God Save the King.* Finally, a large 3D hologram of King George 7th popped out of the screen. It was time for his annual Libion Day address from the balcony of Buckingham Palace. He waved to the excited spectators that could be seen crowding outside of the palace gates before the image pixelated and rearranged to show the Kings face and upper body. He was dressed gallantly in white formal wear adorned with a golden sash and colourful military badges.

'Good afternoon, ladies, and gentlemen.' The crowd cheered enthusiastically as they gazed up at the animated hologram. 'Firstly, I would like to a huge thank you to the BFP for their tremendous work over the years, and to Reconco for keeping our institution safe from infiltration, insurrection, and sabotage!' The crowd clapped in agreement and some waved up at the imposing image of king high above them. 'I would also like to show my greatest appreciation to all of you. My glorious subjects, the public backbone of our glorious country! I will be ever grateful for your ongoing support, trust, and loyalty because we couldn't have achieved this almighty feat without you! We, the British have accomplished something that no one can take away from us! This achievement can never be diminished, and for as long as my family lives we will remain a united Anglican family!' The crowd roared and burst into a round of applause that seemed to last for an unnecessary amount of time. The king cleared his throat as he waited for them to settle down. 'So, my dear people without further ado, I now declare the Libion Day carnival open!' A knot formed in the pit of my stomach as my eyes fixed on the rows of Recons removing the orchestra and lining the lower platform in front of the stage. Something was happening and I glanced back over at the Black Gate quickly noticing that the accumulating crowd seemed restless.

'Phoenix wants to speak to you...' I jumped, startled by the voice coming from behind me. I turned around almost bumping into Swallow head on. I backed away from the balcony ledge, wondering why she had crept up behind me instead of just summoning me from inside. She crossed her arms and stepped aside as I took one more glance over the balcony wall.

'Oh, now he wants to speak to me?' I mumbled as I walked through the double French doors.

'Well, he knows where I am.' I said sitting down on the bed and crossing my legs.

'Don't play with me!' she said aggressively as she grabbed me by the arm and pushed a pistol into my side. 'Get. Up. Now!' I sighed as I reluctantly stood, allowing her to frogmarch me into the lounge.

'So, am I a hostage now?' I asked Phoenix as Swallow pushed me into the adjacent room. I'd been a hostage from the moment I stepped onto that train.

'Where the hell is he!' Phoenix barked as he rapidly turned around to face me. He was enraged, and the rest of his crew turned towards me, as if awaiting my reaction.

'What the hell are you talking about!' I said looking around at their masked faces confused.

'Rook!' He roared marching towards me. 'He's not where *you* said he would be!' His pupils were dilated and I wondered if he was on something.

'I… I have no idea what you're on about!' I wailed mystified, unsure of whether to be worried or elated by the fact that they couldn't find Ryan, 'I told you everything I know!'

'Don't lie to me!' phoenix spat as he grabbed my chin viciously, squeezing my jaw until it began to ache. 'Where the hell is Rook!' He bellowed spraying hot saliva into my face.

'I'm, I'm not lying… I don't know.' I stuttered, 'he should be there, in the hotel room… room 313, like I told you!' I cried; my voice muffled as he held my mouth tightly.

'No, you're lying I know you set me up!' He grunted, his eyes wildly darting in between my own as he stared right into the depths of my soul. 'Didn't you!' He roared making me close my eyes.

'No, that's not true!' I pleaded, peeping at him as my eyes filled with tears. 'I have no idea what's happening Phoenix, I'm not lying this time, you have to believe me!'

'Weaver, read her!' Phoenix hissed angrily. Weaver suddenly jumped to attention and walked across the room. He stood a few feet away from me as his contact lenses glowed, briefly turning from a turquoise blue to an emerald green.

'No deceit detected.' he announced after a few seconds of analysing me.

'Read her again!' Phoenix breathed loudly, and Weaver did as he was told.

'She doesn't know anything…' Weaver said cautiously. 'So, whatever's going on, she's not, I don't think she's behind it.' He said slowly backing away as he fiddled with his telekom. 'Think about it,' he said as he paused next to Phoenix, 'If Rook somehow devised a new plan why would he tell a little whore like her?' Phoenix didn't respond and Weaver quickly retreated across the room. He stationed himself in between an onlooking Parus and Wren, who stood behind the crystal coffee table covered with weapons. Phoenix abruptly pushed my face away, and shoved me down onto the couch as he let out a raucous grunt. 'Keep scanning the rooms!' He commanded Wren, Parus, and Weaver as he began to pace back and forth.

'If you'd have stuck to the original plan this wouldn't have happened...' I mumbled as tears streamed down my cheeks, regretting it as soon as I had uttered it.

'Shut your dirty little mouth!' Swallow said slapping me across the face before pushing her weapon into the middle of my forehead. 'Phoenix, what should we do about the ground team?' She asked, not taking her eyes off me as she spoke. He remained silent, not even acknowledging her question.

'Should I make contact? Give them new orders?' Wren inquired, stepping away from the window. But still, Phoenix didn't respond as he marched out of the room and began to pace in the tiny foyer. His tinny footsteps echoing around the quiet suite. Swallow lowered her gun as she exchanged glances with Weaver, and taking a deep breath, I slowly got to my feet.

'Did I give you permission to move?' Swallow hissed as stood up.

'I need to use the bathroom.' I snivelled, unable to stop the salty tears brimming over my eyelids. I gazed at the lavish carpet as I waited for her to say something, but he was clearly distracted. When she failed to respond I wiped my face and cautiously walked towards the foyer.

'Where the hell do you think you're going?' Swallow exclaimed pointing her gun at me again.

'I said, I need to use the bathroom.' I declared, a little more sternly than before as I clenched my fists.

'Not alone, I'll help you,' Swallow said chuckling sadistically as she began to follow me.

'I don't need your frigging help!' I cried, whipping around to face her as she pressed the gun right into my temple. I stood very still as I looked into her cold emotionless eyes. 'You're going to have to shoot me if you won't let me use the bloody toilet, ALONE!' I screeched as the rest of the crew looked on silently. Swallow narrowed her eyes at me, and then looked around at the others before she proceeded to cock her weapon. 'I said get that gun out of my damn face,' I hissed with my teeth clenched as tight as my fists.

'Woah ladies. Easy now!' Wren said chuckling nervously as he slowly approached and tentatively put his hand on Swallow's shoulder.

'Don't touch me!' She barked violently shaking him off.

'Ok Swallow calm down, just relax ok… I don't want you to do anything your gonna regret.' He said holding his hands up in submission.

'Who says I'll regret it, trust me, Phoenix *will* thank me… Its better this way.' She chuckled as a manic smile spread across her face. I closed my eyes as my breath became laboured.

'Swallow… Swallow! you need to refocus ok!' Wren said stepping around me to face her directly. 'I can't reach the ground team!' He breathed and I

427

opened my eyes to see her looking up at him with fur-rowed eyebrows. Her smile faded as she allowed him to push the hand with the gun away from my temple. 'Now, I need you to talk to Phoenix… you're the only one that can deal with him when he's like this!' He spoke softly but assertively as he looked deep into her eyes. 'Find out if he wants us to move to plan b, or the contingency ok, and, I'll take toilet duty.' She eyed me suspiciously barely nodding as she placed the large gun onto her back. 'I'll stand outside the bathroom.' Wren said turning to me as Swallow walked towards Phoenix who was still pacing around the foyer. I shrugged and marched away, catching eyes with Swal-low as I brushed by her in the hallway.

The bathroom was an ensuite attached to the bedroom, and I strode towards it with Wren following closely be-hind. You had to walk through the walk-in closet to enter it, making it just out of view from the foyer and the fancy lounge area. I went to slam the bathroom door on Wren but his hand quickly blocked it from closing.

'What are you doing!' I barked as Wren forced the door back open. 'You said you'd wait outside!' I hissed as he suddenly grabbed me. Before I could react, he had covered my mouth and enclosed me inside his muscular arms, forcing me inside the bathroom.

'Be quiet!' he hissed into my ear as he shut the door behind us. I struggled to get away as he dragged me across the room and over to the large sink. 'I'm not going to hurt you!' He whispered as I caught his reflec-tion in the mirror and saw him place his index finger over his lips. 'I'll let you go, but you need to shut up and listen… ok?' After struggling for a few more seconds, I finally calmed down and slowly nodded my head. I could hear him breathing heavily behind me as he cautiously released me.

'What do you want?' I asked uneasily, backing right up against the shower cubicle door as soon as I was out of his grasp.

'Didn't I tell you to keep your mouth shut and just listen!' Weaver hissed eyeballing me. 'Here, take this…' He whispered stepping towards me. He quickly thrust his hand out, and I flinched, hesitating as he leaned forward. 'Take it!' He snapped, grabbing my arm as he dropped my confiscated telekom into my hand.

'How did you?' I asked looking up at him. 'What's going on?' demanded, looking down at the telecom and plug in confusion. 'Why are you helping me?'

'Rook, sent me.' He said slowly.

'How?' I gasped looking up at him in shock.

'The less you know the better,' he replied as he rolled his mask up onto his forehead.

'But how can I be sure that I can trust you?' I asked looking him up and down suspiciously.

'Because I've been on *your* side! If it weren't for me, Swallow would've…' He trailed off as he rubbed his face agitatedly. 'Rook had to change the plan,' he continued after clearing his throat.

'Nah, you don't say!' I snapped sarcastically. 'And why didn't Rook tell me about this *change of plan*

himself? Before he left up shit creek without a paddle?'
I demanded angrily, crossing my arms over my chest.
Ryan knew that I hated being kept in the dark.

'It was too risky!' Wren said rolling his eyes as
if it was obvious. 'How would you have passed
Weaver's reading if you knew?' I sighed submissively;
he did have a point there. 'Anyway, all you need to
worry about now is getting the hell out of here.'

'And how exactly am I supposed to do that?'
I said cynically.

'There's gonna be an ambush, any minute now,
and that'll be your chance to make a run for it.'

'What! In the middle of a bloody ambush?'

'Take this.' He said tossing a small cylinder at
me. 'It's a force-shield, press the lever and hold this
button and it will shield you from gunfire.'

'Hold on a bloody minute!' I said in bewilderment.

'Look, it's either you run, or wait for Rooks men
to get to you.' He said as he searched his pockets.'

'And how long will that take…'

'Who knows.' He answered casually, making
me roll my eyes.

'Well, what's the likelihood of his men even
reaching me?' I sighed squeezing the bridge of my
nose.

'Well, Phoenix has a stronger, more experienced
crew that's for sure,' he said nonchalantly. 'But your
brother's smart… resourceful, prepared for anything!
So, it's anyone's game really… and winner takes all.'

'Rook told you I was his sister?' I asked letting my guard down a little more.

'Me and Ryan go way back ok, so just trust me, I'm here to help you.'

'Ok so, where am I running too then?' I asked after I let out an exasperated sigh.

'Here.' Wren said shoving a small fibreglass tube containing new contact lenses inside of my hand. 'They're already programmed to open room 175, down the hall. When you get there look in the wardrobe and you'll find a bag. You will need to sync your plug when you're suited, booted, and geared up, you understand?' I nodded and he held eye contact for a moment before heading towards the door.

'Wait hold on a second, geared up?' I said following, 'then what?'

'I'll do my best to help you get out of the suite. just stay low and use the shield.' I began to hesitate as my stomach began to twist into knots.

'I'm not sure about this–'

'Look, if you don't go now, you won't live long enough to see your daughter's 1st birthday! Do you want that?' Wren cut me off as he turned back to face me.

'Swallow's just itching for an excuse to–'

'Kill me,' I interjected as he avoided my gaze. I rubbed my face. Ryan was right, Phoenix really did want me dead. He probably regretted not finishing me off when he followed me back to the dorm room.

'But what about–'

'Ryan wasn't lying when he said you'd ask a lot of questions.' Wren said shaking his head as he cut me off again. 'We don't have time for this,' he exhaled as he reached out for the door. 'I've been in here too long already.'

'But what if I can't escape,' I probed desperately as he unlocked it, 'what do I do then?'

'Remember your training.' Wren said as he pulled the handle. 'Now stay here until the ambush starts, and I'll tell the rest of the crew that you had a breakdown and locked yourself inside. I'll stall for as long as I can before Swallow insists on blowing the flipping door off its hinges.' He smiled at me sympathetically before pulling down his mask and opening the door. I watched him walk through it and then hastily closed it behind him making sure that I had turned the lock properly. I put my telekom in my breast pocket and swapped out my contact lenses, flushing the old pair down the toilet. I then leant over to the marble sink and inspected my reflection in the mirror. One of my eyes was blackening from where Swallow had backhanded me. I turned on the taps and proceeded to wash the dried tears off my skin, grabbing one of the fancy towels off the rack to wipe face dry. Then I waited in silence for what seemed like an age. My stomach was doing summersaults and I sat down on the toilet, are pacing the length of the bathroom several times. I put my head into my hands as I continued to wait, listening the heavy rhythm of my heartbeat as I grew even more anxious.

The first bang came a few minutes later and even though I was anticipating it, it took me completely by surprise. The ruckus was much louder than I had expected, and I jumped up, convinced that I had heard an explosion. A barrage of gunshots followed as I cautiously inched toward the bathroom door. I could smell smoke, and trembling, I psyched myself up and slowly eased it open. The smoke billowed inside and dust was flying everywhere as I tiptoed through the walk-in wardrobe. The gunfire continued, and I dropped down to my knees as I approached the bedroom doorway. I hastily pressed the buttons on the force-shield but nothing happened. I pressed them harder, flicking the lever and striking the small pen like cylinder against my other hand several times, but still nothing happened. *Maybe I was doing it wrong,* I thought trying a different a combination. I was distracted and panicked as an array of stray bullets flew into the room piercing right through the furniture. I dove onto my stomach as white-hot lasers from plasma guns cut right through the walls and into wooden wardrobe doors. I landed with a heavy thud next to the bed, the force-shield flying out of my hand and rolling across the floor. I slithered underneath the bed, gazing at the force-shield which had rolled into the doorway and out of my reach, ironically it had now activated. But there was no way that I could get to it without being shot or sliced through with a laser beam. From my position I could see that the front door to the suite was wide open, and gunfire was flying back and forth from the communal hallway and into the lounge area. *How would I get out!* I started to panic, and my heart was beating so fast that I began to hyperventilate. I cowered there covering my ears with my hands as the gun fire continued. I had nowhere to go, there was no way I could get out of the front door without being killed! Wren could be dead for all I knew, and I was beginning to believe that I would die here too. I looked back over at the walk-in wardrobe as a ray of sunshine streamed in through the balcony doors and caught my eye. I looked in both directions knowing that I had a decision to make. Should I run or should I hide? I wiped the stray tears away from my face and forced myself to move, quickly scurrying across the floor and outside onto the balcony. Still crouching I closed the doors and took a deep breath of fresh air as I tried to collect my scattered thoughts. I slowly stood up and peaked over the side of the balcony wall to scan the adjacent balcony. I glanced down feeling slightly nauseous as I contemplated climbing over. I turned to retreat into the suite but saw a body in the foyer strewn just in front of the bedroom door. I instinctively dropped down to my knees as I watched a masked silhouette rapidly leap over the body and run straight towards the walk-in wardrobe. I backed away from the glass and cowered by the balcony wall, whoever it was, I knew they were searching for me, and I had no idea which side they were on. I had to move quickly, so I jumped up and tentatively heaved myself over the side of the balcony. I refused to look down as I brought my remaining leg over, wobbling slightly as the wind suddenly picked up and whipped around my trembling body.

I stood frozen as the blustery breeze intensified, and I had to swallow the bile that was rising in my throat. I clutched at the smooth concrete behind me as I steadied myself against the wall. I stood on a small narrow ledge in between the balconies. It was about the size of my foot give or take an inch, and I began to cautiously shuffle sideways to reach the next balcony. I kept my back pressed against the concrete wall as the wind continued to whistle around me. A couple of pigeons flew by startling me, and I froze as my life flashed before my eyes. I kept my eyelids clamped shut for a second and silently prayed as my falling tears flew back up my face and rapidly dried onto my cheeks. I had to force myself to open them, and to keep going, edging ever closer to the next balcony. After a few more steps I finally felt the wall beside me, and I clumsily hurled myself over it, falling on the and kissing the ground. I quickly got up and ran towards the balcony doors to see if anyone was inside. I began to bang on the glass but there was no answer, so I took one of the patio chairs and tried to break through the doors, but it practically bounced off the glass and almost hit me. I decided to try the table but it was fastened to the paving, and I knew that I had to try the next balcony along if I had any chance of getting inside. I dreaded doing it again but I was able to move quicker this time, launching myself over the wall standing in between me and the next balcony with slightly more confidence. I swiftly slid along the ledge and climbed into the next balcony without too much trouble. I stood with my back against the glass patio doors thanking God that I had made it a second time. My ears pricked up as the sound of gunfire stopped abruptly, and I glanced back to see the balcony doors of Phoenix's suite swing wide open. I immediately ducked down and scurried over to the corner of the balcony where I had climbed over.

'She must have gone over!' I heard Swallow's strained voice first, followed by two I didn't recognise.

'What makes you think that?' The unfamiliar one asked seemingly unconvinced.

'Well, where the hell is she then?' Swallow demanded loudly.

'Maybe she got out after when the smoke bombs went off,'

'They did retreat immediately after… maybe they took her.' The other alien voice concurred.

'And I found this by the bedroom door.' The first strange voice added, and I assumed he was speaking about the force-shield that had rolled across the floor.

'Impossible, I'm not buying it! Check the whole suite again, the whole floor in fact, then the whole bloody hotel.' Swallow ordered, her voice disappearing as she moved inside.

'You heard her. Move, check everywhere!' My ears pricked up as Wren's voice wafted over the balcony. I quickly peaked over the ridge and whistled at him just as he was heading back inside behind the others.

'What the hell are you still doing here!' He hissed as he rushed over to the edge of the balcony. I went to speak but he shushed me as he glanced back over his shoulder inside the suite. 'You need to be gone yesterday! give it a few minutes before you break the glass.' he whispered as he threw a small handgun over the edge. It landed with a clatter in the middle of the balcony, and by the time I grabbed it and stood up he was gone. I studied it, but quickly turned toward the balcony doors as I saw the curtain move out of the corner of my eye. I quickly ran over to the glass and tapped on it with my fingernails.

'Hello?' I whispered as I saw it twitch again, glancing behind me to keep an eye on the other balcony. I quickly turned back around and caught a child peaking at me through the long white curtain. A woman instantly appeared and abruptly pulled the little girl away from the window.

'Please, open the door!' I asked desperately, and the woman wearing a maid's uniform reappeared at the glass looking visibly shaken.

'Sorry…I, I can't.' She mouthed shaking her head and eyeing the gun in my hand as she moved out of sight. I quickly put it into my jumpsuit and tapped on the glass again.

'No, please listen you don't understand… I won't hurt you…' I called suddenly sensing someone behind me. I turned around just in time to see Swallow take aim at me from the balcony two doors down. I gasped as I fell to the ground and rolled toward the wall as she began to fire, her laser gun chipping chunks of concrete off the balcony. Dust fell on top of me as she fired several rounds in my direction, but then, it suddenly fell silent and I slowly got up to peek over the side. She was nowhere to be seen, so I darted across the balcony and began to pound on the window as hard as I could. 'Please open up!' I pleaded knowing that I didn't have much time to get inside. 'She's going to kill me!' I screamed leaning up against the glass as I continued to hammer on the window. Tears streamed out of my eyes as I looked back to check that Swallow hadn't reappeared. Suddenly, I abruptly stumbled into the room almost falling onto the plush bedroom carpet. 'Thank you!' I sobbed, 'But you need to hide now!' I ordered surprised to see her child staring at me from the bed. The woman grabbed her daughter and pushed her underneath it as ran towards the bedroom door and locked it. 'No not here, in there!' I cried frantically pointing towards the bathroom as I heard a loud noise outside of the bedroom door. The sound the hotel door being blasted through. The woman dragged her daughter out from underneath the bed and ran towards the walk-in wardrobe as several shots blew the bedroom door off its hinges.

'I've got you now bitch!' Swallow yelled manically as she came gliding into the room shooting aimlessly, the laser bullets cutting through furniture and making ornaments explode. I heard the bathroom door slam as I dived behind the bed and pulled out the mini gun. Swallow didn't spot me as she flew towards the walk-in wardrobe assuming that it was me that had run away from her. So, I took my chance and fired into the back of her head, aiming a round of bullets at her unmasked, unprotected skull. She had begun to spin around when she heard the shots but it was too late.

She immediately dropped her gun as her body fell out of the air, landing with a loud thud on the carpeted floor. I held my gun on her, my hands shaking in shock as she lay facing me with her blank eyes meeting mine. Blood seeped out of her forehead and I paused for a long moment frozen in disbelief that I had killed her. My heart was pumping blood loudly in my ear drums as I slowly caught my breath and put the gun away. I cautiously crawled out from underneath the bed and slowly approached her body, the blood oozing out of her head wound already forming a crimson halo on the thick cream carpet around her hair. I spat on her, she was the second person I had killed and it felt easier this time, almost guiltless. I took a deep calming breath before hastily heading towards the bathroom, suddenly alarmed by the trail of blood speckled across the floor the walk-in wardrobe.

'It's alright, you can come out now.' I called anxiously, my heart beat picking up again as I got closer to the door. I didn't get a response, and my mouth dried up as I put my ear against the bullet riddled door. There was complete silence inside. 'It's safe to come out now...' I said again, but still I got no answer and I nervously looked through the bullet holes. It looked as if no one was inside, and I uneasily tried the handle. It was open. But as I pushed it, something blocked the door. I forced my way in and gasped as I saw the body of the maid lying face down on the tiled floor. I rushed to turn her over, but deep down I knew that she was already dead. She had a round of charred wounds in her back where the lasered bullets had burnt through her flesh. The tiles around her body were slippery with blood, her white uniform was already soaked in it. Her eyes were vacantly deadpan, and a tear rolled down my cheek as I brushed my hand over her forehead to close her eyelids.

'I'm so sorry… *Gabriella,*' I said reading her name tag out loud as I grabbed a towel and lay it over her body. It only covered the top half, and I sighed loudly as it quickly began to soak up the scarlet blood like an oversized sponge. I jumped as I spotted her daughter staring at me from underneath the sink. My eyes immediately welled up with tears, and I turned away to wipe them dry before trying to coax her out. She wouldn't come.

'Is… mummy dead?' she asked staring over at her mother's partially covered body.

'I'm so sorry, this is all my fault… I… I didn't mean for this to happen.' I cried swallowing the hard lump in my throat as I wiped my eyes again. The little girl just stared at me blankly, her eyes vacant, and her cheeks flushed red from crying. Her mother's blood was quickly creeping across the floor towards her hiding spot, it had already stained her hands, face, and clothes.

'I'm Raine…' I sniffled, pulling myself together, 'you can come out now ok, I promise its safe.' She didn't move and sighed loudly, trying to figure out what to do with her. 'Can you tell me your name?' I asked gently as I crept a little closer, she was silent for few seconds refusing to look up at me.

'Zara,' she finally whispered without making eye contact.

'Zara?' I repeated to make sure I had heard correctly, and she nodded. 'How old are you Zara?' She slowly held up one hand in response, showing me her small palm with five open fingers, and I sighed to myself guiltily. 'It's not safe for you here Zara...' I said trying to coax her out again, but she ignored me, so I contemplated if I should just leave her here alone.

I felt conflicted, maybe she'd be better of here where a family could find her and look after her. I pushed the thoughts out of my head, knowing that she'd probably end up as a hired slave or in Hermitage Hill's children's wing. 'We have to go.' I said firmly grabbing her by the hand and pulling her out from underneath the sink. She didn't resist my grasp as I directed her around the body and stood her in front of me. 'You can't stay here.' I whispered, 'if you come with me, I promise to keep you safe....' She didn't respond. 'Zara, do you understand what I'm saying?' I asked, crouching down to her level. She nodded distantly as she allowed me to usher her through the walk-in wardrobe. I lifted her over Swallow's body and into the foyer but paused at the front door of the suite as I heard voices in the corridor. I put Zara down before approaching the hallway. The front door had been kicked off and it swung ajar on its top hinges. I peeked outside and saw uniformed men going in and out of Phoenix's suite. Phoenix's men were nowhere to be seen and it was only a matter of time before uniformed got to us. I waited a few minutes until the passage was empty, and then ran across the hall dragging Zara by the hand behind me. I quickly located room 175, and then scanned my eye to unlock the door before we slipped inside. I sat Zara down on the bed and gathered my thoughts as I paced the room.

I then frantically began to pull open the doors inside the walk-in wardrobe looking for this so-called bag.

I quickly found it and then emptied it out on the bed. It contained food rations, goggles, nun chucks, and an albatross suit. I laid the suit out on the bed, I had never seen one up close before, a Loelife had to become a Junior before they would be given wings. I sighed, giving one of the chocolate energy bars to Zara as activated my telecom. It lit up, instantly notifying me of a pre-recorded hologram stored in my mind mailbox. I popped my plug into my ear, glancing back at Zara who had already finished the energy bar and was unwrapping another one. She must be hungry, who knows when she would have eaten last.

As the hologram pixelated, I walked out onto the balcony to view the message, closing the French doors behind me.

'Raine, if you're viewing seeing, you've spoken to Wren and you're exactly where you need to be. But you don't have long to get away…' Ryan looked remorseful, his holographic image gazing at me as if in real time. 'I'm sorry, I couldn't tell you the whole plan, I just couldn't risk Phoenix reading you and finding out the truth. If anything went wrong, I couldn't have you implicated.' I sighed and shook my head as I covered my empty ear to block out the commotion from the park below. 'You need to get to this location.' A 3D map and a line of coordinates materialized above the telekom, replacing the image of his face. 'I will meet you there.' He said as his face reappeared and the important info automatically uploaded onto my plug. 'I'm so sorry I had to keep this from you, and I'm sorry that we couldn't find Tia before the shit hit the fan. But I swear on my life that we'll get her back ok! I promise you that! We *will* find her!' I began to pace up and down on the balcony as sinking feeling washed over me, a feeling of despair that told me that I may have lost my baby forever. I almost threw the telekom over the ledge.

'Please don't be angry Raine, just try to understand that it had to go down like this.' I stopped pacing and took a long deep sigh as I looked down at his image again.

'And whatever you do, don't go after Phoenix alone ok, do not go back to the slums! Just come and meet me at those coordinates, and I promise I'll explain everything... I'll tell you anything you want to know. No more secrets.' The hologram flickered and then cut off abruptly. I sighed again and put pad away as my ears picked up the commotion below. I peered into the distance, and my eyes focused on a legion of Recons trying to hold back the Loelife' led crowd forcing their way through the Black Gate. The chaos was starting, A hologram of King George was still smiling jovially on the screen, but I could see Recons departing the stage and rushing across the park towards the disturbance.

So far everything seemed to be going to plan, and I continued to watch as the Black Gate suddenly burst open and the crowd quickly dispersed into the park. The crowd trampled the battling Recons underneath the gate before the multitude of reinforcements could arrive. I ran back into the bedroom, knowing that I didn't have much time to make my escape. Zara froze as I entered the suite abruptly, staring at me sheepishly, having eaten over half the rations already. I forced a smile as I tore off my clothes to put on the albatross suit.

'I'm going to get you out of here.' I said hurriedly fastening the hidden boot zips around the legs of the suit. I now knew why Ryan had bought me a pair of Dynamo sliders; they matched the albatross suit.

As soon as I zipped myself inside and pulled the hood over my head, a clear membrane enveloped my face and ballooned into a hardened helmet. Another membrane appeared between my thighs with two larger pieces of unidentifiable skin-like cloth connecting my arms to my lower legs. I gasped, catching a glimpse of myself in the dressing table mirror. This was the first time I had tried on an albatross suit. Let alone seeing in the flesh, and since I had just made it to the Inferior rank, I had never received any flight training. I spread my arms out and studied the wings as a digital menu popped up on the visor in front of my eyes. I hurriedly scanned the instructions knowing that hesitation was not an option. Luckily, it seemed as though Ryan had already programmed it for me, but I had no idea how to carry a passenger. I groaned loudly as a speaker icon suddenly popped up, prompting me to sync my plug to the suit interface. I pressed the flashing symbol and it suddenly began to speak.

'Greetings Raine Montrose, I believe this function will be of use to you.' The suit said reading my thought stream as it showed me an animated diagram of tandem flying. Harness restraints immediately popped out of the front of the suit, and I turned towards Zara who was looking at me with a dumbfounded look on her face. Before I had a chance to speak an alarm went off over our heads. Making Zara fly into my arms as a deep robotic voice spoke through covert speakers we could not see.

'This is a routine emergency announcement, please do not alarmed. Would all guests get ready for an immediate inspection. Hotel security is in pursuit of several hostiles. Only open your door for uniformed hotel security, I repeat only open your door to identifiable hotel personnel. Please do not panic, the authorities have been informed and Reconco is on route.'

'We have to go!' I said as I threw my jacket over Zara's shoulders and zipped it up. I pulled the hood up over her head and adjusted the flight goggles to fit her face. I placed the rest of the rations in a large pocket in the front of my suit and strapped the pair of nun chucks to a metal hook on the side.

'I don't want to go?' Zara said timidly. She was facing the floor and I sighed hesitantly as I sat on the end of the bed and pulled her in for a hug. 'I want my mummy,' She sniffled as she started to cry and I hugged her tighter.

What I was about to do was dangerous, and I knew that I couldn't just leave her behind. Her mother saved my life and was now dead because of me. Zara was my responsibility now, I owed her that much. But still, I didn't want to take her against her will.

'Your Mum can't look after you anymore… remember?' I said gently tilting her face up towards mine as I wiped her tears away. 'She's gone for good now, so she can't come with us…' Zara looked back down at the carpet as I let go of her chin. 'But if you let me… I'll take you somewhere safe, ok? I promise I will take care of you.' She wiped the snort from her nose in the sleeve of my jacket as she gave me a slight nod. I went to stand up but I froze, suddenly hearing a loud thump on the front door of the suite. I put my index finger over my mouth as Zara's watery brown eyes quickly glanced up to meet mine. She looked at me worriedly as I dashed over to the bedroom door. I frantically closed it and turned the lock as a deep voice wafted into the suite.

'Hotel security… we're here to do the safety inspection.' I darted back across the room in a wild panic, flinging open the balcony doors as the muffled knock came again. I then hoisted Zara into the harness at the front of the suit, the restraints automatically fastened around her and clipping themselves together.

'Ready to fly in manual mode?' the suit asked and I blinked yes on my visor menu as the loud knock at the door came again.

'Open up Miss Davies! We must check the rooms because of a major incident a few doors down.

We're truly sorry for the disturbance, but it's just routine protocol, intruders may be still hiding in the hotel.' I felt the albatross suit come to life, like an electrical current ran through it as soon as I clicked on my sliders. I backed up into the walk-in wardrobe all the way up to the bathroom door.

'Miss Davies?' The stern voice called through the door again. 'I'm picking up two moving heat signatures inside your room and there is only one person on your booking. If you're harbouring any fugitives, please note that you will be prosecuted to the full extent of the law. Now were coming in! So, stand back against the wall with your right hand on the palm scanner!'

I began striding towards the bedroom just as I heard the front door of the suite fly open. I picked up speed heading straight towards the balcony, barely passing the bedroom door as it flew off its hinges and several uniformed security guards barged inside. I heard the hotel security lunging behind me as I sailed through the double doors and onto the balcony. I took a deep breath and Zara screamed loudly as I leapt over the edge, spreading out my winged limbs as we rapidly began to lift into the air. A thermal updraft took us high into the sky, and we rapidly soared high above the treetops and over Hyde Park. I couldn't believe we were flying. The visor pointed out the hidden thermal streams in the air allowing us to rise higher and higher with total ease. I gazed around at the cloud scattered sky in fleeting awe. The green grass shimmered in the sunlight beneath us but for a moment as it was quickly blighted by the rapidly spreading chaos below.

I saw the panicked public trampling each other as we careered over the main stage, just above a helicopter that was hovering over the frenzied crowd. The hologram of King George was no longer above the stage, and there was a small ring of Recons encircling the prime minister and his party as the helicopter coasted above them in mid-air. The aircraft had let down a rope ladder as the Recons tried to beat back the clambering crowd. Thick plumes of smoke were rising from burning trees, and there was a frantic stampede forming in the distance, rolling right across the park like an unstoppable tidal wave. The turbulence was stronger the higher we went and a strong wind blew us straight towards the chaos ensuing at the black gate. The Recons around the BFP had begun to use their laser guns on the crowd, as a barrage of reinforcements emerged from the street, spilling into the park like a colony of marching ants. The Recons around the main stage continued to tranquilize the unruly horde fighting to get closer to the helicopter ladder swinging above the stage. The prime minister had already begun to climb with his son tied onto his back, and I began to panic as a handful of shots were fired in our direction from an army of drones that had suddenly appeared on the horizon. Luckily, the suit sensed the danger before I did and activated its force field, the laser beams narrowly missed us as I swerved out of the way. But I lost my equilibrium, and we started to descend rapidly as I lost control. Zara let out a shrill scream as a few more laser beams shot past us and we suddenly fell into free-fall. I tried to balance myself out but we involuntarily plunged into a nose dive as more drones followed us across the sky. Fortunately, the flight suit had an auto-pilot mode, and it activated a few seconds after I lost complete control. The suit suddenly took over my limbs, forcing me to spread them out rigidly as we sped up. It activated camouflage mode and the confused drones quickly fell away, and made a descent towards the anarchy below. Suit made me do a sharp turn, the auto pilot program immediately trying to steer us away from danger, but it was too late. As we circled back towards stage, I saw another beam of light travelling through the air. It moved so fast my eyes couldn't even follow it, and as I craned my neck to track it, the stage suddenly erupted not long after we had passed overhead. I closed my eyes against the dazzling burst of light. The blast thrusting us forward as we were catapulted by such a sudden surge of energy emanating from the explosion.

I woke up to a burning chest and stabbing pain inside of my head. all I could see was a reddish blackness under my eyelids, so I was afraid to open them.

Was I dead? I could feel the heat of the sun shining down on me and my ears were ringing loudly, so I couldn't be. A strong breeze rushed over my body and I shivered as I began to wheeze and cough, trying to relieve the burning sensation in my chest.

I felt the cold hard ground beneath me and my eyelids shot open as I quickly reached out for Zara. I worriedly grabbed the empty harness as my eyes flickered violently against the harsh sunlight.

I couldn't feel her next to me.

'ZARA!' I screamed panicking knowing we must have fallen out of the sky. *What if she fell out of the harness? What if she was lying dead somewhere!*

I sat up, surprised that I didn't feel any pain except for the rapid thumping inside my head, as the smell of sulphur and burning flesh suddenly assaulted my nostrils.

'Zara!' I called again as I shakily struggled to my feet, covering my brow as my eyes came into focus. I whipped my head whipped around and finally saw Zara standing several feet behind me. There were still plumes of smoke billowing in the distance and it took me a few seconds to gather my bearings and work out where we were. I woozily walked towards her as a strong gust nearly took me off my feet. I crouched down, suddenly realising that we were standing on top of a tall building. The suit was on sleep mode and the helmet had retracted itself off my head. I pulled it back on and immediately retracted the wings of the suit before dashing over to Zara as I beckoned her away from the edge. She was still watching the turmoil below as I pulled her face towards me to check her over.

'Zara! Are you ok?' I asked as I brushed the black soot off her face and inspected the superficial scratches on her ashy arms and legs. I barely heard myself speak over the ringing in my ears but at least we were both ok. Zara nodded before continuing to stare over the edge of the building as the albatross suit's AI showed me instant replay of the last events recorded on my visor. The backlash of the blast had knocked us both out but the autopilot had miraculously managed to land us here safely, circling the roof and releasing Zara a few feet into the air above the concrete before taking me in for a surprisingly smooth landing while completely unconscious. Besides a few superficial grazes, we were completely unharmed and the suit didn't seem to have any external damage either. We had landed on the other side of the park, but the uproar below had inevitably spread into the surrounding streets. The smoke was finally clearing, and people were now scaling the gates of Buckingham Palace and being shot down. I pulled up the visor, and my contacts zoomed as I gazed across the park. The explosion had most definitely killed the prime minister and the BFP party, the wreckage of the helicopter that had been blown out of the sky was now a burning centrepiece atop the rubble that was once the main stage. Limbs and body parts lay strewn across the grass, and scavengers were picking the pockets of dead bodies and fighting amongst each other. There was confusion and absolute panic everywhere, and I could see Recons fighting back a horde of people around the burning ruins. In the distance another legion of Recons on gilders were now quickly advancing across the expanse of the park, forcing panicked survivors to scatter wildly in front of them. I froze, watching the determined army seemingly moving in slow motion. They were encroached as a unified force, a mirage of demons seemingly conjured up by the billowing plumes of smoke rising from the streets behind them.

My focus moved towards the Black Gate as a swarm of masked Loelifes flew inside. The second wave had begun. The inferiors had cleared the way for the Junior Loelifes to wreak havoc and unleash their wrath. They were destroying the carnival attractions, hijacking hotels, and tying the blue papered Londoners to burning trees, all the while chanting, LOE live forever, forever live LOE repeatedly. I saw them skating like a black sand storm coming on the horizon. They were heading straight towards the multitude of charging recons, trampling any confused bystanders caught in their way. I ducked, covering Zara as a helicopter and squadron of drones suddenly flew overhead, spraying laser beams into the rioters along the nearby streets as they flew into the park. The helicopter hovered above the rubble of the main stage and shone a beam of light over the site of the wreckage as the drones opened fire on the stragglers below. Another loud explosion went off somewhere close by, and I held Zara to my chest, covering her against any flying debris.

'It's time to go!' I said anxiously, as several large pieces of metal landed around us. I quickly uploaded the map from my plug onto the flight suit, and pulled down the visor. It immediately showed up on the screen, calculating the fastest and safest route as the AI zeroed in on the coordinates. I tried to switch on the autopilot mode but the suit rejected my request, ordering me to take off in manual mode first. Sighing nervously, I clicked on my sliders as I lifted Zara into the harness, this time using the one on my back as per the suit's suggestion. The restraints secured themselves as I took a couple of deep slow breaths. I felt the current in the suit again just before I began to glide vigorously towards the far side of the building. I rapidly picked up speed, running across the surface of the large rooftop and in the direction of the blowing wind. The hover quickly elevated me above the surface of the concrete, and just before I surfed over the edge of the roof, I activated the albatross wings, and we instantly rose into the sky.

I immediately set the autopilot to take over as we climbed in altitude, relaxing my arms and legs as the suit gained total control.

I sighed as I looked down at the clashing multitudes below, noticing the huge bird-like shadow following us along the ground. Thankfully, nobody seemed to notice us amongst the ensuing havoc, too busy baying for blood to gaze up at us as we made our elaborate escape. But I activated the cloaking mechanism just to be on the safe side. I could feel Zara clinging to my back, as we continued to ascend rising higher and higher into the sky. My eyes widened as we finally broke through the scattered cloud cover to reveal the vivid London skyline and horizon beyond it. I sighed as I felt the familiar feeling of angst and dread creep into my stomach, wondering what lay in store for me next. I spotted the river Thames in the distance as a cold gust of wind blew in off the open water. There was a dark grey cloud drifting towards us, and I closed my eyes. Briefly basking in the sun's disappearing rays which warmed my skin for but a few moments, before immediately being followed by a torrent of thundering acid rain.

GLOSSARY

Albatross Suit – A type of flight suit that enables the wearer to fly.

Amber Order – An amber order is to notify the holder of yellow papers that they have been revoked, and that they have now been served with orange papers.

Beefeater – Vigilante/ terrorist organisation opposed to parliament and loyal to the crown.

BFP – British Fundamentalist Party comprised of a coalition of Conservative Fundamentalists and the British Freedom Parties.

Blue Papers – Leave to remain in the UK and freedom to roam.

Crim/ Crimson – Heroin derived drug that is smoked or snorted, known for its bright red colour.

Force Shield – devise that protects the user from gunfire by creating forcefield like barrier.

GMA – Genetically modified animals.

Ghost – Illegal immigrant/ overstayer, or someone untagged and unknown to the government.

Hybrid Contacts – Contact lenses with unique high-tech functions.

Junior – Second level position within the LOE Society.

Inferior – 1st level position for new initiates into the LOE Society.

LOE – League of Equality, also known by common abbreviation the LOE Society, L.O.E or simply the LOE.

Libion Day – Day of Liberation and Union, and an annual celebration of the coalition resulting in the creation of the BFP.

Minion – Inductees who have pledged their life to The LOE and sworn allegiance, but have no rank

Mortis rod – baton like device that paralyses a person by causing the sensation of paralysis like rigor mortis.

MP – Member of British parliament.

Orange Papers – Restricted temporary leave, physically tagged while investigated. No local travel privileges/ under house arrest.

Underclass – Anyone who is not a part of accepted society.

Plug – Telepathic earpiece counterpart to telecom.

Quid – Metallic money like tokens, colour coded and restricted by the government to control purchases.

Recon – Reconciliation enforcement officer.

Reconco – The National Department of Recovery, Reconstitution and Reconciliation.

Red Papers – Papers turn red when individuals refuse to comply or have failed investigation. Red papers mean you are illegal and will be detained if found.

Senior – Third level within the LOE society.

Sliders – Hover boots or footwear used to get relatively airborne.

Spasm Stick – baton type weapon that causes the victims muscles to spasm and cause inhibiting body cramps.

Superior – Forth level within the LOE Society.

Telekom – Telepathic phone device/ computer device used along with or without the plug earpiece. (i.e., kompad counterpart to plug)

Yellow Papers – Conditional stay to work in the UK or stay with a spouse, confined to movement within 'home' district.

ABOUT THE AUTHOR

Cleo Crombie was born and raised in North London, and has always had a passion for writing stories. She studied Creative and Media Writing at Middlesex University where she discovered her love for science fiction. This is her first novel.